INTERGALACTIC NEBULA WARS

Initial Attack On the Forefathers

A Novel

Shaun R Desouza

First Edition

Fulton Books
Meadville, PA

Published by Fulton Books 2024

ISBN 979-8-88505-709-7 (paperback)
ISBN 979-8-88505-745-5 (hardcover)
ISBN 979-8-88505-710-3 (digital)

Printed in the United States of America

PREFACE

Intergalactic Nebula Wars is about three savants, one from a wealthy family, one from a medium-income family, and one from a low-income family. Their lives become intertwined after they meet each other during a spectacular college brain bowl competition. Eventually, these three scientists begin working for the International Government on various top secret projects. A devious government organization, Rouge Hein, learns about scientists and some of their top secret projects. Knowing the power and strength this government can obtain with the help of these three scientists, they embark on a mission of death threats and dubious crimes to convince the three scientists to turn their back on their government and work with them. To protect the three scientists from the sinister plot of the Rouge Hein government, a special force of the International Government called the elite regime whisks the scientist away to a top secret, secluded government-controlled area. The International Government informs the three scientists that the government is working on a new project called Nowhere, confidential information that cannot leak out to society. The three scientists discover that the government plans to take humans to different planets to sustain life. Finally, the three scientists meet a group of aliens called Legendaries, followed by Iquestorians, who murder and kill male specifics for their heinous games. The three scientists and other scientists make a scheme of things to prevent the human race from dying off.

CHAPTER 1

ORIGIN OF THE FOREFATHERS THE MEANING OF NMJ

The year is 2135. The human race has evolved through the way they live with vast technological advancements that harness the human brainpower manifesting over 30 percent that guides them into the twenty-second century. Looking back at the past, humans were evolving rapidly, but first, we must adhere to how that was happening through three different families that changed the course of events. We begin our journey with three young superintelligent savants who specialize in other parts of science in the specific areas of chemical engineering, physics, and biology. These three young people have different upbringings belonging to three distinct families from different parts of the United States.

The first family, called the Normalics, live in a three-story brick mansion in Washington, DC, with a gated guardhouse in the front of their estate. The gated area is a long road to the front of the house with a massive fountain of dolphin statues in the middle of the circular driveway.

The house has several guard dogs at the front entrance, an entranceway of vast glass, and wooden doors that seem fit for a giant. Inside the house is a white banister stairway going to the second and third floors, with giant TV screens on each floor. Around the left side of the house are several small deep moats that carry several species of fish in it that the groundkeepers feed. A wooden bridge leads to an in-ground pool. The deck shows a huge Olympic-size saltwater pool that can be accessed from from inside or outside the home in the backyard.

The Normalic family consists of about seven members of the household. All rooms in the house have large walk-in closets with thousands of wardrobes for all family members, including the youngest, Mary. The house furnishing is put together well, with a huge island kitchen on the first floor. There is a remarkable butcher kitchen to the back of the house where staff takes livestock and butcher them up, making all special foods for the family daily, except for the weekends that are special for the family.

Exceptional chefs cook for the Normalics' special occasions every weekend. Mr. and Mrs. Normalic are specialty doctors who own a specific practice in downtown Washington called the Genetic Speciality Inc.

The American Version company deals with genetic awareness in different family genes, whether families are wealthy or poor. These babies are what families look for to better that family name and make a stigma or stamp in history. They improve gene values in these families to give society a well-grounded human race with intellectual offspring in every aspect of life's ventures, whether it be music, history, math, chemistry, physics, etc. After a fourteen-hour day, Mr. and Mrs. Normalic leave the office, heading home for an extravagant weekend with the family. While retiring for the night from their office, the night guard at the front desk looks at the monitor and says, "Ah, Mr. and Mrs. Normalic, same as usual, letting the scientist work twenty-four-hour weekends again?"

Mr. Normalic has his hands around his wife's waist as he turns his neck to the left and tells the guard, "Oh yes, Jerry, let them work through if they want to, okay."

Jerry replies, "No problem. Have a great weekend, sir."

Mrs. Normalic replies, "You too, Jerry, bye-bye."

An hour later, Mr. and Mrs. Normalic drive up to their house in a $200,000 baby blue Mercedes-Benz, as the guard comes out of the guardhouse with a greeting.

"Good evening, sir and ma'am. You have a wonderful evening and weekend."

Mr. Normalic turns to speak to his wife while interrupting the guard at the time, "Hold a sec, George. Yes, honey, I know you are right. We have to spend time this weekend with the family, and I get it!"

With this, Mrs. Normalic returns, "Okay! I appreciate it, honey. Love you." With this, Mrs. Normalic kisses her husband passionately.

Mr. Normalic says to George, the guard, "Okay, George, would you like to come in for dinner?"

George replies respectfully, "I appreciate it, sir, but my wife and kids have planned something tonight that is very special to my family."

Mr. and Mrs. Normalic simultaneously reply, "Bye-bye, George. Have a great evening."

George walks over to open the gate for them, slowly waves, and says, "Thank you."

The Mercedes-Benz drives around the circular driveway up to the house's front entrance as the dogs begin to approach the car, barking while slowing down. Mr. and Mrs. Normalic exit the car discussing their plans for the night with their children. Mr. Normalic, walking toward the house, remarks to his wife, "Why don't we relax with the children tonight after dinner? Instead of discussing work, why don't we watch a movie, okay?"

Mrs. Normalic, with a smile on her face, slowly puts her arms around her husband and tells him, "Okay, no problem. I will not discuss work, and we will have fun tonight, I promise, my love."

Mr. Normalic, opening the front door, replies with a sweet kiss on his wife's cheek, "Thanks."

As the parents enter the door, Samantha, the oldest daughter, awaits her parents at the front door. She is six feet, five inches tall and is constantly nagging her mother to go shopping with her; in other words, she is a spoiled brat. Samantha does not give her mother time to relax. As she comes in from the front door, Samantha says to her mother, "Mom! Can we go shopping tomorrow morning, please?"

Mrs. Normalic replies, "Honey, can I get in the door first before you bombard me with shopping, please? I will think about it, okay, honey."

Samantha walks away with a shoulder shrug like a spoiled brat, saying, "Fine!"

Mr. and Mrs. Normalic start to take their coats off when their maid, Mrs. Garcia, takes their warm wardrobes from them and hangs them up in the front entrance closet. The maid remarks, "Ma'am, will you be lounging in your studies this evening?"

Mrs. Normalic responds, "No, I will be overseeing dinner tonight because the family will be eating while enticing themselves to watch a movie or two in the downstairs theater room."

The maid nods. "Okay, ma'am, will there be anything else I can help you and Mr. Normalic with this evening?"

Mrs. Normalic, with a blunt look, makes a short statement to the maid, "Jennifer, we will not need you this evening. If you wish, you may take a leave of absence, or you may join us for dinner."

The maid replies with a gentle gesture of gratitude, "I appreciate you and your family so much. You and Mr. Normalic have done so much for my family and me. I will be dining with my family for the weekend."

Mrs. Normalic responds, "Very well. Have a wonderful evening, and say hi to the family for us."

"Yes, ma'am, I will," says the maid and exits the front door.

Meanwhile, Samantha calls her younger sister Mary, as Mary is in the hallway studying in the study room area. At the same time, Mr. Normalic heads to the couch area, where his two sons are watching a football game. Mrs. Normalic leads to the kitchen to discuss with the cook regarding appetizers for dinner. Samantha calls out to Mary quietly, "Hey, Mary, come here. I want to tell you something."

Not wanting to be disturbed since she is studying for her finals, Mary says impatiently, "What is it, Sam? I don't have time for anything. I have to study for my finals coming up."

Samantha sighs. "Mary, it will only take a second, and besides, it is something good for you too."

Mary jumps out of her chair without hesitation and quickly emerges from the room excitedly toward Samantha and shouts, "I want it! I want it bad! Tell me it is something good."

Samantha sees her sister excited and tries to calm her down because Samantha does not want her parents to know that she is persuading her little sister to manipulate her parents into going shopping tomorrow. "Okay, look, I want you to go over to Dad and tell him you want Mom to go shopping tomorrow because you want to get a new dress for your birthday party next week."

Mary looks at her sister bewildered and replies, "Sam, I don't need a dress. I have many clothes already, and besides, what do I get out of this?"

Samantha, a bit impatient, says, "Mary, I need a new look because a particular boy is interested in me, and if you do this, I will give you my old school notes to help you with your finals, okay?"

With a broad smile, Mary exclaims excitedly, "Okay, I will do it then."

Samantha sighs in relief. "Thank you, little sis, you're the greatest."

Mary strolls over to her dad and sits by him while the boys and their dad shout out, "Go, go, go! Yeah! Yeah! Touchdown!"

Mary gently taps her dad on the arm. "Daddy, Daddy, I want to ask you something."

Mr. Normalic, excited over the game, replies, "Hold on, honey, hold on."

Mary taps her dad again. "But, Daddy, I have to ask you a question."

Mr. Normalic, frustrated by the constant interruption by Mary, slowly turns to his daughter. "What! What is it, Mary?"

Mary, a little frightened by her dad's expression on his face, slowly swallows and says, "Ah, Daddy...uh...um...can you please ask Mommy to take me shopping tomorrow, please, Daddy, please."

Mr. Normalic excuses himself. "Boys, give me a minute. I will be right back to watch the game with you guys. Okay, I have to take care of something for my little princess here."

Both boys reply simultaneously, "Okay, Dad."

Mr. Normalic apologizes to his daughter. "I am so sorry I got mad at you, princess. Let me go and talk to your mother for you."

Mr. Normalic gets up from the couch with his daughter and walks with her to find her mother. Mr. Normalic passes by Samantha. Samantha is staring in the mirror, admiring herself. Mr. Normalic asks her, "Sam, have you seen your mother?"

Samantha turns toward her dad and says, "I think Mom is with the cook in the food preparation room."

Mr. Normalic nods and heads toward that area, telling Samantha, "Thank you."

Mary looks back at her sister when, suddenly, Samantha gives Mary a slight wink. Mr. Normalic, a few minutes later, enters a room similar to the kitchen that looks like a butcher's shop and steps on a mat that opens the doors automatically, interrupting his wife as she is talking to the cook. Mrs. Normalic says, "Jeff, remember we want some appetizers with a tasty twist for the family tonight, okay."

Jeff enthusiastically responds, "Yes, ma'am, I promise to give you and your family the best treat tonight."

Mr. Normalic then interrupts, "Ah, excuse me, honey, Mary and I have a question for you."

Mrs. Normalic, a little annoyed at being interrupted by her husband and because she wanted it to be a surprise for them, turns around and says, "Honey, don't you see that I am busy?"

Mr. Normalic, trying to speak up for his beautiful daughter, says, "Honey, it will only take a second, I promise."

Mrs. Normalic sighs and speaks gently, "Okay, how can I help you, honey?"

Mr. Normalic, pleased that he's got her attention, says, "Mary here has something to tell you and what she would like to do tomorrow with you."

"Mommy, I want to go back to the clothing store, and get a certain item along with some other stuff." Mrs. Normalic hears Mary out thoroughly with a drab look. With puppy eyes, Mary stares at her mom.

Mrs. Normalic responds, with a weird look, "Some other stuff, stuff like what?"

Mary moves her eyes left to right. "Ah, stuff like those hip jeans that Samantha wears."

Mrs. Normalic, "Oh, I see now. You want to be like your oldest sister."

Mary tries to tell her mom she is trying to be different. "No, Mom, I like some of her stuff. Of course I want to be different than Samantha."

Holding Mary's face with both hands, Mrs. Normalic kisses her cheeks. "Okay, dear, whatever you like is okay with me."

Mr. Normalic looks into both Mary's and his wife's eyes and says, "Everything is now taken care. You girls have fun tomorrow. Tomorrow, the boys and I will go to a football game because our friend Joe gave me ten tickets to see the game in a booth where the boys can eat their favorite foods and enjoy the game with their father."

Mrs. Normalic grabs her husband's cheeks, pinches them, and taps him on his rear. "You have fun with the boys tomorrow, and I will have fun with Mary, and I am sure Samantha has a date tomorrow with some boy." Mr. Normalic nods with a no motion, disgust, and a confused look toward his wife.

Mr. Normalic heads back to the couch where his two boys are watching the game. Meanwhile, upstairs on the second floor, humming to himself a tune from *Star Wars*, is an incredible savant brushing his teeth, combing his hair, and taking a leak. It's Lucas Normalic, who is the nerd of the family and a genius in chemical engineering. Lucas's room, located on the second floor near his parents' bedroom, has all sorts of awards from the principal of his school and the national foundation of chemical engineers called the American Institute of Chemical Engineers.

Lucas discovered a chemical breakthrough particle by working in his home lab while attending a high school called Phesian. This fragment has made headline news in an article when he was young, which holds a mysterious substance for humans to sustain life a little longer before heading to death. His discovery marks the chemical society as possibly the substance for living longer and reversing old age. Lucas has gotten a Nobel Prize for the youngest scientist to discover a chemical to help humanity in the late 2129 awards ceremony during his first year in school. Lucas's lab attached to his room is full of chemistry instruments from glass tubes to a flask, even computer software to conduct chemical components that see the different chemicals interacting, producing a new compound. Lucas is always conducting chemical experiments in his lab, conducting new formulations that someday benefit humankind. He has three older brothers and two sisters, out of which one sister is more senior than Lucas and the other younger than him. Lucas's oldest brother, Todd, always tries to mess with Lucas by either wrestling with him or patting Lucas on the head when Lucas makes intelligent statements regarding chemical finds and how Lucas seems to know so much about the ladies.

Todd, who is six feet, seven inches tall, with rusty blond and brown hair and blue eyes, is in Lucas's room, and he tells Lucas, "Hey, Lucas, come here a minute. I want to ask you a question, little bud."

Lucas is a bit nervous since his older brother, sometimes, tries to rough him, so he says, "Yes? How can I ah help you, big brother?"

Todd tells Lucas, "Lucas, you have to help me out. Please come to my room now! Ah, please."

Lucas replies as he slowly puts down his mixing of chemicals while wearing a smock and goggles for a project, "Okay, I'm coming. What are you having problems with this time, Todd?"

Lucas comes into Todd's room. Todd hides in a dark corner of the room, and as Lucas opens the door slowly, Todd then jumps on top of Lucas and grabs him, slamming him down on the bed. Then he picks Lucas up again to slam him down when Lucas cries out, "Stop! Todd, stop!"

Todd, who is about to stop, accidentally hits Lucas's head on the ceiling fan by mistake. Lucas cries out, "Oww! Oww!"

Todd grabs his little brother like a baby and says, "I am so sorry, little brother, so sorry, I am sorry." Todd rubs Lucas's head lightly, letting go of him. Lucas runs out of the room. Todd calls Lucas one more time with a severe look on his face.

Todd goes behind Lucas and says, "Little brother, I need your help dealing with a girl you want but can't get because she likes girls."

Lucas replies politely, "Well, my soft-spoken brother of mine, you've got to invite her and her girlfriend to get a girl like that. You can invite them to your place or a party and tell them you can satisfy her needs like a woman. Also, invite her and her girlfriend to shows, special events, and so forth, and maybe they would invite you into their little clique, and you might get lucky." Lucas laughs under his breath. "Playing dress-up with them is a fun activity. It might benefit you."

Todd replies with a striking look of disbelief at how his little brother can know so much about women, although he deals with nerdy stuff. "Oh man, why didn't I think about that? Thanks, genius, you're the greatest." Lucas walks back to his room like a smooth operator, as Todd realizes that he has a little brother who is astute in chemistry and an inventive person in relationships. However, he has never seen his brother with girls yet.

Mrs. Normalic, with her arm around Mary, is talking about a funny multicolor dress Mrs. Normalic had once worn and is laughing over it. "Now that dress was surprising, wasn't it, Mary."

With a peal of huge laughter, Mary says, "Oh yeah, and it is the type of dress that would fit a clown in the circus." Mary and Mrs. Normalic head down the hallway. They pass Samantha, who seems to be checking herself in the mirror.

Mrs. Normalic strangely looks at her daughter Samantha looking at herself in the mirror, and asks her, "Why are you looking at yourself in the mirror, honey?"

Samantha is admiring herself in the mirror. "Don't I look good, Mom?"

With a smile, her mom replies, "Honey, makeup does not make a person. You should love how you look and forget what people think of you. You should love yourself for you and nobody else, honey."

Samantha stops applying the lipstick. "I guess you're right, Mom."

Mary excuses herself from her mother. "Excuse me for one minute, Mom. I have to ask Samantha something." Mrs. Normalic continues down the hall to tell Mary a secret when Samantha touches Mary on her shoulder to get her attention.

Mrs. Normalic, about to tell Mary the secret of her hors d'oeuvres, remarks, "Yes, dear, I guess I will tell you the rest later."

Unexpectedly, running downstairs while Samantha and Mary are almost at the top of the stairway, Lucas is in a hurry, nearly toppling them, as he has to ask his dad and mom a question. Mary calls out to him, "Lucas, slow down. Can't you see sensible ladies walking up the stairs where you almost made Sam and I fall? What is your hurry, Speedy Gonzales?"

At the bottom of the stairs, Lucas calls back to Mary as Mary and Samantha turn to go to their rooms. "Hey, Mary, Mary."

With her head around the corner, Mary asks, "What is it, Lucas?"

With a witty remark, Lucas says, "Mary, maybe your medical attentiveness can accommodate me when I fall with your stupid clumsiness."

Mary not-so-caringly states, "Whatever, brain butt with a hole in the heart."

Samantha grabs Mary from arguing with Lucas and asks Mary, "Did you tell Mom that you want to take me shopping with you? Did you tell Mom?"

Mary, with a selfish type of attitude, tells Samantha, "I said, 'Mom, I want to go shopping.' I didn't include you, was I supposed to?"

With a what-the-heck attitude, Samantha says, "Yes, dummy, what do you think I put you up for the task in the first place."

Mary gives her a mediocre look. "Don't you ever call me dummy. You got it!"

"You're brilliant in schoolwork, but you're way off the mark when it comes to common sense." Samantha, with a disappointment look on her face, "And you need to go back downstairs and ask Mom if I can go shopping with you tomorrow because I have to pick out some stuff to look good for this boy I want to see, which I am hoping to date one day."

Mary replies, "I will try to accomplish the task this time, and for your information, I have more common sense since you didn't know how to tie a knot in your hair, remember."

Samantha throws raspberries. "You got me. Now go!"

Before heading downstairs, both girls look for clothes in their closets to go on that shopping spree with their mom tomorrow.

Lucas, downstairs, says, "Hello, family. How is everybody doing tonight?"

Mr. Normalic—watching the game in the fourth quarter, where his favorite team, the Redskins, is up 48 to 24 with five minutes left in the game—turns to his favorite genius son with a smile, telling Lucas to come to sit down. "Lucas, I haven't seen you all day. How is my favorite, boy wonder, doing? What's going on, son? Come sit down."

In a bit of a low tone, Lucas, heads toward his dad to hug him with a small remark, "I'm just working on a small project, Dad."

Mr. Normalic says, "Oh, you're working on that project for your finals, correct? That's right, and you're graduating in the next couple of weeks. Aren't you excited to go to college?"

Lucas, a bit hesitant, says, "Of course I am excited. I can't wait to see which colleges will accept me."

With assurance, Mr. Normalic says, "With all the scholarships coming in, I'm pretty sure you're going to choose the best son."

Lucas crosses his finger to his back. "I sure hope MIT comes through."

Mr. Normalic says, "That would be my son of the highest caliber. Well, son, let me get back to my game. Why don't you see what your mother is doing okay, son."

Lucas is missing the closeness of his dad. "Will do, Dad. Talk to you later, Pops."

Lucas heads to his mother, getting special plates for tonight's family gathering they will be attending downstairs in the home theater room. The home theater room has weights on one side, a Jacuzzi on the other side, and in the middle is the home theater room for movies with seating and folded tables to place food onto it. Lucas greets his mom in the kitchen. "Hey, Mom, how was your day at work today?"

Mrs. Normalic is a bit busy. "Oh, I have had better days, son, a bit stressful. What is going on with you this evening?"

Lucas, a bit upbeat, says, "My day is not so stressful. You know I like messing with chemicals."

Mrs. Normalic, with much respect, responds, "Son, you have a brilliant mind indeed. You not only have the mind of a super Einstein but one of the greatest minds that ever came into this world."

With a fondness for his mom, Lucas says, "Whatever you say, Mom. I just know I am good at the chemical engineering, that's all."

Mrs. Normalic asks him, "Are you going to go with your dad tomorrow to see the game?"

Lucas is not a bit excited. "I want to stay home tomorrow so I can finish my final project for school, Mom."

Mrs. Normalic, a bit concerned, says, "Lucas! You will be home alone tomorrow because everyone is doing something tomorrow."

Lucas is a bit overzealous. "Mom, I want to get this project done tomorrow. Getting this project done means a lot to me. I'm sure Dad understands. It is not that I don't want to go to the game with him tomorrow. I don't mind watching a game here and there, but it bores me a bit, Mom. Besides, I have to get this project done. You know what I mean, right, Mom?"

Mrs. Normalic says in an understanding way, "I know you, son. You like to come up with formulas and determine chemical finds, right?"

Lucas is nodding his head. "Yes, Mom, you're right."

Mary walks down the stairs and into the kitchen, where Lucas and Mrs. Normalic are conversing. Mrs. Normalic stops what she is doing for a second as she remembers something, "Sorry, son, I forgot to hug you today."

Mary interrupts Mrs. Normalic. "Mom, I have a question to ask you."

Mrs. Normailic turns around toward Mary. "What is it, honey?"

Mary apologetically says, "Oh, excuse me, Lucas, I just want to ask Mom something real quick."

Lucas accepts the apology. "Not a problem, sister."

Mrs. Normalic says, "How can I help, bright eyes?"

Mary says with a slight smile, "Mom, I have to ask you if it will be okay for Samantha to tag along with us tomorrow."

Mrs. Normalic is looking suspicious. "Well, Mary, did she put you up to this?"

Mary, without hesitation, responds, "No, Mom, I want her to come because I want her to help me pick some hip clothes."

Mrs. Normalic left eyebrow up. "Tell her I said it is okay to come with us tomorrow, but still, I am sure she put you up because this is not how you are, daughter."

With a bewildered look, Mary says, "Thanks, Mom, okay."

Mrs. Normalic, still in her work clothes, tells Lucas gently, "Lucas, honey, can you please go downstairs in the movie room and prepare it for the family get-together, son."

Lucas comes up with an intelligent reply. "I see that you brats got your way again." He quietly whispers into Mary's ears. Mary, with a cold shoulder, shrugs at him.

Lucas looks away, eyes rolling. "Not a problem, Mom. I will head downstairs now." Still, Lucas heads downstairs to prepare the movie room for a family night in his pajamas. Mrs. Normalic is running to the back room where the butcher kitchen is. Samantha and Mary catch up with their mother in the hallway, and Samantha hugs her mother and tells her, "Thanks, Mom."

Mrs. Normalic says in a rush, "You're welcome, darling. Can both of you help Lucas prepare the movie room downstairs? I believe he would need your help. Thank you."

Mary, without hesitation, says, "You got it, Mom." Both girls head downstairs to help Lucas prepare the home theater room. Downstairs, Lucas seems to have everything under control. Mary and Samantha hit the last step, running over to see if they can help Lucas.

"Lucas, what can we do to help you?"

Lucas is a bit busy organizing everything from crockery and napkins to picking a few movies they could watch but answers, "Well, Sam, you can help pick out another film because I already picked one out. Mary, you can get the drinks and set them in the holders."

Mary turns around to get the drinks and says, "Okay, Lucas, you got it."

In the kitchen, Mrs. Normalic is super excited to see what the cook has for dinner and desserts. "What, oh my god, that is amazing. Caviar with a bisque. I love it. Thank you so much."

The cook smiles and says, "Why, thank you, ma'am. Glad you liked it."

Mrs. Normalic, with a big smile, reminds the cook, "Remember to bring it down in about forty-five minutes."

Cook answers calmly, "Not a problem."

Lucas and the girls have everything downstairs in order, as Mr. Normalic and the two other boys sit in the chairs while Lucas and Samantha have chosen the movies they will watch. Lucas is the type of boy that loves movies like comedies, true life, science fiction, action, and fantasy. Todd and Joe, the two older brothers, ask Lucas what movie he's picked for the family this weekend. Todd, rubbing his head, says, "Hey, Lucas, what type of dramatic or action movie did you pick for us this weekend, smarty pants?"

Not liking his witty remark, Lucas says, "Well, big brother, I have an action war movie called *The Invisible Ones*. The movie is about soldiers in an Iran covert operation that has not been recognized yet for their bravery due to the Middle East cover-ups of nuclear by the Iranians."

Joe is seemingly interested. "Really! To me, little brother, it fits family night. You're unique, Lucas, because you have the brains to choose a film like this that highlights the gallantry and victory of our war heroes. Picking a movie like this tells me you have a heart for our war heroes."

Lucas, with a thankful attitude, replies, "Why, thanks, Joe, it didn't seem that you would be interested in such a movie."

Joe with thumbs up, "Of course I am, little brother."

All the family members are gathered around the home theater area of the room now. Samantha interrupts, "Well, I picked out a good movie called *The Screwed-Up Cat*. It is an excellent comedy about a cat burglar who robs people, but screws up by leaving clues."

Mr. Normalic, resting his right arm on his chair and hand on his chin, says, "That is sweet, honey, I'm sure we will enjoy it, but Lucas has one that deals with real events about how our soldiers are not well appreciated since they sacrifice their lives for our country."

Samantha, with a not-so-caring remark, "Oh wow, men, huh, how about the women, Dad."

Mr. Normalic looks at Samantha with a caring look, and says, "When I spoke of military people, I meant the women of the military as well."

Lucas elaborates, "Oh, of course, he meant the women."

Mrs. Normalic passes the unique hors d'oeuvres as the cook later comes with the special dessert. The family all cheers simultaneously for Lucas. Lucas smiles cheerfully at them, but the next moment, a trade-off by the families' intrigued intervention of celebrating Lucas as a chemical engineer, almost as if there is an intuition of some upcoming event about to take place.

"Congratulations, the exclusive valedictorian with honors who's an exceptional student, you're among the top 1 percent of the populations intelligence that will be graduating in the next two weeks. We love you, Lucas Marcus Normalic."

CHAPTER 2

THE SAVANT OF PHYSICS

We now turn to the second family of the trio of a scientist who lives in Buffalo, New York. They are a middle-class family with a farm with a few horses and farm animals. They have a two-story farmhouse with chickens, cows, sheep, llamas, goats, and deer. Their house is again a two-story aluminum siding red-and-white house, the interiors of which have a very rustic look with wooden floors and animal trophies hung up throughout the house. The family is a black family that dresses up like cowboys on a farm. Melba, the wife, works at a hospital as a registered nurse, and her husband, Dustin Justick, manages the farm and sells fresh meats to the markets in town. Mr. and Mrs. Justick have three children; two teenagers, and a young child. This family believes in lighting their house with generators, and living off the farm. Having gotten up around 5:00 a.m., Melba went over to the chicken coop and picked out the good eggs, while her son Torin collected the remaining rotten eggs and threw them in a separate basket to use as slop for the pigs.

With a basket under her arm, Melba says, "Torin, grab the remaining eggs and throw them in this basket, son."

Torin makes a slight mistake taking an egg from the excellent basket. "Mommy, do I take these too as well?"

Melba grabs the good egg from Torin's hand. "No, son, do not ever take the eggs from this basket. These are the good eggs. You see, this basket is brown, meaning it has the good eggs, and the black basket that you have has the bad eggs that are meant for the other animals to eat because they are bad for people to eat."

Torin is a bit confused. "Mommy, if it is bad for people, why isn't it for the animals?"

Melba is coming up with an explanation. "Well, Torin, if we eat, we will get sick, but the animals don't need to cook food, and thus their digestive system is different from ours and can handle awful things that are bad for people. Do you understand, Torin?"

Torin realizes the animals are there to consume the bad stuff so people don't get sick. "I understand. The animals help the people from getting sick with bad food, right, Mommy?"

Melba agrees with Torin. "You are right, son. Now let's finish because the rest of the family will be getting up pretty soon for breakfast, and we have to get it done before that. All right, baby?"

Torin agrees again. "Okay, Mommy."

Melba and Torin go back inside the house to fix breakfast for the family. After about an hour of preparing breakfast, the rest of the family wakes up, still wearing their pajamas and nightwear as they start to sit around the table for breakfast.

Darin, with a sweet attitude, says, "Good morning, honey. How are you this morning? The breakfast looks wonderful, babe."

Melba says with an upbeat attitude, "I am fine this morning, darling. Are you ready for a tasty breakfast?"

Darin, without question, replies, "Of course, I am ready to fill this big stomach up." Darin pats his stomach and starts to sit down at the head of the table.

Melba begins to serve the family at the table. Although the food is on the table, she asks her husband, "Do you want pancakes?"

Starving and ready to work the farm, her husband answers with gratitude, "Oh, definitely yes, and butter, bacon, eggs. Oh, how I love this breakfast. You know a brother has to have his meats on the plate."

Melba is brushing off the brother's comment. "Honey, whatever fills that tummy of yours." Melba pats her husband's stomach fondly. The kids are around the table, waiting for their mom, Melba, to serve them. Melba serves the children, and one of the children, Cynthia the second oldest, wants more bacon.

Cynthia is licking her lips, and says, "Hey, Mom, give me some more bacon, please. I want more, please."

Melba looks at Cynthia, and sees Cynthia taking almost all the bacon. "Child, I told you all that bacon is not suitable for you. Upon reaching a certain age, your arteries will harden and you will die prematurely. Now put that back! I said right now!"

Cynthia quickly puts the bacon back on the plate because she doesn't want her mother to get mad at her. Cynthia, almost getting a spanking from her mom, asks hesitantly in a whisper, "Mom, all right! Mom, can I go to the teen square dance at the cavern tomorrow night?"

Melba points over to Darin with her right index finger. "You have to ask your dad."

Cynthia, with sad eyes, replies, "I'll ask my dad in a little bit, Mom."

Darin, who overhears, is surprised. "What is it, child?"

Cynthia tries not to interrupt while her father is eating. "Oh, nothing, Dad. I'll let you know, Dad."

With a confused look, Darin says, "All right, darling."

Jewel Justick, their son, the second scientist in the field of study of physics, is having breakfast and tells his mother, Melba, "Mom? Why do I have to eat sausage instead of bacon? Isn't it the same thing?"

Melba, with a caring look toward Jewel, says, "Look, son, I know it is the same thing, but sausage has less fat than bacon, and it won't hurt you in the long run."

Jewel, who seems to know better than his mother, remarks, "Well, if it is better, why is there fat?"

Melba and her husband, Darin, tell Jewel, "Jewel, why don't you let us worry about that!"

"All right," Jewel replied in a shallow tone.

Cynthia goes to the refrigerator and asks, "Does anyone want juice?"

Jewel quickly replies, "I'll have a Coke!"

Melba knows that Coke is awful and says, "You know Coke is bad for you, right?"

Jewel knows the dangers of too much Coke and says, "Mom, drinking Coke twice a week is not too bad. I drink it a couple of times a week, and besides, I drink a lot of water during the week. Mom, I have to finish my physics finals within the next two weeks. So I have to work on this project this weekend and next weekend."

With concern in her voice, Melba says, "I understand, so you will not be helping your dad prepare the meat to sell to the sellers who will be picking it up this weekend?"

Jewel, with a stern face, says, "I don't have time. I have to finish my final physics project, and it is very intense work, Mom."

Melba sympathizes with her son. "I understand, son, you have a keen mind, and I am glad you are my son. You amaze me. I wish I were as smart as you, but you know, with the internet and everything, your IQ is 220 in physics, correct?"

Jewel is a bit confused. "Ah yeah."

Melba continues further, "But you have something like 180 in other subjects or comparable to that. You are so gifted, and I am so proud of you, Jewel, that you're graduating early, at seventeen years of age. Although they wanted you to graduate at twelve, that still amazes me. Since your graduation is in two weeks, have you decided on what college you want to attend yet?"

Jewel, wanting his dad's point of view on it, says, "I have to talk to Dad about that."

Darin is steadily eating and not paying attention and asks, "Talk to me about what?"

Jewel sighs and says, "Nothing, Dad, nothing."

Melba intervenes, "Nothing at all! Well, I think it's important."

Darin looks at Jewel square in the face with a stare. "So what is this nothing about, Jewel?"

Jewel slowly lifts his head upward, and Jewel's Adam's apple appears and disappears while he gulps. He takes a deep breath. "Well, Dad, ah, about college after graduation, that is what Mom wanted me to talk to you about."

Darin is somewhat ecstatic. "Well, have you thought about one yet, son?"

Jewel is not too worried. "I am sure many will come. Then I have to decide, right?"

Darin sees his son with a good attitude. "That's the attitude, son, a winner's goal. Love it! Well, I have to get some items checked in the study." He picks up his remaining breakfast as he goes into his study room area to do some calculations regarding the farm's meat he has to sell. It is over the next few weeks, so he excuses himself from the discussion. "Excuse me, family, but I must take care of some business on the computer."

Melba and Jewel say, in unison, "You're excused from the table, no problem."

As Darin gets up from the table, he accidentally farts, and the entire family holds their nose with disgust.

"Yuck!"

"Whew!"

The family fans their nose at the foul odor. Before Jewel exits the door with his sister Cynthia, Cynthia heads over to her dad, Darin, in the study. She asks him about the teen square dance. "Dad, I wonder if I can attend the teen square dance next weekend. I promise I will be in by curfew. Please, Daddy, please, I beg you."

Darin sits back down and calmly tells Cynthia, with hardly any enthusiasm, "When it comes down to it, boys only have one thing on their minds, and they don't think logically about family situations. There is always another. You know you can't go to the dance without your big brother or me."

Cynthia holds her breath and exhales slowly, hearing her dad lecture her. "Dad, I would never put myself in a predicament like that. This is something I would never do. I promise you that. I am going there to have fun, and besides, my grades will be better, and I will follow everything you have said."

Darin notices his daughter is maturing. "Well, good, and you have a good day at school. Remember to get those grades up, and I will reconsider it."

Cynthia skips to her room. "Thanks, Daddy."

The following day, Jewel is brushing his teeth, while his sister Cynthia gradually gets out of bed.

While getting ready for school, Jewel says, "Cynthia, we will be late as I have a meeting with some teachers today, so we can't be late!"

Quickly, Cynthia gets ready within ten minutes; putting on her clothes and sneakers while running downstairs, and brushing her hair

Cynthia apologizes, "Okay, I'll be there, Jewel."

Melba calls out to the kids as they run to catch the school bus, "Kids, you forgot your lunch!"

The bus driver overhears the mother. "It's okay, kids. Go ahead and grab your lunch. I will wait," exclaims the bus driver.

Jewel tells Cynthia to grab the lunch bags. "Cynthia, go ahead and grab our lunch from mom. I will go ahead and grab our seats on the bus."

Cynthia holds the lunch bags while she asks a question. "You put Cokes in the bags for Jewel and me, right, Mom?"

With concern for their health, Melba says, "Dear, too much Coke is not suitable for the both of you. Again, it can harm your stomach." Melba cares so much for her children. "I did put a Coke. I also put two bottles of water to wash it down along with your food, okay, honey."

Cynthia grabs the bag and runs back onto the bus. "Mom, got it. Thanks."

The bus drives from the Justick home, and Jewel calls Cynthia to sit in their regular seat. "Over here, sister, I kept it warm for you."

Cynthia gives an intelligent remark, "Well, if it is so warm, why aren't you cooking on it, huh!"

Jewel makes a brilliant retort, "Well, if I were cooking, you would have to survive with my precious meat and bone, huh, sister."

Cynthia is trying to shut her brother up. "You know what? That is plain disgusting. You might be smart, but you're horrible at witty comebacks, brother."

Jewel is trying to make a final clever remark toward his sister. "Well, if I am horrible, I learned it from the best, my sister, who plays softball and tries to bat like a man."

Cynthia, with a snarly reply, "Listen, Jewel, I at least have fun, unlike you, who is always studying for something that may or may not appear in history. Oh, just because you received an award for a physics calculation by the president of the United States for your achievement, and you think that's so remarkable."

According to Jewel, he'll make history. "And in the meantime, I will be memorable to many people throughout history and spend most of my time playing golf, coming up with new ideas for entertainment for young and old. I'm sure you'll nod along with approval."

In response, Cynthia tells her side. "As a neurosurgeon doctor, I will also make people happy by leaving my mark in history. It may not be as well-known, but I will be remembered for years." Despite Cynthia's surprise at Jewel's reaction, she continues, "People were surprised by everything in one way or another, whether it was great leaders throughout history, charlatans in our communities, or parents who made their children smile. In addition, human beings encourage their children to emulate them as role models throughout life. When we leave this world, we should also leave something meaningful for our children."

The bus reaches the school. All the schoolchildren run off the bus, hearing the bell ringing, as they enter their first class. Jewel Justick enters his homeroom classroom as the teacher is taking attendance.

"Daryl Jerick."

Daryl raises his right hand and says, "Here."

The teacher mentions Jewel afterward. "Jewel Justick."

Jewel, with right hand up high, says, "Here. Am I late?"

The teacher admires his punctuality. "Jewel, ah, there you are on time." Science project assignments are passed out by the teacher, and the class discusses their science project. "Students, I am passing out the projects that everyone will be doing this weekend. Everyone understands their project, right?"

All students nod their heads in agreement with a "Yes." Cynthia is in her class, wondering how she will pull her grades from a C minus to at least a B or B minus. The bell rings for the second period, and Cynthia waits until all the students leave the classroom and notices that the teacher is looking down at the roll call sheet. Cynthia gently halts.

"Excuse me, Professor Wildon. I have a question."

Mr. Wildon slowly looks at Cynthia. "How can I help you?"

Cynthia, a bit troubled, says, "I was wondering if there is any way that I can bring my grade up to at least a B or B minus average."

Mr. Wildon is impressed by her willingness to improve her grade and says, "Well, my dear, there is." Mr. Wildon grabs a book he took from his studies at home called *Secrets of a Detective.*

Cynthia, a bit bewildered, asks, "What's this?"

When she receives her the papers, her math and science teacher, Mr. Wildon, tells her, "I know you're a bit confused since you're not in an English class. Anyhow, this reading is intended to address the mathematical and scientific questions in this assignment. The fifty math and science questions you need to complete by the weekend will boost your grade by one grade. Please complete these questions by the weekend and bring them in first thing on Monday."

Cynthia, a bit relieved she does not have to do a book report, is excited. "Oh, thank you, you don't know how much this means to me. I appreciate it. Thank you, thank you so much, Professor." Cynthia is grateful and leaves the classroom with a smile, heading toward her next classroom.

Jewel enters the conference room, running out of breath, and one of the teachers sees Jewel and questions him, "Jewel, why the hurry? You're okay."

Jewel, trying to sound typical, says, "Yeah, phew, okay, I thought I was late."

The teacher tells Jewel he is not late and that two other professors are running late to get the lesson started. She continues, "Well, everyone is here, except Professor Goldman and Professor Stewart."

Jewel notices some donuts kept there as snacks, grabs a few, and eats them, waiting for the other professors to appear. One teacher asks Jewel, "Well, Jewel, let me ask you how the force measure in water appears to gain constant gravity of rotation to be an ongoing movement without stopping the motion."

Jewel enlightens the teachers. "Well, let's say...ah...uh, hum...excuse me, ah, let's see here. Let's say, Professor, let me, show you in a minute."

The teacher waits patiently for the other teachers to keep his question in mind. Within fifteen minutes, the two latecomer teachers enter the classroom. One teacher says with humor, "What happened to you two? Did you find a portal to enter?

Because we are wasting this intelligent genius's precious time." The female professor points to Jewel.

With a bit of a chuckle, Professor Goldman says, "Amusing, now let's get down to business, please."

All eleven professors who had their previous classes excused by looking at a physics movie start to sit around the conference room as Jewel takes the floor. Jewel replies to the teacher's questions about manipulating an equation invented by one of the greats, like Newton, saying, "I had a professor ask me a question about how constant gravity in water appears to be an ongoing movement without stopping it." Jewel starts to write on the board, explaining how this is possible. He says, "Well, let's consider this idea to understand the formulation. The force is equal to the pressure taking the acceleration and dividing it by two. In layman's terms, pressure equals what force times that of the acceleration. When the mass is in parenthesis, it equals density times area times velocity times rotation divided by constant times 360 degrees. Is there anything we need to clarify so far?" As Jewel turns toward the eleven professors, Professor Stewart raises an important question.

"Okay, if the rotation constant is 360 degrees, how does the pressure determine when or where to stop?"

Jewel gazes up at the professor with admiration because Stewart is one of his favorites. "Well, Professor, as a result of pressure inputted into the rotational force, the constants of measurement stop based on that specific pressure, like pressing the gas pedal of a car. The pressure you put on the pedal of a car determines how fast that car can go. That is why the pressure determines how hard you press that gas, right?"

Professor Stewart agrees, "Right, now I understand, and very interesting indeed."

Another professor, Sir William, a British physicist who teaches at Jewel's school so he can get his green card, asks, "Well, the physicist Maxwell, the forefather of several equations, especially the equation of electrical waves that travel at the speed of light, gave me an idea that you might know. A turbine engine, for instance, is designed to turn and rotate in milliseconds. How would one gauge the airwave's velocity?"

Jewel, realizing the professor is writing down on paper as though he is writing for his PhD class, explains the theory, "Let's see here. For one, to determine the milliseconds of a turbine engine flowing with just air instead of maybe the fuel is defined by the constant of air pushing through, let's say, the axle of a car while transferring the air back and forth throughout the vehicle as is captures the ventilation through a different kind of metallic radiator grill that pushes the air back into the axle as one presses the pedal for acceleration. However, we use A equal V instead of electricity to contribute air to the calculation of milliseconds, based on Maxwell's theory of speed of light. Did that answer your question, Professor William?"

Sir William catches a glimpse of the formulation, writes it down, and gives a quick answer as he responds, "Yes, that answered my question, thank you very much."

The meeting within the conference room ends with the professors who ask Jewel where he would like to be within the avenue of expertise he will be taking. Jewel answers one of their physics questions, "Well, Professors, I will pursue my interest and expertise in physics. So I am looking forward to improving several equations and coming up with new and improved ones as well."

Jewel and Cynthia continue to go to their classes throughout the day, as Cynthia gets permission from all her teachers to do extra credit work to bring up her grades, bringing up most of them to Bs and a few of her quality point average to A minus. On the other hand, Jewel has various teachers' classes throughout his other courses, paying attention to what Jewel has to offer them with his knowledge in the other subjects.

Back at the Justick home, Mr. and Mrs. Justick and their youngest child, Torin, are helping Darin with the animals, cleaning up the barn, and feeding them. Darin, who looks a bit tired, says, "Melba and Torin, we are almost done feeding the animals." Darin, who knows that Melba has to go to work in a couple of hours, says, "Why don't you begin dinner so when the kids come home from school, they can warm it up before bedtime so you don't have to worry about them warming up leftovers. Torin and I will take care of the rest of the feeding. Thanks, babe."

Looking at her husband working so hard, Melba doesn't feel like leaving his side. "Well, I know you're exhausted. Would it be possible for me to help you complete everything since it seems like we have most of the work completed already?"

Darin looks at Melba seriously and points toward the house. "Now, go! I got this, I am sure!"

Melba notices he is serious. "Okay, I will go. I will take care of dinner since you have it. You are sure, right?"

Darin, as serious as he can get, replies, "Woman, go! Now!" Melba heads toward the house to start dinner. Darin asks Torin, "Torin, do you know why we homeschool you and why your mother does not want you to attend a school where other children go and why you children attend martial arts classes? So that you don't get kidnapped or killed by strangers who have their eyes on vulnerable young kids like you. You can't attend school physically until you're old enough to take care of yourself then, you understand?"

Torin tries to follow what his dad says. "I guess. I don't know what kidnapping is. Can you explain that?"

Darin explains in simple layman's terms, "Son, kidnapping is when a stranger who does not know you tries to steal you away from your family, may even hurt you. You may never see your family again."

With a lump in his throat, Torin says, "Oh wow! Yeah, I don't think I ever want to go to school. I would rather be home for school. My friends are my brother and sister."

Darin, with sympathy, says, "Well, I guess you got it, son. Go ahead and get that slop over there. We have to feed the goats and ox."

Torin grabs two buckets of slop and puts them in a wheelbarrow, pushing it to the animal feed area and pouring it out slowly with his father along with the long feeding stalls. After pouring the slop for the animals, Darin grabs a ladder, climbs up to the top of the barn, and grabs three stacks of hay for the cows. As he throws the feed down to the ground, Darin watches out for Torin. "Watch out, Torin. Please move out of the way, son." Torin moves out of the way as the father throws down the hay. While coming back down the ladder, Darin happens to fall off the ladder suddenly, dropping to the ground. "Ow, ow, ah! Torin, call someone nearby, please, son, get someone to hurry up! Your mom's preparing dinner. Quick, you need to go get her."

Torin, afraid his dad is hurt badly, runs to the house, while his mother, Melba, prepares dinner for the family. Torin screams, "Mom! Mom! Hurry! Hurry!"

Melba drops what she is doing and asks Torin, "What's the matter? What is it!"

Torin explains his dad's situation, "Mom, Dad fell, and he can't move."

Melba runs out of the house with Torin toward the farm; she grabs a few pillows and blankets with her in case it's something severe. She grabs her cell phone—depending on the circumstance that he has to be rushed to the hospital. Melba says with her husband at the barn, "I explained to you, Darin, your orthopedic surgeon warned you to be careful while climbing. I told you not to do any of that without me. Now relax as I gently lift your head and put this pillow under your head."

Darin says in a bit of pain, "Okay, dear, it feels like I broke something."

Melba puts the blanket on him so that he keeps warm. Melba knows that her husband has backache problems. "Are you sure it's not your back pain acting up again?"

Knowing it might be his back pain, Darin says, "I didn't think of that. Can you get my medicine?"

Melba is about to leave the barn to get Darin's medicine in the house and says, "Torin, watch your dad."

Torin, with a concerned look on his face, replies, "Okay, Mommy."

When Melba gets to the house, the other children, namely Cynthia and Jewel, are coming off the bus after school. Melba screams to them from the doorway, "Children, put your bags down and go over to where your father is in the barn because he fell from the ladder! Go!"

Cynthia and Jewel drop their book bags inside the house near the doorway and rush to their dad's barn area. Jewel is a little frightened. "Dad, you should have waited until I got home."

Darin looks up at his son Jewel, "I know I should have waited, but I wanted to get it done before you came home from school, and I didn't want to disturb Melba from preparing dinner for us."

Cynthia has a way with words. "You know what they say, Dad? patience is a virtue."

Knowing he's impatient, Darin says, "Yep, you're right, honey."

Melba runs back to the barn with the medicine, takes her husband's head in her lap, pops the pill in his mouth with the other hand, and gives him some water to drink it.

Melba, a bit nervous, says, "Honey, hopefully, this will help. Otherwise, we have to call an ambulance."

Darin is a bit worried. "I hope and pray that it is my back and nothing else." Fifteen minutes go by, and Darin starts to feel much better. He starts to move a bit more, and within minutes, a miracle happens as he stands up.

Melba exclaims loudly, "Thank God."

The entire family is happy that Darin is all right and heads back to the house, where Melba continues with dinner, as the older children are helping their mother as much as possible since she has to go to work in a couple of hours. Jewel is helping his mother cut up some vegetables. "Well, Mom, today's school was fascinating."

Melba asks with curiosity, "How's that Jewel?"

Cynthia, who is seasoning the meat, says, "He was teaching again, ha, ha."

Jewel looks at Cynthia with a rugged look. "Yep, you are right, Cynthia. You hit the nail on the spot."

Melba raises her eyebrows. "So, Jewel, what did you teach the teachers today? Just curious, son."

Jewel grabs the onions to chop. "Well, I introduced some fascinating physics today."

Melba interjects a bit, "Why was it so interesting?"

Jewel says with excitement, "Well, a teacher wanted to know the pressure of water and the force to turn a vehicle to move without ever needing gas instead through the water."

Melba, interested, says, "How's that, son?"

Jewel is not trying to explain to his mother because her field is nursing, not physics. "Mom, you wouldn't understand it. It's a very high level of physics and is complicated."

Darin stretches his back a bit, and continues, "Well, I see that is an exciting day, son. Also, aren't you supposed to be graduating in the next two weeks?"

Jewel nods his head. "Yes, I am graduating in the next two weeks, and I am busy this weekend to finish my final project within a week."

Melba asks Jewel seriously, "Have you decided on what college you want to go to, Jewel?"

Jewel stares down at the floor a bit. "Well, Mom, I haven't decided yet, but I am sure many colleges will want to accept me, and I will have many to choose. I am pretty sure."

Darin curiously asks Jewel. "So what type of project are you doing, son?"

Jewel tells his dad what type of project it is. "I am doing a project for physics regarding the motion of water that can move a vehicle."

Darin sees a super achiever. "Hmm, I would like to see how that works, son."

Jewel brushes his dad's shoulder. "You will see it work before I take it to school the next day, Dad."

Darin looks at his son with surprise even as Jewel nods at him confidently.

CHAPTER 3

THE BIOLOGIST SAVANT WITH EXTREME BEAUTY

The third and final family lives in the poorest neighborhood of Camden, New Jersey, in a dilapidated bluish-white siding house with certain parts of the house falling off. The inside of the house seems decorated in an old modern Victorian look, with a tiny kitchen to cook in and two bathrooms. The family, called the Mellomystics, consists of six family members: The father, Lu, a carpenter, has a business doing odd jobs for neighbors, friends, and family members. Su Ang Mellomystic, the wife, is a stay-at-home mother who cares for the house and the children when they come home from school. Sandra, the oldest, is twenty-two years old and helps her mom around the house. Sandra is a college schoolteacher who graduated early and will marry another teacher. The other three kids attend Camden elementary, middle, and high school. Bing-Yu, the youngest brother, goes to elementary school and is only nine years old. Charlie, who goes to middle school, loves martial arts, and he is twelve years old. And finally, Merna Mellomystic, the last of the three savants who loves biology, attends Camden High School. Merna loves studying the human muscular system and loves studying other creatures. She is fascinated with the electrical impulses of the movement of muscles and how tiny cellular structures from the brain can move those muscles.

It is Thursday after 4:00 p.m., and Lu Mellomystic comes home from a hard day at work and kisses his wife on the cheeks. "Wow, it took almost a full day to get all that work done for the neighbor."

Su says, smiling, "Well, I was about to ask you. Did it go well with the neighbor today?"

Lu says with confidence, "It went very well. I made quite a bit of money."

Su asks abruptly, "So how much did you make?"

Lu is crunching the numbers in his head. "I made about $2,000 today."

Su Ang raises her eyebrows and says with disbelief, "Oh really, how'd you manage that one?"

"I know you don't believe me." Lu can't believe his wife is questioning him like that. "Look at these bills I have in my hand, do you want to count it?"

Su Ang notices Lu waving a bunch of money in her face, and she cannot fathom him making that amount of cash in one day. Su Ang with a positive attitude, "Wow, I can't believe you made this much money. I am utterly amazed at you, and you have to be good to get paid this much in one day." Su counts the money.

Lu changes the subject. "Hopefully, I can have a crew of men working for me, making it easier on myself one day."

Su Ang agrees with him. "Yes, I hope you do one day. When you're making money like this, I am sure you will have people working for you in no time."

Sandra overhears them in the kitchen and shouts, "I'm impressed, Dad. We are proud of you. I believe you will be a successful, Dad, one day."

Lu thanks his daughter, saying, "I appreciate that coming from a profoundly wonderful lady."

Sandra blushes. "Why, thank you, Daddy."

Lu speaks Cantonese, telling his daughter how beautiful she is. "Wo de piàoliang baobèi lán Yanjing de nuhái shén liwù duì shìjiè." That means "My captivating baby-blue-eyed girl, God's gift to the world."

Sandra thanks her father in Cantonese. "Xièxiè."

Su Ang gently nods her head in agreement. The other three kids are back home while shouting as they enter the front door, "We're home!"

Lu asks his son Charlie, "Do you want to work with me this weekend, son?"

Charlie is excited because he likes working with his dad. "Yeah, sure, Dad. Will it be all day?"

Lu explains to Charlie, "Charlie, my boy, it is only a few hours this weekend, not an entire day."

Charlie frowns and asks him, "What if I do all my homework tonight? Will I be able to work the whole day with you?"

Lu realizes his son's zeal for work. "Well, son, to be honest with you, it is only a four-hour job anyway."

Charlie is disappointed. Seeing his son down, Lu says, "You can still work with me, so although it isn't an all-day job, you're still working with your dad, right?" Lu hugs Charlie and snuggles him.

With a weak smile, Charlie says, "Right, Dad."

In the kitchen, Sandra asks her mom a question, "Mom? Would it be all right if I took the family to a restaurant tomorrow evening?"

In her yellow butterfly dress, Su Ang points to it. "You see these butterflies, Sandra, aren't they beautiful? Still, they don't care because they are happy, just like the real ones flying around Mother Earth. They are comfortable and content and don't have to prove anything."

Sandra looks at her mother with a puzzled expression and asks, "What are you saying? Are you saying that you do not wish to go?"

Su Ang elaborates, "I am saying, dear, that since we are poor, you do not have to prove yourself to us."

With a small smile, Sandra replies, "Not at all, Mom. What I want to do is take the family out to a nice dinner. Besides that, I want you guys to meet my boyfriend whom I have been dating for months. That is why I want to bring the family, so you can get to know him. He's a nice guy."

Su Ang is surprised. "Oh, okay, we will think about it, dear."

Sandra begs her mom, "Please, Mom, please, you will have fun. I assure you, you will have a good time."

Su Ang feels terrible for her daughter. "I will talk to your dad tonight. It depends on when he gets back from the job he has to do tomorrow."

Sandra gives the benefit of the doubt. "I will let you think about it with Dad and then make reservations for tomorrow once you and Dad talk about it. Please let me know as soon as possible."

Su Ang hugs her daughter. "Yes, dear, I will let you know in a couple of hours." Su Ang turns around and starts cleaning fish for dinner as she asks, "So what is your boyfriend's name? You never told us."

While chopping some other vegetables, Sandra turns toward her mother. "Well, his name is Chang."

Su Ang is surprised. "Oh, he is Chinese, eh?"

Sandra knows her mom has a thing with names. "No, Mom, he is Spanish."

Su Ang again is surprised. "Spanish, no! You got to be kidding me."

Sandra's lips pucked out. "Why does that surprise you, Mom."

Su Ang is still in disbelief. "Because no Spanish or black man has that type of name. Only Chinese people have that name."

Sandra briefs her mother about the changing times. "Well, Mom, times are changing, and people aren't like the previous generation. People are naming their kids what they think sounds good."

Merna walks over to her mother and asks her a question, "Mom, I wanted to know if I can use the kitchen table to dissect a few critters. Will that be all right, Mom?"

Su Ang has a confused look. "What did you say?"

Merna explains again, "I would like to use the dining room table to dissect some little creatures, Mom."

With a shocked look, Su Ang says, "You got to be kidding me, right? We eat at that table. Are you on another planet or what?"

Merna pleads, "Mom, I will move the cloth and put down a plastic material of my own so I don't get the mess over the table. I need to accomplish my final project before I graduate, Mom."

Su Ang, disgusted, says, "You know that stuff grosses me out. You can do it when everyone is asleep on Saturday night or even Friday so I don't have to see and get nightmares."

Merna concurs with Su Ang. "Thank you, Mom, you are the greatest." Merna kisses her mom and is thrilled by getting this opportunity to get her project done. Su Ang calls out to her husband, who happens to be looking under the Craigslist ads under the job section, where people are looking to hire carpenters and odd jobs.

Su Ang calls her husband, "Lu...Lu, can you come here a minute."

Lu is typing on Craigslist for carpentry jobs. "What is it, Su? what is so important?"

Su Ang tries to get his attention from the kitchen area. "Lu! Lu! Come here! It will only take a second. I have to ask you something."

Not wanting to be bothered, Lu replies, "Why can't you ask me the question from there?"

Su Ang is a bit frustrated. "Lu, come here. It is a secret, and I don't want the children to hear."

The two little boys are doing their homework at the dining room table. Lu gets up and heads to the kitchen to see the interest of what his wife wants. On his way to the kitchen, Lu enters the kitchen, as Sandra walks to her room. Merna goes to the bathroom.

In a low tone, Su Ang says, "Honey, Sandra wants us all to go out to dinner together."

Lu is not so thrilled. "Well, that is good. Where is she taking us, to McDonald's?"

Su Ang giggles a bit. "No."

Lu is serious and replies, "What is so funny?"

Su Ang clarifies, "No, Lu, she wants to take us to some fancy restaurant. She feels the family should meet that boy she has been dating for six months."

Lu is enthusiastic. "Wow, we are finally going to meet the man who might be taking our little girl away, huh."

Su Ang tries to get her husband to agree to his daughter's wishes. "Look, Lu, she is the apple of your eye, and it would make her happy if we go."

Lu considers. "Okay, tell her we will go."

With excitement, Su Ang says, "Let me tell Sandra the good news so she can make reservations for tomorrow evening."

Lu hugs his wife and says, "Tomorrow evening? I should be home on time, but I will meet you guys there if I am not. Leave the directions through MapQuest, and I will follow it to the restaurant." Lu heads back to the couch to finish looking up jobs for carpenters, as Su Ang calls out to Sandra, who happens to be in her room preparing what to wear for her special evening with her boyfriend. Merna looks at her sister in disbelief.

"Well, I never. I will never do anything special with you again."

"Merna, come here. Please forgive me for brushing you off, but I am working to make sure that the evening is a memorable one for the family. I hope you understand," says Sandra.

Merna, who is very intelligent, states her thoughts, "Look, Sandra, make sure you don't disappoint Mom and Dad. They don't want any more disappointments, and you know what I am talking about."

Sandra remembers when she had her last boyfriend, who cheated on her, and how her parents were disappointed in her choosing such a loser. "Don't worry, Merna. I learned from my last boyfriend's affair with my best friend long ago. I'll never repeat that mistake. This guy is cordial, and he only thinks about me."

Merna doesn't want her sister to be hurt again. "If he does you wrong, I will dissect his body and feed it to the sharks."

Sandra kisses and hugs Merna. "I know, little sis, you can pick up on things right away, and I am sure you will tell me the vibes you get from him, hmm."

Merna hugs her sister. "You got it!"

Meanwhile, Lu walks over to the two boys doing homework at the table. "Charlie, what can I help you with, buddy?"

Charlie is doing his English homework, and Bing is doing his math homework. A subject for Charlie's essay is eluding him. "Dad, do you have any idea?"

Lu, who isn't good at English, asks his daughter Merna to help. "Hey, Merna, your brother Charlie needs your help figuring out a subject to write about in his English class."

Merna answers, "Sure, Dad, I will be right there."

Lu asks his other son. "Bing, can I help you with something?"

Charlie comes up with a title for his English paper with the help of his sister Merna and begins writing about martial arts and how it helped him with his confidence and self-esteem.

Lu turns to Merna. "What are you doing these days, female version of Albert Einstein?"

Merna tries to make her dad happy. "Dad, you're pretty funny."

Lu questions Merna deeply in her biology subject. "What are you doing this weekend, my extraordinary daughter, on the topic of biology?"

Merna has not known that her father is interested in her work. "Hmm, wow, Dad, I didn't know you were interested in biology, and I am dissecting some small frozen mammals and examining brain activity with an electrode miniscope," with motivation, Merna explains with excitement. "It is amazing, Dad, how our muscular system works. It is fascinating to me. It is what I would love to do."

With joy in his eyes, Lu comments, "You have the hearts of the teachers at your school and students from other schools. However, you are a brilliant young adult who is good in all subjects. You are giving competition to those who are bigwigs in the subject of biology expertise. I am so proud of you. I am waiting for the day when the president of the United States will recognize your gift one day."

On the other hand, Sandra goes into her room and notices something missing. Sandra thinks she knows the culprit. "Merna! Merna!"

Merna, busy in her room looking over her final project for school, responds to Sandra, "What is it, Sandra? I am busy."

Sandra suspects her sister moved her anatomy model. "Merna, did you move my anatomy model from my room?"

Merna messes with her sister because she likes to play games. "No! Did you check the garbage disposal, or better yet, under your car?"

Sandra does not find her sister amusing. "Come on! I know you had to have taken it. I am coming to your room to look for it now!" Sandra goes into Merna's room and looks behind the door. She sees nothing. She looks inside the closet, and finds nothing. She questions her one more time. "Look, if you have it, I don't mind. However, I suppose that you're lying to me."

Merna, a bit frightened of her sister, points under the bed and says, "I hid it under the bed because I need it this weekend to work on a project for my finals. I hope you aren't mad at me."

Sandra, a little upset, forgets about the situation. "So what kind of project are you doing this weekend?" Merna, relieved that her sister is no longer mad at her, shows Sandra the miniscope for the specimens. Sandra is a bit disgusted like her mom. "Well, good luck with that. As you know, we have a family outing this Saturday, and you know the plan already."

Merna is full of herself. "Biology is a gift given by God for us to study and find out what makes people, insects, reptiles, birds, and fishes communicate with Mother Earth."

Sandra is not so interested. "It sounds like a winner, Merna. Good luck with it."

Merna giggles a little. "Thanks."

Su Ang calls everyone to dinner. "Dinner time, come and get it."

Everyone sits around the table to eat. Lu asks his daughter Merna over dinner, "So you're graduating in the next couple of weeks. Have you decided on what college you would like to attend? You are going to have so many to choose from."

Merna is chewing on food. "Honestly, I don't know what to choose among the many. I would have to choose the college with the best biology criteria."

Everyone has a good dinner that evening and goes early to bed later.

The next day is Friday at Merna's high school. Merna gets bullied by some senior girl who wants her to do her homework. "Hey, Merna, have you done my homework yet?"

Merna stands up to the bully for once in her life. "Look, Susan, you might think I am small and fragile, but I am not doing your homework. It will make you even dumber than rocks. How do you think you'll get by in life like this?"

Susan, the bully, grabs Merna and pushes her up against the locker. "Listen, you little scrawny Merna, I want that homework to be done before the following two classes, got it!"

Merna gives one hard-hitting reply, "You know bullying does not get you anywhere with me. How about I don't do the work, and you could fail, and if you touch me, I will go to the officer and tell them you tried to threaten my life. You fool!"

Susan, not wanting to go back to juvie, lets her down. "I beg you, don't tell. I will do anything. I don't want to go back to that hideous juvie place where there is hardly any fun." Merna heads to her biology class and waits for several fond teachers of Merna's work.

Merna enters the classroom, and the professor asks her to stand in front of her classroom. She explains her findings for the upcoming project. "Merna, please let us know what type of speculation you have discovered over the weekend regarding the final project coming up."

"Well, my decision, Professor, once translated into action by a nervous system which must decide how to interact with the physical world. This world that consists of neurons that process and operate multiple levels of muscular impulses," explains Merna in front of the class. "That's it." Merna humbly bows her head. The entire class claps, along with some professors sitting and paying attention to Merna. These professors are blown away and excited to hear what they heard from a brilliant savant who had mastered all aspects of biology.

Merna is to be called to the principal's office while attending classes all day,. "Merna Mellomystic, please report to the principal's office." Merna gets excused from her seventh-period class. Merna enters the principal's office, where she meets up with several of the professors from the biology department; they have put together a substantial plaque award with a trophy from the principal, stating, "A Great and Upstanding Futuristic Mind: Merna Mellomystic."

He hands Merna the award regarding her accomplishments and proudly says, "We have seen a young mind excel beyond extraordinary measures. As someone whose mind grasps new and improved links to material, she has helped great professors not only at this school but even at well-known colleges in the United States. Merna Mellomystic will one day teach the greats of our generation with these significant accomplishments. Congrats, young lady!"

The principal and the professors recognize Merna's pride in these words: "I would like to thank both Principal Lacy and the whole biology department for this great award. I will cherish it for the rest of my life and thank this great school for developing my career. Thank you all for the years I have spent at Camden High School. It will be a staple throughout my life."

One professor asks without prejudice, "Do you think biology can make any more progress than it already has? Do we know everything that has to be unstated about the human body?"

Merna confidentially smiles and says, "My journey has just begun, and I am excited to see where this will take me shortly. But I can assure you it will be something the world has never seen or imagined in the future before. Very soon, sir, very soon."

CHAPTER 4

ONWARD TO A SPECIAL OCCASION

At the Mellomystics' house, the entire family prepares for that special dinner at the restaurant. Sandra grabs Merna and heads to her room on the bed. Sandra has a beautiful blue-and-white gown with sparkling dark-black shoes on the bed for her sister Merna. "Hey, try this on. I think you look pretty in it." Sandra then puts on a beige-and-silver dress with white high heel shoes. Surprised at the new dress, Merna grabs and hugs Sandra with a kiss.

"Wow, you're the greatest. I am so blessed to have an awesome big sister."

"I love you, little sis." Sandra gently hugs her back. The rest of the family is getting ready for the evening. Lu is dressed in jeans with a dress shirt and shoes since he could make it on time for the occasion. He had finished the extra work for the day, where he made $1,500. Excited with the money and ready for the experience, Lu tells Su Ang how gorgeous she looks in her dress. "Mm, you look good. You look good enough to eat."

Su Ang blushes as Lu puts his arms around her waist. "You're too much, young man."

Lu lets go of his wife, and grabs her purse. "Are you ready to go?"

Su Ang says, "Yes, I am."

The two little boys, Bing and Charlie, are dressed in slacks, a dress shirt, and shoes. While Charlie is putting on his shoes by the door of the Mellomystics' house, a car honks outside. Charlie opens the door and looks out and is surprised at what he sees and comes running back inside the house, screaming, "Mom! Dad! You're not going to believe this!"

Lu asks, "What is it, boy?"

Charlie explains to his dad an expensive car is waiting for the family in front of the house. "Dad, I've never been in a car like that. What is it exactly?"

Lu describes what kind of car it is. He looks out the window at the car and says, "Well, son, it's a limo. It's roomy, and many people like the president and celebrities are driven around by chauffeur drivers."

What Charlie's dad said stunned him. "Wow, I wonder who got us a car like that. It must be unique for us to drive in a car like that, huh, Dad."

Lu, second looks through the window, and says, "Well, yes, son."

In disbelief, Sandra overhears them talking, heads to the front door, looks outside, and turns toward her dad. "I can't believe he did this."

With an odd look, Lu asks, "You can't believe what?"

In a roundabout way, Sandra tells her dad, "Well, someone special did this for me, that's all."

Lu gets an inclination or idea of who it could be. "Hmm, he did this. Wow, I am beside myself."

Sandra excuses herself, heads back inside, and asks the family, "Okay, is everyone ready to go? Because I am ready. Let's go, everyone."

The entire family gets into the limousine with a chauffeur who drives the whole family to Big Louie's Barbecue Pit restaurant. Chang stands in front of the restaurant, who happens to be waiting at the restaurant's door. The entire family gets out of the limo at the front of the restaurant and meets Chang. Chang, a gentleman, greets the family, "Great meeting you, Mr. and Mrs. Mellomystic, boys, young lady. Hello, baby." Chang kisses his girlfriend, Sandra, on the lips after greeting her.

Lu and Su Ang say politely, "Nice to meet you too, son."

The entire family enters. A hostess greets them at the front desk of the restaurant. The hostess comes around and asks, "May I help you?"

Chang replies, "Yes, Rodriquez, party of seven. I have a reservation."

The hostess looks at her handheld iPad. "Yes, Rodriquez, reservations for 7:00 p.m. Please follow me." In the middle of the restaurant, the hostess seats the family. It is a beautiful, relaxing, sultry atmosphere with basket woven lights, and a jazz band. As the family sits at the table, Chang pulls out the chair for Sandra, Merna sits in the middle of her two brothers, and the mother and father sit at the ends of the table. Merna, sitting across from Chang, stares and gloats at how handsome Chang is while trying to figure him out. Chang, smiling and looking at Sandra, puts his left hand on Sandra's hand and expresses his love in detail to Sandra.

"Sandra, your beauty beholds me in a way I can't ignore. Your smile is always gleaming with love."

Su Ang breaks into Chang's romantic discourse and exclaims politely, "Excuse me, Chang, I understand that you're a professor where my daughter teaches also."

Lu cuts over his wife and asks Chang, "What do you teach exactly?"

Chang comments with a good look, "I teach biochemistry. Why?"

Lu, a bit enthused, says, "Biochemistry is very interesting. I think you and my young savant of a daughter have something in common, right, Merna?"

With her eyebrows furrowed, Merna thinks to herself, *Biochemistry, what does a biochemistry teacher have to do with an English teacher, hmm. Now that is complicated.* Merna starts to ask Chang a question. "Pardon me, Chang, and biochemistry is the study of chemistry within living organisms?"

Chang replies calmly, "That is correct. Ah, Merna, what would you major in when you attend college?"

Without missing a beat, Merna says, "I will be majoring in biology."

It surprises Chang, he replies, "It's good that you're studying biology, good for you."

Sandra gets Merna's attention. "Excuse me, Merna. We're having dinner with the family. We don't want to talk about biology." Sandra wonders if the entire family is ready to order their meal. "Is everyone ready to order?" The waiter at the table is prepared to take the order from the family. Lu is the first to order.

"I think I will have steak and egg. What will you have, honey?"

Su Ang looks at the menu and picks out the unusual for herself. "Never tried it before. I think I will have barbecue ribs and chicken combo."

Sandra is a bit curious. "Wow, I am surprised, Mom, but you will love it. I promise you."

Su Ang orders the meals for the boys. "The boys will have wings."

Bing wants more. "Can I have fries with that?"

Su agrees with Bing. "Sure, son. Add fries with those wings, please."

Charlie wants something different. "Can I have fish and chips instead?"

Su Ang looks at the menu and notices that fish and chips are not expensive. "Sure, son, you can have that instead of wings. Not a problem, right, Chang?"

Chang is not paying attention to the price. "No, not a problem, ma'am." Chang wants to find out what Sandra will be eating. "What will you have, honey?"

Sandra, who likes her mother's meal choice, responds, "As for my dinner, I'll have the same as my mom's except that I'll substitute steak for ribs. Would that be okay, waiter?"

The waiter, with no hesitation, says, "Yes, that would be all right."

Chang looks at the waiter, and without even looking at the menu a second time, he decides, "I will take the same thing as well."

Thirty minutes go by as the waiter brings out the dinners with their drinks and serve them around the table. Merna asks her dad, "Dad, I was wondering if Sandra could take me shopping a few days before graduation and buy me clothes for that occasion. I don't want to look too poor. You know what I mean."

Lu replies with a mouthful, "Sure, as long as it is okay with Sandra."

Sandra replies without any hesitancy, "Sure she can."

Chang swallows a small bite of food, and says, "Graduating in a couple of weeks, Merna?"

As Merna gets fired up about graduation, she uses a fork to rattle against her soda glass to grab everyone's attention. "My first thanks to all of you is for organizing such an enjoyable evening. I am confident that my career in biology will be fulfilling and rewarding since I am graduating in a few weeks. Someday, we will stand up in history and tell the world that biology is not just about studying animals and people. It's more about helping humans and animals live together harmoniously by understanding all living things through communication. I appreciate this time with family and a future brother-in-law. Thank you for listening."

Su Ang is delighted with her daughter Merna. "Very well said, Merna."

As Su Ang gets up after dinner, everyone hugs Merna.

And so we see that the three families are having a good time several weeks before graduation preparing for their intelligent children's future goals.

We continue with the Normalic, who have had several great weekends with the family on various outings and family gatherings at the house. It has been several weeks and a few days before graduation on a Wednesday. It is Monday morning, and Mr. and Mrs. Normalic are heading out to work at their Genetic Specialty Inc. The maid, Mrs. Garcia, hears Mrs. Normalic cleaning the upstairs bathroom, and she goes to their room and gently wakes them up, first going to Mary. While Lucas and Mary get ready for school and leave in the limo, Mary asks Lucas, "Hey, Lucas, you want to get drunk with some liquor before school?"

Lucas grabs the liquor bottle from Mary. "This is not good for your young mind. It destroys your brain. Have you heard of the wet brain?"

Mary is not paying any attention. "Ah, come on, Lucas, just once. Have some fun."

Lucas is standing his ground. "No, Mary, it is not good. It will destroy your brain cells."

Mary winds down. "You're no fun. I guess you're right."

They get out of the limo. As the school bell rings, they head to their respective classes. Mary runs to her usual class, as Lucas heads to a substantial scientific lab where he teaches professors for his final project. Lucas enters the lab and begins teaching about a chemical he had discovered at home, its mixture of compounds and how it can help the human population. Lucas says, "Ladies, gentlemen, and faculty, what I have to present to you on these slides, along with actually performing the compound I have at hand, is furthering the life expectancy experiments on the frog and the cricket I have in front of you. As this cricket digests argon and silver mixed with boron and salt, aging starts to occur in the frog as it consumes the cricket."

At the same time, everyone in the classroom claps and is in awe. A teacher asks Lucas a weird and unintelligent question.

"Lucas, let me ask you a question, wouldn't silver 4 and boron 5 kill anything?"

Lucas responds with an intelligent answer, "Professor, the silver I use is silver 10. In my experiments, I use is boron 7, which boosts the aging process, reduces the lifespan, and accelerates the death process. For living longer, it is just the reverse of the chemical numbers."

According to Lucas's teacher, the project will lead to humans being able to sustain life expectancy longer once the method is reversed, so the project gets an A+. Later that day, Mary and Lucas are having their last lunch together in the lunch-room. Lucas hands his pudding to Mary. "Here, this is the last time we would have to share any item in this place, Mary."

After hearing what he said, Mary realizes what he meant. "The last time in a lunchroom? Don't be ridiculous. In the future, I will become a doctor, and you will visit me, right?"

Lucas is just catching what Mary is saying. "You know what! I'm sure this is not the last time we will have lunch, but it is the last time in middle school for you and high school for me."

Mary agrees, and gets up from the table. "Yep, definitely the last time in junior school."

The bell rings, and the principal announces a half day for the students. "Students, we will not have a full day of school because of graduation in a couple of days, so I am announcing the half day. As soon as lunch is over, you may go home."

Mary and Lucas eat fast as Lucas calls on his cell phone to have the limo pick them up early. "Hello, Mike, we have half a day at school. Can you pick us up in twenty minutes?"

Mike, eating donuts, replies, "Sure, will be there in twenty, sir." Twenty minutes go by, and the limousine reaches the school. Mike, the limo driver, gets out of the limo and opens the door for Mary and Lucas. "Sir, ma'am, good day."

Mary is getting into the limousine. "Thanks, Mike."

Lucas does not say anything and gets into the car.

After half an hour, the limousine enters the on-ramp and drives to Mary and Lucas's parents' business. As the limousine exits the highway, it pulls up to the location's front door.

He thanks the driver after exiting the limousine. "Thanks, Mike. Let me open the door for you, Mary." Lucas has compassion for his sister.

Mary returns with politeness, "Thanks, Lucas."

Lucas and Mary walk past the guard station, as the guard remarks, "Hey, you two, come here!"

Mary, who doesn't want to explain herself, says, "We're Mary and Lucas Normalic. You can call our parents upstairs. They're expecting us."

Guard, a bit impatient, and says, "I started here a few years back."

Mary states an intelligent observation, "It figures. Still, it will be all right, sir."

Again, guard shows his dumb side. "You say Mrs. Normalic, right?"

Mary is getting a bit impatient. "Yes!" The guard calls upstairs for the Normalics, as Mary turns to Lucas. "Hey, Lucas, this guy is pretty dumb." Lucas looks at Mary with one eye on the guard. "Why is he working here?"

Lucas replies while with a fake smile at the guard, "I don't know, Mary. It is weird indeed."

The guard is on a conference call with Mrs. Normalic. "Mrs. Normalic, we have Mary and Lucas down here waiting for you."

Mrs. Normalic, on the other end, responds, "Send them up, please. We are expecting them."

Guard has a confused look on his face. "Sorry, you two can go up."

Lucas and Mary head to the elevator, going up several floors. They both head toward the chemistry area, where DNA sequences prepare the ideal DNA strands to implement into newborns by injecting them to make them the ideal savants in their expertise. Mrs. Normalic greets the two at the front of the chemical sequencing lab.

Mrs. Normalic smiles and says, "Hello, you two. It was a pleasure to hear from you both. Lucas, are you ready to work while Mary waits in the lounge area?"

Lucas sighs a bit. "You don't need Mary this time, Mom?"

Mrs. Normalic gestures with her right index finger for Lucas only, and replies, "No, son, she can read some medical magazines while we take care of the chemical sequencing. Okay, Lucas?"

Lucas is interested. "Got it, Mom!" Lucas puts on a lab coat, as Mary heads to the lounge area. He helps his dad with his brother Joe with DNA sequencing, defining a chemical balance. He heads to the back of the lab, where he finds his father and Joe.

Joe, who seems to be staring at the chemical sequence modular, notices Lucas in the mirror. "Lucas, we are at 38 percent on gene molecular DNA sequencing to discover a final chemical to fit these two babies' DNA, making them a viable treasure to society."

Mr. Normalic slowly turns around and interrupts the two. "We're at 78 percent of DNA sequence so far. Is there any way you could help Lucas get it to 100 percent so we can use the centrifuges to separate the compound needed to put into the babies' DNA?"

A scientific approach is taken by Lucas. "In fact, Father, when cerium 10 and indium 5 are combined with selenium and praseodymium 3, they will produce hydrogen 5 upon liquefaction. After 45 to 55 cycles of amplification, every gram of 2000bp, where bp is blood pressure, will produce a product from 106 grams of template DNA. In this case, you will obtain a 100 percent liquid mix that will produce a millionfold amplification of the DNA sequence." A computer takes the sequence, showing several beeps as the DNA sequencing begins. The splice of the DNA on the computer combines the chemical sequencing with the final compound needed to liquefy into an injectable liquid taken by robotic needle arms that are then injected into the babies, completing the task at hand.

Mr. Normalic, excited with the outcome, turns to Lucas. "You did it, son. You got it to 100 percent. We will have some excellent savants for families who have struggled throughout their history. I fathom that you will go a long way in history, Lucas. You are a gift to society."

Lucas, trilled, says with much appreciation, "Whatever I can do, I will do for the success of our family, Dad."

Mr. Normalic compassionately hugs his son, appreciating his gift. He calls the parents of the two babies to come and get them since they are ready to be taken home.

Meanwhile, Joe puts his arms around Lucas. "Lucas, have I told you how much you mean to me, little brother?"

Lucas turns toward his brother Joe. "No, why, Joe?"

Joe is a bit teary-eyed. "Brother, you are the greatest and the best little brother of them all."

Lucas grabs a tissue box and takes a tissue out for Joe. "I love you too, brother."

Thirty minutes have passed, and the two families have arrived to pick up their children. Mr. Normalic and Mrs. Normalic greet them. "Mr. and Mrs. Frazen, and Mr. and Mrs. Gallup, here are your babies, and they are ready to be taken home to grow up into savants who will significantly contribute to society."

Both parents say with appreciation, "Thank you so much." The parents sign a release form and are off with their children. The Normalics also leave at the same time for their house, where Samantha prepares dinner with the cook. Lucas is still thoughtful even as the Normalics look on with pride in their significant contribution to society. All this gave him more impetus for what he would do for his upcoming project that would change the course of history forever.

Meanwhile, while Mr. Normalic, Joe, and Lucas leave the front of the building, they see something flying across the skies like a meteorite, followed by some object that seems to blink in and out of sight. They look across the street with amazement as two black vans look up with binoculars and with no license plates. Mr. Normalic then sprints with his boys to the car. That evening, Samantha and the cook bring out the roast, potatoes, salad, and greens, as the family sits around the eight-seat table for an exciting dinner. Everyone has a beautiful evening that night.

CHAPTER 5

DAY OF GRADUATION

It is the day of graduation. Finally, as luck would have it, Lucas's mom, Mrs. Normalic, who happens to be upstairs in her bedroom, grabs Lucas's cap and gown and heads downstairs. At the same time, Lucas gets out of the shower. A stunning suit catches his eye as he puts on his bathrobe. Lucas heads down the stairs in a new suit. Everyone looks at how amazing Lucas looks in his tuxedo. Mrs. Normalic gives Lucas the cap and gown to put on. "Here you go, son. Put this over your suit, and we will head out the door." The entire family is all in attire suitable for the graduation ceremony.

Everyone except the students is seated in the auditorium at the graduation ceremony. Then outside the auditorium doors, the students are lined up on the sides of the hall. Then on the stage, the principal gets up and says, "Students, faculty, parents, and graduates, welcome to the 2138 graduation. Let the ceremony begin." The ceremony starts with an ambiance of a piano playing, and the calling of names begins as they grab their diplomas.

The principal and leading faculty advisor call the graduating students in alphabetical order. "Amber Amos, Brenda Burns, Charlie Channon, Cynthia Kahn, Lisa Garmon, Orrin Haywood, Michael Jannese, Kyle. Kingman, Lucas Normalic, Maurice Lovell, Sharon Naron." They keep calling names until the last person; the principal speaks to the parents, faculty, and students. "Can our double valedictorian graduate, Mr. Lucas Normalic, come up and read your speech to your classmates."

Lucas nods and comes forward to propose an address of wisdom to his classmates. "Dear classmates, class of 2138, may you endure in your endeavors with the fulfillment of your journey. Our generation will overcome everything that life brings us, and we will make a mark in history, as we enlighten those who need to hear us. Let's join hands right now in our ceremony, continually bringing contrition to humanity through achieving our goals and fulfilling our destiny to surpass the previous several generations that are in front of us! For I know while going to this school in my chemical engineering days throughout my four years of high school that I had made a mark in chemistry that all of you may inspire someone to make a mark in their history. One day, unlike any of your study subjects, I may find that everlasting cure to endless youth and never get any older for generations to come. For it is our time to upraise and conquer and make history. May we make a stand in society. Thank you, fellow graduates, faculty, teachers, parents, and continuing students. May the higher power be with you all. I am grateful for your attention." Lucas gets off the pulpit as the students clap and cheer.

The principal stands up from his seat and walks to the podium. "Thank you very much, Lucas. Please let me mount that speech inside the trophy cabinet so that future students will know about this extraordinary student who made history, in this school, and around the world." Lucas hands the speech to the principal. The principal puts it in his pocket for safekeeping. The principal starts to pronounce the ceremony's ending. "I want to thank all the parents, faculty, fellow teachers, continuing students, and graduates for coming to the 2138 graduates ceremony. We'll have some food available for everyone who cares to mingle and stay for a short time. It's up to you whether you wish to purchase graduation pictures or go home if you have other obligations. Nevertheless, we are taking some pictures by professionals if you want to buy graduation pictures for your family. It is a pleasure to see you all today, and we appreciate your presence. It will be nice to see you all or at least some of you at the luncheon."

Everyone gets up from the auditorium and starts to leave. Most people enter the luncheon area, where the food is, and very few leave to go home.

The following week on a Tuesday, Mr. Normalic gets a bunch of mail in their mailbox, which he picks up after work while his wife goes inside for the evening. "So many colleges are considering my son. I must notify the family and Lucas immediately." Mr. Normalic thinks about all the mail coming from not just the United States but also England, Britain, and other countries. Mr. Normalic heads inside the house and says with excitement, "Everyone, I mean everyone, wherever you are, please come. I have some great news!" All the family members come running toward Mr. Normalic, as Mr. Normalic points to the mail on the table.

Joe cries out excitedly, "Wow, Yale, oh my god, incredible, Dad."

Todd yells out, "Harvard, sweet."

Samantha yells out, "Oxford! Going abroad."

Astonished with these colleges, Mary says, "I am still too young to go to college." She sees Stanford University. "Oh my, Stanford, how so soon."

Mr. Normalic reassures his kids that the mail is all for Lucas. "Children, all these colleges are for Lucas."

All the children except Lucas say, "Ah, man, are you kidding me." The siblings hug and congratulate Lucas. "You go, boy!"

Mrs. Normalic opens some of them up, and they all offer Lucas 100 percent scholarships until he gets his PhD, with free room and board throughout the years.

Lucas looks down as though defeated. "Mom, that is great, but there is one school that I have been researching online since ninth grade."

Mr. Normalic's intuitive mind asks, "What school is that, Lucas?"

Samantha gets a little in the conversation. "Yeah, what school is that, Lucas?"

Lucas looks through the mail haphazardly and stumbles across a manila folder that states across the top, "MIT." Lucas jumps out of his skin and kneels on the floor. "Man, I got it! I got it!"

Todd sees Lucas's excitement and picks him up onto his shoulders. "What! You must tell." Todd lets him down as Lucas opens and reads it to the family.

"MIT is offering me a full scholarship throughout my career until I obtain my PhD, free room and board, and a car of my choice."

Mr. and Mrs. Normalic are beside themselves. "Wow, that's great, son!"

Mr. Normalic says, justifying himself, "I never got an offer like that when I went to college. It's fantastic. Son, you have already made history, and I don't know anyone in college who got an offer for a scholarship that paid all their college, free room, and board, and a car of their choice. That in itself is history in the making, son. Do you agree, honey?"

Mrs. Normalic is shocked. "I don't know anyone like that either." With amazement in their eyes, the entire family hugs and pats Lucas, congratulating him on his success so far. Lucas, of course, takes MIT as his school of choice.

As for the Justicks, will Jewel meet the same fate as Lucas regarding college? Soon we will see it, but for the Justicks, two weeks that have gone by, and a few days before graduation. Melba grabs Torin and puts him in bed, clasping the medicine in the cabinet since he has a severe cold.

The next day is Wednesday. Jewel is sitting in a conference room with a bunch of physics professors as he tries to give them an observation or reasoning regarding saltwater as an energy source within his report.

"Ladies, gentlemen, and faculty, I have a small gadget that will rotate across the room using saltwater as an energy source. Please watch and learn as the motion rotates 360 degrees and then slightly adjusts its turn at the end." Jewel shows how an object that runs on saltwater can gently turn like a car. With great sounds in the room, Jewel gets a lot of applause.

A well-known physicist says, "As long as we can build saltwater boats in factories, we can switch all boats from burning fuel to saltwater. We'll avoid a lot of crises."

Jewel agrees. "We can also do away with electricity, but only by hydroelectricity, like the Hoover Dam." Everyone gets up and claps again. Jewel receives an A+ from all professors in his classes. Back at the house, Cynthia gets her report card later that day and shows her dad, Dustin.

"Hey, Daddy, I got my report card, which I know you will be delighted with."

Dustin reads some stuff on the computer. "Dear, you can leave it on my desk." He points to his smaller desk by the door. As Cynthia, a little disappointed, is about to leave, Dustin turns around and stops her by the door. "Hold on a second there. Let me look at what you put on my desk, young lady." Dustin gets up from his main desk, walks, and looks at Cynthia's report card. Looking at the report card, he says, "Oh my god, Cynthia, you brought your grades up, I see. No Cs and no Ds, dear. I see B- and A-. I am so proud of you. I knew you could do it."

With a smile on her face, Cynthia says, "Thanks, Daddy, so I will be able to go to the teen square dance this weekend, right?"

With a broad smile, Dustin says, "Of course, and I will be taking you, right?"

Cynthia hugs her dad. "Of course, Daddy."

Jewel overhears them while walking by. "You are coming to my graduation, right, Cynthia?"

Cynthia wants to back out. "Well, I don't know, Jewel. I have to get ready for the teen square dance this Saturday."

With a nice gesture, Jewel says, "You owe me, sis."

Cynthia remembers when Jewel helped her out at school. "Okay, I will come then."

Jewel responds with excitement, "That's just like my sister."

Cynthia, not knowing when Jewel's graduation is, asks, "When is your graduation?"

Jewel tells her excitedly, "It is tomorrow evening."

Cynthia exclaims, "Wow, already that soon."

Jewel purses his lips. "Yep, that soon, sister."

Dustin calls Jewel, "Hey, Jewel, I need your help on the farm."

Jewel replies quickly, "Okay, Dad."

Dustin takes Jewel out to the farm area, meeting some more people that want to buy some meat from Dustin since he is selling the meat so cheap. Dustin turns to Jewel. "So, Jewel."

Jewel answers, "Yes, Dad?"

Dustin looks Jewel up and down and says, "You should go with your mom because you need clothes for graduation, don't you?"

When it comes to clothes, Jewel is not so rushed. "I could wear jeans, something like that."

Dustin tries to push Jewel along. "Go ahead with your mother. We're doing fine. Pick out something." So finally, that evening, Jewel goes with his mom to Walmart. It takes another twenty minutes to get to Walmart. Melba parks the car in a parking spot, and Jewel gets out of the car with his mom. As they walk to the store's front door, Melba grabs a shopping cart to do some shopping for the house and get Jewel something to wear to his graduation. Melba picks up a few things while shopping for canned tuna, coffee, etc. Then they both head over to the young men's section to pick something out for Jewel; then Jewel bumps into a young girl, spilling her Coke drink.

"Oh, I am so sorry."

The little girl looks at Jewel with a smile. "That's all right. I was not too fond of that drink. I wanted a Mountain Dew, but my mommy likes Coke, and I hate Coke."

Jewel is surprised at how intelligent this six-year-old is. "Wow, I am astonished that you know the difference."

The little girl giggles. "Yeah, I drank Mountain Dew since I was two, so that is my favorite soda drink." The little girl's mother calls to her as her baby sister waves at Jewel. Jewel waves back and heads back to shopping with his mom.

Melba asks Jewel, "So, Jewel, do you like this outfit?" Melba picks up a few different garments, slacks, and shirts. "Do you like these slacks, son, with this gray shirt?"

Jewel is grateful. "Anything is fine, Mom. I would wear anything you get me, Mom."

Melba tries being funny. "Oh, you would wear a clown outfit too, huh." Melba chuckles a bit.

Jewel says with a childish smirk, "Whatever, mom. Can we finish shopping already?"

Melba goes back to her serious shopping.

The next day is Jewel's graduation. His cap and gown are gray and white, which his mom, Melba, put on his bed. During a conversation in Dustin's office, he asks his son, "Do you have your speech ready, son?"

Jewel, preparing his speech, says, "It will be ready soon. I've been working on it for several days."

Dustin pats Jewel on the head as he heads to the kitchen. "Good luck with it, son."

Jewel meets up with his classmates for the graduation ceremony, as the coordinator arranges everyone alphabetically at the auditorium entrance. All the students' families are sitting in the audience, and Jewel's family sits in the middle area of the theater. The principal greets the families, "Good evening, staff and graduates. Let us begin our ceremony."

The director starts to call names as the graduates come up for their diplomas. "Michael Ware, Jerome Dart, Lady Fingers, Jewel Justick, Oscar Myers, Leroy Sanchez, Dominic Wafer, Flores Zarea."

At the end of the names called, the principal gets up from his seat and mentions the star pupil of the grading class on the pulpit. "In an address on the conduct of the graduating class, Jewel Justick will speak. Would you mind standing up, please?" Jewel sets his eyes on the stage, his robe trailing behind him almost as if he is about to break dance. Still, he strolls up the stage while pulling up his robe with both hands, situating the microphone to his level of height.

"Uh hum, class of 2138, I first want to say good luck on your future majors, and may the will of the great and mighty God be with you. You are the fulfillment of the greatest generation that has come to be. We are the class of 2138 for a reason. Since the ninth grade, we have moved to more critical aspiring goals to fit our needs or wants. Even in ninth grade, we were dunderheaded, but we learned more in tenth and eleventh grade, and now we're the few that will make history."

The entire class of 2138 cheers back and forth as some students shout, "Haha! We did it!" Jewel adjusts his gown again.

"I am convinced that my physics will make a mark in history. My sole purpose is to make the physics society aware that we are not the only beings in this giant universe," Jewel adjusts his speech and continues. "We have come a long way to fulfill destiny with the physics endeavors. I plan to seek out dimensions of worlds where others have failed and prove that we are not the only ones in this universe. I, Jewel, will fulfill the need of our generation to see the truth that our government has been hiding since the creation of time. We are the class of 2138 for that reason. We must reach what no human has achieved before. Humanity must excel on the next level and power our minds with the sense of discovery that will come into existence, using our brainpower to overcome any issue and fix all problem areas. Filling the void of our ancestors, and taking that mark in history is what we want, and by my example, we will. I want to thank you all and congratulate the class of 2138. Have a great night."

The principal gets up as everyone in the auditorium claps and cheers for Jewel's speech. The principal tells everyone, "Please proceed to the lounge area in the auditorium. If you want pictures, please go there."

With her mouth full, Cynthia walks over to Jewel as she notices the principal walking over to Jewel's family, shaking the family's hand, and introducing himself.

"Hi, you must be Jewel's mother, father, and siblings."

At the same time, both Dustin and Melba say, "Yes, we are."

Jewel is held in high regard, and respected by the principal when speaking with the family. "Your son Jewel here has an extraordinary brain that people want to harness that type of intelligence. He has made this school a mark in history so far."

Melba pleased, says, "It was nice meeting you, and we want to thank this school for having our son."

The principal smiles, saying, "You folks have a great night."

The next day, there are envelopes from colleges like Yale, Harvard, and Arizona State. As you can see Jewel is accepted to a huge variety of colleges. These colleges want to pay for Jewel's college until he gets a PhD. Jewel picks up an envelope from MIT and says to his mom and sister, "Hmm, I wonder what MIT has to offer." Surprised, he opens up the envelope and reads, "Wow, Mom, Dad, Cynthia, and Torin, they want to offer me free room and board, physics lab throughout my school years, and a book publishing company on my research. I am astonished."

Melba's eyes widen in surprise. "That is good, son. You are on your way to making an entire race of human beings know your knowledge, son."

Cynthia is a bit skeptical. "Hmm, they are giving you a book publisher. Why?"

Jewel explains in layman's terms, "Look, sister, they want me to write a book because they want humanity to know the things I come up with that can enhance humankind and improve our society."

Dustin, grabs the MIT envelope, looks inside, and sees another paper. "Jewel, did you know this paper? I think this one is significant." He hands the piece to Jewel.

Jewel jumps up with joy. "Dad, Mom! You're not going to believe this."

Melba is so excited for her son. "What is it? What more can they possibly give you, son?"

Jewel takes a red marker off the table, circles a part of the paper, and shows his mom in her face. Melba jumps with excitement again as though she has won the lottery. "Oh my god, are you kidding me? A brand-new car! What!"

Dustin and Cynthia, with excitement, simultaneously exclaim, "Are you kidding?"

Jewel explains the paper more. "I get to pick any car up to $100,000, man! Dad, you'll help me get my license, right?"

Dustin replies without any hesitation, "We will go tomorrow to get it."

Jewel, with deligted face, says, "Thanks, Dad."

It is Wednesday afternoon at the Mellomystics, two days before graduation. Charlie whose a purple belt wailing on his opponent at the tournament. Lu is cheering Charlie on. "Go get him, son!"

Su Ang cheers, "Go, Charlie, go!"

Bing and Merna are saying, "Get him! Get him!"

Charlie is fighting a red belt and is whipping the red belt with natural talent. Charlie fights with chi in his stance while attacking the opponent. Charlie finally does a roundhouse and scores the final blow to his opponent. In all this sparring, Charlie, of course, is wearing protective gear. Lu enjoys his son's combat.

"This is very enjoyable to watch, right, Su Ang?"

Su Ang responds fast as she jumps with joy, "Of course, yes, Charlie, you won! Hahaha!"

Lu turns to Chang, Sandra's boyfriend. "Wasn't that enjoyable, Chang?"

Chang is talking to Sandra, and Lu interrupts them. "Oh, excuse me. Wasn't it enjoyable, Chang?"

Chang is very pleased with Charlie's performance. "Oh yes, I loved it."

Lu says with a polite voice toward Chang, "Do you like martial arts, Chang?"

Again, Chang excuses himself from Sandra. "Excuse me, honey. Yes, Lu, I love martial arts. Besides, I am a black belt."

Su Ang turns around in disbelief after overhearing the conversation. "Wow, a Spanish person with a Chinese name that loves martial arts. Now that is weird."

Sandra turns around and asks, "Why is that weird, Mom?"

Su Ang figures, "Chang does not have the smoothness of water like Bruce Lee or any other Chinese person."

With a bit of overreaction, Chang says, "Hold on a minute, not smooth like water, hmm. Let me show you."

Chang grabs the instructor and tells him something in his ear. The instructor and Chang square off on the red mat. The instructor starts with an attack move, as Chang smoothly moves to his right with a triple kick to the groin, chest, and face. Su Ang is amazed at how smoothly Chang works on the floor as she cheers him on. "I can't believe it, a Spanish guy with a Chinese name performing Bruce Lee. I am shocked. I have total respect for you, Chang." Su Ang hugs Chang. "Thank you for loving my daughter Sandra."

Chang hugs Su Ang back. "I would do anything for your daughter, Mrs. Mellomystic."

Merna pulls Sandra to the side. "He is a keeper, sister. He worships the floor you walk on."

Sandra is getting ready to leave. "I know, Merna." Merna laughs a bit. Sandra playfully taps Merna. "You crazy girl." They all go with Charlie from the Kim Komp Mixed Martial Arts school. The family leaves the martial arts school, and Chang drops the family off at the house in his purple Mercedes Benz, which he just bought the day before since Sandra loves the color purple.

The next day, Merna is at school preparing for her biology finals, where she has already done her finals for her other classes. Her biology final is the last final of the day. Merna has prepared a monitoring system that monitors the reaction of a dead mouse's brain that still has activity in it even though it has been dead for months. The biology class and other science classes are interested in her theory in the classroom. Merna explains how mammals can evolve to having memory put into living species. Using the electrodes and the computer monitor, Merna gently demonstrates the results through her computer program. Merna explains the hypothesis, "Teachers and faculty, my biology final involves taking a dead mouse's brain and capturing the impulse sent by the remaining living cells and planting them on a computer program to create the image of the dead brain. Ladies and gentlemen, now I am going to take the positive and negative electrodes along with this wire in the center and place it around the mouse on the dead tissue. With amazement, we will get a relayed image to my computer screen of the mouse scampering for life."

With great amazement, the class, teachers, and faculty clap in awe as the image appears on the screen. The professor of this class, who had taught at Yale, immediately gets up and claps with tremendous enjoyment as he walks up to the front of the room.

"Bravo, bravo, Merna, loved it. My colleagues and I enjoyed your final, which I give you an A plus. Oh, by the way, can we get a copy of that program?"

Merna knows the patent laws. "Professor, I would love to give you a copy of this program, but I haven't patented it yet."

The professor apologizes for the mistake. "I am so sorry about that, Merna. I should not ask you for a copy before you patent it." The bell rings. Merna leaves the classroom and rushes to her school bus to go home.

Merna gets in the door. As Sandra grabs her hand immediately, they both run to the car to take Merna shopping. Forty-five minutes go by as Sandra pulls into the parking lot of Macy's. Merna is a bit stunned. "How! How is it possible for you to afford to shop here? This store is expensive."

They both enter the store and head up the escalator to the third floor, where the women's dresses are. Merna gets off the escalator and almost bumps into a mannequin. Sandra grabs a unique beige dress for Merna, pays for it, and leaves, returning home.

The weekend goes by, and it is Monday, the day of Merna's graduation. Merna and the family, during midday, head out the door. Merna is getting ready. "Mom, can you grab my cap? I got my clothes on."

Su Ang holds Merna's cap on the bed and puts it in her oversize purse. "I got your cap, dear." Su Ang helps Merna with her blouse, zipping it up. "Are you sure it is tight enough?"

Merna notices that the blouse is not tight at all. "No, it is not close-fitting at all, Mom. It is perfect."

Su Ang is ready for the family to leave out of the door. "Is everyone ready to go yet?"

Lu, with his tie untidily tied, says, "I'm ready to go already."

Su Ang notices his tie is crocked. "Let me fix your tie."

Lu let Su Ang fix the bond. "Sure, thank you." The cool breeze blows the blouse over Merna's head as her dad puts the graduation gown over her head. "You look amazing, Merna. You are a double valedictorian graduating at seventeen. I am so proud of you. Your mom and I are forever excited about this moment. I could never be that intelligent."

Merna, with a gentle smile, says, "Thanks, Dad. I couldn't have had better parents in the world. I am glad I am part of this beautiful family. Dad, you are intelligent in your way. Never forget that, Pops."

The conversation kind of gets skipped by Sandra. "Merna, we got to go now. The graduation starts in an hour." Sandra calls out to Charlie and Bing, "Charlie and Bing, you guys are ready?"

Charlie responds quickly, "Yes, I am ready."

Bing is grabbing his jacket. "Ready."

In a limousine, Chang waits outside for the entire family, and the car heads to the school, where the graduation will occur. Families tend to occupy the corner seats near the stage, arranged in a caddy's corner configuration. Ten minutes in, the music begins. Graduating students enter the auditorium from the side, ending up on the right side in a single line. In addition to principal Lacy addressing the audience, several parents are looking at the pamphlet of the graduating program.

"Ladies, gentlemen, faculty, and parents, thank you for coming to the 2138 graduation class at Camden High. We appreciate everyone today. Now we will begin the graduating ceremony."

The music slowly plays low as the students' names while receiving their diplomas are called. The administrator calls names. "Billy Ashone, Rachel Bedara, Charlie Dawns, Anthony Frazier. Anthony Leon, Merna Mellomystic."

Then suddenly, the principal takes to the pulpit. "Mrs. Mellomystic, double valedictorian of the graduating class of 2138, please convey your message to the graduating class after all diplomas are received." The principal motions for Merna to go up to the pulpit.

"Thank you, Dean Lacy," Merna says as she steps up to the pulpit. "Faculty, families, and particularly the 2138 graduating class," she adjusts the microphone, says. "We're graduates of 2138 for a reason. We have come far from elementary, middle, to high school. We will make a staple in this century that we will fulfill the needs of every person we encounter throughout our endeavors in life. We will make a mark in our history of what we will do. We have come so far to say we are seniors who have made those significant steps from childhood to adulthood. We are the epitome of what's to come. We are the jolt in the new age of the human race. Through my biology learning, I've learned that we would be sharing our knowledge with the world that needs our expertise. It is a gift from God and us, and a gift we take our faith in knowing the priority of what we learned is a communication of our life to teach those and help those that require what we have learned. The work within our momentum that we threaten with our brains, the electrical impulses that all species on the Earth on how they communicate, will communicate with Mother Earth and the entire universe, whether it be this Milky Way universe or any other universe out there. Every living organism worldwide can communicate by understanding the biology of different creatures, not simply humans, but all living organisms. Thank you very much, faculty, parents, and graduating class of 2138, and may all our goals be realized. Congratulations, all."

After the ceremonies have concluded, Principal Lacy turns to Merna and says, "Thank you, Merna. We want everyone to head to the lounge area for refreshments and photographs."

Merna texts on her phone to one of the students. "Yes, ah, excuse me, Dean Lacy. How can I help you?"

Dean Lacy replies with a gracious left-hand gesture, "I want to thank you for that beautiful speech, which I would like a copy of and put in the cabinet in front of the trophy room for students to see as long as this school exists. There is no doubt that this speech will go down in history." Merna hands principal Dean Lacy the copy without regard to her address since she already has a copy on her laptop. Later at the lounge area where the celebration is on, Principal Lacy comes up to the parents of Merna. "At this school, we are pleased with Merna's education. We have learned so much from her."

Su Ang shakes Principal Lacy's hand. "We are so blessed to have a gifted child like Merna. We're very proud of her achievements."

Principal Lacy is about to get teary-eyed. "She is a gift to your family and humanity as well."

Lu is grateful. "Coming from a great person like yourself. Principal Lacy, it means a lot to us."

Principal Lacy responds kindly, "I appreciate that, Mr. Mellomystic. You have a wonderful family. Please go ahead and enjoy yourselves."

Lu picks up a sandwich and says, "We will, thank you." The entire family sits down, eats some food, and takes photos with Merna.

Several days later, the Mellomystic family, like the previous two, get a ton of mail from similar prominent universities. They offer her a full scholarship covering a bachelor's degree to a PhD with free room and board. Merna screams, "I can't believe I got accepted to even Harvard."

Su Ang grabs the letter from Merna and reads the letter. She notices in the letter that Merna would have to change her major to law. "Merna, the letter says that you would have to change your major to becoming a lawyer instead of biology, honey."

Merna is surprised, with a disappointed look. "What! You've got to be kidding, right?"

Su Ang is reassuring her that she has to change her major. "Yes, dear. You must adjust to their curriculum since it is a law school."

Merna notices MIT and opens it up. She sees the letter stating biology. Merna laughs with excitement in her voice. "Mom, they have biology and the most intense program. I am going here."

The letter reads further, "'Merna, in addition to the free program and study hall, we would like to offer you this great gift—a brand-new automobile of your choice. We will also give you a personal office where you can teach biology and further your findings in improving the foundation of biology. Using your discoveries, you will write a book that will teach students how biology will change the world.' I am shocked and amazed with excitement. I love this school." Merna's tears flow off her cheeks.

With joy in his eyes like he wants to cry, Lu also reads the MIT letter and notices that Merna forgot to read one more section. "Hey, Merna, you forgot one more section. Take a look at this." Merna jumps up with joy as Lu shows her the section she forgot to read.

In a positive way, Merna exclaims, "I can't believe they are giving me $15,000 for shopping for clothes too. I love, love this school."

The family that night has a small party for Merna, congratulating her on her future with MIT. The three students are now accepted and are ready for their future with MIT. They will be an asset not only to the school but also to humanity. The three savants are about to embark on an entirely different journey as they prepare to leave for MIT with respect to their respective scholarships, but it is far from simple. Almost beyond their wildest expectations, they can't imagine what will soon await them.

CHAPTER 6

JOURNEY BEGINS FOR THREE SCIENTISTS

Finally, it's time to say goodbye to the families. It is the spring of 2140, as per the MIT scholarships, all three savants get a car of their choice, with Lucas going in for a two-year-old red Ferrari, Jewel going for a hybrid sports car, and Merna settling for a periwinkle-blue sporty coupe. During Lucas's last day at home at the Normalics, all the family is outside the house, wishing Lucas lots of luck at MIT. Mrs. Normalic is hugging Lucas as she gives him a cell phone to keep in contact with them every week.

"Son, good luck at MIT, and here is a gift from your dad and me for you to keep in touch with us daily. We want to know every detail of what is going on. Please make sure that you call us." Mrs. Normalic hands the iPhone ultra, the new age cell phone with the latest technology, to Lucas as he puts it in his pocket.

"I will keep the family informed, I promise."

Mr. Normalic shakes and hugs Lucas. "Be very careful in this car, and do not speed. I want my son in one piece."

Along with Joe, Sandra and Todd hug Lucas as Todd gives Lucas a little knock on his head.

Sandra is chiding Todd. "Todd, that is enough already."

"Just having one last memory with my little brother. Let me have that at least, Sandra." Todd enjoys his little brother because he will probably not see him for years.

Lucas pats Todd's hands, puts his luggage into his car, and waves goodbye to his family, throwing kisses at his mom and sisters.

Similarly, at Justick's home, Jewel is packing his stuff to get ready to leave for the purchase of his car with MIT allowance. As they all get into the family SUV, Jewel says with compassion, "Dad, Mom, Torin, and Cynthia, you know I love you guys."

About an hour later, they reach the dealership, and a saleswoman approaches them while getting out of the family car.

The saleswoman escorts the entire family to her office. "Hello, there. How can I help you all?"

Dustin says with a low tone, "My son, who will be attending college at MIT, wants a car."

The saleswoman talks to them for a while and shows them a car. Jewel is excited as the saleswoman draws up the final paperwork."Let's go back to my office and sign some paperwork then."

The entire family strolls to the saleswoman's office while the family chats about Jewel leaving for MIT.

Melba is sad that her baby is leaving home. "Please make sure you do not forget to call us. I want to know how everything is coming along."

Jewel reassures his mom. "Not to worry, Mom, I will. I will keep in touch weekly to inform you of my progress." In tears, Jewel says, "It's okay, Dad. I can always count on Mom's cooking."

Torin and Cynthia embraced him as he climbed into his new car and entered the coordinates for MIT.

Similarly, the Mellomystic family is preparing for Merna to leave the house for MIT. Lu and Su Ang, especially Su Ang, help Merna pack up in the morning, as Bing and Charlie start to cry because they will miss their sister. Sandra hugs her sister. "I will miss you, sunflower. Better call me to give me some updates, my precious sunflower."

Merna starts to cry a bit. "I'm going to miss you too, Sandra. I love you. I will keep in touch and let you know how I'm doing."

Sandra warns Merna about college boys. "Be careful not to get involved with sororities and wild parties. Especially rousing boys."

Merna, who has read up on those parties, says, "Yeah, I am pretty cautious about those things. You don't have to worry about it. I'll be fine."

Sandra hugs Merna for a lengthy time. Bing and Charlie are teary-eyed. "We love you, Merna. We will miss you."

Merna embraces her two little brothers. "I'm going to miss both of you very much. Mom and Dad will call me, and I will talk to you both."

With sadness in his eyes, Charlie says, "Don't forget."

Merna, with a broad smile, says "I won't." Merna hugs and kisses her mom, sister, and brothers as Lu takes Merna's luggage to her car. Lu puts the bags in Merna's trunk, then turns, holds, and kisses her on the cheeks.

"Remember, we may be thousands of miles away, but only a dial away if you need us."

Merna kisses her dad on the cheek. "I know, Daddy. I will keep you posted on my progress every week. Love you, Daddy." As she gets into the car, Merna waves goodbye to her family on the porch.

The three young scientists drive off to MIT, and it takes them hours to reach the campus on various day. At MIT, there seems to be a gathering with food, entertainment, and different organizations a student can join. The first savant to pull up in the parking lot in his E Concept Infiniti car is Jewel, who happens to be wearing a button-down shirt with a gold chain and jeans. He comes out of the car and heads to the events that are on campus. Jewel suddenly bumps into a pretty brunette girl named Laura.

"Sorry about that."

She looks into Jewel's eyes with dreamy eyes. "That's okay. Are you new here?"

Jewel looks at the girl as though she is a model. "Yeah, I am new. What's going on here?"

Laura grabs Jewel's hand with a slight smirk. "Let me show you."

Jewel walks with Laura to the engineering group booth called Elite Engineers. Inquiring what the organization is all about, Jewel asks, "Does it only have engineers or are there students from all fields of study?"

The gentleman at the booth says, "Since there is no science division, the organization is for students of all disciplines, such as programming, science, engineering, and any specialized technology."

As a mechanical engineering major, Laura joined the group and informed Jewel about the organization. Jewel, however, already knows.

"Ah, what's your name again?"

Jewel is a bit shallow. "My name is Jewel."

Laura giggles and explains the program. "This organization helps students understand how these areas will benefit society. This organization also has competitions with other universities as well."

After reading the pamphlet, Jewel already knows a bit about the organization. "Yes, I figured that. Looking forward to the events. I'm joining."

Laura pats Jewel on the shoulder. "Now that's the spirit."

In her brand-new Mercedes-Benz, the next savant arrives at MIT's parking lot in a skirt and blouse showing some of her cleavage. She starts to head over to the event with her luggage, thinking that she should go to her dorm room first and then come back to the campus event to see what is happening. She enters her room and notices two other beds. One has football memorabilia; the other has science trophies and awards. She feels equal to the science trophies than to the football trophies she sees in her roommate's room. Merna starts to put her stuff up in the dresser's drawers by her bed since each roommate has their own. Suddenly entering the room are both the roomies laughing about something that will happen at the school's competition that will be coming up in a month. The two girls, not noticing, are taken aback when they see Merna suddenly in the room and let out a shout.

One of the girls asks, "Who are you? Are you some aberration, a ghostly form that came back to life? You seem so real."

Merna is gracefully approached by the other girl who touches her to sure she is real. Merna calmly says, "I am real. I'm just starting new at this school this year. I am a freshman, and you two are my roommates, right?"

The girls are relieved, calming down as she introduces herself. "Oh, hi, it looks like we got off on the wrong foot. My name is Jill, and that is Penny. And your name is?"

Merna, relaxing a bit, says, "My name is Merna."

Jill introduces Penny to Merna. "Penny, this is Merna, our roommate. She is a freshman just starting here."

Penny caresses her science trophy, and says, "Well, hello, Merna. I'm sure you'll love this school. There is so much stuff to do here. Do you want to go outside and look at the different organizations they have?"

Merna, charmed by the two girls, heads outside with them. Penny takes Merna and Jill to the organization that Jill and Penny have joined. In a girly way, Penny introduces Merna to her organization. "Jill and I belong to this organization, Merna. They are the Elite Engineers. In addition to scientists, and programmers, there are some roboticists on the team. Other organizations include English literature, mathematics, politics, astrology, and other disciplines. Give this one a shot because our first competition coming up soon against Harvard and Yale."

Merna is fascinated and signs up. The three girls walk around and come up to the snack area. Merna buys the two girls some snacks. The third and final scientist, with music blaring in his Ferrari, enters his parking space as the wheels squeal.

Lucas looks in the mirror as he brushes his hair back with his hands, then exits the vehicle, noting that he will get his luggage later and wanting to know what all the commotion is about on campus. Lucas stops at a snack vendor before walking to the various organizations as he stops by a snack vendor. "What do you have here?" As Lucas asks the vendor, the vendor, who was talking to some girls, turns around to Lucas and explains fast what he has.

"Well, we have hot dogs, cheddar bacon hamburgers, ice cream bars, and this lovely dish is some coconut dessert. What would you like to order?"

A bit rational, Lucas says, "I would like a juicy hamburger with an ice cream bar and a root beer soda on my plate."

The vendor puts the plate together for Lucas with some condiments in a napkin and tells him the price. "That will be $8.25 bitcoins, please." Lucas hands taps the vendor's iPhone Ultra and pays $10 of bitcoins, then the vendor gives him the exact change automatically to Lucas iPhone. Lucas takes the napkin, puts it in his shirt pocket, and puts the condiments of salt and pepper on his burger as he sits by a tree and eats. A guy and girl come over and sit by him, laughing with joy.

Lucas asks the couple. "What's so funny? I have to know."

The guy chuckles, ignoring Lucas, and says, "There is a group on campus called Picture-Perfect Photographers. They work with newspapers or sporting events, but it doesn't earn much money."

The female then points to the booth. Lucas returns with a witty remark after leaving the two chatting, "Your conversation with your friend makes no sense. There is a lot of money to be made by wedding photographers." The male and female then ignore Lucas's comment at the tree. Lucas finishes eating his food. He gets up and stands beside the Elite Engineers booth taking an interest in another booth called Ancient Digs.

A curious Lucas asks, "Excuse me, what is your organization about, and what do you guys do?"

In a simple way for Lucas to understand the organization's representative at the Ancient Digs booth gives details. "We have studied the Inca Indians and the ancient Chinese who came to the East Coast centuries ago. We specialize in diggings and uncovering memory sites of the ancient ancestors." Suddenly, Lucas is tempted to join, when he sees two guys and a girl from the elite engineering booth trying to get his attention.

The girl and two guys from the Elite Engineering group say simultaneously, "We are a science, engineering, programming, and robotics group that looks for brilliant members who want to make a difference in this world."

Lucas wants to know more about it and turns his attention to the Elite Engineering group. "What is this group that's so selective to many on campus? I want to know more about this organization." The girl explains in detail to Lucas as he gets excited and immediately signs up. All three to-be scientists have signed up for the Elite Engineering Group, where they get to know each other better. And in the coming days, that will also catapult their lives into the most unexpected interstellar adventure known to humanity. During that time, the government intercepts an alien craft close to Washington, DC, mountaintop, with guns and lasers out the door of the spaceship that opens slowly. As the spacecraft doors open, feet of enormous aliens with mist around them come forward.

CHAPTER 7

THE WAR OF THE BRAINS

Months have gone by, and the three savants are now acquainted through college activities together. It is the third month of their first academic year, and they are attending their third competition against other universities such as Yale, Harvard, and UCLA. The proctor conducts the question, "What state gave birth to the Constitution?"

A male student from Yale answers, "It is Maine."

With a slight grin and a profound look, the proctor says, "That, sir, is wrong." Proctor turns his attention to a female Harvard student with fifteen seconds to answer the question. "Yes, it is your turn, ma'am. What state was the Constitution born in, young lady? You have fifteen seconds to answer."

A timer ticks away as the young lady hums to herself. "Uh, hum." The ticker has five seconds left, and then the girl at one second answers the question, "It is Philadelphia."

With a strange sense of humor, in a loud tone, proctor shouts out, "That young lady *is correct*!" The proctor sees that Yale has four out of seven right, eliminating them from the competition. UCLA has Harvard beat by two points, MIT is ahead of UCLA by one point, and it is up to MIT and UCLA to answer a chemical engineering question. The proctor distributes the question to both teams for the win.

"The final question of the day is, what tetra chloroform formula is responsible for hydrogen bromide?"

The proctor notices two UCLA students buzz in to answer the question. The first female student answers, "The formula responsible is H3B4C5."

The next UCLA male student answers consecutively, "The answer is H10B6C4."

The proctor replies to their answers, "Well, one of you is pretty close, but both of you are *wrong*!" The proctor rephrases the question to the MIT team. "If tetra chloroform is similar to bromide, okay, what symbol can one erase from the formula?"

Lucas, without hesitation, buzzes in with a great answer. "Okay, the minus sign is a small r minus two molecules that would equal the two chlorine and bromide formulas responsible for hydrogen bromide to operate with tetra chloroform to react with a stable molecule of the bromide."

Amazed by Lucas's response, the proctor awards the final point to MIT, giving MIT the victory and trophies their team deserves.

Later that day, after the competition, Jewel is giving a physics lecture, and while he is teaching class, he starts to write his dissertation for his book. During his course, Jewel covered Einstein's theory: E = MC squared and Newton's second law of motion, which states force equal mass times acceleration. Jewel gives a physics lecture on the day after the competition, and while he is teaching class, he records his dissertation for his book. A blackboard happens to contain Jewel's writing.

"Okay, class, does anyone know the derivative of these two equations?" As Jewel writes the equations, one student in the class raises his hand, so Jewel calls him to the blackboard to explain it. "John, please explain by writing it on the board."

John walks up to the board, and Jewel hands him the holographic chalk. John explains as efficiently as possible, "Well, if energy equals mass times the speed of light, which is 186,000 miles per second, and Newton's law of motion is force equals mass times the acceleration, then what we have is mass that is constant between the two. Next, we have energy, defined as the speed of light divided by the force, which is acceleration. Is that correct, Professor?"

Jewel answers John with bright eyes. "Wow, wow, you are right, John." Jewel, unaware that John knows the answer, is stunned since this student is a C student in this particular class.

John is excited. "All right! I got it. Yeah!"

Jewel gives a mini test to the students. "All right, go and sit down, John. I have something to hand out to the class right now. I have a mini test regarding the many theories we have gone over in the past month." Students talk among themselves as though they aren't ready for a test. Jewel hands the paperwork to the front row to pass it to the entire class while Jewel thinks to himself writing his book, *Ah, how do I debunk Einstein's theory? If the speed of light is divided by two, Einstein's theory will be incorrect. Regardless of theory or practice, dividing it by ten would prove my point.*

Laura is staring Jewel right in the face as Jewel glances up at the class to see if all students have completed the quiz. Except for Laura, 99 percent of students complete the five-question test. Jewel, who happens to stare back at Laura gracefully, remarks to Laura as she approaches his desk turning in her paper. "All done there?"

Laura smiles demurely and nods a yes. The last student steps out of the door, and strangely Laura asks Jewel out on a date. "Please excuse me, Professor, but would you like to have coffee with me tomorrow?"

Jewel sees her interest in him. "Well, I have a lot of work to do tonight. I don't know if I will have time in the morning."

Laura insists. "It will only take, like, twenty minutes of your time."

Jewel notices her persistence. "In that case, I will join you at the cafeteria for twenty minutes before the first class I have to attend. Is that okay?"

Laura is beside herself. "That is great. See you in the morning around, ah, around eight thirty."

Jewel nods his head in agreement. "See you then."

It's now the year before the three savants graduate with their PhD. Lucas is teaching a class on chemical engineering while continuing his dissertation or book. Lucas writes a simple chemical reaction on the board.

"Class, I have two hydrogen atoms and a carbon atom. What reaction do we get when we combine the two?" A female student raises her hand. Lucas picks the student to explain. "All right, you there, what do we have?"

The female student stands up and explains the reaction. "We have carbonation."

Lucas is surprised. "Well, that is correct." Lucas starts to pass out a quiz of ten questions. "The quiz for this week is going to be simple and to the point, since it is our twentieth week of classes."

In his book *Chemical's A New Reaction*, Lucas writes "we have arsenic silver representing the integration of a solid consumption by a liquid. With the addition of boron, it will replace the intensity of the silver."

Suddenly the class has finished their quiz, and Lucas gets ready for his weekend of rest and grading of examinations. Merna is lecturing a biology class with spiritual enlightenment with many students surrounding a tank full of rodents. Merna explains to the class what happens when something dies. "Class, what I am about to do, no one has ever tried. I will take these two electrodes and attach them to this healthy mouse. Then, I will take these other electrodes and connect them to the dead mouse. We are going to find out if they still communicate."

Upon looking at the projector, the students discover two stimulations instead of one. Several students jump back as though they are finding out that the living can communicate with the dead. Merna asks a student, "Can you tell me what's going on now?"

A female student slowly tells Merna what her analogy of the find means. "Ms. Mellomystic, I find that the living can strangely communicate with the dead, but what if you can bring that spirit back from the dead into a cloned body?"

Merna is a bit mixed up. "A clone that would host a spirit?"

The female student repeats herself, "Yes, a clone can host a spirit that comes back to life, right?"

Merna is a bit shaken up by the young girl's comment. "Look, a spirit has to be born in a body. A clone cannot host it. It never was done."

Female student starts wondering with a dreamy look. "The goal will achieved one day, I am sure."

Merna, thinking the girl is a little strange, responds, "Yeah, maybe one day. Yeah, okay."

And so the three to-be scientists conduct their lectures throughout their school years while teaching professors on other subjects. It is the last year of school for these three who are about to get their PhDs and book publishing deals. A final milestone occurs when each announces his or her book during their graduation ceremony, where publishers from all over the world seek to sign their books in the grand auditorium. They will become either bestsellers or taken by Washington, DC government officials. The latter also is in the room listening. The deans of the different departments are at the graduation that is taking place in the year 2142, who deliberate about their most esteemed students throughout the school years. The students are in their seats as the dean of student affairs announces each student at graduation as they take their degree. Of our three savants, each scientist makes a speech regarding their roles and contributions to the college. They also mention their book as well. The dean of student affairs commences, calling students' names as they approach him to receive their PhD.

"Allen Todd, congratulations, sir, as doctor of economics."

Allen Todd accepts the degree, shaking the hand of the dean of student affairs. "Thank you, sir."

The dean calls the following two people, "Charles McCabe, doctor of geometry. Michael Gill, doctor of leadership." Then finally, the dean calls each new scientists in an unordered fashion. "Lucas Normalic, doctor of chemical engineering with an emphasis on chemical reactions. Congratulations, Doctor."

Lucas shakes hands with the dean of student affairs as the dean makes an announcement introducing Lucas to the public, book publishers, and government agencies. The dean then announces Lucas, "Ladies and gentlemen, faculty and officials, please welcome to the podium Dr. Lucas Normalic."

"I want to thank MIT for its support throughout these six years of learning and teaching. Throughout my years here, I have found and developed students of interest in chemical engineering and chemical reactions that I have contributed to the field throughout my career here."

Lucas turns to the other side of the podium. "I want to thank all faculty who have given me insight and followed my curriculum from my classes. I want you all to know that my book, *Chemical a New Reaction*, will soon be a textbook taught by teachers here at MIT and hopefully quickly published. It is a well-developed book that shows new insight into new ways to develop chemical reactions that soon be a curriculum here through its fundamental core structures. I want to thank all who have attended my class and congratulate all who contribute to society by getting their doctorate degrees. Congratulations, all!" Lucas steps away from the microphone as the dean keeps calling names for people to accept their degrees. Then soon after, he announces Merna Mellomystic.

"Ladies and gentlemen, I would like to invite the second most essential scientist to the podium and accept her doctorate in the study of insight of body organs, Merna Mellomystic. Merna, please accept this degree, and please announce your book and future endeavors."

Merna walks up the stairs to receive her degree and almost falls into the arms of the dean before gracefully standing up, fixing herself, and accepting her degree. She then turns to the podium, gets up, and speaks about her book and endeavors. Merna pulls the microphone closer to her face because she is excited about helping people.

"Ladies, gentlemen, staff, publishers, and government agencies, I am pleased to have taught at this university. What I plan to accomplish, hopefully shortly, is longevity. Studying not only how to increase brain activity from 10 percent to 40 percent but also how to strengthen our immune system and body organs to operate at potentially youthlike levels for the rest of our lives could prolong our lives. As for my students, they have acquired a newfound outlook on possibly sustaining life after death. As for my book, which will tell you how we preserve and prolong life's brain activity, I present my book, *How to Increase Body Organ Activities.* This book will tell you what steps are needed to not only increase brain activity but how to keep your organs operating like a child's organ forever, which will help keep you young, but I can't tell you if it will keep you alive for eternity, but I sure can tell you it may expand your life another forty years, say for example from sixty years old to a hundred years old."

A book publisher in the audience raises her hand to ask a question. Merna sees a lady raising her hand in the audience and picks the lady. She has a question regarding the book.

"Yes, ma'am, you have a question?"

The lady with a red blouse with blonde hair responds with concern. "Well, don't you think you are playing God, and isn't it God's way to decide for us if we live long or not?"

Merna sees the lady's point of view and throws a hypothetical question to the lady. "Let me ask you, ma'am, are you close to anyone in your family?"

The lady responds in a normal tone, "Yes, I am close to my mother and father, why?"

Merna asked further questions, "Okay, let's see now, what if you could have your parents around for another forty years, enjoying their company without having to worry about them dying from some disease or something taking them out other than a car accident? Wouldn't you love to have your parents around to see their grandchildren, great-grandchildren, or even their great-great-grandchildren and have those memories live long in your memories forever?"

The lady takes her index finger and thumb, putting them to her head as she thinks of Merna's answer. "You know what, at least you're not trying to be God and having them live for eternity. I get your point now, ma'am." The lady sits down as Merna leaves the podium, asking if anyone else has a question.

"Does anyone else have a question?"

The audience claps as Merna leaves the podium, and the dean calls people to get their degrees, then finally, the last scientist is called by the dean.

"Final book writer and outstanding doctor of science, Jewel Justicks, will be receive a doctorate degree in Jules physics, which is known to be ten times faster than the speed of light."

The dean introduces Jewel Justicks to the audience as he shakes his right hand before he receives his degree from the dean.

"Ladies and gentlemen, faculty, students, publishers, and government agencies, I am privileged to announce our final brilliant scientist at MIT and well-known in the physics area, Jewel Justicks." Everyone claps as Jewel gracefully approaches the podium to speak. Jewel will speak on the subject of Jules, which is faster than the speed of light.

"Good evening, all and graduates. I am pleased to announce that on my journey throughout my study at MIT, I have learned from my students the different variations of speed and how speed can go faster than the speed of light. From my research, I have noticed a neutrino find that extends to the speed of light by ten times the rate. My students have discovered and named a new neutrino version called speedrinos with the help of Dr. Lucas and his chemical students, which has sought the attention of probably going a hundred times faster with the probable cause of an equation that has yet within its specific findings. Still, of course, I will somehow find a way, with the help of Dr. Lucas, a chemical or something that can spark such an equation to get to that point, at least. Nevertheless, as you already know, my book *Jules: Faster than the Speed of Light* will be published soon, about the causes and solutions for such a problem. Thanks to my former classmates, who are now doctors in their fields, faculty, teachers, publishers, and government agencies for coming to our celebration. I hope you will all hear about our discoveries in the future that will solve many issues not only for our world but also for our universe. I want to thank you all, and have a great evening."

The doctor turns away from the audience as a woman in the audience excuses herself to get his attention. "Excuse me, excuse me, Dr. Jewel! I have a question regarding your equation."

Jewel, rubbing his face with a handkerchief, turns back to the podium to answer this one question. "Huh, hum, well, let me see, what is your question, ma'am?"

The lady in the audience asks the question of concern, "Wouldn't the new equation make you the father, or the founder, of this new hundred times the speed of light?"

Jewel doesn't take sides on the issue. "My first thanks go out to my students for astonishingly finding a find in that area, and if I could prove the theory, I would be the founder, or if the solution was another type of equation, I would be the creator. My student would still get some credit as the sole forefather of that equation, because I am not self-centered, nor am I a believer that one individual should be given all credit if others first noticed it. Does that answer your question, ma'am?"

Feeling a bit shallow, the lady in the audience, replies, "That is very generous of you. To begin with, few people are like that,. I humbly respect your decisions. That would be all that I would need. Thank you."

Jewel slowly turns around and leaves the podium to sit down. The dean then closes the celebration and tells everyone to meet the graduating students in the lounge. "We wish to thank everyone who attended today's graduation ceremony. As a publisher, I encourage you to check out your booth, and as a government representative, please let me know where the various government agencies will be meeting." The dean shouts, "Mr. Kimp, would you please come up to the podium? Thank you."

Mr. Kimp walks toward the front of the room, waving his left hand at the audience; he quickly adjusts his tie. He then fluctuates his voice. "Thank you all for your kind words. Congratulations to all the graduates."

Mr. Kimp tries to adjust his squeaky voice. "In the lounge, we will have a meeting room where we can automatically accept applications."

Mr. Kimp points to a door far south side of the room, replies, "When I recruit for the CIA, I put a sign outside my door. The doors adjacent to mine are for agencies in other countries. I encourage you to consider who or which agency you would like to work for the rest of your lives before deciding. I want to thank you all, and again, congratulations." Mr. Kimp leaves the podium.

Exiting the auditorium, people enter the lounge area at the opposite corner to sit in the booths. The three scientists walk around each booth to see what they offered for their book as a government official comes up behind them with an offer they can't refuse. Two agents walk up to Jewel, Merna, and Lucas to talk about their contribution to society through their books. A female government agent interjects as the male agent, with arms crossed, stands next to the female agent. As she interrupts, the agent speaks spontaneously, "Yeah, that would be a good idea, Dr. Merna."

Dr. Merna sees this person rudely interrupt and says, "Well, we were talking about extending human life through brain activity along with DNA sequencing with Dr. Lucas."

The female agent curtly replies, "I am so sorry that I interrupted that, but I must tell the three of you that we have something in store for you all."

A male agent concurs, "We are offering you the chance to work with the world's greatest minds, and the most influential government leaders in different parts of the world, not only for humanity, but also for the entire universe. Would you three be interested in this?"

Lucas feels a bit rushed into such a situation, wondering, "Would we have our own homes where we can rest after a hard day of work, or would we be on a tight schedule?"

In a roundabout way, the female agent gives Lucas a probable answer. "Dr. Lucas, it is possible indeed."

Lucas is unsure of himself. "I guess we would have to find out, huh."

.The male agent walks them to his office. "Yes, you would have to hear us out, Dr. Lucas, now! Please, you three follow me right this way, and the different government agencies will be debriefing you on the job descriptions." The three are intrigued beyond words as to what awaits them in the room ahead.

CHAPTER 8

GOVERNMENT OWNED

The three scientists enter the agent's office, and at the round table are other government officials from around the globe. A bearded white man who resembles Santa Claus opens a black folder, while the male agent walks to the back of the room. "Please sit. We have a lot to discuss regarding your work and what the initial stages can do for governments worldwide." The three scientists sit across from each other with some document in front of them. In the old gentleman's words at the head of the table, "The government needs your assistance. Hmm, let's look here. Let's open up page one. This page clearly states that you will be the government's property forever. You will be working with other scientists in various fields to help government officials develop cures and help prolong the human race so that we don't become extinct. The next ten pages show you your job descriptions. It says that you will work extensive hours, days, and nights around the clock to help find solutions. We will provide you with a mansion, a car, robotic maids, and butlers. We put you higher on the pedestal of all department officials. Government officials will only see your books. Therefore, we are giving you a home of your choice in a destination we choose, along with leisure activities protected by government officials around the clock. So please read the fifty-page report and sign all documents. Jennifer here will tell you the next step and how we determine priorities among the three of you. Please follow her after you have signed the paperwork." The three scientists talk silently among themselves and sign all paperwork.

Lucas helps Merna get up from her chair to follow the agent Jennifer to another room, where Jennifer gives them advice on their loyalty to the government officials. "Now, you three will conduct a test with your students regarding a particular task of questions. A few of us will judge your student's outcome. We will decide which one of you will be head over all the various scientists across the globe."

Lucas is a bit shaken by this question. "Why do we have to do that? Why can't you people ask us questions instead of our students? That does not make any sense."

Specifically, Jennifer explains, "We're testing your ability to give orders and the students' ability to understand your orders. Doing this will show us your type of leadership roles."

Understanding the question now, Jewel is ready to accomplish the task. "I fully understand the objective, and we will oblige by it with no prejudice."

During the next few weeks, the three scientists prepare their team members through phone calls, which prepare them for a two-hour match against the other scientists. The three scientists have to put together strategic questions that took several weeks for the overall competition. They are complex questions that the average or above-average person could not understand. It is Wednesday afternoon, and the three scientists are getting together in their area as the students enter the room for the rigorous questions. About eight agents from different agencies on the panel will judge the outcome. The three scientists are ready for the challenge as the agents prepare for the several hours of rigorous work that the scientists' teams have to complete. We now begin as the lights of the room dim. A disco light glow appears around the room, and glowing lights hit all science team members and scientists, resembling the show *Family Feud*, except that there are three sections to answer. Three scientists as the host and the agents are mainly the audience that tallies the scores regarding the questions. The first scientist, Merna, asks the members of all teams a biology question. A quick glance on Merna's face prompted her to ask a challenging question, "What component of plasma decreases blood's water potential most significant amount?"

One of the team members from Merna's team quickly answers the question. "Carbon dioxide component of plasma will, by all means, decrease the water potential of blood by the most significant amount." One of the agents raises his eyebrow, and all agents put a mark on their paper for Merna.

Merna flips the report to the next question, which involves a more intense answer. Merna says into the microphone in a low voice, "My response to the next question is much more enthusiastic, so if multiple candidates are interested, we and the agents watching are likely to accept whatever team answers." The teams simultaneously reply with a yes.

Merna begins to give a historical question. "Who was Gregor Mendel?"

A team member from Jewel's team answers the question, "He was a great biologist who developed the genetics that a pea plant can be split into several stages conforming to different pea sizes."

Another team member from Merna's team also responded, "He was a very talented geneticist, and after his death, he became known for implementing different colors in peas due to his pea structures."

The final person comes to the point of the question at hand from Lucas's team. "He is considered the father of genetics. Having been born in Austria in 1822 and dying in 1884, this monk was a botanist and biologist. For use in his research, he practiced pea cultivation in the gardens of his monastery from 1853 to 1863. His ultimate experiments consisted of crossing pea plants of distinct characteristics such as size, the color of the seeds, and the type of peas cataloged as results and interpreting them by their strains. The experiments led him to enunciate his laws, which resulted in a publication in 1886 with no scientific repercussions. He was the father of genetics in the nineteenth century."

The agents use scorecards for Merna with regard to which teammates answer the questions. The second row of questions comes from the other scientist, the doctor of chemical engineering; of course, Lucas begins his task of questions to the various team members on the panel. Looking closely at his question sheet, Lucas starts his first question in a blatant voice, "Teams, of course, anyone can answer this. What jobs can chemical engineers do? It seems simple, but it is by far not the most straightforward question. Before responding, please consider your response carefully."

The random teammates begin to think. Bruin, a teammate of Merna's, explains, "Chemical engineers can work in fields ranging from medical, dental, to the military and even in mother nature." Agent Wayne looks over at a female agent and discusses the topic with her. Agent Wayne whispers close to her right ear, "I think he almost got it but not yet."

The female agent agrees. "I believe so, sir."

A student from Jewel's group named Patricia has a go at the question. "Chemical jobs that are preliminaries of chemistry are jobs such as atmospheric pressures, military equipment, and so forth in the fields of domestic and foreign threats."

Agents look at each other and write down their information regarding that answer on paper. Finally, a member of Lucas's team, whom he remembers having breakfast with years ago, Laura, a robotic engineer, comes up with a precise answer. "Several jobs can be done by them, including chemistry, organics, civil engineering, cryogenics, and various kinds of equipment that deals with atmospheric pressures, and military equipment that has never been seen before. There can be an emphasis on multiple jobs that deal with chemical engineering on different levels in the medical field, dental, military, and even for mammals."

Some agents saw the extra effort and marked a blue circle around Laura's name and a red checkmark on the panel next to Lucas's name. Lucas flips through his five-page questionnaire to the next-to-last question and smiles as he initiates his last inquiry for the teams.

"Last question, a very straightforward question, mind you. What type of jobs can chemical engineers do in the computer field?"

The agent on the panel marks Jordan from team Jewel as nearly correct but does not get any marks. Jordan predicts, "Chemical engineer jobs could include DNA sequencing, finding lost relatives, ancestry, even through hair follicles."

Lucy comes close to answering correctly from Merna's team. "You can work in chemical engineering that corresponds to computers to discover lost relatives, family ancestry, criminal backgrounds, facial recognition, and organ donation matches." So from a legal standpoint, the central thrust of it all is to inform you that one of Lucas's most insightful students, Beth, has the proper answer according to the agents panel. Lucas's mark is shown on a blue circle, while Beth's is red. "It can go on and on regarding even splicing DNA to design a new animal or species."

Some agents want to clap, but the captain of the agents gestures. In a low tone, he says, "Calm down, not now, please."

The third scientist begins his battery of questions. Jewel puts his paperwork on the table and begins to randomly look through his paperwork for questions he would like to ask the diverse teammates. "The first question I will be asking you is about radioactivity. However, it may seem simple. We are all looking for an answer, so with all due respect, I will begin. What is radioactivity?"

Michael from Merna's team answers because he thinks he knows it all. He gives a direct definition for the agents, trying to find out more about radioactivity in a rare way. Michael responds, "It involves the spontaneous decomposition of an unstable atomic nucleus into a more stable form, in one of three decays: alpha, beta, gamma."

The agents on the panel do not regard that as an initial response.

Jewel's teammate Laura points out, "Radioactivity involves more than gamma, beta, and alpha rays; these methods are needed to initiate chemical reactions toward many nuclear reactors and even produce medical devices today. As with the red, green, and blue rays, radioactivity is similar to the gamma, beta, and alpha rays. Radioactivity has multiple uses in medicine, warfare, the working sector, and even homes. Its basics are fundamental to our lives whether we want it or not. There are no loose holes in radioactivity in our society."

Now the agents get up and clap loud because Laura answered such a relevant question with simplicity and preciseness. Later that evening, the major general of all the agents brings the three scientists into a closed room and comments on their outstanding questions and who will be the lead scientist over all scientists worldwide.

Master Chief Yufer says, "Please take a seat. I have a lot to discuss with you three as my fellow agents sit with us to discuss a few things. I want first to point out how your accomplishments vary by the government sector. As you know, I oversee many federal agencies within specific sectors of the globe, which means I have to ensure the best results for our worldwide information systems. Several government sectors contribute to the advancing aspects of our global society. For example, ways exist to determine the aircraft, cars, boats, and other types of vehicles' speeds. Other parts include chemical warfare, medication for doctors to use on patients, and cloning. Lastly, we have splicing of mammals, breathing underwater, and prolonging brain activities. That is a few, but we have scientists worldwide who have their place in society to do assorted stuff for the government."

Merna raises an eyebrow but says, "I wonder if that would be me because I am proficient in all aspects of biology!"

Chief Yufer fixes his shirt and says, "However, it may seem helpful to all scientists. Still, it is only a limited field of knowledge. So sorry it will not be you, Merna."

Merna feels a bit shameful and is beside herself, thinking Master Yufer does not recognize the skills she can contribute to society. He then turns to see if Jewel has anything to say. Master Yufer says kindly, "Jewel, would you like to confabulate any details you may have while I discover your scientist ambassador?"

Jewel, with a large gulp as eyes stares toward Master Yufer, "First of all, as an ambassador, I would explain to the various scientists around the world how physics is a good area to justify every aspect of science, whether it be chemical, electrical, biology, robotics, astrophysics, or quantum mechanics."

Jewel is not chosen either, according to Master Chief Yufer through a roundabout explanation. "Jewel, you have my admiration but not the skill we are looking for."

Lucas is confused. "Who else can it be except one of us? Who can it be, then? Can it be someone we don't know, or one of our students?"

Dramatic music plays in the background as the chief and several of his sergeants walk up with a blue-and-white lab coat that reads "Dr. Lucas Normalic, Ambassador to the Scientist" with a globe emblem and a red, white, and blue ribbon going through it. Master Chief Yufer congratulates Lucas as he shakes his right hand.

"Lucas, you are the chosen ambassador to the global scientists of the world, and please accept this lab coat."

Lucas has no words to say. "What! I can't believe it. It will be a pleasure working internationally."

Master Yufer, with wrinkled brows, says, "You're welcome, Doctor. Doctor, you will be working with us here in the United States and conference with all scientists through a network similar to Skype on our private web."

Lucas is relieved that he will not be traveling too much. "Well, that is good. What will become of my two friends here?" Lucas puts his arms around his friends while they sit, and he is standing. Master Chief explains where Merna and Jewel will be assigned.

"Merna will have a briefing with one of my colleagues to go to China regarding her biology research. They have a great team there. Jewel will be assigned to Russia and travel between Russia and Spain in connection with his physics projects," Master Yufer confides in Lucas. "Well, Lucas, you may travel at that facility from time to time if needed."

Jewel sucks his lips as though not excited, says, "Great, and I figured that out."

After being briefed about their missions, the three scientists leave the room, and the government owns their books. Jewel meets up with Laura after the briefing. Laura politely speaks to Jewel.

"Would you like to go grab some coffee since it will be a long evening at our favorite café?"

Jewel accepts Laura's offer. "Sure, why not? I will soon be leaving to my research facility. We will have one final coffee together."

As the aliens arrive at their secret mountain base, General Boulder welcomes them and walks along the corridor until they reach a massive elevator that descends near the Earth's core. General Boulder looks up at an eight-foot alien and says, "Is the human race in some trouble, my outer worldly friend?" The aliens look down and nod in a yes motion.

CHAPTER 9

GOVERNMENT CANDY

The three scientists visit their homes to say their final goodbyes to their families for a while. Dr. Lucas Normalic is on a flight to go back home. Several hours have passed, and Lucas's aircraft lands where his family greets him at the gate. The entire family hugs Lucas, as Todd gently grabs him to pick him up, except Lucas is no longer into that.

"What's up, little buddy? As far as gate numbers go, it appears you are the lucky seven."

Lucas, a little impatient, responds, "Not now, Todd, not now."

Joe and Todd load Lucas's bags into the trunk area of the car and drive home. Lucas will only be staying for a couple of weeks. Later, the military will escort him by a Humvee that will take him to his destination where the government has him assigned.

At the house, Mr. and Mrs. Normalic are having dinner with Lucas. Mrs. Normalic cuts a piece of steak and begins to chew when she asks, "So, Lucas, have you found any new developments on a solution regarding atmospheric pressures that may cause the ozone layer to lose its ground with global warming?"

Lucas, with a strategic look, replies, "Mom, what I have found is that not only do we have green gas, but if we put a chemical called hydrogen iodine with a catalyst of sodium zeonic, these chemicals will help change the ozone layer. It can heal our atmosphere into a more beneficial solution for the human race within a hundred years."

With an odd look, Mrs. Normalic replies, "Now that sounds like a winner, Lucas."

Lucas looks analytical as Joe asks, "So how are you doing, Lucas? Are you getting enough sleep or continuously researching day and night?"

Knowing his brothers and sisters are concerned for his well-being, Lucas says, "Well, for one, you don't have to worry about me. I drink enough water and exercise to keep my body fit and let me explain further. My computer does my calculations, so I don't miss my eight hours of sleep anyway."

Mr. Normalic interferes in the subject. "Good for you, son. It is good to have a computer program to think for you. That is smart to make a program like that, son."

With a final word before they head to bed, Lucas says, "I am glad to see everyone is doing well. I guess I will be turning in for the night. Good night, everyone."

The day before he has to leave with the military, Lucas cooks breakfast for the family as the entire family sits around the table on a Saturday. Samantha asks, "What's cooking, Lucas?"

Lucas is busy in the kitchen. "Well, I am making frittatas with waffles in bacon blankets. Why?"

"Sounds good. That's all I wanted to know. No reason." Samantha exclaims when she smells the familiar aroma of the food cooking.

Lucas starts serving the family, but his mother intervenes in the kitchen just as Lucas prepares his plate. "Lucas, go and sit down. I will bring the dish to you, son. You have done enough. It is good to have you these two weeks. You should take a load off of yourself and relax since you will be leaving tomorrow. I didn't get the full detail of what you will be doing now that you have graduated."

Lucas starts to sit down at the table where he begins to eat and slowly tells his family what he will be doing for work. "Well, Mom, Dad, Joe, Todd, and Samantha, and little sister, I want you all to know the type of job I have taken is a classified government job."

Mr. Normalic is a bit worried. "What! A government job. What are they going to have you do, son?"

Lucas calms his dad down. "Dad, it is nothing like that. First, they made me the ambassador to all scientists around the globe. My goal is to provide feedback on ideas that will help society today, for example, starvation, the ozone layer, diseases, and warfare."

Todd is amazed at his brother. "That sounds like a plan, little brother."

Mr. Normalic is so impressed by his son's service to society that he asks his son an exciting question. "So will they be giving you credit for your finds or not?"

Lucas does not want to tell his dad the truth. "Hmm, for one, Dad, they will give me credit where credit is due."

Mr. Normalic, not liking that answer, objects for a moment. "We are a family that has a rich history, so it is only fair they give you credit"

Lucas is not worried. "Dad, don't worry, I will make a mark in history in the long run throughout the world. The military will pick me up around 0400 in the morning to take me to the airport tomorrow. I must start packing up now." The family gives their last hugs since they've had two weeks with Lucas.

Now it's 4:00 a.m. Sunday, the military personnel calls Lucas on his cell phone, the military man says, "Sir, we will be in the area in about thirty minutes."

Lucas, who is not trying to wake the family up from their sleep, quietly exits the front door with his three bags. "Okay, I will be outside waiting."

Another military man says, "All right!"

As a Humvee pulls up to the gate, three military people get his bags and open the Humvee door, putting the luggage in the back. A tough-looking female military officer greets Lucas once he steps into the Humvee and says, "We are now heading to Fort Hood Airfield in Texas, where we'll inform you about where you'll be living and working."

Lucas, already missing his family, is not paying much attention to the female officer. "Yeah, sounds good." The Humvee exits the gate, traveling to Fort Hood, Texas.

At that same instance, Master Chief Yufer is interrupted by an alien index finger showing him what the Inquestorians are and their intentions on a holographic wall. It breaks down their food chain when conquering many universes. Chief Yufer has a frightened look on his face.

Dr. Jewel Justicks has landed about half an hour before the family can get to the airport. Jewel, greeted by a flight attendant who sees him in a donut shop, says, "Excuse me, weren't you on my flight?"

Jewel is chewing a piece of donut. "Ah, yeah. Why?"

The flight attendant asks. "I went to school with you at MIT and saw you in the hallways."

Jewel is concerned about why she is a flight attendant. "What happened to you? Why are you a flight attendant?"

The flight attendant, a bit embarrassed, says, "Well, I didn't get hired by any government agencies because I couldn't answer the routine questions, so I ended up being a flight attendant."

Jewel feels terrible for her. "I am sorry to hear that. Maybe another agency would take you, right?"

The flight attendant is a bit embarrassed, and says, "Anyhow, I've to go. It's great to see you again. Would you mind telling me your name again?"

Jewel notices the flight attendant is in a rush. "Sure, no problem, nice meeting you again too. My name is Dr. Jewel."

The flight attendant grabs her baggage. "Bye, see you around."

Jewel waves at her. "Yeah, okay."

Jewel's little brother Torin, who is about to graduate high school, finds Jewel in the donut shop. He comes around the corner and surprises Jewel. "Hey! Hey! You're Jewel, right?"

Jewel is unaware that Torin is his brother. "Yes, I am Jewel. Who are you?"

With excitement in his voice, Torin bends his knees and says, "It's me, your younger brother Torin."

Jewel, surprised and shocked, says, "Oh my god, look at you. How grown you've gotten. Where are Mom, Dad, and my beautiful sister Cynthia?"

Torin grabs Jewel's bags as Jewel holds the other two bags. "They are outside the airport waiting for you. I came in to look for you. So they didn't want to walk around the airport looking for you to find out that your flight was the next day. You know what I mean, right?"

Jewel understands. "I know. Let's go already because I am excited to see everybody. Let's move, young man." Twenty-five minutes go by as Torin and Jewel are at the van, where Jewel hugs his family as they head back to the farm. Once they reach the farmhouse, renovated nicely, they all get out of the van, where Torin and Cynthia help carry Jewel's luggage to the house as Melba and Darin are behind them. Both Jewel and Darin put the bags in the guest room, Darin asks questions about the school where he will work since graduation.

"Jewel, now that you are a doctor in physics, what has been happening with your book, and do you have a job since you graduated from MIT?"

Jewel feels overwhelmed by his dad's questions. "As an example, Dad, the school remembers me for the work I have done within the school, such as a brain competition among students. As for my book, well, let's say the government has a say on that, at this point, as to where I am going to be working. I will be working for the government, Dad. Anything else you have for me?"

Darin is pleased with his son. "Now that is an excellent thing, son. What exactly will you be doing for the government?"

Jewel is trying to get a quick wink. "Can we talk about this later, Dad, please I am exhausted. I want to relax a bit."

Darin gets up from the couch to prepare for the business rush. "Okay, son, get some rest. I will come back to this question at a later time." Darin calls out to Melba as Cynthia and Torin run out of the door to help the family at the store.

Almost a week has passed, and Jewel is helping the family run the business, apart from putting hay together in the barn to sell and feed the cattle. Melba walks toward Jewel and puts down the milk to ask him, "Jewel, so what kind of work will you be doing now, son?"

Jewel, kind of out of breath, answers, "Mom, I guess I can tell the family what I will be doing now. The type of work I will be doing is working for the government."

Melba looks into Jewel's eyes and tells him, "Jewel, be careful because the government can own your life, especially if you are an asset. Would it be for the rest of your life, or will it be for many years?"

Jewel ponders. "I don't know, Mom."

Melba is concerned. "You should know, son."

Jewel is trying to brush it off. "Can we talk about this later, Mom? I need to get this stuff to the front of the store."

Melba knows that Jewel is trying to get the stuff done. "We will talk about it later, son."

Jewel, tired of the questioning, says, "I appreciate that." Jewel takes the pallet of hay to the front of the store. Later that evening, the family is around the table having dinner, about to say their last goodbyes before Jewel leaves tomorrow.

Cynthia asks Jewel, "So what exactly will you be doing for the government, Jewel?"

Jewel takes a deep breath and says, "The exact thing I will be doing for the government is research regarding physics."

Darin then asks, "So, where will you live while doing that research, son?"

Jewel gives his dad, Darin, the breakdown. "In exchange for research for the government, the house becomes mine. For my research, I will live and work in two countries, Russia and Spain, where the government will provide the necessary utilities and living quarters. Furthermore, I will be able to have fun, too, including working out and doing anything else I choose to do for my work. Dad, do you have anything else to ask?"

Melba is getting the plates up. When everyone has almost finished dinner, she asks Jewel a tricky question, "How long do you have to do this for, son?"

Jewel, in layman's terms, says, "It seems as though they will keep me until the world finds solutions."

Cynthia is almost spitting up some food. "What! You have to resolve that soon because I want to see you on holidays when I get married. You hear me, Jewel."

Jewel is getting scolded by his sister. "Yes, I will resolve it as soon as they brief me on the issue and location."

Darin is relieved. "Good, take care of that as quickly as possible and let us know."

Jewel feels the pressure, and says, "I will take care of it, Dad. I want to go to sleep right now. I feel tired and have to get up early because the military people will be coming for me."

The following morning, Jewel gets a phone call on his private phone that rings loudly in his briefcase while he is getting dressed to get ready to leave and meet the military personnel. Jewel answers the phone. "Hello."

A male voice on the other line answers, "Sir, we will be in the area at 0700, which is seven in the morning. There is a military vehicle on its way there."

Feeling a bit hurried, Jewel replies, "It's right now 6:00 a.m. And I am hardly ready."

"It's okay, they'll wait outside until you're ready to leave." the voice on the other end says.

Jewel is packing up quickly. "That is good, thank you."

Torin and Cynthia see Jewel taking his luggage to the front door as Cynthia says her final goodbyes to her brother Jewel. "When will I see you again, Jewel?" Everyone is up early in the morning and says their last goodbyes.

Cynthia hugs her brother, Jewel. Jewel helps his sister feel a bit comfortable. "You will, or I will be able to visit hopefully on holidays and birthdays. I will make some arrangements. All right, sister."

Cynthia feels a bit better about the situation. "You better."

Torin hugs Jewel. In their half awake state, the parents, say their last goodbyes from the window upstairs. Forty-five minutes pass, and Jewel holds and hugs his sister and brother before jumping into the military vehicle. The soldier explains where Jewel will be heading next.

"The trip will take us to Fort Hood, Texas, where you will be on a flight to your destination. You will meet other military personnel who will take you to your operational base later that night, the living quarters where your house location is."

Jewel is very pleased. "I appreciate it. Let's get on the way already."

The vehicle drives off as Jewel's brother and sister wave goodbye.

In the meantime, General Boulder is debriefed by the alien entities, where one seems to be an alpha male and a head female for each alien race that is on the good side of things. A female alien is seen behind her back as she describes universes that the evil aliens from the past had conquered, saying, "We must be careful this time that the insurrection of these evil aliens does not extinguish our predecessors or ancestors from being eliminated. This time, we must eradicate these aliens once and for all to have peace in all galaxies and universes."

With a curious look, General Boulder says, "How are we going to do that?"

The male alien notices his curiosity. "The Praetorian and human DNA are needed to raise mutated aliens, unlike the DNA of other aliens. They may also be immune to weapons. We don't know the outcome. We can only speculate."

General Boulder rubs his nose, and says, "Hmm, okay, when do we start?"

The aliens create a wavy holographic world surrounding the general as though he sees the future of things to come.

Merna has landed at New Jersey airport, and her excited family happily receives her. On the way to the house, Merna and her family discuss the family business's prosperity. The family reaches their home an hour later, no longer in Camden, New Jersey, but rather in an upscale area of Longport, New Jersey. Coming out of their new Luxury SUV, Charlie taps Merna on the shoulder.

"Do you like our big home, Merna?"

Merna is stunned. "Oh my god, what a tremendous change, Dad. I love it. It is enormous!"

Lu grabs a suitcase from the back of the car. "Glad you love it, dear. Worked hard to get something like this for four years now."

Upon entering the house, they see it is immaculate. It has seven bedrooms and four full bathrooms, a fish tank around one critical part of the house, a gigantic eighty-inch television in the middle, a huge den, and colorful furniture with beautiful paintings on its two floors. Merna enters the house, and her jaw drops to the floor. "My gosh, Mom, Dad, I am amazed at how gorgeous this house is."

Merna hugs her dad and mom, and Lu gets Merna settled in.

"Well, Merna, your room will always be upstairs. Go look at it, honey."

Merna and the two boys head upstairs to look at Merna's room, while Lu, Su Ang, and Sandra get dinner together. At the dinner table, Lu inquires Merna about her future work. "Merna, honey, now that you have graduated and are a doctor of biology, what are your plans for work?"

Merna eats some of her food as she puts the fork into her mouth, chewing. "Ah, hold on a minute, Dad." Merna swallows. "My work plans have been assigned to me already. Don't worry about it, Dad."

Lu is just a little emotional about seeing his daughter after so long. "That is okay, daughter, talk to you about your job another time. You look so beautiful."

Merna glows. "Why, thanks, Dad. So since business is doing well, can you show me where its location is?"

Lu is confident. "Indeed, I'd be happy to show you the location of the business in a couple of days. Okay."

Merna says, yawning, "Okay, sure thing, Dad. Right now, I am tired from jet lag. Want to turn in early."

Lu kisses his daughter on her forehead. "No problem, honey, get some rest."

In the next couple of days, Lu drives Merna and the boys to his business. In Lu's car, a gray-and-black Royal Royce, Merna is talking to Charlie. "Charlie, I'm proud of you for graduating high school and all. What are you going to do for college?"

Charlie sighs. "Ah, I want to go to technical school."

Merna is pretty interested in Charlie's schooling. "What are you going to take up at this specialized school?"

Charlie is thrilled at how Merna is interested in hiseducation. "Well, I want to go to school for robotics."

Merna's eyes are on Charlie. "Please tell me more."

Twenty-five minutes have passed while Charlie talks about his schooling, and Lu has reached his business parking lot, where workers are preparing for a job. Lu gets out of the car.

"Here we are, Merna. This entire building is my business and paid for."

Merna is elated at what her father has accomplished in life. "I'm proud of you, Dad. So let's go inside and see the entire operation, Dad." As Merna and the boys learn about Lu's successful business at the business building lunch hall, the waitress comes by to get drinks. Merna is elated at what her father has accomplished in life. "I'm proud of you, Dad."

"Can I get you folks something to drink?" After long hesitation and pondering, Lu looks up at the waitress. "And, Mr. Mellomystic, would you like the usual?"

Lu turns his head slightly to the waitress. "Yes, the usual, and these two boys will have Cokes, and what would you like, Merna?"

Merna tells the waitress what she wants. "I will have a screwdriver, please." Merna orders quickly. "Well, I will have pasta fettuccine with garlic bread." The waitress nods and goes.

Lu asks Merna about her work. "So what kind of work will you do, dear?"

Merna tells Lu, "Dad, I will work for the government. I will be at my faculty researching wherever they place me."

Charlie exclaims, "You're working for the government doing research. Holy cow. What level of clearance do they have you?"

Merna acts confused. "Clearance! What do you mean? I know there are different levels. Sorry, I have no idea what level I will be working at, Charlie."

Bing furthers the conversation. "What type of research will you do? Is it research for what you went to college for, like biology?"

Merna is nodding her head. "Yes, Bing, exactly."

Lu, a little concerned, tells Merna, "Well, honey, be careful because they like to own everything you do."

Merna assures him, "Dad, don't worry. I have it all under control. I met some friends in college who will be working in other areas of the globe, and they will keep in touch with me and make sure credit is due where necessary."

Lu is feeling good about the situation. "That is good you have friends like that. Remember, they want you, and you have rein over the government since they want your research, right?"

Merna agrees with her dad. "Absolutely correct, Dad. I am in control, and no one else can get the knowledge I have in my head except me."

Lu agrees with the comment. "Good, that's my little girl." As soon as Lu, the boys, and Merna finish eating, they head back home.

Merna takes a phone call, saying, "Yes, I can talk."

Voice of military personnel on the phone. "Ma'am, we will be there at 7:00 a.m. sharp tomorrow morning to pick you up."

Merna stutters a bit, and says, "Okay. My sister's wedding is taking up all of my time right now." Merna says, "Okay. Can we talk later?"

The voice over the phone says, "Not a problem, ma'am, be ready in the morning."

Merna hangs the phone up. Pictures are being taken in the hallway as the ceremony is over. As Merna makes it in time to take photographs, Sandra whispers, "What was that?"

Merna responds, "Nothing, dear sis, you enjoy."

At 7:00 a.m. the following day, Merna is ready with her luggage. A few military vehicles approach as the house's main gate opens. All the family members gather together except Sandra, who said her goodbyes and left with her husband, Chang, after the wedding last night. Merna says her final goodbyes to her family.

"Bye, Dad, Mom, Charlie, Bing."

These four people wave goodbye to Merna, whose eyes are moist. The military man comes up to Merna as Merna is saying goodbye. "Ma'am, we're on a tight schedule. We have to leave right now, ma'am." In the military vehicle, Merna enters. Another military officer informs her of her location for today.

"Our next stop is Fort Hood, Texas, where you'll meet up with the other scientists and receive your designated living and working areas."

Merna says with an intent smile, "Thank you."

The vehicle continues to its destination. In the interim, General Boulder, with some of his lieutenants, is sitting around a table dazed with what the future will bring humanity, especially if the future rift is to shift, giving the enemy the upper hand. As the general and his men are in the fog of what will happen in the not-so-distant future, the enormous alien called the Praetorian offers a solution to the problem. In shock, the general and his men look at each other n horror.

CHAPTER 10

THE PLAN IN ACTION

It has taken several days, but the three scientists have finally arrived at Fort Hood, Texas, in their military vehicles. There has been speculation that the human race will become extinct if the Praetorians fail to get it right the first time, leaving future alien races in perdition if the Praetorians fail to do it right the first time. Boulder and some of his military men struggled to escape the bubble of time hours earlier. Within that very moment, Legendary aliens voice a plea for their ancestors to listen to the warning signals about the evil Inquestorians slaughtering many of the Legendaries on their planet as most of them escape off the world with ships toward their brethren's invisible galaxy.

Lucas, Jewel, and Merna greet Master Chief Yufer, who has guards on each side of the entrance of the ramp of the carrier plane. As the scientists walk up the ramp, they salute several military personnel. In a short conversation with the three scientists, Yufer walks with the three scientists up the ramp with them.

"Well, Drs. Lucas, Jewel, and Merna, there will be a briefing with General Boulder near the front of the plane, where we have several seats waiting for you all."

As Jewel rubs his hair back, he asks, "What else can we discuss?"

Master Chief Yufer wants the scientists to wait until they reach the front of the plane. "Wait until all are present, and we will debrief you on the situation at hand for your new endeavors."

Lucas and Merna say simultaneously, "We got it."

Three scientists and Master Chief Yufer enter the cockpit onboard the plane. They greet General Boulder, "Nice to finally meet the three of the most talented people on the face of the Earth. Please! Sit! We have a lot to talk about."

The three scientists, along with Yufer, sit at a small round table with the general and a few men to review the proposals the scientists should make as a result of their research. Lucas is concerned about family holidays. "Let me ask a quick question before we get started, General Boulder."

General Boulder responds, "Please do ask me."

Lucas continues, "When we move to these locations, will family members be able to visit us during the holidays?"

With a poignant look, General Boulder says, "Well, you see, that can be a small problem because you are dealing with confidential military stuff. It could hinder humanity if a family member took any vital information or acknowledged it. What you will be looking at on a computer and given to you will be other technological advances to help with your research. Of course, if it gets leaked out to rogue governments, on the other hand, you will be able to visit your family on special occasions like holidays with a military chaperone that will be by your side at all times wherever you go. Here is the contract you three had signed when you signed up with us after graduation."

Before the briefing starts, Merna asks, "What about calling family members on our cell phones weekly rather than on Skype?"

General Boulder sees the scientists' concern about communication with family members. "You can use a private line similar to Skype to contact family members. All communications are submitted to a computer program for analysis to prevent information from being leaked. I hope you don't mind how the government operates worldwide. Okay, let's get started on where you will live for the next fifty to sixty years. Remember, where you live is solely your own. You can sell it, or give it to family members, except all government information will be cleared out. On that point, I will say once, you three will become world-famous, just as Einstein and other prominent scientists did throughout centuries. We intend to preserve you three scientists' names, Merna, Lucas, and Jewel, your first and surnames throughout history in textbooks for college, history books, and other textbooks deemed appropriate for the general public."

Lucas is feeling relieved. "That is great. Let's get started."

General Boulder begins the proposition of the briefing for the three scientists. "All right, let's chat about what we will do for the three of you. Various measuring technologies will monitor you, and you can access $5 million in your bank account to use as you wish with your research. Let's talk about the money. You can use it in your personal life, so if you want to buy an expensive car, that's fine with me. We only warn you not to share the information with outsiders. Using a private channel and collaborating with other scientists worldwide, you will only share with us after completing your research. Lucas here will give us a daily report every six days a week. One of my men here or I will pick it up and report it to the International Union personnel only. Any questions?"

Jewel has an odd question. "Will you be monitoring our personnel training as well?"

When Bouldersays, "Well, Dr. Jewel, everything technical is monitored," Jewel is surprised. "Any other odd answers or questions?"

With a blush look, Merna asks, "Will you look at us when we change clothes?"

General Boulder seems amused. "Hmm, good question. We will not look at your wardrobe at all, unfortunately."

Merna says, relieved, "Thank God."

Boulder finishes it up. "If no other questions arise, we will be landing first in Moscow, Russia, in about ten hours, where you will be living, Dr. Jewel. The Russians love physics, and they have a lot of research you can use there to help you and hopefully help things on our planet as well."

Jewel is excited. "Can't wait to see where I will be living, General Boulder. I look forward to it."

Hours later, a plane lands in Moscow, Russia. Four military vehicles enter a huge gold-and-silver mansion that flourished with white trimmings. Jewel's eyes widen as the cars get closer to where he will likely live the rest of his life. After the vehicles stopped, the military men entered the mansion, grabbing his bags. A holographic library and research equipment adorn two floors of Jewel's mansion. Jewel is beside himself. "I am truly amazed at all this luxury and state-of-the-art technology. All for me?"

With a slight smile, General Boulder says, "Yep, all for you, and over in this room is all your communication stuff."

Jewel looks in a huge den area. "Oh Jesus, my god, I feel like I am in a government cover-up."

General Boulder, with a grin, says, "Well, let's say you are, Dr. Jewel."

Jewel is going to another room. "This is my play area and gym for me to get in shape, huh."

General Boulder replies, "Yes, sir. Must keep that body and brain intact training twenty-four hours, seven days a week, Doc."

Jewel calls the family on the brief comm. "Hey, Mom, Dad, Torin, and Cynthia, how are you guys doing?"

Darin talks for the family. "We're doing fine, son. Hope to see you within the next few months."

A gasps of air escapes Jewel's throat. "Sure thing." he replies. "So I just wanted to let you know I am doing fine and residing in my living quarters. My mansion, I apologize. I'll talk to you all later." Jewel hangs up. Boulder is on a schedule.

"Well, good luck, Dr. Jewel. I must drop off the other scientists and head back to our main headquarters in two days."

Military personnel from the United States and Russia stay behind for Jewel to see if he would need anything for his research. General Boulder heads back to the carrier plane to drop Merna off in Hong Kong, China. It takes them about eight hours from Moscow to Hong Kong to drop off Merna. General Boulder and his team of military men get off the plane's ramp and head with Chinese military coordinates to Merna's living space. With disbelief in her eyes, she sees her mansion as a castle. Merna and military personnel get out of the vehicles enter the domain, and inside, Merna sees red and silver all over with superior technologies she can't even fathom. Merna sees her research area and asks General Boulder a question.

"Will I be able to get biological living organisms to work on for my research?"

General Boulder suggests to Merna, "The good thing about the Chinese government is that they have a plentiful of creatures for you to work on that would benefit our societies. Remember, they have cloning facilities."

Merna, not knowing all about it, states, "Really? That is good because it will help me better understand certain species that can camouflage specific ailments, where Dr. Lucas's chemical engineering can help me." Merna looks around the place, and it is like a giant dollhouse for a doll; she loves it so much she wants to tell her family. "I want to call my family to tell them about my living space. May I?"

As he sucks his lips, General Boulder replies, "You can call them on the brief comm, similar to Skype but a secure line."

Merna is calling her family. "Hello, Mom, Dad, Bing, Charlie, Sandra, and Chang. I am in my beautiful living space, a lovely mansion in Hong Kong, China. Hopefully, I will be home for the holidays sometime next year."

Lu and Su Ang say, "It sounds good, honey."

They speak for some time, and Merna continues to look at her new house and surroundings. Merna notices a huge Olympic-sized pool. "Wow, I can get some swimming done. I love it, General Boulder."

General Boulder looks at Merna as though he just set his only daughter on the loose. "I'm glad you love it. Remember, I am only a brief comm away if you need something other than what the Chinese has to offer you."

Merna graciously says, "I appreciate it all. It is like a dream come true."

General Boulder heads back with the military personnel to the plane and heads to Hollywood, California, to drop off Lucas at the last location. Seven vehicles drive off the aircraft to a remote mansion, where Lucas will be doing some research for the government. An army of two guards greets each vehicle at a colossal gate and eamines each van inside.

People in vehicle 1, "Please move on."

"Thank you."

All vehicles move through, and the middle vehicle with Lucas moves to the main gate of the guard. "Yes, General Boulder and Dr. Lucas, welcome. You can move along." After driving up the winding road to the mansion, General Boulder and Lucas enter through a massive door. After entering the estate, Lucas notices similarities with his parents' house.

"I am amazed at how much this structure resembles my parents' house." Dr. Lucas inspects his new home with a few military personnel.

General Boulder grazes his right hand against the luxurious furniture.

"As you can see, there are a lot of guards around this room in case someone tries to intrude, and you also have state-of-the-art technologies to help with your chemical analyses. I hope it will be beneficial for you, Doctor."

Lucas goes into an office area with holographic panels, where he calls his family on the brief comm. "Hello, Mom, Dad. I am at my place of residence. Take a gander. Do you like it?"

Mr. and Mrs. Normalic both simultaneously, "It is so much like home. We love it, son."

Lucas is on a time crunch. "Basically, I just called to let you know I am okay and that I am well placed."

Eight years have passed, and the scientists have come up with great discoveries as Lucas takes notes of all findings. In a brief comm, Lucas is in touch with all scientists around the world.

"What do we have, teammates?"

Researchers John and Merna have devised a way to maintain the culture of defending against diseases and rapidly reverse the aging process, so people can become teenagers and start over again. John gives his findings to Lucas. "My discovery, Lucas, is a particle called periello2, which would defend us against disease. In addition to fighting cancer, it also resists many other disorders."

Lucas then gets Merna's attention on the brief comm. "Merna, what do you have?"

As she prepares to report, proud Merna shares, "I have found a biological culture that can reverse the aging process to the point that it can make an elderly person look like a teenager. It is working on a live subject."

As a spur-of-the-moment, Dr. Lucas creates a report. General Boulder's commanders enter Lucas's house.

"Dr. Lucas, it comes to our attention that your discoveries can be of great use to us. I will forward this report to General Boulder as soon as I receive it. Beneficiaries and other government officials will benefit from these discoveries. Our plan is not to leak this information yet. The public is not ready for this for at least one hundred years."

Lucas hands over the paperwork and files, transferring them to the commander's computer so that the other part of the government can get those files. Lucas slowly and slyly puts a copy to his computer's hidden area. In a remote file on his laptop.

"Here, it is all there. All three gigabytes of material."

The commander takes a good look and nods with satisfaction. But a couple of months later, the word escapes Lucas's facility, and some devious governments catch wind of the findings. Almost every government in the Middle East is aware of the news, including Saudi Arabia, Venezuela, Cuba, and Africa. To find these scientists, Rogue Hein sends out devious mercenaries to infiltrate their facilities and gather more information. Rebecca, a Sunni Arab spy, disguises herself as a fellow scientist and visits Jewel in Russia. Jewel has sent for her as she seems to want more information, so she has a meeting with Jewel since they have been in touch for some time now. Jewel opens the door for Rebecca.

"Hello, Rebecca, right?"

With a short skirt and sexy legs with long black hair, Rebecca says, "Yes, I'm Rebecca. Do you have those files for me?"

A bit skeptical of her, Jewel gives her a copy of a temporary USB file. "Yes, I have that information for you. Let me download it to your computer." Jewel downloads the information to her laptop, which has various files from different projects. Jewel feels she has a conflict of interest with humanity and a selfish demand for his work. There is a conscious effort on Rebecca's part to be nice.

"It looks like you have a lovely place here, so how has it been working out?" Rebecca slowly brushes the furniture with her right hand, as Jewel tries to be social but very careful.

"Yes, it gets the work done. That is all I need."

Rebecca says, "Thanks for the information. Will talk to you soon for more details."

Jewel replies as he pulls his hand back from giving Rebecca the information, "I look forward to that."

Jewel gets several more visits from outside sources that he thinks the International Government had sent him. They get by the facial recognition into Jewel's place that Master Chief Yufer men guard tightly with their lives. After many such visits, the military finally scans for bugs in Jewel's mansion and finds several listening devices. One of the men calls Master Chief Yufer to tell him the estate is compromised.

A military man on the phone with Master Chief Yufer says, "Sir, the estate is compromised. It has a bunch of listening devices."

In a concerned tone, Chief Yufer says, "To prevent such an incident from occurring again, I will send an elite force to satisfy the matter and protect the scientist more effectively. Only my men will be allowed to talk to him, and no strangers will be able to come into his lab. That's it. Give Jewel that notice."

The military man quickly hangs up. "Yes, sir."

During this time, Merna receives a visit from Suko and Maria, a Japanese man and Venezuelan woman. Suko and Maria, unaware of Merna's other projects, are standing on the doorstep as Merna opens the door of her house. When the two enter her residence, Merna greets them.

"Hello, you are Suko, Maria, right?"

Suko bows to Merna. "Pleasure to meet you."

Maria gently gives her hand for Merna to kiss. "Pleased to meet you, milady."

Merna bows to Suko and kisses Maria's right hand. Merna welcomes them into her home. "Please come in. We have a lot to discuss."

Maria wants to know the location of Merna's research area. "Where is your research area located, Merna? I am interested in your findings."

Merna is feeling a bit weird and cautious. "Well, let us first get acquainted, and we will get to that point in a bit."

Suko stares abruptly at Merna, then turns away and agrees. "Yes, Doctor. Let's have some sake, relax, and then get down to business."

Merna sits down as her back slams the couch, and agrees. "Okay, let's sit here."

Suko talks with his hands, and asks, "So what motivated you to get such a find?"

Merna observes Suko's delicate taste in her work. "Well, I have examined different animal cells, like other starfish and lobster, and they don't age, so I found a chemical in their DNA sequence that corresponded to the lathem8 cell. In my laboratoty, I am working with an old adult female human who is rapidly deteriorating and whose DNA seems to collapse due to my discovery's conversion within the cellular level."

Maria is amused. "I'm in awe with this finding." Suko impatiently requests an explanation, "Let's see what your research says."

Not knowing Suko's ulterior motive, Merna replies, "No problem, we just need to walk around this corner of mirrors to where my office is."

Maria, who has to use the bathroom, asks, "Where is your bathroom?"

Merna is a bit suspicious now about why she's waited to use the restroom. At the last second of the visit, she gets wary of the situation. "Sure, it is three doors down on the left side." Merna goes with Suko to her area of research. "Here we are. Let me get that information for you." Merna, a bit vigilant, gives them a small copy of the work. Meanwhile, Maria is trying to put bugs in Merna's house. "Let me transfer the information for you since you have to leave abruptly."

Suko is taking the data and transferring it to his computer. "I am grateful to you. I look forward to working with you in the future."

Merna meets up with Maria at the door. "You two have a good time. It should be beneficial to you both."

Maria says smoothly, "I am sure it will be, Dr. Merna."

Both Suko and Maria leave with no red flags. Later that week, Merna gets a visit from Frank and several other people. Merna meets Frank at her door. "Hello, everyone else. Feel free to enter. We should discuss the research. Hello, do you have that information for me?"

Frank and the other people head to Merna's office. They discuss scientific notations to help slow down aging and additional valuable information for humans to have a long life. Merna has one of the military men search for bugs hours later when they all have left, and they find at least fifteen throughout the downstairs area.

"Hmm, I knew something was fishy with the people I invited. Now how did they get past you guys?"

Military guy replies with a scared look, "Ma'am, I have no idea. Next time, we will use body and facial recognition to ensure that they are the people they say they are."

CHAPTER 11

PROTECTION OF THE SAVANTS

Lucas gets several visitors to his California, Los Angeles, heavily unpenetrated mansion. A young African woman named Nadine is visiting Lucas, and a few other people. In the meantime, Nadine is with Lucas, having hot tea, while the others look around his compound, asking, "So what exactly do you do?"

Nadine gives Lucas an eye. "I deal with various technologies in the science area. Why?"

Lucas is trying to pinpoint the exact location of technology that she is in "That is so general. Give me a narrow area of expertise."

Nadine gives Lucas what she does. "Well, I do rigorously maintain all new and used technologies."

Lucas is impressed. "That's amazing."

Nadine cuts to the chase. "Would you be interested in me updating your area for you, if that is okay with you."

Lucas is a bit mistrustful. "Please give me a minute to gather some information for you, all right?" Lucas notices a man near his work area and asks, "What are you looking for exactly?"

The man, who has put a listening device in his house, wants to find the bathroom. "Oh, I am just looking for the bathroom."

Lucas directs him to the toilet. "The bathroom is down the hall this way." Lucas points in the direction. She was trying to get information from Lucas's computer. Nadine tries one other trick in the book.

"Can I see your research area and see what I am working with?"

Lucas takes Nadine to the site. "Sure, you can look, but don't touch, okay."

Nadine is delighted. "Not a problem." They enter the area as Nadine puts a device near the computer to pick up information so that the Rogue Hein government can transfer that information to them. Nadine begins to leave after thirty minutes of looking around. Lucas says goodbye to Nadine at the door.

"Will talk to you later. Maybe we can have a cup of tea sometime, huh?"

Nadine, who would love it, says, "Sure." She leaves, and several military personnel search for bugs as one military personnel finds a device near his computer.

"Dr. Lucas, we just found a listening device here."

Lucas, feeling awful, has no idea who would do such a thing. "What is that?"

Military personnel gives him the lowdown. "The device picks up data when you type it in or when you transfer them to your computer, Doctor."

Lucas, who likes Nadine, is dumbfounded. "I can't believe it." He sits down, feeling foolish and embarrassed. Lucas stares into space, wondering if either the man or Nadine could have planted or one of the other people.

Nadine reports to the Rogue Hein government in regard to Lucas's research. She calls in. "Did you get it, General?"

Rogue Hein General Papsi replies, "Yes, except it seems to be erasing itself as I try to download it."

With a confused look, Nadine says, "But how is that possible?"

Papsi on the holographic phone says, "Looks like they had a failed safe protection on the transfer if someone was to steal it. Damn it!"

Nadine slowly takes a breath and gulps. "How, really, how is that? Unless the scientists put some temporary file on the download."

Papsi says with a violent temper, "Now I can't report to the higher people. We must try a different way to get some of their research or kidnap them somehow."

Nadine, in agreement, says, "I agree, Counselor." They both hang up their phones abruptly.

The next day, Master Chief Yufer locks down all three scientists' facilities with military vehicles and choppers surrounding several areas within a five-mile radius to ensure any cars that visit the scientists have a thorough check before entering. Furthermore, Master Chief Yufer also ensures that all computers that acquire any threats or hackers would notify his team and trace the information back to its source. Jewel, who happens to be sleeping in his bed with several pillows, gets an alarm on his computer. He slowly gets out of bed and opens the top of his laptop to see the message. He yells out loud, and a military man who happens to be down the hall comes running. Jewel yells, "No!"

Suddenly, drawn by Jewel's attention, a military man says, "What is it? Please tell me what is it, Doctor!"

Jewel stares at the screen of the computer. "Look there!" As Jewel points to the e-mail message. The military man reads the news as the letter says:

> To: Jewel Justicks
> From:
> Subject: Regarding Hydroelectricity
> Date: Unknown
>
> Dr. Jewel Justick, if you don't comply with our demands to get the information on the hydroelectricity formula, we will not only stop you but take out your family unless you do as we say.
>
> We will not hurt your family if you work for us. Give us what we want—we want your incredible mind—and we will leave your family alone; otherwise, there will be consequences if you don't comply!
>
> Regards,
> Mr. P——

Master Chief Yufer sees someone has infiltrated Jewel's communication system. He gets a real sound techie guy to find out what's happening. Master Chief Yufer comes running in the door and looks at the message. He notices that the From is through a portal e-mail where the sender is not recognized. After hours of waiting, the technician arrives and examines the location of the hacked e-mail.

"It says here, sir, that the site is in Iran."

In his mind, Master Chief Yufer ponders, *A government called Rogue Heins must have done this. They would stop at nothing until they get what they want.* Master Chief Yufer calls General Boulder. "We have a problem, sir."

General Boulder says in a meeting with the International Government officials, "Excuse me, gentlemen and ladies."

General Boulder answers his holographic brief comm on his phone. "What is it, Chief Yufer?"

Chief Yufer stares at the information on the screen. "Sir, we have infiltration from Rogue Hein through e-mail."

General Boulder appears to be very cautious. "Are you on secure lines?"

Master Yufer replies, "Yes, I am."

General Boulder is calling an urgent meeting with the International Government Council. "People, we have a problem. A malicious intrusion within our computers systems must be dealt with immediately!"

Not so far in Hong Kong, Merna receives immense threats through her holographic brief comm showing various people with masks. Merna's dangers are similar to terrorist ones; one such threat tells her that if she doesn't comply with their demands, her family will die one by one until she works for them and do what they say. The two men say simultaneously on the video, "Dr. Merna Mellomystic, we need aging information. If you do not work for us exclusively, we will kill one of your family members one at a time."

Merna, scared for her family's safety, calls the chief guard to look at the video. Merna reaches the top guard. "Peter, we have a problem."

Peter, an armed forces member, responds with, "What is the issue at hand, Doctor?"

Merna explains to him what came over her holographic brief comm. "It looks like someone is trying to threaten me by not showing their faces, Peter. Here, look!" She is badly shaking.

Peter calls Master Chief Yufer, "Sir, we have a problem. There have been threats to Dr. Mellomystic. What should I do?"

Master Chief Yufer says on the holographic brief comm, "Keep the doctor safe, and we will take care of the situation. I made a call to General Boulder, who is in the process of taking care of it."

Peter accepts his duties. "I will take care of the doctor and protect her."

Lucas, scattering his papers all over the floor to find a specific formula for his zeonic chemical trace at the other site, suddenly gets a phone message with a no-name person video chat threatening him with his family's lives. Incoming video chat from an unknown source with a scrambled picture.

"Lucas Normalic, you must follow these orders due to this. If you do not comply, your family members will no longer be noticed by face as we disfigure them. Besides this, you must arrange for us to pick you up in a particular area, resulting in your family being returned safely and soundly to their homes."

Lucas listens to the brief comm threat and wonders what to do. He calls one of the military personnel into the room to hear the message again. "Hey, can you come here? I have a threat on my life that you need to hear." The lieutenant rushes to Lucas's aid and looks at the message on the holographic brief comm. He then calls Master Chief Yufer to tell him about the threat to Dr. Lucas Normalic.

Lieutenant Mike, a little hazy, repeats the threat video message to Master Yufer. "It says, sir, 'We need the zeonic formula on the holographic brief comm, or your entire family will be beheaded.' What should I do?"

As an answer to the lieutenant, Yufer says, "I will send further notices to extract the doctor, as well as further instructions in the next ninety-six hours with further instructions."

Lieutenant Mike says, "Anything else I need to do?"

Master Yufer says, "I will call until then. Keep all threats at bay with the help of Hacker Johnson, who will be there in twelve hours and will try to find the locations of these threats. Nothing else, for now, Lieutenant."

Lieutenant Mike hangs up from the holographic brief comm and starts to get tactical reinforcement to surround the area within a five-mile radius protecting the doctor. Meanwhile, it has been forty-eight hours, and the Rogue Hein government has moved to extract the families of the doctors for ransom.

On December 31, 2148, a spy spots Lucas's family going to see a major league baseball game. At a vendor, Mr. Normalic is getting some hotdogs for the family.

"I'll have six hotdogs and five sodas, please."

The vendor worker making the hotdogs puts the hotdogs and sodas on the counter a few minutes later and starts to ring up the total for Mr. Normalic. "Will that be all, sir?"

As Mr. Normalic hands over the cash to the worker and grabs the sodas in the carrying box, six men in black suits with guns concealed near their hips approach him and whisper, "Excuse me. Is that you, Mr. Normalic?"

Mr. Normalic, not seeing the gun, asks, "Who's asking?"

One of the gunmen says, "Oh, a good friend of your son. We want you to follow us because your son has been affected by an injury, and he would like you to see him."

Mr. Normalic is trying to grab the drinks. "Wait, I have to pay for this and give this to my family."

The vendor is trying to get the money when one gunman throws it at the vendor. Without warning, Mr. Normalic feels a pistol by his ribs. "Now follow me right this way." Mr. Normalic, who is very careful, starts to follow two men as one gunman walks him out of the stadium. The other four gunmen stay behind as they search Mr. Normalic's jacket for tickets to find the rest of the family. When the family realizes their father is taking too long to return, one of the gunmen searches for where they are seated and whaits until they get up. Forty-five minutes have passed, and the two boys get up to find their father. They both look for Mr. Normalic, while one heads to the bathroom. Suddenly, Todd bumps into a man in a black suit as he looks for his father.

The black suit man puts a gun to Todd's ribs and tells Todd softly, "Todd Normalic, please follow me. Your brother Lucas wants to see you."

Todd, a bit nervous, asks, "What is it with the gun? There is no need for that."

The gunman, given the situation, explains, "first of all, as a precaution, we have to abide by the rules, so this is our rule of taking you to a hidden area to see your brother."

Todd, understanding, responds, "All right, let's go."

On the other hand, Joe is coming out of the bathroom when another gunman walks up behind him, slowly putting a gun to his rib. "Careful now, do not make a move."

Joe wants to fight back, Who are you, and what do you want with me?"

The gunman tries to hold Joe back from wrestling with him. "Take it easy. I am trying to bring you to your brother Lucas."

Joe relieves. "Okay, I will do that, but I first have to tell my dad and mom."

The gunman is trying to keep Joe calm. "No worries, and they are safe in our vehicles just around from the stadium. Now come." The gunman takes Joe out of the stadium to his car, meeting several men. The last two gunmen in the stadium are waiting for the women to get out of their seats.

It has been two hours, and Sandra and Mrs. Normalic notice the guys are not back yet. They both get up with concerns as they look at each other.

Mrs. Normalic says, "I wonder where the guys are. It's taking them too long."

Sandra, a bit worried, says, "Yeah, way too long. Let's find them. They must be horsing around somewhere." Both women go to the concession stands. One woman goes in one direction, and the other in another direction. The last two gunmen follow each of the women. A gunman points and tells Mrs. Normalic where her family location is.

"Excuse me, ma'am, are you looking for two boys?"

Mrs. Normalic looks at the gunman as though he is a lovely gentleman. "Please, can you show me where they may be?"

The gunman has Mrs. Normalic follow him near some dark vehicles. As a van door opens, two men grab her real quick. Mrs. Normalic screams, "Help! Help!" As the door of the vehicle closes.

As Sandra's last gunman approaches, there are hardly any people walking because the second inning is starting, and most people are heading back to the stadium. Sandra sees a gun by his side and runs, but the gunman runs after her. She is screaming for help. "Help! Help! Help! Someone!"

The gunman lunges toward her, grabbing her feet, trying to calm Sandra down. "Ma'am, take it easy, take it easy."

Sandra tries to calm down. "Who...what do you want?"

"Look, I'm here to pick you up to see Lucas." The gunman brushes his clothing off. "He's in danger, and we have to protect you." Sandra is relieved and replies, "Really? Seeing my brother would be nice. Hopefully, he is okay."

Gunman reassures her. "He is okay. You have to follow me to see him again." Sandra follows the gunman to the identical dark vehicles. As the door opens, two men grab her as she tries to scream, putting a dark cloth over her head. Sandra screamed, "Help! Help!" while her hoarsed voice became muffled. Almost all Normalic family has been captured, except for the youngest daughter. The latter appears to be in college. The family is held in an undisclosed compound under the city while the men in black suits await further orders from the Rogue Hein government.

CHAPTER 12

THE SWITCH-UP GOVERNMENT

Jewel's family is taking a road trip toward Florida to Disney World. Unaware of it, they have been followed by three black vehicles for several hours now. The family makes a stop at a restaurant to eat. They enter the restaurant and sit at a table. Dustin orders food for the family as the waitress takes their orders.

"My daughter will have eggs and pancakes. My son Torin will have a big breakfast. Melba will have steak and eggs with fries, and I will have steak and ribs with two sides of mashed potatoes. That will be it."

The waitress picks up the menus and asks, "And what will you folks have to drink?"

Melba tells the waitress, "My daughter here will have a soda, my son Torin will have a lemonade, my husband will have wine, and I will have wine. That will be all."

Fifty minutes go by, and the family gets up from eating and heads back to their car to continue driving to Disney World, as the black vehicles continue to follow them. Several hours have gone by, and the family enters Disney World. There are five men in black suits following them inside the park. The family gets on a few rides, enjoying themselves, then without warning, one of the black outfit men grabs Cynthia and tells her, "Excuse me, small girl, would you like to meet your brother Jewel?"

Cynthia excitedly says, "Yes, where is he? Is he all right?"

The black suit man gets Cynthia's attention. "Well, your brother is nearby, and he would like to meet the family."

Cynthia is trying to get her family's attention by waving at them. "Hey, wait a minute, I need to get the other family to respond."

The black-suit man is not giving much attention to Cynthia. "No, he only has a short time. He asked for you. Let's go."

Cynthia follows the man. As they exit the park, two other men grab her quick, putting a black sackcloth over her face as she faints in their hands. Similarly, the men from the rogue government pick up each family member and put them into the vehicles. The vehicles then drive off to a hidden building for further instruction from the Rogue Hein people. During this time, Merna's family enjoys lunch at Lu's restaurant, where three dark vehicles park outside. Talking at the table, Su Ang asks, "What are we going to do about the guy who doesn't do the work needed for the customer?"

Lu is looking at Su Ang. "We think we should give him a second chance."

Bing tries to get Lu's attention. "Can I go to the bathroom? I have to pee. Can you excuse me, Dad?" Lu moves to make room for Bing to go to the bathroom, even as another man from the black van goes inside without anyone's knowledge. He quickly follows Bing to the toilet. Bing is in the bathroom peeing when the man in the black suit grabs Bing without any indication, putting something over his face, and knocking him out.

He quickly and in a sneaky way takes Bing to the van, as Lu and Su Ang discuss through the restaurant's window, not noticing what is happening around them. Lu goes to the bathroom to check on Bing.

Charlie wonders where his brother is and asks Lu loudly, "Where is Bing? He's taking a long time coming back from the toilet."

Su Ang and Charlie wait patiently for Bing and Lu to come, as Su Ang looks at the time and notices they have been sitting there for almost an hour. She gets up and searches the area to see if they can find them. Consequently, once he walks into the bathroom, another man from the van goes inside the building of Lu's company to get Lu's attention.

"Excuse me, sir, are you looking for your son?"

Lu looks at the man up and down. "Who are you, and what do you know about my son?"

Black suit man is trying to get Lu to follow him. "Your son ran outside and seems to be around those cars there." The man in the black suit points to the black vehicles as Lu goes out around those vans to see when one of the van's doors opens, grabbing Lu with a black hood over his head, and as Lu struggles, one of the men knocks him out.

Su Ang figures they must have gone home in the other car when suddenly one of the black vehicles comes up behind them slowly. Su Ang notices the man wanting to talk to her. "Excuse me, ma'am, can you tell me how to get to the highway?"

Su Ang is being polite. "You have to go right at the Stop sign, then go south for about two miles, and the route is on the right." While Su Ang is talking to the man, Charlie goes around to the black van's other side, where his mother's car is. Two men grab him, and Charlie tries to fight them martial art style as the man sprays something in Charlie's eyes, slowing him down and putting a hood over his head. Su Ang notices a struggle on the other side of the van and begins to run as one man from the other vehicle runs after her as she tramples over herself. The man ties her hands with handcuffs. The man puts Su Ang in the van, and the van continues to look for the last family member, Sandra, who is pregnant.

Chang has rushed from work there to take his wife to the hospital because suddenly her water burst, and she is about to have twins. A black vehicles sees Sandra being lifted on a stretcher in the ambulance and follows to the hospital. Suddenly, two men in black suits emerge from the vehicle, carefully avoiding nurses as they rush Sandra to the baby delivery area. Sandra is screaming, "Oh, oh, oh, oh!" The nurse tries to keep her calm as they wheel her into the room.

"It is okay, ma'am. It will be all right. Keep breathing in and out fast."

The doctor puts on scrubs to deliver the twin babies; a boy, and a girl. The baby comes out screaming; then, the second baby comes out, and Chang watches with awe after some time. Soon after, Sandra holds both babies in each arm on the bed. Sandra hands over to Chang one of the babies.

"Here, hold her, your daughter."

Chang, with teary eyes, looks at his small child as he kisses her forehead.

Meanwhile, the two men in black suits change into doctors' scrubs. The actual doctor and nurse leave the room. As the two imposters come in, one of them says to Sandra, "Ma'am, you are Sandra Mellomystic Rodriguez, right?"

Sandra answers, "Yes, I am. Why?"

Imposter doctor says, "Well, ma'am, we have to take you and the children to another room. Would you like to follow, sir? I assume you're the father, right?"

Chang is a bit nervous. "Yes, I am. What's going on?"

The other imposter doctor says, "Well, there is a problem with the baby room, and we have to take you to another building."

Chang gets worried. "All right, can you tell me what's going on, please?"

The first imposter doctor responds, "Not to worry. We have to take you for your protection in these black vehicles right outside, okay."

Sandra looks at her husband with fear and confusion on her face. The imposter doctors take them and go by the nursing station, as people are unaware of what is happening. Once they reach the black vehicles, Chang and Sandra are apprehended at gunpoint and loaded into the crossover SUV. There was a screeching sound coming from the car as the other two vehicles scraped along the road; as they sped toward an abandoned private area where there was a wreckage building, the caravan then waited for further orders from the Rogue Hein government.

As guns are blazing, the military and Rogue Hein's men are shooting up the place in Moscow, while Master Chief Yufer is also getting calls stating, "We are under attack. We are under attack. What should we do?"

Master Chief Yufer calls General Boulder and lets him know things are heating up. Master Chief Yufer says on the holographic brief comm, "General, we have gunfire. The scientists are no longer safe in their mansions. What should we do?"

General replies on the holographic brief comm, "We need to send in the elite counsel."

Over in Hong Kong, the same situation is going on at Merna's compound, except the military men here seem to have some victory going on. They are targeting the enemies even as more come out of the woods with blazing guns. Merna is frightened for her life. "What are we going to do?" Her ears filled with guns blazing in the distance made her body tremble with fright. In front of Merna's research area stands one military man and eight others.

"Not to worry, Doctor. We have it under control."

Over in Hollywood, California, Lucas is also undergoing the same dilemma, except Lucas wants to be a hero.

"It's time for me to pounce those jackals."

A military lady is holding back the doctor. "Not a good idea, Doctor. These men are living mercenaries, and they will kill you instantly."

In all three locations, fighting continues for more than twenty-four hours.

General Boulder gets on a private line after discussing with International Government personnel and diplomats. General Boulder says on the remote holographic phone, "Sergeant, we have a problem. We must go to DEFCON 5. We have issues with the doctors in Moscow, Hong Kong, and Hollywood, California. We have to try to extract them quickly."

On the other line, the sergeant says, "I have the men ready to go, General. Should we eliminate the threat at hand?"

General Boulder commands the sergeant, "Delta extra altera terrain at all cost." It means to destroy all threats possible over the doctors. The sergeant gets the order and relays it to his men. Hours later, fighting intensifies to the point of the recon men intercepting the enemy's attack. Sergeant Bobo takes the other men on the other side of the enemies to surround them. One of Sergeant Bobo's men, who happens to be on a roof nearby, is waiting for the signal from Sergeant Bobo. Two minutes go by, and then he gives the motion. The sniper then takes out about ten of the threats nearby. Sergeant Bobo and his men infiltrate the rest of the enemy, knocking them off one by one on a large scale with several of Sergeant Bobo's snipers and men on the ground. They have silencers for the new Z38 guns similar to an M16, except for double barrels with a barrel silencer at each end that can fire eighteen rounds at a time. So imagine a roll of bullets through a circular belt around the hips of the men.

Another sergeant, Sergeant Sash, infiltrates an enemy near a five-mile radius near the other side of the world where his teams are holding the enemy at bay. The military has a hard time getting a good grip on the situation. Sergeant Sash and his men throw silent grenades to blow up the men nearby; he tells his men to make a circular combat move that will surround the enemies in that five-mile radius.

"Go to the west and the east. Slowly throw the silent grenades toward the enemy." Sash continues, "That should knock each enemy down, striking them and eliminating them once and for all if they don't back down. Got it, Lieutenant?"

The lieutenant responds with caution, "Got it, Sergeant."

On the United States soil, recon five takes out the threat by sneaking up on each enemy one by one, grabbing them and tying them up with cable cords and twist ties, handcuffing them. They realize several enemies have noticed them and begin firing back; the recon five men are yelling, "Get back, fall back, call up the snipers!"

Sergeant Cold calls the snipers, "We have a situation, corner of southwest Monroe Avenue near some vehicles. We need five threats taken out."

The sniper responds, "On it, Sergeant." The sniper takes out the five men, and the men on the ground continue to take out the threat within the five-mile radius.

The figure holding Jewel's family hostage demands a ransom. "If you surrender yourself to one of our men, we will return your family. Otherwise, we will negotiate another method. You have fifteen hours to meet my demands."

Watching his family on the brief comm, he has no idea what to do. He then goes to Master Chief Yufer for advice. "Master Chief Yufer, I just got another threat. This time they have my family. They said if I don't let one of their men take me, something will happen to my family."

Master Chief Yufer calms down Jewel. "Not to worry. They are only threatening you. Remember, they want you to work for them. They will do nothing to harm your family. If they do, we will put a decoy in and get your family out. So don't worry about it." Not feeling good about it, Jewel sits down for a second as Master Chief Yufer tries to get the doctor out of the location.

There is also a threat from the holographic brief comm for Merna in Hong Kong, but the demand from Rogue Hein are more intense for her. A man with a black mask over his face gives Merna an order. If she doesn't meet that demand, one of her family members will not be alive anymore. The man in the black mask appears on the brief comm screen.

"Dr. Merna Mellomystic, we have a demand. We want your intelligence to work for us solely. We also know that you designed a way to prolong aging, and we want your brainpower. I will send one of my men to your location ten miles away in a gold and black car. One of my men will cut the head of one of your family members if you do not meet this demand within twelve hours."

Merna is petrified. "Okay, what do I have to do? I don't want my family members to lose their heads."

The masked man says, "Go now! Ten miles south, and he will meet you."

The man hangs up, and Merna begins to get ready. The chief guard focuses on Merna as he realizes she is packing up. He then tells her, "Ma'am, sorry, Dr. Merna, you can't leave. There is a war in our backyard."

Merna is afraid for her family and her life. "I must leave right away. My family is in danger."

Chief guard calms Merna down. "Look, Doctor, they aren't going to hurt your family. It is a tactic so you would go on their side, and they would return your family. Don't think on their level. The enemy wants you. If they destroy your family, they will not succeed in obtaining you. So don't worry, okay."

Merna says with relief. "If that is the case, why don't you guys get my family out?"

The chief guard replies, "Unfortunately, at this point we cannot locate them since they are well concealed." Merna frowns at this and is still nervous.

Furthermore, mad as hell, Lucas sees his family bonded in chains, blindfolded, and muzzled. He is stomping around in fury as he sees his family on the brief comm with a message from a masked man. The man relays the statement, "Since you found the zeonic chemicalwe discussed, Dr. Lucas Normalic, we are not interested in that. We want your intelligent brain. If we cannot have you working for us, there will be uncontrollable measures where your family will suffer greatly. You have ten hours to meet our demands, or something terrible will happen."

The lieutenant, coming from the bathroom area, sees Dr. Lucas in a rage of fury. "What seems to be the problem, Doctor?"

Lucas is not feeling like chatting much. "I got another threat, and they have my family this time. What am I supposed to do now?"

The lieutenant gestures. "What we can do is first calm down, then let me say, it seems that they want you, not your family. Trust me, they aren't going to do anything to your family, and if they did, they would lose hope of getting you to work for them. Get it?"

Lucas realizes the situation and uses it to his advantage. "The next time they call, I will have them by the tail."

The lieutenant rubs his nose in a sour mood, saying, "I don't think there will be another time. I have a strong sense of confidence that everything will work out in the end. The situation is under control. I am confident."

The fighting seems to dwindle in Moscow as the military and the regime council take out the last threats. A few helicopters lower into the grassy way of the mansion to extract the doctor. Master Chief Yufer tells the doctor to follow him.

"This way, Dr. Jewel."

Jewel grabs several essential things that mean something to him and his research. "All right, coming right away." Jewel and Master Chief Yufer duck slightly from the helicopter's blades and enter the aircraft.

The helicopter man clicks some switches on the aircraft. "Ready to go."

Master Chief Yufer says, "Go! Go!" The helicopter goes up safely.

The chief in Hong Kong is protecting Merna in Hong Kong as they cautiously emerge from the mansion and walk through the yard toward some blue and black vehicles. Merna is rushing toward the car. As they get into the dark-colored vehicle, Chief tells Merna to hold on. "Hold on, Merna, the ride will get intense." The elite regimen drives the other two cars. The vehicles are out into the five-mile radius, where silver and gray vehicles follow them. Then two men in the black cars put a missile launcher out of the sunroof and fire it at the oncoming vehicles trying to shoot at them, and they continue shooting back and forth until they overturn the three cars following them.

Lucas waits for the lieutenant in Hollywood, California, to get word on what to do. The lieutenant gets a call from Master Chief Yufer.

"Lieutenant, a helicopter will land in your backyard in about an hour. Get the doctor onto the helicopter as quickly as you can."

The lieutenant gets Dr. Lucas ready for extraction. "Doctor, we need to be on the lawn area in an hour."

Dr. Lucas is excited. "I will be prepared to go in that hour. Let me get my research work together and a few cases of clothes."

Lieutenant is about to tell the doctor he would have too much to carry. "We only need to take a few things as there is not much room on the helicopter, and we must hurry."

After fifty-nine minutes, two helicopters touch down, as the doctor and lieutenant enter the aircraft. All three locations have secured the doctors. The elite regime takes all three doctors to a hidden classified base underground, where they meet with General Boulder. General Boulder talks to the three scientists.

"I have already met the two gentlemen and this fine woman. We have extracted you from the threat, and we need the plan to make you disappear off the face of the Earth."

Lucas scratches his head. "How is that possible, General?"

General Boulder taps Master Chief Yufer on the shoulder. "Master Chief Yufer will explain what will take part in your disappearance."

While in warp speed toward planet Earth are the Inquestorians to demolish humanity's ancestors. Meanwhile, near a hidden door at the underground base, an alien arm quickly shakes its arms at General Boulder, who comes running toward him as he excuses himself from the scientists.

"Please excuse me for a second." General Boulder slams the door behind him quickly. "What is it?"

The Legendary female in charge says, "We have a problem. Intel tells us the enemy will soon be here. We need to prepare for war."

General Boulder's eyes widen as though in shock as his body numbs simultaneously.

CHAPTER 13

NEW ENLIGHTENMENT

Master Yufer walks with the three scientists through the hidden base area and explains the detail of the issue at hand. "We intend to have you disappear by cloning you three and telling the world that you all have died. That way, the Rogue Hein government cannot pursue you three and restore your family to their proper homes."

In the scientific section of the facility, the scientists look eager, as if they have just hit the jackpot. Hundreds of units show scientific research, from cryogenics to significant research on supersoldiers, cloning, and designing species. There's also a private area that looks for new technologies that are at least two hundred years out of reach of humanity today. Jewel's mind is ticking, going a million miles per second, about how the cloning process works and other things in this facility. Finally, he questions Master Chief Yufer mostly about the cloning area.

"Master Yufer, exactly how does your cloning process work? Several books have described the process but on a speculation basis. Could you please elaborate?"

He explains how cloning works. "First, we take a blood sample that carries your DNA, then put it in a tube to detect your DNA structure. We have built your identical twin several hours later with all your thinking and characteristics."

With curiosity, Merna, from time to time, leaves the other two scientists behind to explore the facility. Several massive generators are powering up during the cloning process. Lucas asks Yufer, "If the plan is for us to die, will we maintain a normal relationship with our families?"

Master Yufer gives Lucas a risk factor for that issue. "However it may seem reasonable to you, Dr. Lucas, it is a security risk because even if we pull off as your clones faking your deaths, it will cause the Rogue Hein government to pursue your family again, putting them at risk again, gaining your knowledge for their evil plot. So, Doctor, it wouldn't be in the government's best interest to fulfill such a demand. You do understand, right, Doctor?"

Lucas heads down, and agrees. "Of course. I comprehend. Okay, let's move on with the process."

The three scientists meet up with a scientist named Gale, who specializes in cloning. Master Chief Yufer introduces the cloning scientist, Gale. "Doctors, this is Gale, who specializes in cloning. In preparation for the death of your twins, she will arrange for several of our men to execute them on a boat excursion, during which a blast of chemicals will supposedly kill you three. Three scientists who specialized in research for the International Government died suddenly, and a news report will explain what happened. Until then, Gale here will get you three together in the next two days, and all you three will do is meet your clones. They will exit our secret facility toward a military craft that will take them to a boat where they will do research with several of our navy SEAL team that will organize a chemical mishap that will send your clones to a fiery grave where we will have men rescue whatever is left of them. Then the Rogue Hein government will believe that you three are dead, returning your families to safety. Remember, you will never see your family again for at least a long time. Gale here has the floor. Go ahead, Gale."

Gale introduces herself and then gives the three scientists the breakdown of what they will be going through in the next few days. "It's nice to meet you, three doctors, and as you can see, we're going to be doing a few things in the next few days." Gale points to a robotic arm extracting the blood from the three scientists and another instrument that takes a folic piece of hair from the scientist's body with another computer taking their height and weight. Gale continues, "Another computer here will take your voice recognition to synthesize your voice with the clone's identity. Oh, I almost forgot, this computer here on the right will take the brainwaves of your consciousness and subconsciousness. Additionally, the machine can produce an identical clone in a couple of hours or twenty-four hours. It all depends on how detailed your DNA sequencing is. Do you have any questions for me?"

Merna asks with concern, "Do these keep data forever in the computers to make duplicates later on?"

Gale helps the doctors to understand. "Well, we can keep the information in a database unless the upper government wants us to erase it from the archives. Otherwise, we have to keep it for years to come. Why?"

Merna is just a little skeptical about why the government would want their DNA or even for a long time. "In what capacity would they need it? Longevity of the DNA."

Gale gives Merna a straight answer. "That is confidential."

Jewel regards that idea. "That is crap. Why does the government have so much cover-up anyway? At least they should let us know since we have to work for them."

Gale, who has no say, tries to give Jewel confidence in the government. "Dr. Jewel, right?"

Jewel says, "Yes."

Gale continues, "Look, wouldn't you want to protect your findings to ensure they didn't get in the hands of someone who would use your work to harm people, right?"

Jewel is trying to come to grips. "Okay, yes. Right."

Gale takes the three doctors to their quarters, where they will rest for the night to prepare for the next day's cloning process. The next day the three scientists wake up and are taken by one of Gale's scientist helpers to an area to withdraw the blood for the DNA sequencing to begin. Gale takes Jewel first, injecting a tiny needle that can go through the core of the bone marrow to draw DNA blood.

Jewel chats with Gale. "How come I am unable to feel anything?"

Gale, on the computer sequencing the DNA pattern, responds, "That is because it is not a needle but a solid metallic hair strung that withdraws the blood, and that is not of this world. That is pretty much all I'm saying."

Jewel stares at the needle slowly withdrawing the blood into a chamber. It looks as though the piece of hair is alive and sucking the blood right out of Jewel. It has a fantastic suction coming from a tiny metallic strain of hair. Next, Jewel goes to another machine that plucks a small strand of hair from his head as Gale matches the sequence in the computer. Furthermore, Jewel goes through a device called the bodiratic machine. This machine calculates an individual's weight and height; this takes roughly about thirty minutes. Jewel then is pushed over to the voice synthesizer for voice recognition saved on a spinning miniature disk drive for usage. As it combines with Gale's computer, it also reads the subconsciousness and the consciousness of the brain through a machine called sublime. That takes roughly an hour to go through. When this is all done, Gale fires up the G200 Clone processor machine. This process takes twenty-four hours.

As a result of Jewel's sequencing, it takes roughly twenty-two hours before his clone is processed. The other doctors on several stations begin their cloning transformation several minutes after Jewel starts. Merna's clone takes about eighteen hours, and Lucas's clone takes about twenty-three hours. Four days later, the three original scientists meet their clones in a hallway, and to tell the actual doctors from the clones, they have to wear black scrubs, while the clones wear white ones. Master Chief Yufer and General Boulder meet all the original cloned scientists in the hallway, with Gale introducing the cloned scientists to the actual scientists.

"Dr. Jewel, Dr. Lucas, and Dr. Merna. Doctors, here are your three clones. Please familiarize yourself with the clones."

Clones, staring at the original doctors, start to introduce themselves. Clone Dr. Lucas shakes the doctor's hands. "Hello, I am Dr. Lucas. I am delighted to meet all of you."

Clone Dr. Jewel also shakes the original doctor's hands. "I am Dr. Jewel. Pleasure is mine."

And finally, Clone Merna shakes the doctor's hands as well. "Hello, Doctors. I am Dr. Merna. Nice to meet our makers." Clone Merna notices that she and the original doctors are up to par on their discoveries. "I see that we are up to par on our discoveries, especially dealing with changing weather. Do I have the gist of what is going on?"

Initially, Dr. Lucas's eyes wander as he watches through a unique technology window. "Yes, you have the idea. That is true. We are up to par in everything."

Clone Lucas is fixing the front of his scrub. "When can we get started on this new research, Doctors?"

Initially, Dr. Jewel tries to stay on target. "We will get started when Master Yufer here gets it together for you."

Dr. Lucas explains the research. "We will be discovering how to limit pressures in hurricane wind storms."

Clone Merna, who can't wait to start the study, asks, "When do we start?"

Original Dr. Jewel points to General Boulder. "As soon as General Boulder here gives us the go."

General Boulder tells Master Chief Yufer what the clones' expectations are, whispering into Master Chief Yufer's ears. Master Chief Yufer then states what the expectation of the clones is. "Doctors, the clones will be going out tonight researching their discoveries of hurricane storms throughout the months on the ocean to distinguish their research findings of wind pressure and how to diminish those pressures within the hurricane before it gets to full strength."

"When we receive word that your families have returned to their homes." Master Chief Yufer speaks to the initial doctors. "You three will be relaxing in this facility for the forseeable future. Gale here will plan your task for you."

Dr. Lucas is awaiting his appointed area. "While waiting for the specified regions, what should we do?"

Master Chief Yufer explains their position, "You will stay here and get to know some people on the base. I am sure you would enjoy meeting some scientists you already know and getting some hands-on experience with some of our new technologies, which I am sure you would be of interest to you."

Dr. Jewel can't wait to see other parts of the facility. "Now that sounds interesting to do."

Master Chief Yufer turns to General Boulder. "General Boulder, do you have any words to say?"

General Boulder turns at an angle toward Master Chief Yufer and the original doctors. "Yes, Master Yufer. Your doctors will be working with our present scientists on specific projects. As Master Yufer said, we will give you word when your family has returned to their homes. Gale will accompany you if you have any questions. For now, you will return to your quarters, where we will have service for dinner for the three of you tonight by our caterers down here. We have to get the clones ready to go out with the navy seals, who will put them on a state-of-the-art boat to do their research. Sounds good?"

Gale takes original Lucas and the other doctors to relax in their quarters.

General Boulder calls his chief navy SEAL officers. "Gentlemen!"

The navy SEAL chief, along with the other navy SEAL officer, walks toward General Boulder from a corridor. "Yes, General."

General Boulder hands the two officers assigned paperwork of what is supposed to be done with the clones. "Go ahead and take these clones out into their projected boats, and they will work on weather hurricane research." General Boulder takes one of the officers to the side in secrecy. "After you have set up the task for the explosion of chemicals, I want you to grab the research first."

Navy officer two says, "Not a problem, General."

General Boulder turns to the clones. "Doctors, please, these officers will take you to your new research area."

All clones follow. "Thank you." The navy SEAL take the clones to a black van exiting the hidden facility base. Part of the base location is in between Arizona to California, where the navy SEAL and the clone doctors get out of the van onto a destroyer naval vessel.

Once aboard, the clone doctors meet with Lieutenant Shaffer, who greets the doctors. "Welcome, Doctors, to destroyer *Merlin*. We will be setting out to your prospective area this evening in about twelve hours. We are expecting a hurricane."

Clone Merna, who can't wait to start on the research, states, "That doesn't sound too soon enough."

Shaffer and several navy SEAL walk the doctors to their location on the ship. "We will first settle you in and be on the way in the next hour."

Clone Lucas looks at the vessel's side into the ocean. "Very well then." The destroyer heads out an hour later to a secluded ocean area. It docks where the water depth is about two miles down. Then several navy men and the doctors climb into several navy boats lowered into the ocean. These navy boats close onto a researchable yacht named *Prairie Dog* with a cloned driver and several cloned guards; it houses six double bunk beds. The navy boats come alongside the vessel with a ledge with some steps to climb aboard. This area has guards stationed 24-7. The clone doctors climb aboard the yacht as one of the navy officers shows them around it. A navy officer enters the wooden doors to the front of the boat with the clone doctors.

"Doctors, on this level of the yacht, you have a dining area with several coolers."

Clone Dr. Jewel asks, "If we run out of food, do we have to go fishing?"

A navy officer opens a secret compartment. "In this section, you'll find other meats. We're a call away if you need more food. But if you like fishing, by all means, please go ahead and fish if you want."

Merna, who enjoys that entertainment, says, "Now that is soothing to know."

The navy SEAL officer and the clone doctors head down some stairs to see the research area. This area has a mass of researchable chemicals and advanced technological equipment. A see-through barrel-looking glass case contains all possible chemicals that the navy officer shows the scientists. "Doctors, in these cases are all known chemicals on the periodic charts and chemical finds that aren't on the chart yet."

Dr. Lucas asks a sedimentary question. "Do we have a chemical separator like a centrifuge for ocean sediments of rocks with findings from the waters as well?"

A navy officer grabs several technologic advanced partitions below the center of the research lab. "Here is a centrifuge where you can separate anything you may find in these waters."

Lucas knows he has all the instruments he needs to do his research. "I appreciate that, Officer."

A navy officer takes the doctors to the lowest deck. "Here are your living quarters for the months to come. Do any of you have questions for me? Now is the time. Otherwise, I will leave you, Doctors, to do your bidding."

Merna speaks for all the doctors. "No, that will be all. We will begin our research this week. Thank you, Officer."

The navy officer leaves the boat and heads back to the destroyer *Merlin*. The doctors turn in for the night. A massive hurricane is coming off the coast of Hawaii at the end of the week. The name of this hurricane is Wendy. The doctors have devised with a researchable chemical called krypton phosphate with a chemical number of 24. The doctors figure if they shoot this chemical into the hurricane's eye, it can kill off the wind pressure, taking a storm from a category 5 to merely a thunderstorm. Dr. Lucas takes the ion gun, which looks similar to a flare gun since the boat is in the eye of the hurricane, and shoots it three miles up. With wonder in his eyes, he begins to see the storm die. The other doctors rejoice.

"Holy cow, it worked! It worked!" The three doctors exclaim with joy.

During this time, Lieutenant Shaffer begins to put together an assassin team, but what is in the water the next day is another boat that has been noticing the doctors; in that boat is a Rouge Hein agent who reports to his superior.

The Rogue Hein agent reports, "We have eyes on the doctors. They are in the southwest coordinates of the Pacific Ocean. What would you like me to do, sir?"

A voice on the other end esays, "Do not engage. We want them alive."

Agent continues, "We also have targets on site about six."

Superior replies, "Again, do not engage. Will tell you when to engage."

The agent has no patience. "Got it."

Early morning about 3:00 a.m. Lieutenant Shaffer is getting the assassins together. "You know your targets, gentlemen, and what needs interception? You got it!"

Assassin navy SEAL officer says, "Got it!"

When the crew members are asleep, a navy SEAL assassin climbs aboard the yacht with his men. Upon boarding the ship, the assassins sneak into the research area, intercepting all paperwork and research work and zip-tying it in a sack.

A chemical explosive is set by taking the onboard chemicals and arranging them so that it appears to be an explosive setup with the potential to char and kill all aboard. In order words, the assassin navy SEAL used nitrogen and sulfuric acid with another chemical that would naturally explode when tapped. The assassin navy SEAL grabs other documents from the computer and files, leaving the boat to head back to the navy vessel and wait for the trap. Hours later, clone Merna gets up around 6:00 a.m. She grabs a fishing pole and begins to fish. An hour later, she catches several flounders and some yellowtails. Merna begins to grill them on the stove in the dining area. One of the doctors gets up because he smells something good cooking. Dr. Jewel smells something good and enters the dining area in his robe.

"What is that you're cooking, Dr. Merna?"

Merna is flipping the fish on the stove. "It's flounder and yellowtail fish with some rice. Smells delicious, right?"

Jewel takes a whiff as he fans the smell near his nose by the pot. "Mm, smells delightful, can't wait to eat it."

In the interim, the other doctor is shaving, and he also smells the aroma of something good. Clone Dr. Lucas comes up the stairs, grabs a plate, and starts to dish himself out a container of that delicious food. All three doctors sit at a table and enjoy the food.

After eating, they change into their research clothes and do some research. Jewel is so clumsy that he taps a jar near his elbow, setting up inertia that causes a massive fire to become an explosion. The Rogue Hein agent catches a glimpse of the explosion and reports to his supervisor, "we have a problem."

Supervisor wants to know the problem. "What is the problem, Agent?"

Agent stares in disbelief. "It seems the doctors had a mishap."

Supervisor, thinking it is not that serious, asks, "What kind of mishap? It can't be that serious."

Agent says, "It is dire, sir. The entire boat containing the doctors has exploded and is on fire."

Superior, "What! It can't be."

Agent, "Yes, it is, sir."

Superior is concerned. "Report back to me with pictures, Agent."

The agent takes a picture to prove to his superior, as the blast of smoke hits the atmosphere. The agent speeds back to park his boat and heads back to his headquarters to note that the doctors have died in a watery tragedy. The yacht continues to burn for hours. The next night, the navy vessel intercepts the boat and, with a crane, picks up the burned ship and puts it on the destroyer. Navy officers go through the boat as they take all valuable technologies. The burned-up bodies of the doctors are taken and put into body bags for honorable burial.

General Boulder gets word from the navy SEAL commander. "General, I am sorry to tell you that the doctors, through an explosion, have been killed. It looks like a chemical mishap. What would you like me to do with the bodies?"

With a short interruption, the general on his holographic brief comm says, "Give them the proper burial they deserve. Let the president know, Commander."

The navy commander calls the president of the United States on a secure line. "Mr. President, sorry to bother you, sir, but we have an urgent problem."

The president responds on the yellow-coded holographic brief comm, "What is the problem, Commander?"

Commander, with an incredibly concerned voice, says, "Sir, the three prevalent scientists that did the bulk of all research had a mishap, Mr. President."

President is not too shocked. "What kind of mishap?"

Commander, zipping up the body bags, says, "The type of mishap that kills you, Mr. President."

Now the commander has the president's full attention. "Okay, I am listening, and please explain."

Commander explains to the president, "The three scientists were researching hurricanes last night. Fire exploded within the boat this morning's research, sending the scientists' bodies up into the air, causing sixth-degree burns to their bodies. Sadly, Mr. President, this was a fatal accident."

The president informs the world leaders and will also give a news announcement regarding the deaths. The news announcer is announcing the end of three terrific individuals that solved society's problems.

"Ladies and gentlemen, this a special breaking news. The three savant scientists that were to help humankind are presumed dead. With a short upcoming announcement, the burial site of these three great savant scientists will shortly take place to where the location will be. These tremendous scientific minds were working on research in the middle of the ocean, where a chemical explosion took their precious lives. This mishap was a tragedy. I hope some scientists of the same caliber as these great scientists in the coming years will come to fruition. Ladies and gentlemen, please welcome the president of the United States."

As soon as the announcer has introduced the president, the president starts talking about the disaster. "This day marked the tragedy of three of our century's most remarkable scientists conquering history's greatest mystery. They were the brains of not only our culture but the brains of our universe, making the greatest minds of not only great savants but a calling to cure all humanity's woes. They have helped, for instance, with diseases, hunger, global warming, and the like. Grievously, these three scientists had to suffer freak destruction that happened on an unsafe boat, but for now, we will remember them as always being the ones that help with government issues. Hopefully, one day, this will allow humanity to seek new areas of cures for the vast problems we have today. I give you my heartfelt condolences to the families of these three scientists. May they be remembered in our history forever. God bless you all, and the United States of America."

A couple of days later, the burials of these scientists are at their place of birth. Rogue Hein reports to their leaders that the scientists have died, and they want to ensure that they are the scientists who died. So what the Rogue Hein government does is dig up the dead scientists' burial sites to ensure that it is indeed the three that died and not any other scientists that looked similar to them. The agents dig up Jewel's grave and report to their leaders.

"Could you please let me know what else we should get besides bone and blood samples?"

Superior responds, "Get a piece of hair as well."

The agent takes a sample of hair back to the lab. Another agent at Lucas's burial site does the same thing. Agent gets a selection of the bone from Merna's body and heads back to headquarters. The Rouge Hein has a piece of the doctors' DNA because they have agents infiltrate their compounds earlier. These agents have taken that sample from their dwelling, and the Rogue Hein headquarters has a database of their work and their DNA in a computer.

The Rogue Hein researches to ensure they are the doctors who died, and finally, after several weeks, finds out that it is them. Several days later, Rogue Hein headquarters give all agents holding the doctors' families the go-ahead to release them back to their homes. Rogue Hein headquarters gives the order to all agents on several patched lines.

"Based on the DNA analysis we performed on the dead doctors, we have determined that they are deceased. You have an order from us to release the families back to their dwellings and return to base."

Jewel's family is thrown out of several black vans into the streets with a black cloth over their heads. The family quickly removes the black material covering them as the truck vanishes round the corner. The family, relieved, calls a taxi from a restaurant and waits for the cab to take them home. In the meantime, the men in a dark van throw out Merna's family near a grassy field. Since Lu already has his cell phone hidden in his shirt pocket, Lu and the rest of the family remove the black cloth off their heads. He then calls for a ride from one of his employees.

"Hey, Roger, we are stuck near some cornfields between Laurel and Nardy Street. Can you pick us up? I would appreciate it."

As for Lucas's family, they also are thrown to the side of the road near some farms. Mr. and Mrs. Normalic untie themselves as the vans screech away on the dirt road. Mr. Normalic unties the rest of the family, and they run toward a farmer's home and knock on the door.

"Can we please use your cell phone, ma'am or sir?"

The male farmer goes to the back of the house to grab his cell phone and brings it to Mr. Normalic. "What happened to you folks?"

Mrs. Normalic gives the farmer the lowdown. "Well, what had happened is that my family were being held at ransom so that they can get our son, who was one of the three scientists that died."

The female farmer asks, "Was it one of the scientists that the president was talking about several weeks ago?"

Mrs. Normalic is nodding her head in sadness. "Yes, it was. It was a shame how they left this world so soon at a young age, not given a chance to live an entire life."

The female farmer responds, "I am so sorry."

Mr. Normalic is getting off the phone. "Our limo driver will be here several hours from now."

The male farmer makes them feel at home. "While you wait, would you lovely folks love to have dinner with us?"

The family agrees.

CHAPTER 14

THE BEGINNING OF THE END?

Back at the hidden base, the three scientists introduce themselves to fellow scientists within the facility who will be working with them, and they discover that a few of the scientists are those they already know. During Jewel's introduction, a scientist introduces himself.

"Wait a minute, I know you. You're John, right?"

John grabs and hugs Jewel as though he hasn't seen him for years. "Hey, how are you doing, Dr. Jewel?"

Jewel asks about John's profession. "So what do you do here, my friend?"

John shows Jewel his work area. "Here,s I work basically on gravity."

Jewel looks at the screen. "It is similar to the type of work I do, physics."

John responds, "Oh, yes, it is."

Jewel, with a jolt, sees someone he hasn't seen since college. "Oh my gosh, can it be?"

Gale introduces Jewel to Dr. Laura, researching the black matter in the universe. "Hey, I know you." Jewel also hugs Laura.

"Laura, wow. I am amazed at you. You made it by working for the government, confidentially this time."

Laura feels good about herself. "Yes, I have made it."

Jewel has a question for Laura. "So what are you doing for the government?"

Laura is showing Jewel on her computer system that tracks a moving satellite moving at the speed of light through the Milky Way galaxy. "Well, I am studying the black matter in our universe."

Jewel, who loves physics, asks, "Anything interesting?"

Laura shows him one attraction. "Well, we have a black matter that bends light, very similar to black holes, except we have noticed meteor rocks enter and come out broken up after months of being in this black matter. It reminds me of a cluster of nebulas being reborn and then destroyed. So the blackness is chaotic to see on the screen."

Jewel chats with Laura and John, while the other doctors introduce themselves to seven other scientists in other facility areas with teams working for them. Merna bumps into someone from her college days named Penny, her roommate. "Wow, can it be? No way, it can't, can it?"

Penny acts like she misses Merna. "Hey, Merna, long time no see. I hear you're doing great things."

With a high-pitched tone, Merna says, "So what's up, girl? What specialty are you doing for the government?"

Penny, with a smile, giggles a bit and takes Merna to her workstation. "What else would I be doing but the science on alien DNA? It is a secret, don't tell anyone."

Merna knows she is sworn to secrecy because she works for the government. "Secrecy, we both know are not going anywhere anytime soon. Wow! Alien DNA. You have to give me the lowdown someday."

Penny, hugging Merna, whispers, "Wait until you see these species called Legendaries. In addition to looking weird and awesome, they also appear to be extemely intelligent beyond our comprehension."

Merna talks in a low tone. "Please tell me more about it."

Gale finally introduces Lucas to a scientist named Beth. Lucas jumps out of his skin, shocked. "No! No! What! Beth, how the hell are you?"

Beth is focused on her work and looks up at Lucas, taking off her goggles as she torches some robotic parts. "Oh my! Dr. Lucas, how are you?"

Lucas shakes Beth's hand gracefully. "You were so amazing on my college team. I figured you would be working on robotics. What type of robotic contraption are you working on now for the government?"

Beth explains what she is working on in a roundabout way. "What I am working on is some robotic dematerialized portal. Don't know what it does yet, but I have some great teachers."

With a confused face, Lucas asks, "Teachers, what are you talking about?"

Beth does not want to give away what is to come, where Lucas will discover who the Legendaries are. "Let's say these teachers are beyond our galaxy."

Lucas muses to himself, *Hmm, can it be a government conspiracy? Have to find out soon, I guess.* The three doctors walk around the facility as Gale introduces them to other scientists throughout the floor. These other scientists deal with astrophysics, alien genetics, warp speeds at the speed of light, and splicing and growing crossed food plant lives and species.

The three scientists, fascinated with all the different technologies at the facility, finally come across the scientist who deals with astrophysics, whose name happens to be George, who looks at various stars in our solar system. Lucas asks him, "What do we have here?"

George is very polite as he gathers information and puts it into another computer for calculation on his right side of the table. "As we travel through our solar system, we find astrophysics anomalies. In the future, I believe that this computer, to my right, will find similar planets where humans may be able to survive. As a result, it calculates atmospheric pressures and elements that do not exist on Earth. On this computer, to my left, you can see that a NASA rover has collected data and released it back to me.

"In contrast, I analyze the probable causes that contribute to growing plants and producing drinking water on the planet."

Jewel, who is interested in George's work, turns to George. "These planets are in our Milky Way galaxy, George. How so?"

George, who happens to be drawn by Jewel, responds, "Three satellites circulate the planet collecting data through a massive telescope. It sends back images to my computer to simulate animal life on Earth but may look different in color, shape, and size. These various planets are what we call Project Nowhere.

"The reason is that the human race has not been there yet. We are just scoping the area for possible worlds to live on if our planet was to be destroyed or suffer extinction sometime in the future. So we have somewhere to go and survive."

Merna looks at the computer screen and sees a very reddish-green and blue planet the size of Earth. She points to it, asking George, "What do you call this one, and why is it red? Can it hold or sustain life?" Merna receives a breakdown of the planet from George.

"There is a reason why I gave it a specific name." He points to a plotted graph on his computer. "Dr. Merna, right?"

Merna sees the plotted graph. "Yes, that is right."

George continues to explain the planet. "You see here, Dr. Merna, it has a reddish hue is because it rains down water and reddish iron dust called femine, which is similar to our compound iron and iodine mix. Our solar system is the ninth planet discovered, but the seventh solar system is where this ninth planet exists within our Milky Way galaxy that provides life with enough conditions. We gave it the name XT-109 because it extends our galaxy."

Merna sees a few more comparable worlds and asks, "What are the names of these other ones that seem plausible for humans to live on?"

George gives Merna the breakdown of the other planets that Merna is pointing to on the plotted graph with their pictures. "This one is three times the size of Earth. It has a bluish-gray atmosphere, and we call it T141 with black mist for clouds. It rains hydrogen argon, and the waters have an extra oxygen molecule. The waters probably taste better than our Earth's water by far, especially for its purity."

Merna's and Jewel's jaws drop as they stare at the picture that can sustain life. This planet is ten times the size of Earth, very similar to Earth, except there seems to be more land mass than water. It has some gray waters that are very similar to liquid cement. George gives Merna and Jewel the secret of this planet.

"Now I know you doctors are excited about this one here. It is ten times the size of Earth with a lot more landmass and half the waters as our Earth. It also has a black hue with more hydrogen molecules but seems breathable to our lungs. I can show you. For now, the other planets seem to be similar to Earth, except those planets are different coloration on the planet's surfaces. Any questions, Doctors?"

All three doctors look at each other in awe and figure out that since the government has been looking at these planets, they have more significant ideas to get the human race to either expand or escape our world because they know that we are doomed sometime in the future. Lucas takes the other two doctors to the side and speaks silently as Gale and the other scientists in the facility talk. Lucas is talking to the other two scientists.

"Boy! Wow! What are they thinking? They must know something we don't. That is why they are doing these experiments on other planets. What do you think, Jewel?"

In a low tone, Jewel says, "I think they are probably going to use clones to colonize these planets with the most intelligent people they have on Earth. That is what I believe. What is your input on this matter, Merna?"

Merna looks around to ensure no one is staring in their direction and comes up with an exquisite solution to the issue. "From what I understand so far, the government is experimenting with different alien DNA. They want to make sure that we can sustain life on these planets. That is what I think is going on here."

Lucas gazes at Merna for a moment, and he finally gets it. "Sounds promising, Merna. For me, that is reason enough to experiment with clones to ensure that we as humans can sustain life on these vast worlds that are similar to ours. I couldn't come up with a better analogy."

The three scientists return to where George and Gale are chatting and interrupt them to diagnose the star system. Gale starts to get the doctors ready for their station area. Jewel interrupts George and Gale. "Excuse, George, how long have you been doing Project Nowhere?"

Gale looks at George as though he wasn't supposed to let that information out. "George, did you let it slip again?"

George is embarrassed. "Yes, Gale."

Gale then covers for George. "George here has been doing this for two years now. Why?"

Jewel is intrigued. "Oh, since I deal with physics, George has helped me realize that life's existence is not only actual, but living among other species is magnificent to me. Several theories from my college professors genuinely proposed to me on other similar planets that may differ from ours in terms of physics."

With laughter in her heart, Gale tells Jewel where his station will be. "Haha! You're just what we are looking for, Dr. Jewel. It takes a physicist to prove these theories for them to become real. We hope to do it sometime shortly. What do you think of that, Dr. Jewel?"

Jewel, beyond his imagination, believes. "Well, given the Earth's names that George has given us, I can bring back that information for us to learn if offered the right to go and research on these similar planets."

With a smirk, Gale raises her eyebrows and says, "Let me tell you, Dr. Jewel, only the government will know about this. Besides, you will work with George and his team to give them more insight into your brilliant mind, Dr. Jewel."

Dr. Jewel accepts it with a slight bow. "Why, I appreciate it, Dr. Gale. I won't let down my superiors."

As George updates Jewel on his research. Gale looks at the two other scientists. Gale reintroduces Penny to Lucas and Merna.

"I know the both of you already met Penny earlier, and she will be the one you two will be working with as a team." Gale proceeds further. "We need insight from both of you since you, Dr. Lucas, deal with chemical engineering, and Merna deals with biology to help our military personnel. With a team of people, I figured you three could help us find a solution toward improving our military and making them impenetrable. Both against enemies domestic and foreign."

Lucas scratches his head with confusion on his face. "Exactly, Dr. Gale, what do you mean?"

Not trying to give away the farm or idea, Gale responds, "I believe Penny here will get you two up to speed. I have to get back to my team, which we have a time crunch to report back to my superiors. Have fun, you three."

Merna, about to talk to Penny, slowly says her goodbyes to Dr. Gale, "Ah, bye-bye. Anyway, Penny, what exactly do we need to catch up on?"

Penny, who from earlier was supposed to give Merna the lowdown, actually gives away the secret of the alien DNA. Penny tells both Merna and Lucas about the aliens called Legendaries. "Okay, you two, let me give you the lowdown, which I was supposed to tell you earlier or wanted to say. First of all, Dr. Lucas, these species called the Legendaries are a race of intelligent beings who have been here since the creation of time. They have slowly taught us about technology and the pros and cons of technology. They have also taught us different scientific compounds and other compounds that aren't known to humanity."

Lucas is very interested. "So what kind of compounds have these alien species discovered?"

Penny shows Lucas the compound structure on a computer screen. "You see, you found the zeonic chemical. Still, instead, we have what is known as zetafrillic."

Lucas tries to wrap his mind around such a weird compound. "Never heard of this compound. What is composed of such a chemical?"

Penny shows him on the computer. "You see here, zetafrillic is a composition of a mixture that is not of our Earth." Penny shortens what the compound is used for, which it uses healing properties. Penny proceeds further. "It can heal wounds in a matter of seconds, and it also cures various diseases and eats up the cells that cause illness."

Merna, along with Penny, grins a bit. "Wow! It seems very interesting to me. It can help me with my find on how to slow aging as well, huh."

Penny concurs with Merna. "That is exactly right. The Legendaries live for thousands of years."

Merna wants a sample of these Legendaries' blood. "How can I get a little bit of their blood? I want to perform an analysis of what I had discovered before the Rogue Hein kidnapped my family."

Lucas interrupts, "Merna, we understand you want to take it to the next level, but shouldn't you find out if it will reverse in our species first? What happens if it speeds up our age?"

Merna keeps calm. "Lucas, we have clones for this purpose, so we can analyze them first and then provide them to our species. I am not sure if the government will allow us to offer it to humanity in the future."

Lucas and Penny approve of Merna's thinking. "Right!"

All of a sudden, General Boulder, comes into the area where the doctors are all located, to give them information regarding what the International Government wants from them. "Pardon me, Doctors. May I have your attention, please." All the doctors in that facility area turn around, including Jewel, Lucas, and Merna, as their attention is on General Boulder. Jewel wants to know what the General wants.

"General Boulder, the look on your face looks like you have a lot of information for us. What can it be, General?"

General Boulder says with anxiety, "For one, I have good news for you all. The good news is that you all will soon get a greeting from the *ones* who are legends in our time. Soon, you will gain insight into the technology you have in front of you and intelligence through these beings. What the International Government wants from you doctors is what your brains can bring to the table regarding your intelligence."

Lucas wants to know more about the mystery beings' intelligence. "Exactly how much intelligence do those beings possess?"

"Well, let me just say their intelligence level is far beyond ours. I also want to express their way of calculation is in another language altogether. Their rate of technology is thousands of years ahead of us right now." General Boulder laughs and chuckles.

Merna and Jewel sigh in unbelief. They are about to meet the mystery beings, the aliens who have fascinated humans for centuries, now face-to-face. Despite the twinkle in Lucas's eyes, this is by far the most mesmerizing discovery in the history of science.

Currently, somewhere deep in space, the evil aliens, the Inquestorians overlord, are looking at his holographic map, identifying a planet to conquer for its resources, unknown to these people lost in their research. In hyperspace, however, a planet-sized asteroid appears, knocking the vast ship out of control. The ship commander says, "Overlord, we have a problem. Our map now points us to another solar system that appears to be similar to the one we were going to."

Not knowing that they had come to the Milky Way galaxy by chance, but now the map points them to a distant planet that has been the ancestors of the aliens—this information stops them in their tracks. Even as they get curious about this planet called Earth, all the smaller ships come out of hyperspace as the sizeable main mother vessel seems lost in the Milky Way galaxy.

CHAPTER 15

INVISIBLE LAYERS DISCOVERED

A couple of years have passed, and the doctors have acclimated to the facility. The doctors have not seen these new beings called the Legendaries yet; all they ever know is that they heard of them and followed what the International Union wanted from the doctors so far. As the year is 2154 approaches, Dr. Jewel and George are working on a physics formula regarding the speed of light. George's team calculates Jewel's theory using an unusual instrument called a celertrino regarding the speed of light. Tiny metallic objects use the speediness of light calculation in the device as its measuring targets. The celertrino shows how fast light increases or decreases when a Jules retention formula is input. So when a positive input pops out mathematically from the procedure compared to a negative, it turns an electron counterclockwise, increasing the light's velocity by one hundred times. Therefore, Jewel's theory proves that the speed of light can travel a hundred times faster within its acceleration.

George is looking at the computer of the celertrino chambers, as Jewel is charting it on his laptop regarding the results. George gives Jewel some calculations. "It looks like we have a burst of electrons and protons moving extremely fast as the light passes through at a hundred times its speed. This calculation gives us a Jule retention minus electron pulse times the rate. We have proved your theory, and now we are ready to report back to our superiors at the International Union. What do you think, Dr. Jewel?"

Jewel is paying attention to the rate on his charts as they come in. "Yes, the Jules times to the hundred is merely the beginning, Dr. George. We have to hit a thousand times, which could be any day now. What do you think of that result?"

George believes in the scarcity of results. "It looks like we have found tiny spectacles of lights. Any tinier, we can hit the tiniest molecule of photon called ferros. These sharpened molecules bring another formula you came up with, Dr. Jewel. It might hit a thousand times the speed of light. Do you know what that means, Dr. Jewel?"

Jewel high-fives George. "I know what this means. We can travel with a spacecraft to another universe in less than a year. For example, we can hop over to the galaxy Andromeda in no time."

George, shaking his hand, high-fives Jewel back. "You got it, man." George calls General Boulder on the holographic brief comm. "General Boulder, we have the results of the Jule Retention formula that the International Union may want."

A brief holographic communication from General Boulder says, "I will be at the location in a few hours to grab charts and formulations. The International Union will also be there. They want to see how the Celertrino machine works."

George is about to turn off the holographic brief comm. "We're waiting patiently for all of you. We will keep it running meanwhile."

General Boulder will click off the brief comm. "Thank you, Dr. George." Right after Dr. George gets off the brief comm, one of his other computers that monitor our galaxy has an alarm that signals any strange anomaly. One computer linked to several other mainframe computers emits an alarming signal so loud that a person's ears can receive a full range of sounds, almost hurting their ears. George sees all the scientists crouch down, holding their ears, trying to get away from the sound, as George runs over to the computer and punches in some numbers fast. With a baffled look on his face as though confused, he sees an out-of-the-ordinary reading coming off the charts on the computer. He pushes Jewel aside as he goes to another computer to contact a five-star general named Snuff. This five-star general is over General Boulder and reports to the dignitaries and diplomats of the International Union.

General Snuff, on the private link, says, "What is the big problem, Dr. George?"

George, on the secret line, replies, "General Snuff, we have a problem. The problem is significant." George gazes at his computer screen. "It's a reading that mystifies my intelligence, General Snuff."

General Snuff thinks George has a sense of humor. "Don't make me laugh, George."

"There is no laughing matter here; this is a serious matter." George urges the general to be serious. "It seems like I am getting some weird reading from my computer that resembles a figment of my imagination, like there are some invisible layers out there, almost like a cluster of nebula stars. I can't tell what they are, but we have come across some universal layer of our Milky Way galaxy. I can't explain it. You would have to see it. It alarmed the heirloom computer, General."

"Is that the heirloom computer you're talking about?" General Snuff asks.

"Did you hear me?" George asks, hoping Snuff heard correctly.

"Sorry, but we'll be there shortly." General Snuff shakes his head.

George hangs up the emergency line as Jewel approaches a table, limping. "What's going on?"

George tells Jewel, "When we get a reading off the heirloom computer, it means either there is an abnormality in our galaxy or something extraordinary is heading our way. Whether a meteor shower, a shooting star, or just weird changes in our universe, it shows us what is going on. Nonetheless, with certainty. This one reading, I can't tell what it is. It was something I had never seen before. That is why I had to call the International Union directly to come to see what was going on."

Jewel wants to see what is on the monitor of the computer. "Oh my, what in God's creation is that?"

George's eyes are wide open. "I have no idea. It is invisible, but you can see the lining of the hidden layer."

"Where in God's green creation is that?" According to his appearance, Jewel is an expatriate. "It seems to show many linings of our Milky Way galaxy in a curvature wavelength."

George knows he will have to sit down with other scientists soon. "It looks like we all need to put our heads together and figure this out, huh." All scientists within the facility are now around where George and Jewel are performing some calculations. Lucas and Penny seem to have developed a solution to the issue.

Lucas scratches his head after talking with Penny. "You know what, Dr. George, it seems this can be a discovery of a new system within our Milky Way galaxy. What do you people think of that?"

Dr. John has another impressionable idea of what it can be. "Maybe it is a way to see into our futures. Hey, you never know. I suggest that what Merna is viewing on the hologram monitors may be a window into something about to happen, but it could also be a portal into another dimension. Is that even possible?"

Dr. Gale tries to get everyone's attention by screaming, "Wait!" Wait! Did you look at this horizon area here, Dr. George?"

The topic Gale is discussing is not precisely clear to George. "What horizon are you talking about, Dr. Gale?"

Upon pointing to the position on the computer, Gale says, "Look here. As it turns out, there is not only a new system but a system outlining our very own galaxy. Merna may have viewed this as the portal to parallel universes or dimensions. I have developed this theory after experiencing parallel universes for several years."

Jewel does not dismiss the analogy as he also looks upon the screen. "If that is so, do you know what this means, Dr. Gale? It means it can either be a passageway to other galaxies within our system or an invisible system beyond what we can comprehend. We can probably visit these universes if it is possible to gain insight into their marvelous treasures of life. I wonder what the International Union would do with this type of data if possible."

Gale looks inside the computer hologram again, but this time, the outlining of the invisible linings turns to different colors of the rainbow and out of the ordinary colors. They turn blue-green with a tint of purple and so forth. She tries to theorize the idea of dimensions and many possibilities with the changing colors on the monitor. Gale is currently formulating her theory.

"Hmm, Doctors, I have concluded that there are hundreds and thousands upon thousands of possible dimensions at hand here. The colors are endless here, and mixing the various colors gives me the idea that there may be millions of dimensions. Does anyone else have any ideas?"

After looking at the computer screen, Penny looks up. "I think it can be a doorway to alien species that harness technology beyond what we can comprehend. What do you think, Dr. Lucas?"

Dr. Lucas plays the devil's advocate. "Wow! Can be possible for different home worlds within our universe to guide us to other Earths within our universe. Now that can be a presumable idea if you ask me."

Gale's computer receives an intermittent comm call near her desk, notifying her through a specific sound the computer makes. Gale walks to her computer and answers the brief comm in a low tone. "How can I help you, General Boulder?"

On the brief comm in a low voice, General Boulder says, "Looks like we have an issue at the facility. According to Dr. George, we have a weird reading coming off our Milky Way galaxy. What's your analysis, Dr. Gale?"

Gale quickly interrupts, "Not sure what the interpretation is trying to achieve here or where it is coming from." Boulder listens quite intently as she tells him her philosophy. "It looks from my approach, General Boulder, that it can be readings sending off either to dimensional worlds or it can lead us to believe that it can be teleportation to different galaxies within our universe through some invisible linings."

"Dr. Gale, according to what I understand, General Snuff and a few International Union agents will be coming to look at that weird reading," General Boulder tells Gale. "Also, looking upon the Celertrino, they hope to discover space travel from this achievement. Hopefully, through traveling at the speed of light, we can take some clones along with actual people through these assumptive possibilities that you have come up with, Dr. Gale."

Gale assumes, "Yes, of course, General Boulder, but they would have to find out once they are here to believe this to happen, I guess."

General Boulder tells Gale, "Dr. Gale, you will expect General Snuff and International Union people there in about 0200 by the next day." Gale dismisses the IC brief comm with General Boulder as she prepares the scientists for what is expected from the new scientists when General Snuff appears.

Gale returns to the scientists and explains to Jewel, Lucas, and Merna what is expected of them when General Snuff arrives. Merna and Lucas simultaneously respond, "Not a problem." Jewel nods his head in a yes motion, giving Gale his understanding of what is needed. Several hours later, General Snuff arrives with five dignitaries and two diplomats at the facility. While he dicusses the facility's technological advancements with the dignitaries and diplomats, General Snuff leads them throughout the facility.

"Right here, ladies and gentlemen, we have our most advanced area where we work on formulas faster than the speed of light. Astronomy, where we monitor the Milky Way galaxy. Clones to use as test subjects in various technologies."

One of the dignitaries has a question for General Snuff. "Which one of the scientists here discovered the hundred times the speed of light as I had read in a report?"

Jewel humbly says with due respect, "That would be me! How can I be of assistance to you, ma'am?"

With a graceful, polite voice, the female dignitary says, "My dear doctor, how have you come up with such great calculation, and how near are you to further accomplishing other tasks?"

Jewel is talking scientifically. "I would say, ma'am, the analysis was the Jules retention formula, which you have read, I am sure, in a report. My team's other accomplishments are gaining closer to one thousand times the speed of light. I believe that to be the hop from one galaxy to another within a year."

The lady dignitary likes those odds. "Now, that is an accomplishment, and I would say it would be a travesty if we don't get to that number fast. Right, ah, Doctor?"

Jewel takes a drink from his computer. "Yes, it would be, ma'am."

Now a diplomat has a question regarding that specific reading earlier that morning. "Which one of you doctors has conviction regarding this weird signal we had received yesterday on the heirloom computer?"

Without a breath, Merna and Gale take action to support that evidence further. "We imagined probable galaxies." Then Gale looks at Merna stealthily and continues the conversation from there. "Dr. Merna and I came up with a theory that these right here"—Gale points to a graph area and a photo shoot of yesterday's image on the hologram computer—"might be what we suspect as possible dimensions or a wormhole that leads to some other galaxies in our universe. We are not too sure yet, but time will only tell if we should ever do space exploration and figure out what these linings are."

A diplomat with dominion over the International Union, Yarmin, wants to take the top scientists on each team into a closed room area to discuss such an anomaly. Yarmin points to Gale to get her attention. "Dr. Gale, can we please meet at our usual closed-door location to discuss this anomaly? Please tell the other new scientists who have been here for years and have never been in our closed discussion to advise them that they need to be there.

"The diplomats, dignitaries, General Snuff, and General Boulder will meet you in the room in fifteen minutes. Got it, Doctor!" Gale feels the pressure like she usually does at these meetings. In preparation for the meeting, she brings together the top scientists from each team and Drs. Jewel, Merna, and Lucas. Gale advises Dr. Jewel, Merna, and Lucas. "Excuse me, Dr. Jewel, Merna, and Lucas, please let me tell you what we will go over at the meeting."

Lucas talks to the other two doctors. "What can be so terrible at this meeting, Dr. Gale, that we must be informed about?"

Gale further explains. "You see, Doctors, they not only want the readout of the anomaly but also how we're going to solve this solution that may cringe on our galaxy. What I mean is it could be a threat or a way out for humanity. We must see what they want us to do to resolve this issue."

Merna sighs a bit. "Well, let us know what they want us to do, Dr. Gale, and proceed with their plan of what they might need."

Gale rallies all the top scientists in each facility section and brings them into the meeting room with the diplomats, dignitaries, and generals. The scientists all sit down facing the front, where the seating is like a small auditorium with a microchip speaker at the forward-facing to accept any questions the scientists may have. Diplomat Yarmin faces the opposite as he goes over the paperwork the scientists gave him earlier regarding the readings to discuss what actions to take to solve the problem in our galaxy. Yarmin is going over the tasks.

"Okay, ladies and gentlemen, we have an issue that we want to resolve quickly so the world does not get wind of what is to come. I want you scientists to come up with a solution to determine if those anomalous readings are actually what Gale and Merna see as dimensions once you find out that report. But suppose it is a way to gain control traveling to other dimensions, by all means. If that was the case, then there is a solution for humanity if we need to relocate our species to other areas of unknown universes that can be helpful or dangerous to our well-being. I'll get back to my people here."

Merna has a question for Yarmin. "Excuse me, sir, but how are we going to do that without sending a clone to find out?"

Yarmin raises his head toward Merna. "That is precisely right. Dr. Merna, right?"

Merna is feeling special. "Yes, that is right."

Continuing, Yarmin says, "We will send a few cloned soldiers to report back to us via a small spaceship aircraft we have developed. The ship's computer system will deliver the information to you. Once they realize it's just a weird lining to nowhere or a possible portal for humankind, they'll give you the information. Then, you will report back to me. It will allow us to further our speculation of those glowing linings. I am leaving General Boulder in command, and he will report all information back to me when we know for sure of this reading of what they are. Does anyone have any other questions for me?"

Lucas talks for the entire scientists' section. "We have no further questions. We will proceed as planned."

Yarmin and the dignitaries leave the room, as General Snuff escorts them back to the vehicles, leaving General Boulder in command. Gale and Lucas rally all the scientists together and somehow resolve the problem at hand. Gale yells to Lucas, "Hey, Dr. Lucas! You got a minute?"

Dr. Lucas heads over to Gale's science area. "What is it, Dr. Gale?"

Gale makes plans with Lucas. "Why don't you go along with Dr. Merna and Dr. Penny and create something that is a chemical compound that would read these linings so that the clones can put it into the colorful lining atmosphere once they are out in space to give a reading that may seem to distinguish it to be a portal to other universes or not."

Lucas, pretty sure of himself and what he can come up with, says, "It looks like I can come up with a chemical compound that might do the trick."

Gale is trying to rush Lucas to get it done. "All right! Let's get it done because we want to get the information back to Yarmin as soon as possible."

While they are busy with their discussions, the hologram computers with the live satellite images of the anomalies, namely the linings in the galaxy, start to flicker erratically, changing color to a dark reddish hue.

CHAPTER 16

THE CLONING JOYRIDE

The following day soldiers come into the scientists' area to conduct a cloning procedure. Penny starts to fuel up the spacecraft with her team to get the clones ready for the mission into the Milky Way galaxy to expose those anomalous readings. Lucas conducts experiments with his squad on a compound that can analyze those weird glowing linings in the Milky Way galaxy, reporting to Jewel's computer to reassure them that they are dimensions. Gale, porting several soldiers to the cloning station, reads their DNA.

"We need to get these soldiers done no later than tomorrow afternoon, people."

Lucas, with his team, conferences on the matter of a specific chemical that can stand the velocity of the cold universe atmosphere. "We have silicone astatine that will give off the reading, people." Lucas's team gets those compounds together to access the reading thoroughly. "Let's get it done, folks."

While Beth and Penny work on building the robotic arm, Penny constructs an instrument that reads anything out of the ordinary in space with a tiny two-mile long component. Penny makes sure by asking, "Are you sure, Dr. Beth, that we have the right length to get the readings? Because it could give us no reading if we don't."

Beth reassures Penny, "It's the correct measurement as long as the spacecraft doesn't get too close to those colorful linings because I don't know if they are dangerous, but it will be all right." Beth then adjusts the arm length to ensure it can go beyond what is needed.

Gale has her clone soldiers the following day, and the spacecraft called Union I is ready for lift-off. The soldiers get on board, while Penny and Beth make sure that the robotic arms are intact, as well as Dr. Lucas and his team put the measuring chemical in the parts of the ship to analyze the colorful lining. The clones take the initiative to start the ship up as the countdown to the bay doors opens. On the speaker, you can hear the countdown initiation beginning.

"Ten, nine, eight, seven, six, five, four, three, two, one, bay doors are open."

The ship takes off as the engines are in silent mode. The ship hits the atmosphere in thirty seconds as it ascends toward space. After reaching the cosmos, the ship goes into hyperdrive for two minutes; several soldiers put on space suits to leave the spaceship reach their destination at an estimated time. These space suits can fly around with inertia gases that slow and speed the person up.

"Setting up tasks now. Go ahead and release it into the aura of colors." Two soldiers on the ship give the go-ahead. These soldiers get out into space and hit a few buttons on the ship's outer exterior; then floating in space is the silicone astatine that seems to grasp the molecules of the colorful linings in outer space that surround the Milky Way galaxy with leaps and bounds. One of the soldiers relays a message back to the ship through his suit communication device.

"We have delivered the element. It is grasping and holding itself to the colorful linings. Commencing our robotic arm for readings now."

One soldier that floats outside the ship with one other soldier hits the button to the door of the robotic arm and, with levers, sends the arm about two and a half miles into the aura of colors. The soldier on the ship starts to get readings as he reports back to the doctors and sends the analysis to his command center at the secret facility where the doctors appear. Soldier relays a message to the scientists, "We have confirmation of the readings, doctors, initiating phase two."

Jewel notices the interpretation on his computer as Gale overlooks it with General Boulder. "It seems from the readings here that it is a projectile alignment. It appears here, Dr. Gale, that your dimension theory appears to be confirmed."

General Boulder wants to be sure. "How do you know that for sure, Dr. Jewel?"

Jewel reaffirms it. "Well, General Boulder, you see right here on this computer screen. You can see a variation of a copy of our Milky Way galaxy. There may be living worlds in these green and blue hue balls that resemble our Milky Way galaxy, although they differ in shape and color, thus giving me the notion that there are patterns of worlds in these shadow copies. I know for sure by dimensions with the color codes of green hue showing us it can be worlds where humanity can live, and the blue hue shades are the suns."

General Boulder looks at it in awe. "Get me a report right away, Dr. Jewel, so I can report back to my superiors and Yarmin."

Jewel says without a beat, "Already on it."

While in space, the soldiers with the robotic arm get a sample of rocks from the colorful hues to take back to the facility on Earth. After the mission has been accomplished and the clone soldiers return to base, one of the soldiers gives the sample to Merna, who then inspects the rock to find tiny life-forms on the colorful stone.

Merna encounters these little creatures under a microscope, naming them crondites. They are tiny critters that look like a firefly with many legs in fluorescent colors that change when they move. Merna concludes that these small specimens seem to live through galaxy mist, whether a universe is born or dies. Then, Merna shouts out in a tone that gets everyone's attention, "Wow! Another life-form different from ours in space. Amazing!"

General Boulder and all the leading scientists go to Merna's station as General Boulder looks at the tiny specimen in the microscope. "What is this thing, Dr. Merna?"

Merna tells General Boulder, "Well, General, I have come up with the name crondites because these tiny little fellas, I assume, were pivotal somewhere in the history of the creation of our universes. So what do you think, Doctors?"

General Boulder needs a report on these tiny critters as well. "Dr. Merna, please give me an account of those small specimens. I appreciate the input on finding a name for these little soldiers. Please report as soon as possible."

Merna, mesmerized by these little beings, gets her information ready to give to General Boulder. Several hours later, Dr. Jewel and Merna give their reports to General Boulder. Then General Boulder takes off to his private jet with some soldiers to the International Union government to provide them with reports as soon as possible.

Several days later, Yarmin returns with some diplomats and a few dignitaries interested in the report. Behind them are a few tall creatures distinct from one another that stands eight and nine feet tall. One of the creatures is a Praetorian, a nine-foot creature that looks like a cat, and has a human resemblance with feet similar to a lion's claw. The eight-foot-tall creature looks like a cat and bat with several small tusks as whiskers, a very furry creature with sharp claws and an intense sound for a voice. The living being is white with black stripes throughout its body. Eye colors are bright, almost glowing, unlike humans. There is a smooth, practically humanlike face, but its skin is identical to a bat.

The enemy can't seem to get a hold of these Praetorians because they instantly go invisible and communicate with a sonic sound that is ear-piercing to any human ear, almost putting a human to the ground. This Praetorian group lived in the tenth century during the time of humanity on Earth as a small window in time allows them to see. However, they have existed since the time began, which is why they speak a million languages. Back then, they had come on ships that could fly at light speed, and they were sent from above to help society advance, sending lightning to start fires, developing gun power, and eventually learning about nuclear bombs.

We can see the Praetorians helping humankind understand technology slowly since humanity was an infant race to learn these technologies. Then, President Kennedy was in power, the Praetorians gave the human race militia technology to their hidden bases, advancing technology to communicate through satellites that can voice over billions of miles to nearby galaxies to see if humanity could sustain life somewhere else. Since then, the government has known about a few stars that humanity can survive. We have found hundreds in the Milky Way galaxy right now.

General Snuff, Yarmin, and the aliens head over to Jewel's area and a few diplomats and dignitaries. Yarmin, delighted with Jewel's report, gives him an appreciation for his hard work and walks up behind Jewel as he is working on some theories from the finds.

"Ah, um, Dr. Jewel."

Startled a bit, Dr. Jewel smiles, not noticing the aliens yet. "Oh, hello, Mr. Yarmin. What can I do for you?"

Yarmin shows appreciation. "First of all, I want to give you this plaque as an appreciation for your hard work and dedication to your team. I have an alien species with me that can help you understand these readings you have found in space."

Jewel looks down at some weird alien feet and furry catlike feet, then slowly, with utter disbelief and awe, he manages to ask shakily, "How can I help you?"

In a heavy tone, the Praetorian creature gives Jewel the breakdown of those readings. "*What we have here, Dr. Jewel, is a reading of a portal to not only other galaxies but endless universes. The only way to get through to them is through a doorway, which Yarmin has told us is almost ready for action.*"

Jewel wants to know why this is happening. "What would we need this for?"

The Praetorian gives the floor to his more knowledgeable colleague. The Legendary creature with a catlike voice then gives Jewel a deeper understanding. "*The reason for this anomaly is because the human race is at risk for extinction in the coming future.*"

Merna overhears the conversation with a look of fear as she approaches the aliens. "I couldn't stop helping what I am hearing, but why would the human race need to escape?"

The Legendary gives more detail. "*You see, Doctor, these things have been happening for centuries through universes. Who knows where it will go next, as it just reached the Milky Way galaxy this time, and who knows where it will go next. It indicates if an impending doom is upon a certain race, in this case, the human race. By taking this path, we can save the race.*"

Merna grasps the concept. "Well, I haven't been around for centuries like you guys, but to think the human race could meet doom. Honestly, I am beside myself in shock. What are the steps we need to take to prepare?"

Yarmin interjects in the conversation, "we're ready. That is why we have advanced technology. These big guys developed most of this technology to help humanity if something happened. So we need to get prepared if it comes."

With a worried look, Jewel says, "Should we be worried right now?"

The uneasy fear Jewel is experiencing is easing, thanks to Yarmin. "No! We must continue our research and prepare to bring our technology up to par. These two big guys will engage all the scientists on what to do."

Jewel converses with the Praetorian for a minute. "Excuse me, giant creature, where do you come from exactly?"

In a strange smile, the Praetorian tells Jewel where it is from as it looks down as Jewel. "*You see, Dr. Jewel, where I come from is a universe so distant it is almost in a system unknown to anything, a system of invisibility.*"

Jewel ponders what the creature means by invisibility and wants to know more. "Does that mean no one can locate it, or is it not there anymore? What do you mean? Please explain?"

The Praetorian creature explains it to Jewel in its own words. "*Well, Doctor, what I mean by invisibility is we are the only creatures that can see it. We have acute sight and hearing none of the creatures throughout any universe can comprehend.*"

Jewel wants more. "How is that, exactly, heightened sound?"

The Praetorian creature continues, "*Our heightened eyes and sound are a thousand times higher than any dog whistle or species on Earth can understand or compare. Fortunately, we can see progress not just today but also in the future.*"

Jewel, astounded at what these creatures could offer, asks the Praetorian one last question. "So what is this invisible universe, and what planet are you from?"

The Praetorian creature looks down at Jewel. "*I will show you a gateway to our invisible world, from where we originate. It's a universe called Innovo. Galiton, the planet's galaxy, contains multiple worlds that orbit it, including Lunair, Cosmo, and Blugana. These are beautiful worlds with stemming plant life, replicated foods that continue to grow daily forever, and species beyond your imagination. It is like Earth when it first was created with the garden of Eden, except it is more colorful."*

As Jewel stares into the creature's hands, his mind goes into a trance. Unfathomable beauty never seen by the human eye engulfs his existence. With the most beautiful array of colors and vivid imagery, strange, petrifying, yet oddly beautiful creatures occupying these so-called invisible planets are seen only through the possible vision of the creature's hands. It can't be seen or located by any other species except the Praetorians. Only a Praetorian can find this universe, and they only let those they want to see it. There is no other way to get there except by a Praetorian species. As the Praetorian begins to close his hand, Jewel's eyes return to reality. Jewel's eyes are wide open. "That is paradise."

The Praetorian is pleased. "Glad you enjoyed it. That is our lovely home."

Jewel gets his team of scientists together, and the other scientists converse with the alien creatures on what technologies they need to develop to make the facility up to par or schedule for when the human race may meet doomsday. Dr. Penny and the Legendary creature adjust the robotic portal. The other scientists and the Praetorian make adjustments to the cloning station, astrophysics computer, speed of light celertrino computer, and others throughout the facility. Finally, scientists gather in a corner with the two aliens as the diplomats and dignitaries head over to a room with General Snuff for deliberation once the facility is up to par.

The Praetorian is taking an instrument from its sack of goodies, as the tool looks like a soft spiral spear metal with computer compartments on it. The creature adds it to the cloning stations to adjust the clones with a filament DNA, giving them special heightened abilities such as speed, agility, and slight invisibility. Merna and Lucas are fine-tuning a gadget that one of the aliens has given them; they can splice alien DNA with various creatures to produce a string of unusual species. This device is hollow in the middle, cylinder circular shape where one can put chemicals in it, splicing the species' DNA with alien DNA compromising the species' DNA to the aliens for fast reproduction. In John and Jewel's area, the computer system has an unknown software called perios-five; it scans all visible and invisible universes for known threats. It will also minimize itself and extract the information to one kilobyte, although it contains ten gigabytes of data. The software communicates within itself, and talks to you in any language for communication purposes.

Merna walks back to the room where the diplomats and dignitaries chat regarding the upgrade and discuss the completion with Yarmin. She says, "We are done upgrading the facility, sir."

Yarmin gets out of his seat. "Ladies and gentlemen, let's go see our facilities upgrade. Please follow me." The other diplomats and dignitaries get out of their seats and begin to follow Yarmin, who is following Merna. Merna gets Gale, who walks the people around the facility to see the upgrades.

Gale first goes by her area as the cloning machines begin to churn up. "Ladies, gentlemen, Yarmin, we have the new device Gyro seven r. It is in place and working fine, as you can see." Gale engages the new device as she touches other buttons while the machine is churning.

One of the diplomats looks and feels the new instrument with astonishment. "What exactly does it do?"

Hours later, Gale shows the diplomats and dignitaries an example of the new soldier's ability. "Ladies and gentlemen, Yarmin, I will now show you what powers they have acquired."

One of the female dignitaries notices their eyes shining in bright blue, green, and purple colors. She concludes to Dr. Gale, "Dr. Gale, I noticed that these soldiers have distinct eyes. Does that tell us that each one has a different ability?"

Gale shows a computer screen graph indicating each soldier's ability according to their eye color and physical build. "This graph on this computer shows us not only what their eyes tell us, but also their physical build."

Lady dignitary does not see a difference in the soldiers' build as she touches them slightly. "I don't see a difference although they are so manly."

Gale explains, "Let me give you insight into their different builds. For one, this build is called cross-haired. You see, his forearms they're a lot bigger than his biceps or triceps. Speed is one of his abilities, as well as his green eye color. According to the charts, he can run about forty to sixty miles per hour and crush huge rocks with his strength. As for this next solider here, his type of build is called invisone. He has a little bit of skinnier legs for stealth movement with the quickness. These soldiers are good for infiltration of enemies and quietness when behind enemy lines. Their eyes are purple for the reason of seeing in dark areas. This third type of solider body built is called radialone, reason is because their body is a bit smaller than the other two and their eye color is bright blue. These third types of soldiers can slightly go invisible. You can barely see the outline of their bodies, and their eyes are bright like a flashlight in darkness. They also can sniff out enemies from afar. I think that is the major update to our cloning machines. Any remaining questions?"

A male diplomat has one question that will cover all other questions from the diplomats and dignitaries. "Since these three soldiers have these abilities, does the machine acquire future abilities for other clones?"

Gale, who has no specific answer for this male diplomat, gives a general answer. "Since it's a new technology, I know we have not learned these things yet, but we will keep you informed of discoveries that will develop. Any other questions?"

The male diplomat is paying attention to the computer graphs. "No, ah, Dr. Gale. Keep us informed on any new development, okay."

Gale responds, "Okay."

Eventully, after seeing the inventions and understanding them, the dignitaries and the diplomats praised the scientists and thanked them for their work. In appreciation for their work so far, Gale takes them to the final issue, the G300 machine, where Dr. Beth and Penny work to calibrate the machine with the alien species' data. At the same time, Penny looks at the onboard computer to monitor the test clone taken through the robotic arm portal into the alien planet.

One of the dignitaries slightly scratches his nose, watching Penny and Beth at work, and excuses himself as the two doctors are very busy. "Excuse me, Doctors, want a quick answer."

Beth asks enthusiastically, "What is the short answer you would like, sir?"

The male dignitary gives Beth what he wants. "What I want to know is, does this machine break down the body when transported, or does it squeeze the matter then expands it on the other side?"

Beth looks at the computer monitor that tells her exactly what the computer does to matter while being transported through it. "Well, according to the computer here, it looks like it breaks down the molecules and then reconstructs it on the other side."

The male dignitary starts to talk to the other International Union people, and a female dignitary lashes out in a loud remark, "Why not send a clone to see what exactly happens when the machine finishes? Let's do it, Dr. Beth!"

When Beth discusses putting a clone through the machine, she taps Gale on the shoulder and looks into Gale's eyes. "Gale, can we get a clone to go through this machine right now so that these government officials can see how it works."

Gale walks over to her station area. "That is not a problem. Let me make a clone from one of these soldiers' DNA on the holographic computer within the hour, okay."

An hour later, the clone is made and is ready to participate in the portal experiment. Gale brings the clone to the area of the robotic portal, putting the clone in the middle of the machine, as Beth explains further to the government officials, "Ladies and gentlemen, we can now proceed with this procedure." Beth sets the machine on automatic as the device analyzes the clone as matter, reading the clone's every part as the engine speeds up the process. The robotic arms begin to sync with the middle device as the device initiates a whirling sound, almost sounding like a thunderstorm, and lo and behold, suddenly, without warning, the clone disappears in a spinning vortex, quickly breaking down the clone's structure as the vortex begins to shrink into thin air.

Minutes later, the machine estimates the arrival of the clone on the other side, wherever it may have entered, to be ten minutes later. Beth gives the government officials the reading. "People, according to the task on the computer, it shows the clone has entered a universe in ten minutes."

A diplomat has a good question for Beth that has the entire facility of people wondering to themselves. "Does the computer have a way to grab the clone and bring it back?"

Beth is looking through the programming of the portal robotic machine to see if there is a way for the clone to return. Her programming design makes her think it may take a thousand years from now for the clone to return. In Beth's words, "The light at the end of the tunnel is that humanity could return in a thousand years, providing another portal is designed on the other side. I don't know why that is, but I hope these alien species can explain it to us."

The Praetorian takes over the conversation. "It's best known that with adjustments in the computer system, humankind can return to Earth in five years or sooner depending on if warning signs still say some enemy is in your galaxy."

Beth, with the Legendary, makes a few adjustments on the computer of the G300 machine to bring man back a few years at a time, depending on if the enemy is no longer on Earth or in the Milky Way galaxy. Penny adjusts the motherboard with other alien species to comprehend humanity's travel back to Earth if there is an Earth to come to in the future. Penny asks, "Does the computer know if the Earth will be safe to return to in the future?"

The Praetorian puts several new components on the processor board to read future events. *"As I install these new components, they will tell the computer software if it is safe to return to or if it's a hostile environment. Only time will tell."* Penny is relieved after hearing what the creature just told her.

Meanwhile, Lucas has an odd question for Yarmin. "What is the origin of these creatures, Yarmin? I know they can't be from our galaxy."

Yarmin laughs. "Let's say it is beyond our reach."

Lucas smirks as he cautions his next question. "So, what planet or planets do they come from exactly?"

"Dr. Lucas, the Legendary beings come from five planets in a galaxy called Xeria. These five planets include Cationic, Rufantic, Baloris, Valorian, and Crestwatonic," He is answered by Yarmin.

Lucas, a tad confused, asks, "How can a Legendary be from five different planets?"

Yarmin answers Lucas's question. "You see, Dr. Lucas, the Legendaries have five home worlds because they consist of several species." With a strange look, Lucas asked," what other creatures can be from their home worlds?"

Yarmin excuses himself from Dr. Lucas and gets the attention of the Legendary chatting with Penny. "Excuse me, Professor, do you have a minute to explain something to my doctor friend about where you come from, as in your home worlds."

The Legendary pardons himself from Penny and turns toward Dr. Lucas. "*Pardon me, good doctor, I am needed somewhere at the moment.*" Penny smiles and nods. Yarmin accompanies the Legendary over to Lucas to explain where its species are from and why there are five planets in the first place.

Lucas, a little dumbfounded, looks up at the creature with an academic eye. "So, um, why is your species from five different planets?"

The Legendary shows Dr. Lucas on a holographic board where his race is from and what type of species live there. *"You see, Dr. Lucas, my species are from five planets. The first is where my species of five different versions of creatures come from called Cationic. It consists of a species called the venerir; they look like your rabbits here. Venerir has eight legs, and a bit of a vicious disposition. The other intelligent species is the crodones. They look like a gorilla and chinchilla mix. The other two creatures look similar to my group, except their faces look like an owl with fur and raccoon eyes. The last species look identical to us, very catlike, except they have four nostrils to breathe. There may be a tusk in the middle of the learmin's face, but our furry comrades on Rufantic look like a hybrid of dogs and humans.*

"As for the other worlds, we find that their female creatures reside in Baloris. Exceptionally smooth and sleek fur gives them a majestic appearance, accompanied by dreamy eyes and skin as smooth as glass. The fourth planet, Valorian, consists of peaceful species like us who look like water horses in the faces, possess humanlike

feet, and can run and swim so fast it is unthinkable. The last planet is our home world called Crestwatonic. It consists of our kind and another kind called gitaaninic. They are larger and taller species of us, except they can withstand any injuries and create homes for us within the planet as well. In out Milky Way galaxy, you'll meet some alien species that protect your homeworld from one of the five planets above."

Lucas turns to Yarmin, confused by what the creature said about its home world. "There are more creatures for you to encounter?"

Yarmin looks at the beast, not knowing some of the information. "Yes, I guess there is." Yarmin stares into space. "What is the reason for these questions, Dr. Lucas?"

Lucas, who is being passive, answers, "Oh, no reason at all. Just wanted to know for my indulgence, that's all." Lucas turns to the other side as he faces Jewel and Merna; the three exchange a knowing look. Dr. Lucas is concerned about much more than his indulgence when he asks questions. A gorilla chinchilla steps off the elevator and approaches a scientist within the corridor of the facility. Taking a double look in that direction, Lucas looks again as though he has seen a clear image of a creature.

CHAPTER 17

A GLIMPSE FROM OUR PAST

Lucas and Yarmin walk back toward Gale to get her attention because Yarmin intends all the new scientists to know more about these species. So Yarmin and Lucas approach Gale and say, "Dr. Gale, I want to gather all the new scientists to learn more about our friendly big guys."

Gale, who is in the middle of setting up her cloning computers to see if there are future abilities that the soldiers can obtain, turns around to talk to Yarmin. "Of course. Same meeting room, right?" Yarmin nods his head. Yarmin takes the two creatures and goes into a meeting room. Gale walks over to Merna and Lucas in a hurry, bumping her knee into a desk by mistake.

Gale limps and says, "Dr. Merna and Dr. Lucas, Mr. Yarmin wants you two to follow me. We have a meeting to attend."

Lucas answers for both him and Merna, "We are at your mercy. Please lead the way."

Gale heads over to the G300 since Penny and Beth missed their last meeting with the aliens years ago. Gale gets their attention since they are working on the machine. "Dr. Penny and Dr. Beth, please follow me. We have a crucial meeting to attend right away."

Beth is tugging at Penny since Penny is deeply engrossed as she works on the machine's programming. "Penny! Penny! We have a meeting to attend right away."

Penny is startled. "What! What!" Penny quickly puts down what she is doing. "Are we going for lunch, huh?"

Gale finally gets Penny's attention. "No, dummy, and we have a crucial meeting with Yarmin right away."

Penny says thoughtfully, "Let's see what he wants right away."

All the other scientists are intrigued to attend this critical meeting, so Gale gathers them all up in no time. A glass floor opening allows furniture to rise through it. When you ask a question, robotic chairs and desks rotate in a circle, giving you a platform to speak. Scientists discovered furniture had been lifted into the meeting room by a robotic entity that emerged from beneath the ground. Scientists have never convened in a meeting room with artificial intelligence of this level. The Praetorians originally built this facility to discuss and debate reactions to the advice of the council from the International Union during wartime. As the Praetorian approaches the pulpit slowly, his face fills with accomplishment.

The creature looks at Yarmin and then asks before turning to Yarmin, "*We have done what needs with the upgrades of the now intact systems. Does anyone have any questions for me on the technologies?*"

With a look of disarray on his face, Jewel says, "I have one question."

The Praetorian guises toward Jewel. "*Yes, Dr. Jewel.*"

Jewel asks a question about the creature's name, "Yes, ah, sir, ah. Do you even have a name, or should I call you creature?"

Knowing that these doctors do not know its name, the Praetorian begins to tell them its name. "*My name is Cokiko. Why is that so important, Dr. Jewel? I received it a millennium of years ago.*"

Dr. Jewel, a little bit meticulous in his speaking, responds, "I was only interested in discovering whether you had names similar to those familiar to humans. Didn't know you guys lived for a millennium year. How's that?"

With a light glare near its face, the Praetorian replies, *"Oh, I see. We live a very long time. We are born when planets are born. We die when worlds die. It is the life cycle of a Praetorian."*

Wide-eyed, Jewel gazes into the distance. "That's an incredibly long life. I wondered, Cokiko, will we be advancing our technology in the physics sector to scan these universes for hostile forces, probably?"

Cokiko, with a loud voice, says, "*I don't know of any hostile forces in these universes from my understanding. The way the program works, it scans for any pressent hostiles before traveling to that universe that may cause harm to humankind, which we have accomplished. After that, any other scanning is on a need-to-know basis.*"

Some papers get ruffled by Jewel as he scatters, looking for something. "What's up with that?"

"No need to know."

Cokiko gives Jewel the necessities of why it's a need-to-know basis. "*You see, Dr. Jewel, you have everything necessary for one. In other words, our planet, or any other creature, does not have any hostility toward your kind.*"

Jewel begins to look down at his paperwork. "Okay, I understand now."

The Praetorian is about to step down from the pulpit. "*Any other questions?*"

Lucas, who has his hands raised, has a question for Cokiko. Cokiko acknowledges Lucas's hand waving back and forth. "*Could you please tell me your name, Doctor? So I can assist you in any way I can?*"

Lucas coughs a bit. "Ah, Dr. Lucas."

Cokiko paraphrases, "*Dr. Lucas, how can I be a help to you?*"

Lucas, who wants to study the DNA of the creature, asks a question that would lead to the history of these aliens. "I understand where you come from, but I would like to know. How long have you been helping humanity? For example, throughout history."

During its presentation to the scientists, Cokiko describes the history of its species with society. "*We have been helping humankind since the tenth century. Are you ready for this, Dr. Lucas?*"

Lucas is waiting patiently. "Shoot away, Cokiko."

Cokiko continues his history lesson. "*Our planet was born billions of years ago. It was like we were the protectors of all universes. Having protection by the supreme being who you call God, God gave us a task to go through all universes and protect the good you see, especially help humankind, the first beings in all universes. In the beginning, we arrived on Earth by ship.*"

Lucas's eyes raise. "Ships!"

Cokiko continues again. "*Yes! We were the wheel in the sky mentioned in some accounts, a wheel within a wheel. What we have done for humanity throughout history is that we visited many times to help humankind at the beginning. We came to study humanity at that time. We checked society to see where they were going in their ways of gasping certain things in life, like feeding themselves and how they reproduce. We do not reproduce, and we are asexual. We have no females.*"

Lucas, Merna, and Jewel say simultaneously, "What!"

Jewel, with a bizarre look, says, "No females! How can you enjoy sex or that sexual drive?"

Cokiko gives Jewel the answer. "*We don't have a sexual purpose. We just can't, even if we wanted to. We aim to help those less fortunate and bring them up to speed on what they need to be as a race. Our history with humanity is to show society what they are missing, not overstepping and bringing them to the proper perspective to see their potential of what they can do on their planet. Throughout history, we have helped humanity from the beginning until now. What we have done to help humanity, for example, is the discovery of modules of flint in the so-called caveman days that can be split and chipped into sharp edges to hunt bison and form spears. We have put those flint sediments near decaying bones so the so-called caveman can discover it."*

"Wow. That is amazing," Lucas says.

Jewel, on top of the conversation, adds, "You guys had a lot to do with helping humanity."

Cokiko brings a lot more to the table about how his species help further advance humanity. "*The next thing we did was send a chemical into Earth's atmosphere that produced lightning at the time. Humankind found that lightning made a fire, and man learned from burning himself that it can be dangerous. Eventually, we showed humanity how to tame fire, giving them the tools to work with, such as fire using it for cooking in 250,000 BC. Hunters took wooden spears to harden them with the fire embers, and this is how man learned to set wood. Later on, in 8,000 BC, they know to use fire to mend pottery, eventually casting metal and healing shapes with higher temperatures to form different pots, and weapons shapes with higher temperatures to form various vessels, creating more weapons. Finally, we showed them how to use clay and mud to build housing to live in a warm and safe area from animal threats."*

With a look of surprise, Merna says, "I never knew you guys helped humanity with that. I was wondering if it came through by way of natural selection. Wow, interesting indeed."

With continuance, Cokiko belches oddly, "*We helped them form the housing and how to construct different rooms within their dwellings. They used fire for warmth. In the first century BC, humanity learned how to use water mills performing gears and axles, creating a wheel to water their crop for food. Society adapted very well so far."*

Cokiko, with a massive smile on his face, proceeds further. "*Later in the sixteenth and seventeenth centuries, we showed them how to form glass out of the sand by blowing it and making vases. Humankind learned how to break glass and reuse it. They would reuse it to make a tile from broken glass to form different tiles and shapes. In the eighteenth century, we helped humanity develop a plan that we have debated for a long time. That debate used wood instead of iron core for the railroad. Of course, humankind saw that iron core would make the tracks withstand a heavy train instead of hardwood that would snap. Iron was put on your Earth by us so that humankind can use its benefits for different instruments used today. In the nineteenth century, in Simi Valley, California, we showed the military to harness the various components of sand quartz to make different computer components, such as ham radios, gadgets, and top secret devices. Did you know that the Internet has always been around since the 1920s? Now your society uses it to look up various things. In the past, its usage was to look up other technical operations. We showed humankind how to use it. We gave your military the insight to use it for the public. Today, we are advancing the human race with technology to expand humanity's knowledge. We finally gave humankind a way to clone things to feed the billions of people you have on Earth. We gave humankind a way to see other astrophysics by showing your people robotics and its usefulness to all industries."*

Merna is feeling a little bit relaxed. "Now that is a lot of knowledge for us. We appreciate your help throughout history. This is why our technology has advanced rapidly through the last one hundred and thirty years, right?"

Cokiko nods his head in a yes motion. Then, Cokiko gives his final statement. "*We have shared with your species the insight for survival in any tragedies that may come upon them. What else would you like to know? I just gave you the rundown of our history."*

He looks toward the Legendary creature in a low tone. "How did the Legendary come about?" Jewel quickly says while mesmerized exquisitely.

Cokiko looks to the Legendary mythical creature and introduces him to the people. "*Let me give my associate a proper introduction to tell you more about his history with us. Please, Professor Wymoym, please."*

Cokiko removes himself from the pulpit as Professor Wymoym approaches the pulpit gently, and cautiously. His arms down to the side with his head up a bit and an undertone growl. "*Yes, Cokiko, I appreciate you sharing the history. Now I will begin with our past. They call us Legendaries because we come in all forms and sizes. We are a species from a different universe. We come from a universe called Mirunda from the galaxy Xeria, where we have five sustainable planets that pertain to eleven planets altogether. The planets that can't pertain to life have bright hues around them that cause their ozone layers to collapse under specific temperatures, for seconds causing flaming gases in the atmosphere. When the Praetorians first found us, it was like redemption that came upon us, for we got attached to some evil creatures unknown to us. These creatures desire to mate with females, killing their male counterparts through heinous crimes. So we had to initiate some plan to preserve our species. The Praetorians protected us from those creatures from annihilating our species through a protective shield of inconspicuousness with their sonic sounds that made those creatures kneel. They fled away from our galaxy due to these guys right here."*

While he points to Cokiko, the Praetorian, Merna wants to know the type of creatures that attacked their galaxy. Professor Wymoym is trying to hush about the evil creatures, not telling her yet. "*In time, we will advise you who they are and what kind of menace they can bring to any planet. Now, all you need to know is that they would bring evil to you. As a species, our friends, the Praetorians, saved us from extinction. Praetorians are peaceful beings. As you have heard, their universe is invisible for a reason. If the enemy were to find them, they may destroy their world and never protect all the universes and galaxies from the plaque of these evil beings. In our story, the Legendaries go back to millions of years, even billions. We are a peaceful race like our friends, the Praetorians. The Praetorians had made ships that came to our universe, and planets that have expanded our species for one day. For a long time, the Praetorians had no way of mating with any female. We, on the other hand, never died. We were just there with no offspring until one day. The Praetorians had researched us. They found a planet in our solar system with female Legendaries that looked similar to us except for a few different appearances."*

"Exactly what did their appearance look like, Professor Wymoym?" Merna wants to know.

Professor Wymoym, through the Praetorian hands, as the Praetorian opens his hand to show the beauty and the subtlety of the female planet with the delightful plantation with creatures of brilliance. We can pet them without being threatened as the scientists are transformed into that world as though walking through it.

Jewel has a not-so-easy question. "These creatures that live on your planet, what do they have for food?"

The professor reveals to Jewel the truth about his world. "*You see, Dr. Jewel, the creatures regurgitate their food and reproduce, making new species. So instead of the same creatures for billions of years, they evolve into something new, like our species. On the female planet, we have plenty of food that could sustain our species for billions and billions of years and your species for billions of years."*

Delighted with the female planet, Jewel wants Professor Wymoym to continue the history lesson. "Please proceed. I would like to know more."

So Professor Wymoym proceeds with the history lesson as the rest of the scientists are intrigued while taking notes. "*The female species, as I was saying, look different from us by their anatomy. Despite their magnificence and splendor, females have a wide variety of species. I mated with a female with the head of a cat, a horse's hair, butterfly's wings, and mule's feet. Another female has branches of a hornet, face of a feline cat or tiger that cannot tell her apart from the rest of her kind, and a scorpion's tail. But the majority of females' faces are beautiful. These female species have given us a chance to survive. The birth accomplishments are primarily the male's responsibility, which is to deliver the offspring, while the females raise the female offspring on the female planet. Our planet has various species of different kinds. As you have seen through the hands of my friend Cokiko, we eat what we call dondines. These dondines are creatures that we eat and survive on. They look like miniature horses that fly around, and there are mingdongs, live vegetables of assorted colors. These vegetables move and talk, also grow old before they die. That is because we absorb their essence by eating themonce they take their last breath. If they die right before their time is up, we lose the nutrients that help sustain our lives.*"

Hmm, interesting, Lucas thinks to himself.

The professor keeps speaking. "*We have no engineering facilities or vehicles. We do not need them. Our species never get tired. We can walk forever, jump, climb, and have a lot of agility ability. One other creature is a Legendary that can fly. The Praetorians took us as soldiers because they had never battled, and they protected us through their invisibility and sonic noises. Using our skill and ability to fight, we defend them. They warn us of any coming doom if there is one. Please, I'll give the floor back to the one and only, Cokiko.*"

Professor Wymoym leaves the podium as Cokiko approaches for his final wording on the history of their two species. Cokiko pulls the microphone close to his lips. "*As you can see, we are here to help humanity from the enemies that we have not talked about yet. If you don't know the enemy, the enemy will know you in a matter of time. We are here to protect your species from imminent doom or extinction. Our advanced technologies will give you the tools of this planet Earth, but if your species were to live off-world, it would give you those advances. We will train your species to protect themselves from all enemies. You are the baby species that have grown in leaps and bounds to almost adulthood regarding technology.*"

Merna, who is totally in the realm of the history of these creatures, looks and gazes at what they have to say. She wants to know why we as a human race have not met adulthood yet in technology.

"Question, why do you not think that we have not reached maturity in technology?"

Cokiko smiles slightly and looks at Merna. *"Dr. Merna, your species have not yet reached adulthood in technology because we have not taught your species everything we know. To grasp most of our knowledge, it will take your species to see a fraction of what we know for at least ten thousand years or more."*

Merna, shocked and bewildered simultaneously, looks down at her holographic tablet, and starts to make notes with a right finger jotting down a fraction of knowledge is all that humankind has learned so far.

CHAPTER 18

THE MINERAL THIEVES

Cokiko further explains why they put the facility together. "*The reason we put this facility together is that we can take humankind living on different universes adapting themselves to their alien environments forming alien beings. Humanity is the ancestors of these new alien beings, becoming a new race, a more advanced race.*"

"Advanced race!" shouted Merna. "Can you explain that?"

Cokiko stares solemnly and says, "*Excuse me, but what I mean by advanced race is when the time comes, the majority of the human race will transport through various universes. In time, they will adapt to their new surroundings that may take them thousands of years when they reach that universe. According to vegetation and food on the planet and any ailments or diseases, they will transform from their human counterpart that first came to that planet to alien species that have transformed them through time. With better adaptation to the environment, whether it be cold, hot, lukewarm, or their food supply, people may die adapting to these conditions and, through time, will see what works and doesn't. Does that explain much to you, Dr. Merna, and the rest?*"

Merna, who was more excited than anyone else, felt relief. "Thank you for explaining in an understanding that I can comprehend. Thank you, Cokiko."

Cokiko is delighted that people in the audience grasp the concept of why they are here to save humankind from the evil ones that want to destroy anything in their way. "*By taking each scientist across every universe and galaxy, the machine G300 accomplishes this through its numerous programs. You scientists and all humanity who go through that portal would be the ancestors of aliens developed throughout history and time. Throughout thousands of years, your future alien-human hybrids will learn different ways and how to build warfare to fight off the evil enemy that comes their way. I am not saying that you wouldn't have wars in your galaxies. It will not be long before those wars turn out to be friends and not foes, and you will either develop or suffer the consequences of their aggression depending on how much technical ability we can teach you. Yes, there will be many Legendaries and my kind, the Praetorians traveling with you into these dark new worlds. Hopefully, you either pass or fail. It depends on the humans who are strong and those that are weak."*

With a feeling of nervousness over her, Merna wants to know what happens to the original scientist. "In contrast, this transition occurs through these travels. You said the actual scientist will end up where exactly?"

In his message to Merna and the other scientist, Cokiko tells them where the original scientist will end up. "*You see, when we put your foremost-cloned scientists in a jam when things get out of control, we will send your original scientists on a journey that will indeed be impossible to traverse. There is another universe called Vaderina next door to ours, where the scientist will report to us while communicating with other universes that hold their replicas by telepathy. It has shades of invisibility, and its specific race will protect the original doctors. But at the same time, the clones teach your hybrid human race how to deal with new and developing technologies that would either help them or be their demise. Whether or not there are wars among them in different universes depends on whether or not the strong survive over the weak."*

Jewel, who wants to know more about this invisible universe, first questions Cokiko. "Would us, the original scientist, be in your universe or one of the other universes that may be similar to yours? Also, are you related to the human race? Are we your ancestors as well, or are you God protectors of all universes?"

Cokiko looks at Jewel with an odd look as if he hit that question on the nail. "*Well, Dr. Jewel, good question. I already told you the original doctors would be in a universe called vaderina, similar to ours, that is merely next door to us. I must say your intuition is almost on target. But no! Let's say we are family, but the human race is not our ancestors. We are the protectors of all universes. Further, I would like to tell you about all the other reasons we are here, not to alarm you, but to let you know that we are aware of our enemy being within the Milky Way galaxy. We have a hunch it may lead them to a cause of a rare mineral they are after."*

Merna looks foolishly at Cokiko while trying to guess what kind of mineral the enemy is looking to grab from Earth. "So let me imagine the enemy is searching for a mineral without warning. Do you think it is gold or silver a precious metal or copper? Could you tell me why they would look for these and the purpose?"

Cokiko smiles a bit and calmly, with a whimpering laugh similar to a hyena, points to Merna as though she got the correct answer and gently gives her the opposite of yes. "Dr. Merna, ah, no!"

Merna, a bit more curious, wants the correct answer, so she continues. "Okay, now this has to be the answer tungsten or iron. Am I right or not?"

Cokiko sees Dr. Merna is a bit frustrated and almost gives her the answer but plays with her a bit regarding a guessing game. "*You are almost there, Dr. Merna. You are hot but not hot enough.*"

Merna looks down at her necklace, looking at the zirconium diamonds, and she has it figured finally. At least she thinks she does. "All right, I think I got it now. It has to be diamonds. What else can it be."

Cokiko, who loves intelligent games, quits messing with Dr. Merna and gives her the mineral the enemy may be looking for on Earth. "*Their only reason for traveling to Earth or a planet similar to it is to fulfill this need. In this scenario, the enemy would be looking for two different types of minerals. One would be platinum. The other would be smithsonite, which is similar to zinc and calcium.*"

Lucas looks at Merna, shrugs his shoulder, and turns back toward Cokiko, wanting more information on why the enemy wants these minerals. "Could you explain to me why these enemies need these minerals?"

Cokiko looks at Lucas's eyes wide open as a Legendary pushes an invisible button in thin air to bring down a holographic chart behind everyone. That chart is like a jigsaw puzzle, with rows of descriptions of the enemy on a clear see-through filament that is wavey in midair, powered up by a small holographic computer that appears to be like a USB drive near the pulpit with shimmering, colorful light as it passes through it. It lights up most of the room so people could walk through it. While the wavy see-through moves with the pattern of wavy filament adjusting to either creature or human body movement, this wavy substance is so focused that the colors are more vivid than anything on Earth. It shows the inside of a massive ship and how these creatures with various alien DNA look. The scientists stare upon the filament with a fearful gaze, as if they had seen the devil himself, as the Praetorians and Legendaries show them what these creatures resemble and their shapes that are similar to humans with odd upper-body torsos. The picture shows a few aliens with eight legs, which resemble spiders and whose pupils have hues of green and gray surrounding their pupils. Like humans, other creatures have facial features with different skin tones and horns on their faces or shoulders.

Cokiko points to a particular area on the chart and explains why the enemy would desire the minerals. "*Well, the reason, ah, Dr. Lucas, is that they would use one mineral to power vessels of destruction, and the other used as a catalyst for firepower. There is no other reason except from what I have just told you.*"

Lucas pries for more information from Cokiko. "How is that possible with zinc and platinum? Please elaborate more."

Rubbing his hands together, Cokiko further explains, "*Well, the first meltdown is the platinum, then they have a heated generator on this massive ship that keeps it hot. Its fuel usage lasts for centuries because it has a long burn. Slower than molasses. As for the smithsonite, these minerals' usage is to fuel their weapons on board, and the type of weapons they carry gives these weapons a long-lasting charge for days, so they would probably need eight mountains full of these to last them a century or two. So why did you need to know, Dr. Lucas, regarding the additional information?*"

With all certainty, Lucas wants the data. "To know more for my knowledge, that's all."

Cokiko shakes his head from side to side as if a fly just passed by and carries on about the giant ships. "*The vessel here come in various sizes. The mother ship here uses platinum for its firepower. As mentioned earlier, these ships use this mineral for firepower and its fuel.*"

Merna looks at the different ships, and wants to know the name of the creatures. "What are these creatures called?"

Cokiko, without hesitation, informs the entire room of the name of these creatures and their reasons for coming to Earth. "*Of course, you already know they would come for minerals and destroy their enemies, the Legendaries. But I don't think they know that the Legendaries are on Earth now. They would come to Earth to replenish their system with foods, with almost any and everything. There is nothing that they cannot eat. If you give them poison, they will eat that too, and nothing will happen. These creatures are almost invincible. It is hard to kill them, but I want to give you the names of these creatures as you have seen here on this picture on the holographic monitor.*"

Cokiko points to the picture of creatures on the monitor as he continues. "*They are strange, and with weird torsos, this is the oddest thing about them, but the big thing about them is that they are violent creatures. Their violence has no end, so they are mainly evil tyrant creatures. The name of this enemy is Inquestorians. Their leader is a warlord called Faloosh. He is the leader of these creatures. He has soldiers, captains, and generals among millions of these creatures. You can see here on this wavy chart that they come in all shapes and sizes. Their goal is to conquer worlds, especially universes. Before I get into why they conquer worlds, let me give you other reasons for them to come to Earth. Unlike sensual beings, these are not emotional beings. Their main characteristics are to dominate and demolish anything in their path. They are very destructive and chaotic when it comes to taking over planets. He is like the God of their world, so basically, if you get rid of him, they are like ants with whom the army becomes confused once you get rid of the queen. Getting rid of Faloosh would confuse his army. You might find good somewhere within these creatures, eventually, who knows.*

"The ultimate reason why they would travel to Earth, where I am sure they are unaware, is to visit Earth's ancestor's. Otherwise, these creatures would try to eradicate all human entities if they were aware. Also, they would grab your supplies as well. As a result of their supplies shorten, they would want food resources. They would take your livestock and animals for food, even insects. Some Inquestorians can eat a whole cow or elephant, even a giraffe."

Merna and Lucas look at each other and blurt out, "Really!"

Lucas, stunned by what Cokiko has mentioned about these enemies, has an excellent question for Cokiko. "Excuse me, Cokiko, let me ask you. Since they are not aware that they approached the ancestors and I do not know why out of all universes they come to ours, I get the part regarding the minerals, but do you think they would try to conquer us still?"

Cokiko gives Lucas the benefit of the doubt. "*Look! I understand you guys are confused about why they would come to Earth. Regarding their computers, our investigation of what I am about to tell you has taken them off course, where they think they are at a planet similar to Earth but are unaware that you are the ancestors. And besides, Earth is the beginning of what is to be. So that would mean that although humanity is the ancestors, what is to be would mean that it gives light to what you are supposed to be in the distant future. Although we may know they are unaware of this location, our agent or spy has infiltrated the site's target location of their computer systems to where the forefathers may originate. This spy has been collecting information about them for hundreds of years. We have heard that our head spy was tortured as reported to us by another Legendary who escaped in time. The only way they might know about your planet is through our spy. The Inquestorian warlord captured and tortured our spy, a Legendary agent who provided the Inquestorian warlord with information. And they probably put the news at that time into his charted holographic computer. Getting here recently after millenniums is perhaps one of two things: the spy confused their computer system or an asteroid took them off course, confusing them entirely."*

Cokiko uses unknown technology to make a virtual monitor in the air, taking them back into the past like a movie screen. At first, they view the ship Omnibus before the agent dies. An enemy soldier happens to overhear a creature communicating on its holographic earpeice, speaking in an unfamiliar language unheard of by Faloosh's guards, who happen to see the Legendary leaned up against a post on the ship speaking to no one but itself. Once it stopped talking, two Inquestorian soldiers first questioned the legendary on the unfamiliar language and escorted him to face the warlord, Faloosh. One of the Inquestorian soldiers forces the mythical creature to kneel facing down in front of Faloosh.

Faloosh says in his alien language, "*Ba mo ka pu ka puta backa, ah sacka ye Macka Seca ba ca Baca ta maca," which interprets into English as "So you're the spy. I want to know the reason you are on my ship. Give me a reason why I shouldn't kill you now."*

In its language, in a high-pitched voice, the Legendary creature says, "*Al te ya te Ayer te."*

The interpreter of Faloosh says, "*Ah se bok, boc se toca."* Basically, the interpreter is telling Faloosh that the Legendary doesn't want to die. Here is the English translation of the interpreter: "Please don't kill me. I will give you anything."

Faloosh, in his alien language, again gets up from his throne, grabs the Legendary by its collar, and looks it in its tiny eyes. "*Why have you come on my ship? Are you here to grab tactics from me, or are you trying to extinguish us or what!"*

The Legendary, at this time, responds with a trembling body. "*No! I'm not trying to harm you at all. I'm trying to get information on your type of species so I can give it to my superiors."*

Faloosh looks deep into the Legendary's eyes. Faloosh's eyes begin to get bigger, speaking in his alien language. "*Yu! Bat ca ta bas tactica, Bat te extin se ce exter se."* Within the translation of the Inquestorian's language to English, "Why would I ever give you information on our species? We have no idea if you want to extinguish or exterminate us."

Of course, as this is all happening, the Inquestorians have never heard of the Legendaries before. The Inquestorian warlord Faloosh finds out through the spy where the Legendary universe location is. Once they have located the universe, they conquer it before he kills the Legendary spy. What Faloosh does is wage war among the Legendaries while showing through a window in space its home world that's beginning to get trampled with warfare from the Inquestorian army. Legendaries who are underground dwellers have to flee to underground mountains and subterranean tunnels to protect them from the oncoming slaughter. Some Legendaries fought back hard, while most of them hid and couldn't be found and had a cloak of invisibility from their neighboring universe, the Praetorians.

The Inquestorians, think they have been extinguished from existence and are no more when the Legendaries gave them a good fight. The Inquestorians have caught several left alive, and they have become enslaved beings on the Omnibus ship. So from this capture, having a spy on the spacecraft showed the warlord Faloosh as an unmerciful tyrant who wanted more creatures worshipping him as though he was God himself. So what Faloosh does with the Legendary spy after his planet has become desolate is to put on a piece of torture equipment called the spindel. The spindel is an instrument that not only stretches a creature and burns electricity through them while being stretched. So from this, Faloosh has a couple of his soldiers performing elasticity on the creature to get more information. Faloosh comes to find out the being is not only spying on them, but the Legendaries have learned that the Inquestorians are an evil race who like to conquer universes. Some other Legendaries have an escape plot and have found some escape pods. The information Faloosh has found out from the Legendary that he has on the spindel torture object is information about a universe where life begins that is the mother of all universes. Hopefully, that will flourish other universes with energy and new technologies with goodness, spreading love throughout the cosmos. Faloosh doesn't like that a world called Earth would spread love, warmth, and superiority to other universes, sprouting up new technologies.

The warlord Faloosh's ultimate goal is to stop the species of the old universe from spreading into other universes. Faloosh wants all universes to belong to his offspring and his kind only. The Inquestorians' ultimate goal is to either stop this old universe from flourishing into other universes or wipe out the new technologies they would develop in the long run. After taking information from the Legendary spy, Faloosh decides not to spare his life. Instead, Faloosh took a device to shoot small balls that attached themselves to the Legendary, burrowing themselves within the fur of the Legendary. The Legendary's entire body seemed to turn a different color within a few minutes. Imploding the mythical creature while it deflates like a balloon, Faloosh looks down at the deflation of the Legendary, picks it up, then drops it down in front of him, using it as a mat to wipe his feet under his throne around his creatures. Faloosh, once he conquered the Legendary planet, he seemed to be not interested in that planet anymore.

Several Legendaries came out of their holes within the ground, tunnels, and mountainous areas as they searched for survivors on the surface. Some Inquestorian ships head back to the surface to ensure no survivors are on the surface. The Legendaries hide in the bushes to see what the enemy wants. A spacecraft from the Legendary female world happens to catch the enemy ships' wind as it floats in space. One of the female Legendaries in the ship notices some males hiding from the spacecraft.

The female Legendary activates her cloaking device to ensure that the spaceship cannot be detected as the Inquestorian soldiers land and exit their ship to scout for survivors. The Inquestorians send out a tiny vessel that seeks if anything is moving. Several male Legendaries see that little vessel approaching them as one of the Legendary males imitating one of their animals. At the same time, he turns a different color so that the female on board sends a small invisible ship to cloak the males present. The Inquestorians are not that easy to fool or give up on their mission to find the last of the Legendaries and eradicate them. So they steadily approach the surface area closer to where the Legendaries are hiding while being intrigue as these two robust species build up some type of commonality.

CHAPTER 19

THE CONQUERING OF THE ENEMY

The Legendaries then start to distract the tiny vessel of the Inquestorians with a bit of blue light running away into a small bush where one of the Legendaries grabs it to destroy it. Suddenly the cloaking vessel hides the male Legendaries as they seem to study the enemy up close. When they get enough information on the Inquestorian's computer from their handheld instrument, it is sent to the Legendaries underground, through the tunnels and mountains. However, as the Legendaries leave the ship, the first Legendary sees the female Legendary trying to help him diverge into another route. Unfortunately, they both become trapped in an ambush where some Inquestorian soldiers happen to have their weapons drawn and capture them. Back at the ship, a soldier gets word from other ground troop. "*No sight of any survivors.*" The Inquestorians that captured these two Legendaries have weapons on them as they take the two Legendaries back to the mother ship.

Meanwhile, a female Legendary with the art of attack attacks one of the Inquestorians' ships, destroying the enemy and its ship with a weapon that vaporizes them. The other Inquestorian ships have not noticed. Meanwhile, 98 percent of the Inquestorians' ships head back to the mother ship as one stays behind. The two Inquestorian soldiers who are left behind hear a weird sound near some tunnels. As the survivors listen, Legendaries are trying to quiet down the inside group. The Legendaries attack the Inquestorian soldier on the surface that is cloaked. The two Inquestorian soldiers are captured and questioned by the Legendary leader Ballisto. Ballisto and some of the Legendary leaders with some of their soldiers happen to mind bend their thoughts, torturing them with good ideas instead of evil thoughts.

The Inquestorian soldiers start to leak out information to the Legendary leader with what information they have stored in their memory. The mother ship and its leading ships leave all the Legendaries' home world. They expect all life-forms to be deceased and the remaining captured Legendaries enslaved to the warlord Faloosh.

Coming back to the present day, Cokiko begins to move on with Inquestorians' threats that may come to Earth. "*They will also take your animals, your water, leaving Earth as dry as possible where habitation is no more. They are rejecting your world where the remaining humans are starving, eating each other if they survive the onslaught of the Inquestorians.*

"*The Inquestorian's ultimate goal is to destroy all life as you would know it. So their main problem would be extinguishing all universes' energy and ruling over them the lives left behind. In other words, they could leave a crew of creatures to control that universe or destroy it if the aliens don't abide by Faloosh's rule.*"

While Cokiko remains grounded in the information he is sharing with Lucas, Lucas is about to say something. "We will fight them no matter how long it takes until we find a way to kill them."

Cokiko, needing to hear Lucas's view, continues. "*This enemy is adamant, and it has hard, impenetrable skin, so thick that it is more comprehensive than wale skin and stiffer than worm silk, which is as strong as steel. Your machine gun bullets will bounce off of them, even your missiles. Some lasers will bounce off of them too. You need something that can attach themselves to them, bury themselves, and implode them from the inside out. Sometimes their inside is just as challenging as it is hard to kill some of them. I'm pretty sure this is one way you can kill this enemy.*"

Cokiko, knowing the doctors are unaware of the other creatures on board the enemies ships, clarifies further, "*A Widgee is a giant creature with four legs that don't have a human torso but an alien torso, very awkward looking. These creatures are very destructive. If you get in their path, you can send a missile or nuclear bomb into them, and they will survive the impact. They are untouchable. We haven't found a way to conquer these creatures yet. Faloosh has these creatures as his bodyguards. But before he would send out his bodyguards, Faloosh would send out his minions first. The minions are his small soldiers that look like ant creatures with six legs torso very alien, and they are pretty quick on the ground. If the minions are losing the war, Faloosh sends out his middle warriors to attack. These look almost human but are various alien species called Gimbocs with their skin thick like a dragon, some of them have feet like an eagle, and some of them have faces like minks. They are hard to kill, and with a tactical team group together we can strike the enemy with their tactical alignments. They bow down to Faloosh in his presence. If these warriors were to lose the war, Lord Faloosh would send out his flying army. These flying beings have sharp claws that shred anything in their path, and when these warriors are losing the war, he then sends out the bodyguards to make the playing field equal."*

Cokiko squats at a fly nearby and proceeds with more information on the enemy. "*These bodyguards are eighteen feet tall and smash, squash, annihilate anything in their path. They have long fingernails to dig up earth to find enemies within holes. We have not figured out how to destroy this creature yet. As for the Praetorians, the reason that we both have come to Earth is for Earth's help. With your species integrated into alien hybrids, we can form an alliance among universes. Hopefully, one day, whether it be a thousand years, a million years, or even a millennium, we can find a way to conquer those bodyguards. Once we have them conquered, we would then destroy Faloosh! Faloosh is a stronger creature than the bodyguards and a lot bigger! Also, Faloosh's offspring. We have a lot to think about and plan ahead of us. If Faloosh ever comes on Earth, watch out! He is evil himself by the meaning of the word. Faloosh has impressive powers. He can grow up to twenty-two feet tall and shrink down to an insect."*

John in the background sighs with disbelief. "Hmm." John then looks at Jewel. "What the hell we are going to do, my friend, with a creature with those smarts?"

Jewel looks back at John. "Yeah, John, with a beast like that, we have no power on Earth that can take on a beast like that at all. What can we do! Maybe we can do the impossible."

John scratches behind his right ear, responds, "Yes, the impossible might be plausible."

While Jewel is uncomfortable in the seat, he expresses, "If they exhaust the resources, we will surely starve to death and possibly even eat each other. Clones and excessive cloning would also benefit the situation. Therefore, if our waters were to run out, we will all be dehydrated, and nothing will grow. The only thing left for man to save us is cloning, and if that would succumb by an insane person who went on a rampage, we would surely die."

John stares at Jewel. "Now that we know there is always a nut within a mass hysteria."

Jewel then looks at Cokiko and says, "What in the name of God could we do if we come across creatures like these?"

Cokiko stares directly at Dr. Jewel as he steps down from the pulpit. "*Dr. Jewel, that's why we need hybrids to come and find out a way or even get rid of these creatures that can cause mass panic in other universes. If your species had to leave Earth to save itself from these creatures, your hybrids could live on planets that don't have life right now. With the guidance of our race, the Praetorians and Legendaries, with proven technological advancement that will take centuries to perfect, we can have a better chance against these creatures on those planets with aliens environments. The open worlds will be your home worlds where you can be integrated and mixed with species for centuries, forming new alien races that will become hybrids to ward off and hopefully defeat these creatures in the long run. You will be far more advanced with these new technologies than the technologies you have on Earth right now. If we combine all your hybrids from the different home worlds of the other universes, then maybe, just maybe, we can conquer these beings."*

Cokiko's lips pucker up while he feels to see if the floating microphone is still in front of him, then says, "*Why we are here is because we need your help. We are teaching you everything we can. However, you are babies of technology. We will teach you a small percentage of our technology for now until your hybrids are ready for us to teach them the vast parts of our technologies in the future. They will roam the universes and destroy everything in their path until they have depleted the resources the local species have. If it comes to that, we would be able to advance our technologies, utilizing them and coming up with new extraordinary technologies beyond imagination to devour this enemy from destroying peaceful worlds."*

Lucas has to refute what Cokiko has said so far. "If they intend to rob our species of resources, we'll retaliate to save ourselves. No one should take our possessions. What is the point of living? Unlike you, we aren't capable of traveling off our planet."

Jewel is reminded of the ships they arrived in by Cokiko. "*In the hangers-on floor 200, there are massive vessels loaded with all the resources we could have ever needed."*

Jewel acknowledges and goes on, "Yes, you came in ships. It would take us decades for all of humanity to reach extreme light speed. But to meet incredible speeds to outrun the enemy is beyond our scope of survival at this time. If we try to fight this enemy or conquer them, it would be like hitting a blocked wall and hardly putting a small dent in several of them. Since they would destroy us from existence, it's not a good idea at this time to worry about that scenario I just mentioned. We would need to defend our grounds with all technologies that we have at our disposal at the time."

The Legendary speaks up on the matter. "*From what I know, they almost conquered us. The truth is that they depleted and took a lot of our resources on the surface of our planet. Many of our resources are below ground for those survivors on our planet, and all we have to do is replenish it back to the surface, which has taken us decades.*"

The Legendary, with sad eyes, continues, "*As for our different animals, we had to repopulate starting from below and spread them throughout the surface. As we fought the enemy, many of my brethren grabbed enormous amounts of food by hand at the surface, like gophers. We take things from the surface and store them underground. That is what we did with many resources. Since we are subterranean creatures, we have to protect ourselves. Otherwise, the Legendaries as we are known would have disappeared without knowledge of our race. The Praetorians came to our aid, yet we know how to fight, but this enemy is very hard. So from what I know or have seen, this enemy has conquered a lot of universes.*"

A tear runs off the Legendary's cheek and he says, "*Your universe was the first universe developed by your God, and other universes followed. From that, it made those universes bearing lands of nothing more than vast wastelands on those planets. That is why there are different creatures mixed with Faloosh's siblings. If these creatures discover that you were the first universe, they will destroy it, and all universes would collapse, causing a domino effect. If they do that, they will wipe themselves out of existence. These creatures want other beings to abide by their laws. They want to be the only universe in all. But they don't know if they will get rid of all universes. So they would eventually destroy all creatures within the outcome.*"

Lucas walks to Jewel to show him something on his tablet. Can you believe this? This information on the tablet shows these creatures have different ways of destroying universes. Just, look at this. It says here that they have a canon the size of five football fields to wipe out an existence on any planet. What do you think of that, Jewel?"

Jewel sneezes for a moment, places his hands on Lucas's shoulders, and puts his head slightly to the right as he slowly says, "The nerve of these creatures. We should take action if they come to Earth. I hope they don't arise because they don't know the human race and our vengefulness. We will find a way to destroy these creatures if it is the last thing the human race does."

Lucas puts both hands on Jewel's shoulder with a serious. "We have these fellow creatures here to help us understand the enemy, prepare for them, and conquer them. Whether a century or a millennium, we have no idea when we would defeat these creatures. However, with their help and guidance, we can eventually triumph against these hoarders of universes. That is why they gave us this technology we have right now, so if we had to flee Earth, it would be possible to save the majority of the human race to fight another day. There will be thousands of years before the enemy even knows of us. We would have had prepared advanced technologies to fight back at the enemy and hopefully conquer them at their own game."

Jewel, wanting to know how long these creatures take to get to a universe, disrupts Wymoym, getting his attention by waving his hands at him. "How long does it take these creatures to get to a universe because they have light speed going about a thousand times the speed of light?"

Wymoym hears him out. "*Well, you see how it takes the speed of light to go through other galaxies.*"

"Yes, go ahead," says Jewel.

Wymoym proceeds further. "*To get to another universe, they have the transcender.*"

In a state of wonder, Jewel asks, "What does this transcender do exactly?"

Wymoym tells his colleagues in the room that it transcends the enemy ships in waves. "*This is like seeing two or three ships going through a universe at once, and what we know so far from our spy is that it takes a regular transcend thousands of years to get to another universe. Their advanced gigawatt transcender takes them with a mirroring image of the ship about two to four weeks to get to a particular universe.*"

Lucas shouts out with extreme amazement, "Two to four weeks! Oh no! We don't have technology like that right now, do we?"

Wymoym explains to the scientist, "*We don't have technology like this either.*" Wymoym tells the scientist. "*As an alternative, we have a parakin, which allows us to travel from universe to universe within three years.*"

Lucas suddenly thinks that is impossible. "We are working on increasing the speed of light. So in a few weeks, this enemy would reach any universe with this transcend technology."

Looking at Cokiko as though looking for advice, Cokiko proceeds further with his speech. "*Excuse me, hum, what I am saying is the transcender can pop into any universe at any time according to Faloosh's technology on his ship. When he pops to that universe, whether it takes them two weeks or several months, going to these different galaxies, he will use a superior speed of light to conquer all universes.*"

As Merna flashes of itch, she asks, "How can this speed of light be blended with transcender technology? According to Dr. Lucas's question, how is this technology used for mirroring? How do they see several universes simultaneously, and how is their technology chosen to enter that curious universe they want to conquer? Please, we would like an explanation. Please give us the answer to that. We are waiting patiently."

In response, Wymoym explains beyond all doubt the technology of the transcender. *"Okay, to jump from one universe to another, they have a liquid called zillerion, according to our spy. Zillerion is a cool or cold liquid in a bluish form put into the engine chamber to accelerate the light speed to ten thousand times its speed. An advanced artificial intelligence technology program pinpoints 89 percent of all universes on a chart where the Inquestorians have only gone to maybe forty of them. They are still conquering other universes to build their mass army, in the interim, stealing from worlds as many resources as their kind can get. That is how they jump from one universe to the next. The Inquestorians' smaller cruisers of fighters jump from one galaxy to the next in a few months. Conquering whatever worlds they can capture, any form of life, making sure they mate with the female species that will serve Faloosh and do his bidding and his siblings' biddings."*

Jewel holds his head in his hand, looking down. In an uproar, a few scientists shout about that situation, "We must stop this enemy wreaking havoc on other worlds, eventually conquering and taking over these worlds, especially if they come here! I'm glad you guys are here to help! But the more we know about this enemy, the more I want to eradicate them and obliterate their very existence! So we have to get to their path on this technology fast."

Wymoym tries to calm the scientists by gently waving his paws at them as several scientists are outraged. Finally, Wymoym puts his mitts on his chin, begins to ponder for a minute, and gradually catches himself to what is going on in the room. *"Please calm down, calm down, everyone, let's get back on track here. Be quiet! Please, thank you."*

Once the scientists hear Wymoym screaming, they calm down and quickly start paying attention. But Jewel is still captivated by the speed of light at ten thousand. It has his mind boggled a bit as he slightly bends his shoulder toward John and looks toward Lucas. "Wow, ten thousand times the speed of light, is that even possible?"

John shrugs his shoulder back to his chair, gently pulls himself upright, then sighs for a minute as he looks at Jewel and says, "I guess, I mean, hey, as Cokiko says, we are lucky to do a hundred times the speed of light, and we are just hitting ten times the speed of light. Besides, who knows, if we will reach that speed in a millennium to get to that speed? I have no idea."

Jewel is unsure what kind of language is coming out of his mouth. "Sheesh! Canaliculus, we have no channel outlet, John! If something were to happen on Earth, how would it affect things? We can observe other planets, analyze other galaxies, and explore other galaxies in record time. However, in light of our Earth's depletion and the fact that we do not know where else to go, we would probably need ship designs to leave the planet. The process of building these ships would probably take hundreds of years. Whenever that occurs, we will need to travel at least one thousand times the speed of light to reach other galaxies in record time."

John tries to listen to Wymoym and turns back to Jewel. "Yes, most definitely."

Jewel turns toward Wymoym and says, "We are a baby race. Why would they come and conquer us anyway? Minerals! Water! Please! There is a lot of that throughout other universes. So why come to our territory!"

The Legendary turns to Jewel. It reiterates from earlier, "*Remember, by way of our spy, they have come to find out Earth, a baby race, will learn new technology. This enemy who wants to destroy technology is preparing itself against the human race as a threat to their race of existence. Their goal is to destroy the baby race before it becomes an adult race. Their main objective is to destroy the human race.*"

"Man, oh man," says Jewel. Then taking a breath. "These guys are dangerous. We have nothing on Earth comparable to what the enemy has on the ship looking at this virtual screen. These guys look like they have superior weaponry. They have a weapon that looks similar to an M16 but much bigger."

Looking at the holographic monitor, the Legendary points with an invisible wand and says, "*This weapon here! It shoots lightning, not lasers. People would be burned flat by this. In their language, the ultimate weapon is a demolition destroyer, which would shatter your neighbors' homes into dust in a blink of an eye. You tell me if they wanted to conquer the human race, they would annihilate the Earth in hours, and not one thing on Earth would be alive, not even in the waters.*"

"What!" exclaims Merna. "No creatures living in the water. How is that possible? This weapon sounds like a disaster for sea creatures."

Wymoym reiterates, "They have a mass destruction weapon containing poisonous gases. When it touches water, everything in the water dies off, turning to filaments of dust, just drifting away like wet dust. All living creatures in the water would be no more."

"Oh my god," replies Lucas. "This is like a fantasy. I hope these creatures don't recognize our Earth and that we're the ancestors."

The Praetorian looks at a tiny computer on its wrist and, with an alarmed voice, says, *"I got bad news for you all."* All the scientists look at each other with fear in their eyes and shocked looks on their faces, as though their facial expressions show hysteria, wanting to know what the bad news is and if it is terrifying news. Wymoym eventually gives the information.

The Legendary reports, "*The bad news is, according to our links, the enemy is definitely within our solar system. With recent news in the last twenty minutes from our trajectory program, I have looked upon Cokiko's wrist computer. They've been here for months now.*"

Merna turns and looks at Penny, eyes wide open. "What the hell are we going to do when these creatures are already here. Since they are here, it will cause mass hysteria throughout Earth. Nobody will be able to survive these creatures."

Penny grabs Merna's hands and, with a friendly smile, says, "I know. I have no idea what we're going to do, either. We might as well live underground as the Legendaries do."

With looks of shock, all scientists drop their jaws with dismay at what this implies. As a result of this imminent threat, the scientists' families and the entire globe are in danger.

CHAPTER 20

THE LURKING ENEMY FROM ABOVE

Legendary Wymoym walks back and forth as he proceeds to educate the scientists and others in the room about the coming doom. "*Since we know they are here right now, let's hope they made a slipup or mistake on their chart system and are unaware that they are within the Milky Way galaxy. Since they are hovering above the Earth, an artificial computer on Cokiko's wrist from the riff says that the Inquestorians are locating Earth. But unfortunately, we have no recourse or any new technology regarding weaponry that can help humanity ward off these creatures. So in that regard, we must prepare society for a possible war. So we're teaching you these technologies to prepare your race to flee, if possible, to save humanity. Now do you understand what we are trying to communicate to you?*"

All the scientists acknowledge by saying yes throughout the auditorium. Then, Cokiko takes over and explains what the enemy's laws are and the details of them. He goes through some rules the enemy has that disturb the human race.

The first rule Cokiko mentions is "*Now their laws are something to worry about because their laws are the opposite of anything good. For instance, let me tell you about their most treacherous laws. If their enemy doesn't comply with their standards, they will slowly torture them in different chambers.*"

Merna thinks to herself first, then she comments on the issue at hand, "What kind of torture can it possibly be? We have things we do in our army if we need to get information from the enemy. We torture them by putting a cloth on their mouth as we pour water over it to get information, it is close to drowning them. We also torture them by cutting their fingers off if they don't comply. What kind of tortures do these aliens use?"

Cokiko, moving the holographic wavy screen in front of him with his paws from left to right, pops up a picture of the horrific torture chambers. On the virtual screen slides, we see some compartments that are inhumane to our human race. Cokiko explains to them, "*These tortures are frequent with burning lasers and some that disintegrate a being. Torture may regenerate an alien's body, then deteriorate the alien being until they constantly receive information from the alien. They have technologies that are beyond this world.*"

Merna looks at Lucas. "That doesn't seem too far away from what we do. Of course, they have different tortures as well."

Cokiko carries on. "*They have tortures of games. We will get into that later. Let me go ahead and tell you some of the laws they have.*"

In the meantime, the scientists sit there and listen clearly as Cokiko continues, "*The different rules they have are if a warrior or enemy refuses Faloosh. The overlord Faloosh and his siblings and their offspring are the leaders of all their creatures. If any beast refuses to worship Faloosh or his family members, that creature is either banished or killed.*"

Lucas scratches behind his left ear and says, "Banish doesn't seem too bad, but killed, hmm, that is absurd. If we don't pick a president, does society go crazy, or do we, ah, you know, we do have ways of impeaching our president, but we don't banish him or anything like that, and he doesn't kill us if we don't pay our taxes. It's bizarre and just plain nuts."

"*You have to understand,*" Cokiko replies, "*these are not humans. They are aliens. First of all, they don't give a crap about how they manage their laws. They have the overlord Faloosh, their leader, and he has key players that know what to do. If they don't comply, he banishes them instead of killing them.*" Cokiko talks about the subsequent law regarding females. "*The overlord's females raise them to be mated from birth because they are born from an Inquestorian's bloodline.*"

Cokiko, a bit teary-eyed, says, "*For females to give birth to children, they must mate with warriors, as all male babies are born to be warriors. The third law reflects that all males will submit to the overlord and his offspring, so if the overlord has ten or fifteen offspring, they must submit to them. Faloosh, the leader to his siblings and his progeny, is down the hierarchical level of the family structure, where the last offspring has minor leadership compared to the rest. In the fourth law, if they are traders, they are put into in the torture chambers, where various dangerous games are present. According to their leader and home world, I know about ten laws, and they must already have over twenty-five. These four laws are the basis of their lifestyle. The last law I will talk about is the tenth law. As I said earlier, there are over twenty-five laws.*

"*These few laws are the most natural for them. The other laws are gruesome. The tenth law states that a creature used in the game will determine whether a warrior survives or dies in a maze traveling through it. If they make it through a maze, they stay another day to worship Faloosh. Otherwise, the creatures tear apart the warriors that don't make it. So any questions regarding these laws?*"

"Hmm," states Lucas. "We have laws that keep us from, you know, going berserk on each other. With their laws, you know they have, I guess, their defiable laws."

"*So, ah,*" Cokiko speaks on, "*let me tell you about their hideous games, the games of choice. According to the Legendary that died to get information, he mentioned some of their games. For instance, a game called the ogala spirit is also called the phantom race.*"

Cokiko cringes on the viewing of the creatures he's about to mention, saying, "*The beasts in this game have seven feet with wings similar to a gargoyle with see-through skin, sharp claws, faces that look leathery of an alien being, and a body full of scales. The scales are gray and black, with a tinge of light blue through its upper body. Their prey is transformed into frightful dark worlds as they drain their blood of their life-force. While attempting to change the spirit lingering in an unknown realm, Faloosh keeps the limbered body within a frozen tomb. However, once a creature survives the horrific game, its body and soul are devoured quickly. The beast spirit will tell Faloosh on his mapped charts its location. Whether it be on a conquered world or a new world will be Faloosh's new destination where he sends out one family member and a ton of soldiers to seek and destroy or submit and worship his family, eventually Faloosh. But if it is a new world that has not been tampered with, Faloosh makes it his priority to have that new world worship him by conquering it and mixing his DNA with a new species for a stronger army.*" Cokiko trembles as his knees knock. "*Here is a game that I think is ridiculous. It's called the glass container. This game is similar to chess. It uses giant water tanks, except there are two notable alien species with eight rows of teeth.*"

Cokiko tries to cover his eyes when viewing these creatures on the holographic board, says, "*Body like a serpent and wings for swimming fast. The game's object is the sole survivor. Enemies go into see-through glass containers on a see-through glass platform. If the enemy falls into the water, that enemy becomes devoured by the giant creature.*"

Lucas looks at Cokiko, saying, "I would never want to be in that game. It's a 99 percent consumption with a 1 percent survival rate. You have to be the lone survivor compared to those other contestants."

Cokiko shows a means chart. "*Yes, that is right. If you are fighting against your friends, you must be that survivor if you want to live. Let me continue, and the next game is called the flying guillotine. The game works in a giant arena with a long twisted runway that goes for miles. The game's object is to make it out of the maze without getting hit by the creature's razor-sharp claws, which can slice a body in half. The creature hunting the prey is a winged alien with sharp claws on its winged tips. If an enemy survives this creature, they will either get to choose to worship Faloosh, or be tortured through a miniature guessing game to serve his siblings for the rest of theier lives.*"

A point of view is taken, regarding the Inqestorians' heinous games, as Cokiko further speaks about them, "*The Inquestorians' beast are near and dear to their five hearts. Mudslingers are their featured pets. This creature resembles a massive frog with midsize arms, a colossal bottom jaw, and an enormous tongue that slushes around the mud and slowly swallows its prey. They have short bodies with three legs. The object of this game is for the target to find weapons within the mud to ward off the creatures. The creatures, at times, will sling mud in the arena to locate through heat signature within the heated soil to find their prey. The weapon would have to lodge within the creature's mouth with a ten-second timer for the target to survive. They are eventually exploding the beast from the inside out.*

"*On the other hand, the mudslinging creature has a hammer tail. When the prey is stuck, it can cripple it for a while so the mudslinger can quickly sloop its target up within the mud. There you have it. I've told you a few games close to the Inquestorians' hearts. There are a lot more games on their ship. They also form games on conquered planets as well.*"

Cokiko waves at Wymoym, who charts the holographic board with invisible pegs, says, "*The best and most dangerous, devious game on any planet they use is the hunt. It features the last resort of creatures called the Inquestorians' body-guards. They are vicious and have no mercy whatsoever. In other words, they may toy with you and then devour you if caught.*"

Scientist John looks at himself then, Jewel. "Bodyguards! What would they need bodyguards for?"

Jewel says out loud, "Why would they need them? That's absurd!"

Cokiko shows a picture of the Inquestorians' bodyguard. A silenced crowd is in the room as fear drives over their eyes that are wide open, and the crowd is silenced in the room. Cokiko clarifies why Faloosh has bodyguards.

"*These bodyguards help Faloosh and his warriors to conquer the galaxies. One bodyguard can take out an entire planet by itself.*"

Merna flinches in her seat as though feeling a wave of uncomfortable heat coming over her body after seeing what these bodyguards look like and can't imagine the destruction they can accomplish. Then with their significant exterior armored skin. She proclaims in a soft tone at Cokiko, "How do we defeat a thing like that? It looks impossible."

Cokiko, with an unlined look on his face, says. "*The good thing you said that this is where the human race comes in to defeat these creatures of impossibility. It's why we are hoping throughout years from now to beat them by their own game. it would be your hybrids that bring them down in the future. Faloosh's bodyguards and his siblings offspring we haven't seen in action within our history. We understand that these bodyguards have leathery skin that is impermeable, a head that looks like a helmet, big stocky arms with stocky hands, strong legs, and huge feet to stomp their grounds. They love to smash, crash, slam, and throw things. The game's object is to outsmart these creatures and either dive or burrow small water holes where the prey can climb out of when the beings don't notice them so that they can go to a safer location where the bodyguards can't get through. These are all the games in detail that our spy located on the Inquestorians' holographic computers. So in all, these are their laws and their violent games. Do you have any questions?*"

John puts up his hands with a very subtle statement. "What kind of games would they make us do if caught?"

Cokiko comments on John's question, "*They probably would choose the game that other captured prey have gone through, a game of death traps. The only way out would be to banish or worship Faloosh and his siblings or be slain. That is all for now. We can move onto the stage by getting up from our seats and dragging into the other room to discuss our female counterparts further.*"

All the scientists gently get out of their seating arrangements along with the dignitaries and soldiers. Minutes later, they now enter another featured advanced technological room. The scientists and others are seated in a dark room as the computer pulls up a holographic screen with the details enclosed. Cokiko proceeds further.

While Cokiko proceeds, a black entity is just waiting in a corner. The scientist has no idea what that entity is in the corner or what it is. The scientists and others are in the process of sitting down. A picture pops up on the holographic screen of a particular species within the Inquestorians. Cokiko starts to talk, pulling the microphone on his head closer to his mouth with his left hand.

Cokiko speaks, "*Ladies and gentlemen, fellow beings, I would like to tell you more about this species, but I will let my fellow partner, Wymoym, tell you more in detail. Please, Professor Wymoym.*"

Professor Wymoym approaches the platform to tell more about the holographic creature at hand. "*This creature that you are seeing is called an Inquestorian. Let me explain something. Once the Inquestorians conquer a universe or planets in that universe, the female species mate with the warriors. Unfortunately, this is how the Inquestorians increased their army. First of all, Faloosh's main queen, who he had conquered within his first universe, had taken her as his mating partner, or may I say, his child-bearer. The queen's name is Bamoosh. She and her daughters and female siblings of Faloosh all maintain the entities of other females from other universes they have conquered. The other females of these conquered planets become like maidens to the conquered females from these other universes. So what happens is the females enter a room containing several of Faloosh's head warriors who then begin to mate with these females as Faloosh chooses each couple.*"

Wymoym, with a stern look, focuses on all in the room, says, "*Other warriors get a mate with them in the long run, and Faloosh male offspring usually gets first pickings. At times you would hear screams coming from the rooms. The females are suited for these warriors by Faloosh and his queen. They only mate with the strong females from these universes that they conquered. The main ingredient to making strong males and females is to weed out the weak ones first. Depending on the different planets, these females are mated with the male warriors and Faloosh offspring for weeks, months, or even years until the female is pregnant. The male continues their daily task around the ship as the females are cared for by Bamoosh maidens. Once impregnated, the females put the younglings into an incubator in a nanny chamber. Once born, the offspring of the strong warriors, especially the male babies, enter another secret room called gatlent. Now the gatlent is a vessel where future warriors with skill training are bred at a young age to fight in Faloosh army.*"

Merna looks at Penny with a troubled look. "Why would it take years when it takes us a month to ovulate to get pregnant?"

Wymoym tries to narrow it down. "*You see, each female from each planet within each universe depending on their composition depends on how long it takes them to get pregnant. Inquestorians have no idea how long it takes these females to have babies. During intercourse, the babies drop out of some alien species, and some maidens have to rush in to grab the baby and take it to the incubator room. At times, Faloosh and his team of interrogators interrogate the male species conquered to get more information on their female vulnerability regarding getting pregnant. The Inquestorians learn from the interrogation about the alien females through the female's composition anatomy makeup. Faloosh's queen, Bamoosh, and Faloosh's female siblings and other females on board cater to these pregnant females with food and what, at times, are considered special drinks that these females are treated as queens on board for the continuation of Faloosh army. When the females are bred and impregnated, Bamoosh and the other females cater to the pregnant female to understand their conquered planet's ways. They make sure they have a good pregnancy, clothe them, bathe them, and even slap, rub, and chant Faloosh ways to the unborn infant. For instance, they chant bongo songs to them. These songs are loud and strange, making the pregnant female sleep so that the unborn infant stands firm in their stomach listening to them. The babies stay in the incubator area for years until they are the right age to play evil games and roll among each other, doing hurtful games like pulling ears and legs until it hurts.*"

Wymoym notices the women in the room start to feel hot with sweat and says, "*If there seem to be good ones in the bunch, which is very odd, it will play having fun and crying when it is not having fun. When they get to a certain age, the male babies enter a young warrior arena, training for the battle for Faloosh's army. Raised with their battle instinct is very helpful because they have the instinct of Faloosh's home world regarding destroying things in their path. These male babies train in the Inquestorians' ways, making them even more fierce to battle against them. The training is very harsh, with evil intentions mostly. The young warriors are banished or put them in horrific games, of course, if their hearts are full of goodness, which rarely happens within Faloosh newborns. If they survive those games, they will allow them to worship Faloosh and his siblings and offspring. So as I move on—*"

"Excuse me," says Lucas, "what happens to the babies that are stillborn or are mongoloids?"

Cokiko turns to Lucas with a horrifying disdainful look.

CHAPTER 21

WHAT IS HEINOUSLY INVOLVED

Wymoym slowly moves his eyes to the dark corner, where there is a figure standing there as he has a blank look on his face trying to answer such a question. "*Well, ah, let me tell you. Hmm. Since I have no idea of that, I have someone here that can tell you more about the female species of the enemy and how or what happens to those types of babies, whether they be stillborn, rejected, or even thrown away. So please let me introduce, with no further ado, the professor.*"

Of course, she is a female Legendary, and it is all of the scientists' first time seeing her.

"*Please welcome Venush. Would you please come forward?*"

The scientists begin to clap loudly as they slowly see the dark entity moving from the corner toward the platform. Their clapping begins to diminish as the dark entity slowly comes out of the dark corner, strutting her body back and forth as though in a Ms. Universe pageant contest. The female alien approaches the platform slowly, brushing into Wymoym's right side. She timidly grabs the microphone to adjust to her comparatively small body as she begins to introduce herself in a sultry voice.

"*Huh, hum, I want to thank you all for meeting with me this evening. As Professor Cokiko left off. Well, as he was saying—*"

Lucas interrupts, "Ah, ma'am, or Professor Venush."

Professor Venush responds, "*Yes, ah, Dr. Lucas, right?*"

Lucas acknowledges, "Yes, that's right. What happens to stillborn, retarded ones, and so forth?"

Venush tells the scientists what the Inquestorians do with those types of babies. "*These babies are either fed to the creatures on board as snacks, or the Inquestorians use them as food. The Inquestorians suck their life energy out of them and harness these energies extracted from them. In turn, this gives the young war-*

riors additional strength. Furthering this information, I would like to explain some of the other things they do. What the den mothers do if a baby has trouble with speech or some unparticular body structure that is uncommon to the Inquestorians is that the den mothers then deem them unique. Regarding the are males, they put them in special warrior groups as a unit like tactic scouts that may pick off the enemy strong points."

Venush brushes back her luscious hair and says, "*The females look upon them as beauty within the Inquestorians' mating rituals. At birth, the Inquestorian females are matched up with certain young male warriors of age for mating purposes in the future. It's not the same as Faloosh assigning his head warriors to mate with a conquered species. Once pregnant, those babies are given from birth a male to a female for future mating rituals. As they would say, you would marry a woman in some of your cultures before meeting her. It's the same scenario. The Inquestorians don't marry, but the females' den mother match themale counterparts from birth.*"

Venush smiles and quivers a bit as though nervous as she speaks and says, "*One last thing I want to leave you with before I go on, especially with the female DNA, is to conclude that the birthing rights of the male and females are divided. At times several warriors can have the same female at once. If an alien youngling dies from an illness, the den mothers either care for the young one, giving it medicines, and if not able to revive, it is given to the beast on board for consumption, but before that, they drain the life force from them, giving it to the young male warriors.*"

Venush looks upon the holographic screen with abhor and says, "*The purpose of the Inquestorians' blood is compelling and overcoming compared to other species' DNA. Their DNA, especially their blood cells, seem to take over other aliens' DNA, transforming them into odd creatures for Faloosh. Using those alien instincts with theirs in combat would significantly make Faloosh's army stronger. The aliens will lose their vitality if they reject those with Faloosh DNA and their bodies are consumed by the creatures aboard. The Inquestorians want strong females only, not weak ones. The vulnerable females are also there for warriors' pleasures before their life force diminishes her. Faloosh wants his DNA among all universes because he wants those who are already trained in his ways to spread throughout the cosmos, worshipping Faloosh and keeping up with his laws, abiding by them. Faloosh's objective, the birthing of the males and females, has a division where the female den mothers take care of the female babies, and the male warriors take care of the males when they have come of age.*"

Venush proceeds with caution and says, "*Meanwhile, the females may cater to the male infants for the first twelve months or however long regarding different conquered species, feeding them nourishing with food and maintaining their vital health before transferring. When the babies are teenagers, they learn the powerful ways of being a warrior, fighting each other in an arena to prove their loyalty to Faloosh. They are different arenas on the ship for the teenagers continuing training and all warriors on board. Suppose a teenager shows weakness and doesn't turn around with strength from their spiritual energies. That teenager in this specific case, their powers are gradually absorbed by the next strongest teen warrior, and their lifeless bodies become food to the creatures on board. Our objective, along with the Praetorians, is to make sure this doesn't happen in the future as we fight the Inquestorians. As you would say, God willing, or I would say Ouna, which is my god. These species have evil intent that comes upon them. In reality, they don't know how to react on their own without Faloosh. We want to maintain the Praetorian ways and keep the peace, so we're praying for victory in the future. We need humanity to form these hybrid species among different universes. If your female hybrids were to be caught by Faloosh, they might turn a lot of warriors around to have a good heart. We would never know unless we tried. It is more like, let me say, hum, you know when you have red ants that the queen mainly controls basically?*"

"Yes, yes," says Jewel. "What about that? What does that do with what we are trying to accomplish here?"

Venush continues, "*Let me say, Dr. Jewel, right?*"

Jewel acknowledges, "That is right."

Venush proceeds, "*When you have a queen, and that queen was to die, the workers are confused.*"

Jewel is trying to see where Venush is going with this. "Yes, what is this about then? If this concerns Faloosh, doesn't he have his siblings and offspring to be worried about too?"

Venush agrees, "*Except, then what if we disrupted Faloosh's operation, having hybrids inside for years and centuries, and all their offspring exhibit goodness? If not, those hybrids of the Inquestorians would either enslave the offspring, banish them, capture them, imprison them, or even kill them. If the amalgams were to take their side, we would be dealing with chaos. Let's hope it doesn't get to that. What if our objective was to get rid of all evil intent? One of our goals is to get to that situation if possible. If not, we are all doomed if they take over. Their DNA is a dark sentiment of reddish, blackish, bluish slicing that takes other alien DNA by its stronghold. That is why they're the evilest creatures throughout all universes. But we, with the Praetorians, must overpower them. We will eventually, with the help of the hybrids. I want to talk to you about what happens mainly to the male species if they don't comply. As I am sure you heard from Cokiko that if they don't comply, they either get killed, banished, or eaten by creatures within the games. Dealing with their crazy stupid laws, I want to talk more about the male species not complying. As our spy was trying to understand these creatures, he found out what happened next from the intel he had gathered on their ship. The truth is that they represent more of a threat to our cause than an ally, finds out they are species of danger? He also discovered what they do on planets they conquered after the battle."*

Venush tries to finish her speech on the evil creatures and says, "*Once captured, the enemy species must bow down to Faloosh as servants. Again, if an enemy doesn't comply, the Inquestorians begin to play the mind and warrior games that Cokiko told you earlier. These games aren't on the ship. Most of the games are on the conquered planets. These games that they have are like war games. They have a big game that deals with land, water, and air tactics. But let me tell you a couple of their insidious games, which are just raunchy. For instance, if they don't comply with the Inquestorians' laws, they are put into a furnace chamber, a massive chamber that they bring out of the ship that storms and blows up the planet's sediments, dust, or sand dirt. It seems to blind you, and it's called the chamber of fire is because it is so windy with fighters in it that it looks like an octagon-shaped chamber. When fighting in this chamber, you are fighting your opponent along with the blowing debris around it. Usually, for an odd reason, if victorious against the warriors, the victor then has to worship Faloosh. Or if refused, leaving them on their planet for dead."*

Venush is a little impatient, continues with details about the enemy, "*Very few had survived this game. Some of our scouts that escaped Faloosh ships have landed on these planets to see if certain species are left alive. Reports to the Praetorians who had attempted to know their intentions at that moment were not aware until later on. The Inquestorians have a weapon that turns any terrain into a forming environment of their choice. If the Inquestorians had found survivors, they would either annihilate them by absorbing their souls or somehow eliminate them. Disabled aliens who survived the games were sometimes buried in quicksand by the Inquestorians. If they were weak, they were either left to fend for themselves or had their life force taken away. The fragile survivors can rebuild themselves if they survive and find survivors on their planet."*

Venush sees the last of her holographic slides, and says, "*Hopefully, we are striving to find survivors on these vast deserted planets to implement the hybrids and other alien DNA. Then, we can train the new amalgams and specialized DNA from that planet. In the long run, we have a new type of hybrid that we can qualify within the new environments, transforming these new hybrids to withstand anything that would be better than their ancestors. In turn, it will ward off the Inquestorians in later battles. Hybrids eventually come together to create an ultimate force with mixtures throughout each universe.*"

Cokiko comes to the pulpit to explain another heinous game. Cokiko gauges a bit. "*There is a game similar to hide and seek. Only through their sense of smell can these intelligent creatures locate their prey if you hide underground. They have several nostrils that smell clean, dirty or heat signatures on a target.*

"*They can see for distances because they have many eyes and one big eye that generates or retracts like a scope. If the creature senses you, they send an ear-aching sound to make you rustle around to seek you out, making the prey scream in its alien voice. When they find you, they use one of their stingers on you, snatching you up, numbing your entire body, or drugging you with their highly toxic venom. They also can destroy the prey if Faloosh gives the order.*"

Incredibly, Beth has not spoken since she learned how the enemy operates, but she shouts out, "Stingers, stingers, who cares! Since these cretins have studied us for months, we only care about knocking them flat and ending their existence. Preparation is crucial. I don't particularly appreciate living on the edge of knowing our human existence may vanish without hope. Give me a break and move on already!"

To calm the scientist, Yarmin pleads, "Please, Dr. Beth, do not be so hostile to us!"

Beth looks over at Yarmin with a bit of a cold shiver but seems to calm down as though she had a hot flash.

Yarmin senses Beth's cold shoulder, brushes it off with a kind look, and says, "Why the destruction? Why kill beings off these planets? For what reason would that gain us by demolishing a creature or creatures from existence? Wouldn't we then become as evil as the enemy?"

Merna looks at Penny in disbelief. "Weren't you listening? They want to dominate all universes and enslave others to worship Faloosh, eliminating any other species' lifestyle but only to know Faloosh's lifestyle. There are planets full of beings that we don't know anything about right now. I'm just shaking my head. I can't understand this at times."

Cokiko notes things on his wrist computer that tells more about Faloosh. "*Faloosh, ah, I feel your pain. With regards to your race, which is the baby race. You're the only universe that we must save its people from being conquered. I want to tell you we will do everything to protect your race.*

"I would also like to discuss why they enslave the males. The enslaved beings not only worship Faloosh but also they do the spring cleaning of the entire ship and take care of the warriors."

Inputting his details while talking, Cokiko recognizes the voice on the holographic tablet, and this is what he says: "*The different enslaved beings are like waiters to Faloosh and his men providing food, hors d'oeuvres that are either dead or moving on the bright glowing plates. Occasionally they hold special performances in front of Faloosh, such as singing, juggling, or a cruel joke. Jumping and skipping over coals that feel hot to the touch make Faloosh giggle. There is a higher level of mating among the more relaxed females. Worshipping Faloosh isn't required. However, having babies is a necessity. If an enslaved being dishonors Faloosh, he rejects them, sending them to the games. Sometimes for entertainment, especially if he doesn't care for that species's weakness. If they are strong, they worship Faloosh, and he loves worshipping. He likes to party, which a party to them is called a Jesup, when young women dance and sing for him. If some enslaved males don't say good jokes, Faloosh throws them in a glass pit below to see them struggle to fight against the creatures below.*"

Cokiko's eyes becomes tired and droopy as he continues, "*Faloosh has an interpreter who can interpret any language, except if he is unsure of an alien language, the interpreter may try to solve it in a broken language format. He may make Faloosh laugh because it may translate as a cruel joke or an evil compliment. translates it. The enslaves of Faloosh and male followers, females, warriors, and youngsters, when they are in the presence of Faloosh, have to bow down to him before going on about their busy days. Faloosh, at times, may put his giant hands out front to be kissed by most crew members except his siblings and offspring. The enslaved beings and some warriors cater to Faloosh's family members when needed to do a task. For example, if Faloosh's sister asks a warrior to hit a baby so it would stop crying, she would hold the baby and kick one of the warriors in his behind to get his attention to slap the baby to stop crying while she cradles it. Some warriors pick on the more diminutive warriors, making fun of them, pushing them around, and tripping them up."*

Cokiko feels a bit of relief after getting through the speech, saying, "*Sometimes Faloosh's queen, Bamoosh, would hit the bullying warriors on their heads, making them look at Bamoosh with fear upon their faces. All in all, this is what Faloosh's terms are with his species. Do you have any other questions for me?"*

A bit relieved, Jewel sighs, putting down his invisible pen tablet on his right side after taking notes. In contrast, the small pen shape instrument shuts down this holographic display. "Yeah, I don't have any questions, but I would like to know if there are female warriors among them, or do they not allow that?"

Venush, with politeness, says, "*That's a good question. It is unheard of, as many female creatures are similar to the bodyguard. These female creatures may come out in a battle once in a blue moon, especially if Faloosh's fourth wave and bodyguards seem to lose ground. These female bodyguards are slender and quick. Their slim bodies can move between crevices of walls and creases. They are a couple of feet shorter than the male bodyguards."*

Venush stretches the story and says, "*They also squeeze their prey to squash their insides out, taking their life force. These creatures are wretched and have no mercy, whereas the bodyguards may have little compassion. At least they don't squeeze you until to the point of dying. With no awareness of how or what is the exact idea of how these female creatures look or their composure, we have never seen one. We know of its tales. If this creature happens to come across centuries from now, we might not have any idea of how to defeat these creatures. We would never know until then. It's almost like a myth, a legend to the Inquestorians warriors. According to the onboard spy, none have ever seen these creatures. This female creature might be the mother to all the bodyguards or can be a set of female bodyguards that Faloosh may be hiding for centuries until the right time that they are needed. Remember, Faloosh himself is a giant creature, of course, the biggest of them all. This female of all females may be the offspring of the first world he conquered. To beat Faloosh from our intel, we wondered how it could be done. In the name of Ouna."*

Merna senses the name of a weird word called Ouna and calls out to Venush with curiosity, "I know you had mentioned this before, so how did your deity Ouna come about?"

Venush puts it lightly as she gives a little history of the name. "*Rasheen, my dear doctor, was a male warrior who wanted all the females to serve him as long as the males were born from the females. He would kill all males who were not strong enough or couldn't produce strong bloodlines to have a strong army of warriors. His ultimate goal was to make sure the males of the planet would see him as the only God to serve, but Camosh, a goddess, would behead this dark lord, turning all the males' and females' hearts to goodness instead of doing evil things. She is the protector of our species. That is why we wear this glowing emblem around the leader's neck of the legendaries within our ribbed skin just below our hearts."*

Merna begins to see similarities between Faloosh and the dark lord Rasheen and, with her intelligence, puts two and two together. "Isn't it ironic that Faloosh has similarities to Rasheen? Can it be that your myth can be a reality? Is it possible?"

Venush eyes Merna and says, "*You know, Dr. Merna, that rarely hits my thoughts, but it is a curiosity that needs further investigation. You know this may lead to a direction of some sort. Thanks, Doctor.*"

Merna looks upon Venush and points her hands toward her with two thumbs up as she winks at her.

Venush continues, "*We will defeat this enemy if it takes us millenniums beating Faloosh, his siblings, and offspring to help make universes peaceful again. Now, that is a big task. First, we must get the hybrid humans who will eventually be from different worlds throughout different universes. The Praetorians, and we will protect you from any doom that may come our way while we see humanity mix with other species from different worlds where those will be our fighters in this fight to bring peace. Since they are here already, from what we know, they are gearing to properly find Earth according to their computers, where they found it but it could be a hiccup on their technological systems.*"

The Praetorians and Legendaries educate everyone in the room on a sense of somberness, and Venush proceeds. "*I will assure you from the Praetorians' solar system, and they have no creature or beast that has ever come close to becoming an enemy to them. That is because you already know their homeworlds and galaxies are invisible to all others, except them. The Praetorians have a cloaking membrane with footsteps as quiet as a piece of cotton lying on soft flooring. That is all for now from my end, and I will return the floor to Cokiko. Cokiko, please.*"

Cokiko grabs the mic as he begins to dismiss all. "*It was a pleasure meeting the new doctors and speaking with everyone. That is all for now. You may exit and proceed with your daily duties.*"

Everyone claps. Cokiko and Venush mingle with the doctors, dignitaries, diplomats, and Wymoym, Yufer, and Snuff. They all exit the room and head back to an advanced scientific laboratory, where some Legendaries and Praetorians put together equipment. Legendaries and Praetorians have to get the scientists ready for the alleged attack upon the Earth from the Inquestorians, based on the technology they gained from their ships recently.

CHAPTER 22

SCIENTISTS CONVEY MANKIND'S HOPE

Cokiko, Venush, Wymoym, some Legendaries, Praetorians, Yufer, and Snuff are walking alongside the diplomats and dignitaries with the scientists putting the final pieces together in the new advanced lab. As the scientist, with the Legendaries and Praetorians, put the final pieces together, one of them is programming its last commands into the computer systems. The only thing the program does not have in its calculations is the Praetorians' home worlds or universe location. The Praetorians have cloaking ships that allow them to escape through the Milky Way galaxy, returning to their universe faster than the speed of light. If the Inquestorians attack, all of this should help humanity. Yufer draws immense attention from other scientists, even those already taught about the Inquestorians and what to expect from them. The program will translate what it is supposed to do for all species recognized by the program, including cloning, projected destinations for humanity, and the number of legendaries for each destination and Praetorians.

Seeing Gale busy working at the cloning computers, Yufer yells to her as she has headphones on and is immensely engrossed in her work. "Dr. Gale, Dr. Gale!" Yufer throws a paper her way, and Gale gets a glimpse of it as it flies by her. Gale removes her headphone and turns her head forty-five degrees to the left with eyebrows raised.

"Who threw that!"

Yufer yells at Gale, "Gale! Dr. Gale! Please!"

Gale finally pulls the headphones off her neck and puts them on the counter. Then, she turns around and says, "Yes, yes."

Yufer is delighted that he got Gale's full attention. "Thank you. As you all know, we must prepare for any embedded doom that may come upon us. What the

Praetorians and Legendaries have done for us was to prepare us for what is to come upon us. We so far have advanced technologies from the Praetorians. Hopefully, this isn't the sole of the advancement. We're hoping our technology will probably take us centuries, if not millenniums, to accomplish. But, the technology we have for now might be able to fight off the Inquestorians if a war was to take place. So what I want to say is—"

Gale interrupts, "Mr. Yufer, sir?"

Yufer looks at Gale. "Yes, Gale, how can I help you?"

Gale examines a chart through her holographic pen. "Well, where the Praetorians are concerned, the Inquestorians have already crossed over to our world. Their ships have passed through five universes in the invisible layers but have transpired right next to our planet. According to the holographic wrist computer, this has transpired, as earlier mentioned.

Yufer replies to Gale's statement, "Yes, we must prepare right now. There is no sitting down on this. First, I want to take the top scientists to a room immediately."

In addition to Gale, Jewel, Beth, John, Lucas, Merna, and Penny, some Praetorians and Legendaries serve as guides who keep them up-to-date. They travel by trans, like a fast train. The train travels in parallel rather than in a straight line. They all get onto the trans that travels several stories below from where they are. Once the trans reaches level 17, about fifty-eight levels down from the top, the fifty-eighth level is where all their scientific research's primary purposes deal with different trials conducted on the various alien technologies. Among these technologies are warp engines, weapons, spacecraft simulations, and machines to help understand alien life, including their DNA, way of life, terraforms, and anything else that catches the attention of humanity. In that regard, this floor's high-end technology is one hundred and twenty years ahead of present-day people here on Earth. Getting to level 17 of the facility, the Praetorian Cokiko meets his superior, Bunuck, when they enter a dark room with bright glowing lights. Bunuck, seen by scientists and important aliens along with high-end human officials, sitting down floating at a vast rounded table, an enormous, chubby creature, seems to be putting calculations within the air along with other alien entities. The military personnel, diplomats, and dignitaries with the scientists slowly begin to sit while chairs automatically adjust to their postures. Observing the aliens calculating the fate of the Earth with concerned looks, diplomats and dignitaries stare in awe.

An elegant robe-like cape cascades down Bunuck's feet, giving the impression of royalty. In his presentation, he makes himself appear as a king or a ruler of the

Praetorians. Banuck puts his left hand out in a soft tone, telling everyone politely to sit down. "*Please, everyone, sit. We have no time to wait. For what's coming on the Earth will cause your people to have mass hysteria with nowhere to run or hide, so I want to prepare you, but first let me explain.*" From the ship's hall, Banuck pulls up a holographic image. The device's communication protocol allows it to connect with the computer of its mother ship to display the calculations the enemies have already transferred to Earth's universe.

A concerned voice says, "*Ladies, gentlemen, and species, the mother ship and several of her ships above the Earth at this present time are very challenging to our existence, our brethren, the Legendaries, and your entire species right here on Earth. This is very alarming to us right now. Based on the pattern on charts months ago, we could see the elongated object just beyond the scope of these various color arrays. So several months ago, before the enemy showed up that has been studying us for months now, their patterns became transferrable into Earth's realm by way of this key factor of the number of warriors onboard. We have gathered information from our spy systems that the ship measures about twenty football fields long, with trailing ships measuring about three football fields. The various spies had speculated the ship size when they used escape pods to view the ship in space.*"

Merna and Gale, especially Gale, take notes on the issue on their holographic tablet. "If these ships are that huge, I can only imagine how many enemies are onboard. The lack of inquorate humans may cause the enemy to overrun or overrule our species. What do we do in that matter?

Banuck in a calm, settled voice, "*You see, Doctor, the most significant point on that matter is that we Praetorians have an emblem on our chest that cause us to go into cloaking mode when we are in danger. For that matter at hand, Doctor, if a mass attack were to happen, our cloaking that we are born with would cover one football field length, causing those protected within the cloak to be invisible from the enemy until they are in a safe area. The veil would last as long as the Praetorian is moving. Otherwise, it uncloaks them when standing still.*"

Gale tries to interrupt while Banuck is talking. "What about, ah—"

Banuck overrides Gale. "*One other thing you need to know about some of the enemies. Some Inquestorians who cannot see to the side. They have blinders when born, a lot of them within their eyes. In the human, eyes you have the white area of the eyes. However, the Inquestorians have blackness that prevents them from seeing in what we call peripheral vision. They can only see straight forward. The Inquestorians are pretty good with hearing.*"

Gale says, with a severe staring face, "Oh, I know. I'm sure we never knew that."

In frustration, Banuck requests, "*Please, no more interruptions, please, let me proceed further.*"

Yufer tries to tell everyone to focus on Banuck and what he has to say. "Please be seated again. Let Banuck finish what he has to say because it is crucial to us right now. So let's continue this journey of what is supposed to be our plan."

Banuck looks from the left to right at everyone in the room and continues, "*With this enemy, it all depends if they come to conquer or take nutrients for its kind. If they feel Earthlings are a threat, they will try to extinguish your kind. If the enemy thinks you are not a threat, they may study you for a while and ponder whether to enslave you or mate with you. But more or less, if not hostile, they might have an easier way of thinking you could worship their overlord. Well, the technology we had put in the G300, for instance, as you already know, if there is doom upon you Earthlings and if they wipe out your planet, we would have to send your species to other worlds for survival purposes. Transforming Earthlings into many different species or hybrids of those species to keep you all recognized as the planet that carried superior beings.*"

Merna, Jewel, and Lucas say simultaneously, "Well, we would need a way off this planet. Let's go on ships that have advanced technologies. I am sure they would shoot our ships down."

Banuck does not hesitate about the power of the enemy ships. "*Yes, they would shoot down the crafts because they have weapons that shoot faster than the speed of light that would destroy the spacecraft in an instant. They have different weaponry other than lasers.*"

Merna wants to know the other types of weapons that they might have. "Oh, I see. What do these other weapons look like?"

Banuck shows a moving image on the holographic monitor and tells Dr. Merna about two weapons that can cause mass destruction. "*What we have here, doctor, is a few different weapons. This one is called the sonic boom generator, and it operates through heavy metals. If these metals were shot on Earth right now, it would transform into a metallic, heated terrain where Earthlings couldn't handle it. Only Inquestorians can because they are born with no feelings regarding temperature changes or extreme temperatures in their feet or legs. Another weapon is the razor blaster. It fires lasers to destroy ships and break them into pieces. The lasers, coming from the belly of the spaceship, turn the craft into ashes or dust.*"

Banuck switches back to what he was supposed to say. "*We have installed is not only cloning devices or computers that help you clone but also advance technology to help doctors. So what happens, as we have said many times, is that your hybrids will become alien-human hybrids, and with these hybrids will come new advanced technologies developed by them. They will also have special abilities. These can help influence or defeat the Inquestorians. That is our objective here. I want to share with you on this holographic map here what Venush and Cokiko shared with you that I have been mapping out these areas for millenniums of various universes, which are crawling with galaxies and universes.*"

Banuck's ears flicks off a flying bug nearby and says, "*The Inquestorians will not return to a planet they have defeated or conquered and wiped out. They can only find out by sending an ogala spirit creature which is then transformed back to that planet. It signals to the Inquestorians that life may be on that planet again or find out if there is a new type of species to be conquered, building up his army to defeat other beings by substantially holding them by the masses of his creatures. The hybrids will not only going to have the DNA splicing of that planet with the human DNA, but we're going to implement in the future through you doctors here the Praetorian's DNA as well. The reason is that is the Praetorians are stealth-like creatures, tough to detect. Due to the amalgam's beneficial properties, capturing the hybrids would be a problem, as Cokiko had mentioned. Just like in your military, specific soldiers splice with our DNA-making hybrid. They will be warrior-type beings that will go against the Inquestorians. While some humans may not adjust well to alien environments, advanced humans can adapt with the help of cloned doctors. So your clones will do their due diligence to help the vigorous hybrids survive against the weak ones. As a result, they are making hybrid armies more robust and versatile. These hybrids are a few that will try and fight off the enemy, but splicing the human DNA and alien DNA along with Praetorian and Legendary DNA would have a new type of recruits to help fight off the enemy Inquestorians in the long run.*"

Banuck, with a huge smile, says, "*Through the G300 warp machine, each human species will be traveling with their belongings, separating them to different planets through different galaxies and universes.*"

Lucas sighs a bit and asks. "Hum, what do you mean one by one? I don't understand the terminology of transferring a human one by one to a universe. Do you indicate families will separate from their loved ones through the G300 machine, or would their family members be transferred or sent to different planets or universes?"

Banuck, in nonspecialists' terms, gives Lucas the rundown. "*Let me explain what I mean one by one. For instance, if you have your entire family with you, it will split them up. How the G300 portal works is that when you go through it, unless you are hugging each other or holding hands, you will go through it one by one, in which people will divide among the different planets, galaxies, and universes. So you won't see loved ones unless they are offspring or hybrids knowing each other in the future through telepathy or features of the same sort.*"

Lucas catches what Banuck is saying. "Wow! Now that is pretty intense."

Banuck adds, "*There are millions of dimensions beyond your comprehension, which may be home to the Inquestorians. When the Legendaries first contacted the enemy, we had no idea these Inquestorians were threats. A billion millennium years later, the hybrids have conquered many universes. By then, the war continues on the Inquestorians. We plan to either slow them down or eliminate them as they advance so they can no longer endanger numerous species or universes. Ultimately, we hope to overthrow their plans by capturing Faloosh himself and his offspring or siblings and turning them around or eliminating them for good with the hybrids infiltrating the enemy's territory.*"

Banuck turns around as two other Praetorians and a Legendary leader handle some calculations regarding future enemy tactics on a holographic future board. Banuck then introduces another more advanced female Legendary whose mind is silent while calculating probable outcomes. Banuck introduces Mynuck. Mynuck, with quickness, turns around and says in a soft voice, almost like a whisper, relaxing all human individuals in the room with a calming pheromone. The creature has the ability on other species, except on other Legendaries, even as she starts to speak.

"*What I want to tell you all today is very, very concerning. Because the whole universe millions of millenniums ago were peaceful, there was no evil intent. We and all universes lived happily ever after with no threat in sight. We were like the guardians of all universes. We had no idea they were turning to a different way of life toward evil intentions. We didn't know they were coming to our Legendary galaxy. The Legendaries were very peaceful in the past. In the interim, they survived the first stage of their defeat by the Inquestorians. There was also destruction on many of the Legendaries' other planets. They were able to save some of their kind through tunneled underground facilities. This first battle left them with four planets out of the eight, in which the other four got obliterated. Let me tell you all that is in this room. You human species are a chosen race because you're an intelligent baby race. You learn fast when we put technology at your forefront. Your intelligence and abilities these different planets will be a force to be reckoned with in the future. Let me further say what else is involved. These cutting-edge technologies that we have thought the original and cloned doctors in these laboratories here will give a head start on each new world as the hybrids train and develop their new fighting skill techniques. It will help provide to the doctors on these tiny computer chips given to each one of you with an opportunity to study and research over a million different abilities that we've already implemented into the charts."*

"We have put DNA codes for each planet where humans will settle." Mynuck blinks at the holographic page. "In the future, new DNA may be discovered due to the centuries-old research.". Samples put into any future DNA found on those planets will be updated. A selection will provide a specialized program where the amalgam's DNA sequence will upgrade to a centralized holographic data center. It will increase the functionality of that amalgam or hybrids from that point in the future. These hybrids will have the qualities of being peaceful, bringing down anything that might pertain to evil in it. We're hoping to build an army of hybrids to come against the Inquestorians and defeat them off each planet, wherever they may be. What happens is Faloosh, their leader, whenever he conquers a universe, he leaves tens of thousands of his men on those planets. That may or may not be a threat to him. Other planets he leaves are desolated and destroyed with nothing growing on."

Mynuck again blinks, brushes off some lint off of her clothing, and says, "*The terrains we have calculated have none of these armies on them. We're going to train the human race in the field of how to battle this enemy through unique DNA sequencing within each planet that lies beyond each universe, and you will learn how to defend yourselves from this enemy and continue the education of how to battle other evil hybrids within Faloosh's ranks. Let's hope we eventually get this going here. What I want to do now is give the floor back to Banuck."*

Banuck takes over the floor. "*I appreciate your comment, Mynuck, giving us the insight into what our human friends are to expect."*

Merna slides a comment before Banuck can continue. "Excuse me!"

Banuck responds, "Yes!"

Merna blatantly says, "That would be Dr. Merna!"

Banuck feels Merna gives off a sense of a strong woman. "Yes, Dr. Merna, how can I assist you?"

Merna wants to know about the clones. "If we have clones portraying us on these different planets, where will we, the original doctors, be then?"

Banuck enlightens Dr. Merna with the solution. "*We want to keep all you doctors' intelligence at bay. We aim to protect all scientists with all the brilliance of the human race from mishaps involving your species. To prevent their extinction, we must protect them. Therefore, even if the human race is defeated, the Praetorians will protect you via an invisible universe, which cannot be seen only by mere human eyes but by the Praetorians' eyes. The invisible brethren galaxies of our neighborhood will keep the original scientists hidden from all beings.*"

Merna catches what the Praetorians are trying to do with the actual scientists. "Oh, I see. So we would be on your planets."

Banuck knows the scientists seem to be pleased with the outcome. "*Yes, you all will be on our planets within our universe. As new technologies emerge, you will learn about them. The Praetorians and Legendaries will join the clones on these worlds and universes that will allow you to communicate with them.*"

Merna suddenly gets what the Praetorians are trying to do. "So this is how we communicate with the rest of humanity and relay our findings."

Banuck simplifies it. "*Yes, if we need to get more DNA sequences from our Praetorian worlds, we can rely on our Praetorian brothers to get it to the clones, eventually helping the humans and the human hybrids as well.*"

Lucas exclaims, "We're like the presidents of the clones, right?"

Banuck reassures the question. "*That's correct. You are like the liaisons to the different worlds.*" Then, Banuck gets the scientists to follow him. "*Please follow me.*"

It takes everyone about fifteen minutes to get down to level 28 on the trans. When they reach level 28, they get off the trans and enter a glass room lit with a bright blue hue as the light reflects off the bright glare. Several scientists, diplomats, military, and dignitaries circle the room as they look near a hovering platform where a few old elderly aliens are working upon an electrifying impulse. The futuristic holographic board with finger calculations displaying futuristic interactions between beings is like a battle in the future before it begins. It tells the outcome of future events in that scenario. The scientists and doctors are amazed at the advanced technology and cannot believe their eyes as to what the elderly aliens have for their knowledge and understanding. In the meantime, many are unattended to the holographic artificial intelligence computer. The time has measured the distance of the Inquestorians, studying them in the Earth's atmosphere, and begins to show an erratic reading.

CHAPTER 23

THE MANY OUTCOMES

Two elderly beings are Legendary, and two are Praetorians at level 28 on the trans floor. There is a coughing sound coming from one of the older creatures. A grid emerges in thin air as these aliens point across an invisible board with various calculations like electrical impulses. A chart shows how long the hybrid races in all universes will live after a mission's outcome is known. Hybrids can change their assignments by changing their DNA structure or switching their behaviors. Each individual determines when and how they want to change their mission. These elderly are the brains of all electrical holographic reappearance charts. One of the elderly creatures does some calculations on their reappearing chart. The Praetorian turns around, looks at everyone in the distance, then turns back as he continues the measures.

Suddenly, with eyes wide open, the elderly female Praetorian speaks, who is a queen to all Praetorian males. "*I've got it!*" She turns around as the two elderly aliens sit at a circular floating table. Meanwhile, everyone else in the room sits quietly, not disturbing them as they wait an hour, then it becomes two hours. The elders have not turned around in that time yet.

"*Listen,*" she says sternly, "*the human race has been on this planet before. We had a superintelligent species here before. Their evolution was so rapid that they ran out of resources trillions of light-years ago and moved on throughout the galaxy. They were so smart that they couldn't comprehend the simplest things.*"

Jewel is confused. "What happened to the first Earth, and where did they go?"

As for the female elderly, she remarks, "*Well, let's say they are the guardians of all universes.*"

Merna, seeming to get an idea of what happened to these intelligent beings, makes a small remark, "I guess they were so clever they escaped to an invisible universe where no beings can find them, right?"

The elderly female smirks a little and gives Merna a left thumbs-up. The female elderly continues, "*We're going to go back to that time and age, but in the future.*"

Pointing to a certain point on the chart, she says, "*Well, I see this calculation here! Using these numbers minus two sig, I calculate BC5 2 Pi 4 echelon tee infinity.*"

An elderly Praetorian says, "*You are not only the baby race but also our new brothers and sisters who must prevail. With the help of Wymoym, Venush, Yufer, and General Snuff, they'll implement this plan as we speak or as we discussed with my comrades. If you do it right, you should produce this." The chart pulls up a few futuristic hybrids moving around on the holographic chart as though they are on the planet already, way in the future. The calculations on the see-through board perform exactly what some hybrids would look like with similarities in the future.*"

Male Praetorian smirks a little at the female queen, flicks a bug off his shoulder, and says, "*One has pointy ears, and another has thick but powerful legs. Showing these hybrids gives the scientists what they will be look forward to working on with these powerful half-breeds.*" They have also calculated if put on suitable planets, and they can produce an incredible array of warriors to help defeat the enemy. The elderly Praetorian says more. "The enemy, as you know, wants the destruction of good planets within these universes."

The third elderly says in a soft tone as he gazes at each scientist, "*I speak of futuristic things. I am a being of what you would call a seer, or spiritualist, in your world. I read the future, and this holographic chart performs the possible outcomes with creatures that aren't born, like your hybrids. If you and your clones do these calculations right, you will have hybrids that can conquer anything and stand anything. If you train them right, they will prevail over the enemy. But if you don't, they will come to the Praetorian home world and destroy us, and we don't need that because they will have the intelligence to know where our invisible universe's location is, and our allies'. So make sure the clones are programmed to gather your intellect and are wired precisely to your specifications because mistakes can cause war. You know how a robot operates. If wired wrong, it can go awry and stray away from the intention of the battle. So with everything in tune here, we're going to go and send you on your way. We have given you all the insight we have told you. For now, the rest will come in spurts among the invisible planets, where you will delegate any findings or issues with the clone's worlds.*"

The other Legendary elder, a serious look on his face, says, "*Would you please enjoy the new facility we have created for you above? Yufer, some military person-*

nel, diplomats, and dignitaries will stay with us for further details as we plan. They will relay those details later on. Now, enjoy."

Yarmin, some diplomats, and some dignitaries stay behind with the elderly as the scientists and other military personnel like Sergeant Snuff and the rest of the diplomats and dignitaries, and Wymoym, Venush, Cokiko head back to the trans. They head up to level 5, where the new and improved laboratory location happens to be. While riding in the trans, Jewel discusses the realities of living in an invisible world with John and Lucas.

"However, you can't see the planets themselves." John shakes his head from side to side as though he has water in his ears and says, "Lucas, I am astonished at this idea of living on an invisible planet. Would we be eating food-living organisms that we can touch and taste? Or yet not be able to see it, or would we have the qualities of seeing things on this planet where no one can see them but us? It makes you wonder, right?"

Lucas is a bit scared of the idea. "It is a bit scary because we have no idea if the atmosphere is even pleasant to our body composition or things may taste differently there. The atmosphere may keep us up for weeks without any sleep. We would never know until we experience it, right?"

John playfully gasps for air and starts to talk as though he is trying to get air in a jokingly. "Well, if we hold our inhales for a long time, it may happen for days before we get any air."

John laughs as Jewel laughs as well, but Lucas has a rugged look upon his face as though it is not a joking matter to him but a serious one. Riding at the speed of sound, they all get to level 5 as the trans stop suddenly without jolts or even feeling of movement.

The scientists go about their business to see the new and improved lab with the latest instruments installed. Along with some military personnel, Praetorian Cokiko, and two Legendaries, General Snuff enters the advanced technology room. The scientists with them, Merna, Lucas, John, Penny, Jewel, and Beth, are pulled alongside the corridor way for a moment to the advanced lab by General Snuff.

"Ladies and gentlemen, I want you to know that these new and improved instruments are for you to enjoy before any severe threat is among us, so please go about the lab and look around you, where I am pretty sure you will like the new toys our alien friends have installed for you. Please go!"

Gale goes back to the clone station, checking out the programming for the clone area, as she talks to Lucas, who approaches her from behind.

"Dr. Lucas, we have a lot of planning to do."

Lucas looks at Gale's new cloning station, impressed. "I know, Dr. Gale, we sure do."

At that time, Professor Wymoym is speaking to General Snuff at the entrance area to the lab. "I guess Yarmin will come back soon and tell us our expectations regarding the enemy's invasion."

Snuff nods in a slight yes and no motion. "We assume it is that, but can it be regarding future endeavors of the hybrids and scientists?"

Wymoym, in a roundabout way, agrees with General Snuff. "It can be either. We won't know until Yarmin returns."

Snuff agrees. "You are right."

Back at the forefront of the glass area of the lab, Lucas is still conversing with Dr. Gale. "Yarmin will give us detail on what tactics we're to handle when it comes to the enemy."

Gale presses some configurations into the computer systems. "Yeah, they will tell us how to go about the scenario if an invasion happened."

Wymoym enters the lab with General Snuff as several military personnel stands attention at each station where the scientists and helpers are. Wymoym presses a red button near the center of the lab to get all the scientists' attention. "*Pardon me, all scientists! Excuse me, Doctors! Please!*" Most scientists stop their work and turn around toward Wymoym's direction. "*We have to strategize on how to attack these beings. We are waiting for Yarmin to give us further instructions on whether we strategize ourselves or use the few hybrids we have. We won't know until he returns from getting the directions from the elderlies below. We have to consider the perspective of this case to determine how to attack these aliens that are already here studying us because, with the weapons they carry, which I am pretty sure have improved throughout centuries, our defenses may not be that strong. We must agree to assist you human beings to overcome this threat if possible. We have to prepare the military in case these attacks do happen.*"

Lucas looks at Gale, then turns to Wymoym with curiosity and speaks toward Wymoym. "I wonder what types of weapons we would have to fight this enemy off? We probably can't do anything with bullets to penetrate these beings."

Gale says in a low tone, "Yeah, I know. That's so true."

Wymoym tells the scientists and Lucas, "*Their bodies are like armored plates. We came up with a solution that might be able to get through to their body armor. Of course, we won't know if it works until we try it."* The scientists are a little worried as they talk about this issue.

There is a brief communication between General Snuff and Yarmin near a wall outlet. "Sir?" he asks. "What is the status of the resolution?"

Yarmin, on the other line, voices of the different elderly's speaking from behind to give the final stages of the plan, replies, "We will be up in twenty minutes. We have an idea."

Yarmin, on the other line, as the elderly are speaking from behind to give the final stages of the plan, replies, "We will be up in twenty minutes. We have an idea."

Twenty minutes go by. And Yarmin, along with the rest of the diplomats and dignitaries, are on level 5 with one of the head elderly Legendary as they enter the lab. They all look at the adjustments of all technologies as they walk around the room. At the same time, the scientists seem to be engaged in their work. As the entire floor of scientists' fixation exists on Yarmin, softly says, "Excuse me. I understand we have been discussing and developing the latest technological advancement. Nevertheless, we must be prepared to face any harm."

An old Legendary alien ascends to the floor through an invisible platform with a solution. Before taking out one of the alien weapons, the ancient Legendary observes the scientists in the room. She pulls out from her vest and explains, "*We have a new alien weapon that may help us fend ourselves instead of being overwhelmed by the first, second, or even a third waves of enemy defenses against the Inquestorians. We do not know if these weapons would work on the enemy. We have no way of running a trial run, but it may be the best defense we have for now from our sources. We are hoping it can hold the third wave of aliens at bay. Several studies have shown that it could eradicate the first and second waves. As I said, we have not tested it on them yet because we have not captured an Inquestorian to test it on yet. They are a tricky species to be caught, and they will not give any information if captured in some odd way. If captured, they would dislocate their jaw or disintegrate themselves to dust, but I have never seen them do that yet because they have never been captured at all so far."*

Another elderly Legendary, with a stern look, says, "*Our technology, the alertness to us, is giving you scientists new insights into discoveries within our systems. Thanks to Legendaries and Praetorians, we have improved our technologies and weaponry for centuries. As you can see, here is the K5-49, and right here is the J-woop weapon. When fired upon an enemy, these two weapons aren't just lasers. They're also a tactic devices, like microrobotics, but intelligent weapons, as you say. Their vulnerability in the their sensors. When fired, the laser is almost like a heat-sinking missile. It finds an area on the enemy that seems weak or can injure the enemy if it cannot find a soft spot. Or it may slow them down. This other weapon here, the J-woop, is like a saw buzzer. It whizzes through the air, similar to a boomerang but with sharp razors. It attaches itself to the enemy within five seconds countdown as it explodes the enemy from outside to inside its core. It may or may not work on the second wave, and we have not yet tested it on an enemy yet. These are two weapons we have for your military defenses. Not only that, but you have clones already that are military warriors we have spoken of earlier that have different abilities. Using these warriors' abilities for your defenses from our research, you can probably stop the first and second waves of the Inquestorians."*

The first elderly Legendary looks over the human scientist and says, "*You will go in strategically through the first pattern of our waves against the enemy with air pilots. If that doesn't work, military men will use specil forces to go in on the next wave. If we can't hold the enemy at bay, we will have to use special soldiers with special weapons. If this fails, we would have to call the Jack-roles who project chewed up chemicals from your land that, when tossed out of their mouths, will be like a nuclear bomb exploding millions of miles on the ground. They would be our only hope, with the Legendaries at their side. If we can't stop them, we will send more superhybrid soldiers with different abilities to destroy this enemy. We will know from their abilities if the hybrids have a chance. We won't know for sure until the time comes. Finally, the Legendaries, with the military along with the amalgams, will either be able to defeat or contain the enemy. So there won't be a fight for all Legendaries. Maybe 75 percent at the time will help humanity survive. Is there anything you'd like to know about these strategic lines of defense?*"

Each scientist shakes their head, except for Jewel. Jewel asks. "What about coming out of the ground in a sneak attack?"

Female old Legendary thinks to herself and points at the doctor. "*That's a good idea. That is why these hybrid soldiers with these different abilities can come from behind enemy lines from the underground with the forces in front, making it hard for the enemy to combat us. If this doesn't slow them down, we must get everyone escorted to these other planets as quickly as possible.*" Continuing, the elder female Legend turns to Wymoym. "*Now, Wymoym will fill you in on mankind.*"

Wymoym gives good insight, saying, "*As you already know, the plan to save humankind is to take every individual on Earth to these various planets throughout the universe. These are the ones where we will have to leave a few Legendaries behind to defend or take their last stand with our resources on the planet. We have underground bases that the Inquestorians have no idea how to locate. Like this one, there are many more throughout the Earth on different continents."*

Wymoym scratches or flicks a particle off his face. "*If they find a hidden base, they will destroy every aspect of Earth since they are intertwined. Almost at the center of the Earth is where they would locate all headquarters. Except for this one, since it is so far below the landmass of the Earth. Due to molten rocks, it is hot going to other levels, which cools down by water vapors from above through ventilation shafts. Our ideal plan is to get each human being through the G300 machine on every hidden base on Earth through these portals as fast as possible. If they have a full-fledge war before getting most humans off the planet, then there may be a few humans or none who survive. There may be little chance that humans could survive the G300 then. Who knows?. Unless full-blown warfare were in progress. Currently, it is unclear what their intentions of accomplishments are."*

Merna responds to this possible situation, "Now then, Wymoym, pardon for the interruption. We will have the waves of attacks, but we may not have the tools yet to immediately wipe them out immediately. But then they have no idea the human race of old since they have been studying us right?"

Wymoym tells the scientists and Merna what they might come for as well. In which the scientists already know if they try to conquer the human race, they may not attack right away. "*The Inquestorians will scan your planet for what minerals they can use and the weaknesses of your defenses. As you may already know, they will use those minerals to replenish their ships and destroy Earth. When we get people through these portals, they will separate individually. If you are three, then I will explain what I mean. You each will travel to Saturn, Pluto, and Uranus. Remarkably, this is how it would happen on the different planets of the various universes. Your race will solely distribute unless you hold hands with your loved ones, where both or several individuals will transport to that individual planet. Some technology will be transported to those planets in different universes, or dimensions as you would call them."*

Merna and Dr. Beth suggest, "Excuse me, Yarmin." Beth looks at Merna intensely and says, "Merna and I have a suggestion for you, Mr. Yarmin."

At the very moment, Yarmin spins around in confusion. Beth asks, "Wouldn't it make more sense if we had an underwater base where we could hide the humans?"

Then Yarmin agrees with Beth. "That's fantastic! We should conceal them there where they are not spotted."

Yarmin looks toward Wymoym while speaking to Beth and says, "There is indeed an underwater base. Inquestorians have only one species in their arsenal that can survive underwater thousands of miles. However, they have a weapon to change the terrain, not the water. That might be a safe life source to save some human species that want to remain on Earth. The aliens traveling thousands of feet in water are deadly if they find the base under the dark, murky waters. These creatures would annihilate the surviving human race."

Merna says with wondering eyes, "Oh, I see."

Wymoym continues, "*But we would have to wait and discuss this among the rest of the Union, when they come up from below on the other sector.*"

Beth acknowledges, "Merna and I understand, Professor Wymoym."

Merna agrees as well. "This may be a saving grace."

Wymoym agrees. "*Of course, we will not know because the intentions are not there yet. However, the worst-case scenario if we have to take our troops and fall back and let some creatures called the bandees intervene. Should the need arise, we'd like to ride back to the submarine that can take us to the underwater military base called Bandsada. Until then, we have to make these plans work.*"

Diplomatic representatives and dignitaries speak with other council members during the interim while the lab finishing touches are in place. The International Union government hears from Yarmin.

"Ladies, gentlemen, fellow military personnel, and far-off world relations aliens. Dr. Beth thinks we should take the remaining human race that would stay behind, and if need be or the war was to intensify to protect the rest of the human race, we would shield them through our underwater military base."

As diplomats, aliens, and scientists watched in amazement; everyone else was in awe. In another part of our Milky Way universe, we see a sinister mother ship preparing to send down some drones and alien scouts.

CHAPTER 24

AN UNDERWATER DESCENT

Yarmin discusses Dr. Beth's idea among the elderly aliens, as one of the elderly Praetorians turns around and says, "Dr. Beth!"

Dr. Beth turns around, while chatting with Gale. "Yes."

Elderly continues, "*We have heard your advice on the underwater military base plan. If worse comes to worst, the remaining humans, military, and aliens will fall back if needed to take submerged alien vessels around the globe to the underwater hidden bases deep within the dark walls of the ocean. The enemy will become blind by an assorted giant octopus ink that will make the military base invisible to any creature, especially the Inquestorians' underwater deadly creature. Does everyone understand? You got it too, Dr. Beth?*"

Beth tries to listen to Gale and the elderly alien. "Yes! Yes!"

Wymoym takes over the conversation of the elderly. "*We do not have enough room to put seven billion humans, but a mere five hundred million only can the base handle.*"

Merna thinks about the impossibility of billions going through G300 and how many humans will stay back on Earth."*I get it. We have to have enough time to make sure we've got an out for eight point seven billion people on Earth. That many people will take a while to get off, huh?*"

Wymoym shocks Merna and the other scientists. "*Well, not precisely. People would go to the various planets scattered throughout the universe. The lights flash ten at a time on the G300. Despite this, they are all placed on different planets. One can travel through the G300 more than ten thousand times faster through space than light. It's almost like time stopped when one clicks a camera, as if a billion pictures simultaneously taken.*"

Beth, while talking, turns toward the rest of the scientists in the room. "We love that you acknowledge the plan and the idea that the G300 can flash ten people simulataneously. First, however, we would love to thank you for helping humanity and helping us save our race."

Wymoym, in a loving voice, says, "*If we're losing the battle, we will go to those plans, and the remaining Legendaries will be protected there. Assuming the Inquestorians establish a base on Earth. If we want to take back the Earth in the future, then the new and improved hybrids, we'll need to design a way to do it. The Inquestorians always leave on most planets some soldiers behind.*"

"How about in the future?" Lucas asks out of the blue, scratching his head. "We can time travel back with the hybrids and take them out."

Wymoym jolts at the statement. "*That sounds good, but at that time, they may have something that we may have missed, so we have to be careful if we were to come back to fight them.*" With an odd look on his face, trying to figure out what can switch the barriers of time with this enemy, he wonders what that information is or what it could be. Wymoym is not too sure. "*We will never know until that place in time. The Inquestorians may leave most of the Earth as dust terrain or try to get as many minerals out of the planet as possible. With that in mind, we have sacred grounds like the underwater base and underground tunnels where Earth will have a fighting chance in the future. Do any of the doctors have any more ideas?*"

Merna blurts out, "I don't think we have any more ideas. It's just that we wish the bases could accommodate eight billion people."

Wymoym sees the concerns of the doctors' and continues, "*Unfortunately, we did not build it for that many people. The result could be many people being underground and underwater. Developing a solution of this magnitude would take centuries. Volcanic eruptions and enormous underwater currents that can cause metal or stone to crumble in some areas, so that shield would be necessary. Sometimes giant waves with crushing currents can destroy our facilities if not made with the proper metals and compounds to withhold them.*"

Yarmin interjects, "Of course, the military has been doing this for years to build an indestructible base with the technology of these aliens that helped us for centuries."

Merna, who gets it, says, "I believe, talking for all the scientists here, that we needed the insight and know-how from our alien visitors in the long run. I'm glad the Praetorians and Legendaries are here. We hope the Earth's creatures, trees, and other things the Inquestorians will not take from us."

Wymoym shows through his holographic pen instrument. "*The Inquestorians come for water, minerals, and vegetation. If they decide to drain your waters, they may find the base. If they deplete everything, including your creatures and so forth, then the surviving human beings in the hidden base will not be able to survive if found."*

Yarmin has an idea. "Why don't we cover the base with giant rocks surrounding it, covering it from anyone entering it? Like it was never there."

The elderly give details. "*Well, let's say the base has cloaking ability."*

Yarmin, who had no idea, says, "Wow! Never knew that."

The entire room of scientists and some of the International Union members are happy as one of the dignitaries has a question. "How or who will be operating it in time of danger?"

The elderly remarks, "*Well, some Legendaries know the code and will protect when the time is right."*

Yarmin also reassures the scientist how the humans will survive. "Inside the underwater base is growing vegetation, fish, some small animals, fowls, and other resources for the remaining humans to survive and eventually replenish Earth. Of course, we have technology in those hidden bases that if our waters were to contain poison, it would test it and find a cure for the oceans' water if they don't take our seas. Still, if they don't see any humans remaining on the planet, and we hide them with just the octopus ink, these giant octopuses can withstand a lot of poisons. They are ancient since prehistoric times. They will protect our bases. Hence, there is no need to worry unless they know how to destroy these octopuses, which I don't think they know how yet. We will see what happens when the time comes."

Lucas is almost like a salesman. "That sounds fair enough. I get it. Does everyone else get it, or do I have to sell you what he just mnetioned?"

Everyone ignores Lucas and proceeds further. One of the diplomats has a question. "As discussed below, the different strategies with achievements. How can we hit them first before they hit us?"

Wymoym replies as he shakes his right hand as though numb, "*We are not up to par with that technology yet. We have the ships. Humans can't fly them yet. We have fighters and so forth, but the human race is not up to par with the technology. Most soldiers are Legendaries, and some human military fighters. We can take our huge ships into battle too.*

"If they capture one of the Praetorians, they will find the invisible universe and destroy all life in all universes. If that comes to fruition, the Inquestorians will indeed win the war. We will not let that happen, people and outerworld friends."

A diplomat agrees. "I agree with you."

The elderly Praetorian says, "*Let us continue our preparation for this battle that is already here above the Earth. According to our computers, the Inquestorians are now scouting the Earth's lands.*"

Knowing the Inquestorians will soon attack the Earth shakes the scientists. They prepare for the upcoming war at hand and what to expect. During this time, Praetorian computers estimate that scientists have been working on cloning for weeks and weeks. Then, approximately six months ago to the year, the Inquestorians hit our Milky Way galaxy. Scientists are taking months and months to clone themselves, preparing millions and millions of cloned scientists to travel with humans to different destinations throughout the various universes. There are hundreds of cloning stations throughout the facility. Gale sets the computers to clone Jewel, Lucas, Merna, Gale, Beth, John, and Penny fast, and the laptop clones them. The clones appear every few seconds.

The G300 portal starts up. All clones start jumping through the portals. Some Praetorians head to their ships to calculate the enemy's ships' positions. Some Praetorians, along with some Legendaries, go through the portals too. A few Praetorians aboard the vessel send messages to Legendary worlds so they can transmit to the planets of the different universes where the clones will appear via their entrances. The clones, Praetorians, and Legendaries will prepare the humans who come through the portal to get acquainted with the planet's environments. These planets are dead or desolated, with hardly any living species. Occasionally, alien races may be present on planets that have not caused the destruction that will ultimately accept humans into their environment. These alien races may have a way of living that will not affect humans long term.

The original scientists do not go through until the last minute after all humans are through the portal. The G300 will recognize them to send them to the invisible Praetorian universe, or better yet, the original scientist will leave with the Praetorians in their ships. They will go to their universe through a cloaking device that makes them invisible so that the Inquestorians will not get a glimpse of their vessels. All the Inquestorians will see out in space is a streak of white light that quickly vanishes into thin air, where they will have no idea where it came from, as the Praetorian of old has already mentioned.

Over the past year and a half, a lot has happened. Billions and billions of clones have gone through the G300 portal to these different universes and planets. Months have gone by as a male Praetorian runs from its ship area down a corridor into a wall that opens up as it drops down a side swindle elevator. It takes the male

Praetorian to a level 5 facility, where the clone doctors and some military personnel prepared in a remote location are military hybrids ready for war. The male Praetorian comes rushing into where dignitary Yarmin and some diplomats oversee the disbursement of the billions of clones going through the portal along with cloned dignitaries and diplomats. The male Praetorians runs toward an open doorway that swings. While the glass door opens, the creature begins to scream out loud in an English and alien language.

"They are here. The enemy is here! Prepare yourselves!"

On the other side of the room is Cokiko, overseeing the operations of a device that will read off future technologies for the future human hybrids. Suddenly getting wind of the male Praetorian words in his language, he begins to scamper around as though an emergency is happening right now. This statement had already been shared by the Praetorian to all of the scientists in the room on a holographic billboard.

"Attention, all personnel in the facility. We have an emergency. That emergency is, the enemy has touched down on planet Earth. They have arrived on our soil. Be prepared for battle!"

The scientists and Gale, prepare with Cokiko a plan to escape the Milky Way galaxy. Cokiko speaks to Gale about their method of escape. *"First of all, Doctors, if a war breaks out and there is no other way of survival, we have to protect you all. So what I want to do here, as you can see on this holographic image, is to take you up on this ship called the Galvaton. This ship here has a cloaking device and with a speed of time to escape the enemy clutches out in space."*

Merna speaks with a concern, "What if they see us out in the open throughout interplanetary? Wouldn't they come after us since they can travel fast themselves?"

Cokiko sees Merna and proceeds, *"As I mentioned, we have a time-stoppage device that can stop time and proceed through, and this is the one technology I have not given away or spoken of yet."*

Jewel, with a shocked look on his face with amazement at the same time, says, "You mean to say you have that type of technology, and you kept it from us. Why?"

Cokiko gives them the reason. *"We only brought enough technology finding from our world on what we had. You will know more about this technology once you know our home worlds."*

Merna and Gale begin to understand why, and Gale speak. "I guess we know why you would keep that technology behind, in case the enemy was to get their hands on it. They would replay time events until they conquer your species, leaving everyone worshipping Faloosh, right?"

Cokiko agrees. "*That is correct, Dr. Gale.*"

Cokiko makes plans with the doctors, while in the corridor of the particular unit where General Snuff, Yarmin, and Yufer are residing as they are making plans with the Praetorian, who had rushed to tell about the enemy's touchdown. Yarmin proceeds with plans to prepare the military for a war that may break out on the planet's surface.

"Okay, to all military personnel here, we must prepare ourselves for the undetermined undermining of the enemy at hand, who is among the humans right now. Therefore, I want your people, General Yufer and five-star general Snuff, to prepare your men for war in the primary areas of the bunker's hidden bases marked within mountainous regions. Hopefully, they could surprise the enemy at hand if war was to break out. You got that, General Yufer?"

General Yufer gets the message from the dignitary Yarmin as a military captain, speaks out, "Sir! According to NASA, there seem to have some vessels in their scope on their radar."

Yarmin turns to the Praetorian, eyes wide open. "What do we do now?"

The male Praetorian gets everyone to calm down as he suggests, "*Let me make a suggestion. Why don't we see what the enemies' intentions are? In contrast, we get our military ready and plan on whether the enemy attacks or not. Is that fair enough?*"

Yarmin and Yufer seem to agree with the Praetorians' plan. "We agree!"

Meanwhile, Yarmin pulls Yufer aside to get the military in the ready stance. "General Yufer, I want you and your men around the world to be in the ready view until further notice from this division. In contrast, Captain George gets more insight from this male Praetorian who will get his commands from Cokiko and his leaders, okay?"

In response, Yufer calls General Snuff to one side and prepares his military personnel. "You got it, General Snuff! I want you to contact military leaders worldwide and prepare them for invasion from the enemy, which could happen any moment."

General Snuff salutes Yufer as he responds, "Got it, sir."

Yufer says one more thing that may concern the military at this time. "We may need a lot of firepower. I want you to bring out the heavy military tanks and land gunships that hovers over land and water as well. We may need those weapons as soon as possible if things get intense. Got it, General Snuff?"

Snuff puts the information into his task holographic computer on his wrist and starts to call to other commanders around the globe as he adheres to Yufer's wishes. "I understand the command. I will start making those calls right away!"

Yufer heads back with Yarmin to the doctors with Cokiko, who continues his brilliant plans to get all original personnel off the planet, leaving a few clones back. Cokiko further discusses the plans for those of importance, "*For example, doctors will be assigned different spots on our homeworlds depending on their specialties. Besides the original dignitaries, diplomats, and confident leaders like the president and former presidents, the other 5 percent of world leaders will have a position there. They will be responsible for sharing information about the hybrids with them and keeping them abreast of current technology. Since our planet would age humans ten years to your Earth's one year, your scientists and all your leaders may die off, eventually leaving your descendants as future leaders of upcoming worlds. They can control clone leaders within these different universes helping future hybrids technologies advance while keeping Inquestorians away from the control of these univereses from being conquered in the future.*"

Yarmin briefs Cokiko and a few dignitaries about the military. "I would like to update the room on what is happening. I have General Yufer and General Snuff relaying messages to all military personnel worldwide regarding the threat that may infiltrate our planet in the coming weeks or months to come."

Even as this conversation continues, two substances head toward the planet's surface in a twinkle of an eye. All turn their ears and attention to Yarmin on a sad note. But, even with the help of the Praetorians and Legendaries, can survival lead to impending doom?

CHAPTER 25

ENEMY ARRIVES IN THE DISTANCE

Yarmin continues the conversation sadly. "In case combat was to brew, we will have our military at a stance near every mountainous facility where the ramps of the mountains will disperse all military personnel on the battlefield when the time comes to it."

Lucas had a question for Yarmin. "What about the hybrids? Will they enter the war zone too?"

Yarmin reassures Lucas, "Actually, in the military plan, they are behind the enemy lines for a surprise attack if it comes down to that."

Lucas sighs in relief. While the doctors, significant people, aliens along with military personnel hash things out, on the other hand, at a NASA division that monitors space activity, a few of NASA's employees happen to see something out of the ordinary appear on their screen, like something whizzing in and out of the holographic monitors. The first employee sees another blip, saying to the guy next to him, "Did you see that?"

The second employee says, "Yes, I did."

The first employee, all of a sudden, gets a long signal on the monitor that is unstoppable. "What can this be? I can't figure it out."

The second employee looks at the monitor strangely. "I have no idea what it can be."

The first employee turns toward the second employee. The first employee thinks it's some emergency and calls his commander. "Hey, since we have no idea what this could be on the monitors, I think we should let Commander Hem know about it. What do you think?"

The second employee agrees. The first employee hits a button at his desk to interrupt Commander Hem if an emergency happens. A green light with a buzzing alarm surrounds the room's ambient.

Fifteen minutes later, Commander Hems comes up to the bridge where the alarm sounds and rushes in the door. Commander Hem says, "I hope you have something this time, Harold!"

Harold, the first employee, responds with uncertainty, "Sir! I have no idea what is happening here. A sudden anomaly appeared on the monitor, sir. These anomalies won't disappear. They appear and disappear as they approach inward of our Milky Way galaxy, sir. I have no idea what it is. What are we supposed to do?"

Commander Hem responds as he looks upon the holographic monitors, "Let me check that out. Move over!" Harold moves over to an empty seat as Commander Hem sits down to see what this anomaly is as others sitting in various NASA seats try to come up with what may be coming into the Milky Way galaxy.

A few females think it might be something more, as Pamela and Sarah yell to Commander Hem, "We believe it is an invasion of some sort, sir!"

Hem responds, "That is nonsense. How can it be? Tell me how long this was on the radar, Harold."

Harold, who seems to stare at a screen for hours and days, slowly, after about a year and a half, Harold finally tells Hem, "About two years, sir."

Hem hurries to his office to make a phone call on a brief emergency communication as he gets up and out of his seat violently. Immediately, Harold hurriedly sits down on the chair that Hem had just vacated.

Commander Hem is in his office. "General Yufer!"

On the call, Yufer responds, "Yes."

Hem explains terrifyingly, "We have some strange activities on the monitors."

"Awe, interesting," says Yufer. "I knew indeed who and what they are, Commander Hem. A little two-year late report, Hem."

Hem questions with trembling fright, "What are they, sir?"

Yufer reminds Hem of a classification file. "Remember classified file 5229?"

"Yes, sir." Hem sparks the memory.

Yufer continues, "Well, it happened."

The future is a bit more frightening for Hem. "What are we supposed to do here, General? Should we let the president know about the situation here?"

Yufer, with a smirk on the brief comm, replies, "I already took care of that years ago."

Hem turns to look at his door and looks back at the holographic brief comm as Harold stands in the doorway. "Yes, hum, hold on a minute. What can I help you with, Harold?"

Harold looks worried. "Those blips on the monitor are gaining ground into our Milky Way galaxy!"

Hem calms Harold down. "Please, Harold, we took care of the situation years ago. Sorry, two years a little too late, buddy."

Harold is a bit uncomfortable. "Will do."

Meanwhile, General Yufer gets attention of Cokiko. "Excuse me, Cokiko."

Cokiko responds, "Yes."

Yufer provides more information, "The monitor is showing the ships are in proximity over our satellites. Two have touched down, and enemies are scouting the planet."

Cokiko says with a harsh concern, "*Just as I suspected, they bought their heavy arsenal ships in our quadrant. According to my holographic wristwatch, I see various vessels like 2991, 2992, 2993, and 2994 out in space right now, just lurking at how to manipulate the planet they think is something besides Earth. So we must prepare now for the extraction of the human population.*"

Yufer hangs up with Commander Hem on the other line and gets back to understanding what these vessels are like, while Cokiko gives more detail. "What are these vessels like, Professor Cokiko?"

Cokiko provides the feature of the ships. "*It strikes me that K994 is the smallest vessel they brought with them, having been here for a while, 2991 and 2992, on the other hand are huge ships that cannot enter the Earth's atmosphere because they contain tons of vessels. As for 2993 and 2994, these ships can enter the Earth's atmosphere.*"

Yufer needs to know what to tell the president about the spaceship. "What should I say to the president about these vessels?"

Cokiko, who does not want mass hysteria to happen yet, responds, "*Do not contact the president as yet. Until a bunch of ships touch down and are in range. Then we will let the president of the United States and all world leaders know what is going on. All Earthlings must immediately perform the following extraction through the G300 in all facilities quadrants.*"

Yufer then instructs his men to contact all quadrants of sectors worldwide to get ready for the human race's extraction from Earth. Yufer further tells military leaders around the globe, "Gentlemen, we must prepare to extricate the human race from Earth and prepare them to leave Earth and find new home worlds." All the generals and lieutenants agree to disperse the human race preparing the bases for human entry to enter and flee through the G300. Yufer is still in the dark about what he should say to NASA on the other line. "What should I tell NASA in the meantime, Cokiko?"

Cokiko tells Yufer what to tell NASA. "Tell NASA they are relaying old news and just hang up, Yufer."

Yufer quickly hangs up with Hem, not telling him anything.

On the other hand, Cokiko gives Yufer a command on what to tell the president. "*Say to the president not to be alarmed. We'll let him know what will transpire in the upcoming events.*"

Yufer talks to the president on the holographic brief comm and updates him. "Mr. President, do not be alarmed. We will let you know any updates on the upcoming events, sir."

President remarks with relief, "Thank you, General Yufer. I will stand by for your call regarding this issue."

Yufer repeat a bit, "Do not be alarmed until it is in range. Let us know when they are in range, or we may let you know."

President looks at his cameraman and says, "Please keep me informed on this end."

Yufer as he massages his hair and says, "Thank you, Mr. President." Yufer hangs up the holographic brief comm. Yufer will know if the enemy's ground troops are in range way before the president ever knows due to the Cokiko's wrist holographic device. When the enemy is in range, Yufer will inform the president about any threats to Earth's population. Hours, days, and even weeks havepassed. Then, one of the Praetorians unexpectedly rushes to Cokiko, who has been monitoring other devices on the doctors' floor of the facility from his ship.

"*Cokiko, they are in range! What now?*"

Cokiko gradually gets up from his seat, gracefully puts both hands on the young Praetorian's chest, and says softly, "*Do not be alarmed. Get all the young and some scouts through the G300 as fast as possible. In the event of war, I will make Earthlings aware that combat is imminent. Let's find out what the enemy's intentions are first. I will inform all bases worldwide and top leaders to prepare to leave Earth as soon as possible. Your job is to prepare, and mine is to go.*"

The young Praetorian nods in a yes motion and begins rounding all species: scientists, young, female Legendaries, and some military through the G300 as fast as possible. Finally, Cokiko informs Yarmin, "*Yarmin! They are in range now. Tell NASA right away if they are getting the same readings.*"

Yarmin heads over to a holographic brief comm and rings into Hem at NASA. Hem is on the line. "Contact is in range. I figured that is why you called."

Yarmin wants to know how close are they. "What is the projection of the enemy ship's closeness to the Earth?"

Hem gives Yarmin the precise coordinates of the enemy. "Their ships have been .25 in range over the Earth."

Yarmin figures it out. "Precisely. Since they have studied us for some time, their ground troops will be in range in a week. We must let the president know as soon as possible."

Hem agrees. "I agree with you."

Yarmin tells Yufer the enemy is in range. Yufer, who already got the information from Cokiko, knows they are in range. Yarmin speaks to Yufer. "Tell your men that the enemy is in scope and will be here in a week."

Yufer responds, "I know, I know. Already on it."

Yarmin gets information regarding the vessels from Cokiko, as Yufer also overhears them as he calls in on his tactical team to get ready for the inbound of the enemy once they close in on their facilities.

Cokiko gives more information on the vessels. "These vessels K2991 and K2992 are enormous. They cannot enter Earth's atmosphere because of their monstrous size. As for K2993 and K2994, they can easily enter Earth's atmosphere with ease."

Yufer questions some of the ships. "What do these K2993 and K2994 ships look like, and are we capable of defending ourselves from them?"

Cokiko gives relief regarding these ships with the right tactical teams in place. "*These vessels are powerful alien aircraft, and with the right tactical team in place, we can hopefully sneak behind enemy lines and steal one of these vessels if possible. The only way to do this is by using our human hybrids. K2993 and K2994 are slightly different in design, as seen on my holographic computer. One drives it by telepathy. The other is get-up-and-go by the energy of the individual who is powering it. The K2993 is a fighter ship with burning lasers that can disintegrate the object. K2994 is a scout ship with minimal firepower used to track and capture anything in its way. Our officials should notify your government that the enemy is within a week of our facilities. We need to move now!*"

Yufer starts to get on the holographic brief comm, but Yarmin stops him. "We should let the president know right away."

Yarmin interjects, "I will let the president know our position on this matter, General Yufer. You need to get tactical together if a war breaks out and start to gather all personnel. The enemy will be within range of our facilities in a week, so we must inform your officials. I am sending intel to warn the people of Earth that we need to evacuate. You got that, General!"

Yufer salutes Yarmin, who heads to another part of the facility to get things rolling as he departs from General Yarmin. Yarmin walks to another part of the facility where he is alone in a room on a brief comm channel where he can contact the president in case of a national emergency.

Yarmin pulls up his holographic brief comm with a touch of his index finger in midair and turns to a channel that is only for the president of the United States as it phones in with an emergency ring on the president's wrist comm. President excuses himself from many influential people as he discusses politics. "Yes, what is the emergency, Yarmin!"

Yarmin shows a channel that links to the facility and Cokiko ship resources. "Mr. President, classified file 109494. As you can see here on the holographic display in front of me, it has reached its destination. Mr. President, we need to let the public know right away."

The president responds with concern. "How close is the enemy to the facilities right now?"

Yarmin gives the president the precise coordinates on a channel. "They are about .25 miles away from the facility."

The president calls in his team of media people to get him on the streaming media. The president will soon gather his staff to inform Earth's people of the looming threat. The president says a final message to Yarmin before he brings his media team into the oval office, "Yarmin, my team will prepare Earth for the removal of its people as you inform the heads of all organizations and facilities to incline on the matter. Furthermore, I will tell all leaders within the International Union and governing entities worldwide that an evacuation is imminent! That is all, Yarmin. My media team just entered the office. Take care of everything on your end, Yarmin."

Yarmin abruptly hangs up from the president, saying one last word, "Way ahead of you, Mr. President."

Yufer calls to Cokiko, "Question, Cokiko, why the numbers for the ships? They must have real names for them, right?"

Cokiko gives Yufer a lowdown on the vessels. "*Well, I would love to provide you with terms of the ships, but each spaceship the enemy has its quality to a specific name. With that in mind, I will have to confer with the elders to give you the certainty of those names, okay, General Yufer."*

General Yufer waits as Cokiko calls one of the elders through his wrist comm. "*Elder Kunash, please, can you explain to General Yufer the names of the ships K2991, K2992, K2993, and K2994, please."*

Kunash is elderly and is the only female Legendary who can give the names of these ships along with their history. "*The k2991 is a ship called the Morando. It is a colossal ship. It is solid with its humungous size, as you have already seen in past holograms. One would have to sneak on board the vessel to find its weakness. The weapons are sophisticated that they fire rays from smaller beams that singe any surface. It also has medium beams that boil the surface, to more giant beams that can blast a hole through the planet's core, causing all kinds of catastrophe for that planet, bringing it at times out of alignment. The Inquestorians' ship K2991 was first seen in the battle of the third universe called Gideon. There were fierce creatures in this universe that gave the Inquestorians a real good fight, almost defeating the Inquestorians until they had to bring out this ship that imploded the planet's surface, destroying tons of worlds in this universe.*

"There are tales that other planets may have survived that attack, but I am guessing that our allies, the Praetorians, had preserved them in a time of need. These creatures are known as Caphlorian and master warriors for their tremendous and mighty supremacy in battle. They only use the Morando weaponry if they lose a fight to a planet with a stronghold, and we only know of a few universes that gave the Inquestorians a run for their money. But the Caphlorians came very close to beating this enemy for good. One thing the enemy does not have that the Praetorians have is a time portal, which you will learn about it later on when we have the future of the hybrids together. The next ship, K2992, that Cokiko is showing you through the holographic wrist comm is called the Catombic. The vessel holds many games Faloosh and his band of rebels enjoy. You see the Morando and Catombic at times connect like a puzzle where Faloosh and his band of warriors and his family enjoy the outcome of the games. Now, when not attached to the giant ship, this ship alone can protect itself with an invisible light that circles the vessel and expands for miles. It destroys the enemy instantly while touching this invisible light.

"The light can interchange by their mercenaries on board through mind control, telling the light what pattern to adjust to while expanding toward the enemy. There is only one way to bypass this light either by a cloaking device or stealing a craft that communicates with the mother ship over, which no one has ever tackled

before. Faloosh has predefined tactics in case someone was to infiltrate his territory. Faloosh learns more technology as he conquers universes that are in the way that he wants to destroy, worshipping his laws. The last two ships, the K993 and K994, are called Mercy and Spy. The Mercy ships are two-person vessels with a few spinning tarot guns on the top, bottom, and sides. Each gun performs a different task. For instance, the top gun shoots out rays that can crisp a being, and the base beam shoots out white lasers that freezes one burning them from the inside out. The two side guns are lasers that rotate back and forth, turning the enemies into dust.

"As for the Spy ship scouts, the area for minerals, anything worthwhile for the taking shoots out two things: an energy web. If this web captures an enemy, it reads the being sending information to Faloosh, two massive vessels giving all possible data about that creature. The spy shoots out the other thing called a stunner ray. Now, this ray can stun an enemy for days. The Mercy ships can capture the enemy and take it back to the mother ship for further study, with the possibility of mating with Faloosh warriors, or worshipping Faloosh. The Mercy ships can turn any terrain into metallic terrain. Although the Mercy ship is a two-person flying crew, it carries about eight hundred to five thousand enemy ships on board. According to our projections, the mother ship has other vessels surrounding it by thousands.

"Well, as you already know, they got here through the transcenders. We do not, so far, know their intent for planet Earth. What I may know is that they may scout the area and hopefully find nothing of value and may find no threat to them or might take over planet Earth for the hell of it, wiping it out if necessary due to the duties they have in conquering all universes, which is their ultimate goal."

Yarmin looks closer at the wrist com on Kunash, wanting to know more about certain ships. "What are these tiny, tiny things surrounding the big vessels?"

Kunash's eyes squint a bit as she moves her wrist com closer to Yarmin's face. *"These small vessels, they are called Madrones. These ships are not similar to drones. They are ships, which I describe as a ship driven by tiny alien beings."*

Even as Kunash explains, in another part of the solar system, those small drone-like ships are moving at an extreme speed—faster than the speed of light descending upon Earth. Yet, as a speck of dust to a human eye, they fluttered with quite eloquent speed. Not even a jet can see them.

CHAPTER 26

THE MINERAL HUNT

Kunash continues, "*These vessels comb the area for any minerals, living beings, or threats to the scouts, which can cause a battle to brew later. The scouts and Madrones report to Faloosh's head soldiers on radars regarding minerals, beings, or threats to the warships if they were to invade. Before invasions, the first waves are usually the first and second waves: the Madrones and Mercy ships. Of the big ships, there are waves three and four: they are the Spy ships and spirals fighters. As for waves five and six are the combatants and destroyers, Faloosh brings out his more reckon mercenaries with the giants if they were to lose. In the interim of it, all is his awful games which Faloosh acknowledges more when he has won a war. As you all already know, wave eight consists of female bodyguards used once during the Gideon war. The hybrids are essential for preparing for this war, so do we have any questions?*"

Yarmin, not holding back, says, "No questions here. We have to find a way to protect ourselves by our soldiers who stand ready at the gates and bridges."

Kunash, with deep understanding, says, "*I understand. We already projected a battle scene on Earth. From what we acknowledge in the near future, A total of 98 percent of Earth's population departs through the G300s all over Earth's underground facilities. We need to prepare right now because if they are near our facilities, the next step for them is to comb the area, and from now, we may need to start a strategy with our combatant plans for whether to conquer them or leave. But they may beat us and desolate our grounds from vegetation or life. It depends on what they do with the planet's terrain. Our president needs an update with the information given to him through our brief communications regarding the enemy's intent before this can happen.*"

Yarmin turns around, heads out the door, and begins to fly his private jet toward the white house.

While Faloosh rallies, his scouts and the Madrones fly into Earth's atmosphere to discover what Earth offers. During that time, above the atmosphere, Faloosh tells his commanders in his alien language, "*Oui jam juju bam giv em tim te ma Ju Maju tu comado,*" which means "*We need to scout the area for minerals. Major and Commanders, If life resists us here, we must devise a strategy to stop them and use them to our benefit.*" The chief and commanders nod their heads in a yes motion.

Back down on Earth, Yarmin enters the Oval Office, as the president sits down with his team of media people to get him on TV to give Earth's people the urgent news. One news media person suggests something for the president to say.

"Mr. President, a suggestion, please."

The president raised his hand as Yarmin was about to speak to him in a silent motion. "Yes, go ahead, Tracy."

Tracy, with the suggestion, says, "Yes, I think you should sit over here near the desk, and according to the prompter, I would reiterate the word *alarm* a few times to get it through to the people at home who may be in the shower, cooking, or have loud noises such as children or music. They would also be warned not to panic and to follow military personnel to hidden bases by following highways."

President gets the picture and asks to speak to Yarmin. At the same time, one of the media people is setting up his timing to be on TV. So, Yarmin goes over to the president with details.

"Mr. President, profile K2995 has appeared over Earth's atmosphere right now. What do you want us to do?"

President looks at Yarmin and sighs. "It seems we have prepared at the gates if the enemy tries to engage us and all other preparations are at hand for the G300 for humanity to leave, right?"

Yarmin nods his head toward the president. "All provisions are in place, sir."

President replies, "Sounds reasonable. I must inform our world about what is happening in the current situation. And what needs to transpire for the human population."

Some media team prepares the camera for the broadcast, and others prepare the president for television. One cameraman starts the countdown. "Five, four, three, two, one. You're on the air."

The president starts to make a state of emergency broadcast as the United States and world leaders on television transmit the same messages in their language. Finally, the president gives his speech.

"Citizens of the United States, I have realized that I have a special urgent message with tonight's state of emergency. The message I am about to give you is not to cause mass hysteria but not only to warn you but get you ready for something that needs to happen right now at this very moment. I am saying that unknown forces may threaten the human race outside our galaxy with utmost urgency. In your area, military personnel who will escort you to secret military bases in the mountains. Please take the necessary belongings with you cause you will be leaving stuff behind. You will be briefed by military personnel once you get to the hidden military bases.

The camera gets a close-up of the President, who says, "According to NASA, please do not panic, but we have to save humankind right now! We need all civilians to rush the military personnel as they gather all citizens right now, but please listen to them. Once again, this is a state of emergency. We have a red terrorist interstellar alert from out of space.

"Whatever you're doing right now, drop it, take your family in their car, and follow the military. For those who do not have a car, many buses will be at cross streets to pick up all families. Please aboard calmly as the military proceeds toward the secret bases with further instructions. Again, do not be alarmed but move fashionably, and things will get done fast. For those of you who decide to stay behind in their homes, some military personnel will remain in the perimeter to protect you from this unknown enemy or help you to escape with further notice. I appreciate your cooperation in this manner. Much regards from the president of the United States. May God be with us all through these frightening and dreaded forthcoming events. From the president of the United States, God bless America, and good night."

Meanwhile, the elderly female Kunash back at the base tells General Yufer about the number of aliens aboard these ships. "*Yufer, let me explain that the number of aliens aboard these ships is hundreds of thousands of occupancy. We would say there are many as the grains of your beach sand, so in other words, there could be billions for all we know. They have hybrids from the many universes entangled within their web of destruction.*"

"Interesting," Yufer says in a low tone as he moves his face to the right, then gently grazes, and slowly, looking up at Kunash, who is about five feet away from him. "We only have seven point five billion people on the Earth. In contrast, the enemy has octillion, the twenty-seventh power to nine hundred and three. It would take us billions and billions of years to conquer such an enemy once we find a solution to finally beat them with the hybrids. If they all come on the Earth, they wouldn't be room for all their species."

Kunash responds, "You are right. I want you to know that we have a way of strategizing as planned earlier. We will, if war was imminent, get at least 98 percent of the Earth's population to the new universes and all species of animals. Until then, we have to strategize our ways off this planet right now!"

Back at the Oval Hall, Yarmin talks to the president after giving his speech of the union address. "I don't want to alarm you, Mr. President, but I think we must prepare all the executives to be escorted to the mountains."

The president agrees and points to one of his staff members. "Jorie, please get all staff members together, and let all Union professionals know it is time to leave our world."

Jorie takes up his silver case as he starts toward the oval door. His body half turns toward the president as he makes one final suggestion to the president. "Yes, sir! But, sir, as you already know, we would need to camouflage our appearance leaving this office. So, if we drive, sir, I suggest you fly to the destination."

The president agrees. "Yes, that is what I intend to do. I appreciate the advice."

Jorie leaves the room. Yarmin proceeds with the issue of the aliens above Earth's atmosphere. "This race of alien beings are very vile and nasty, from what I understand, according to our foreign friends."

Once informed, the president starts to walk out of the Oval Office with some agents and Yarmin. They reach the outside area where both aircraft are parked. Yarmin looks at the president with a very frightful stare. Yarmin says, "I will keep you up to date, Mr. President." All personnel enters each plane as both planes take off toward the hidden bases in the mountains.

Meanwhile, the military is picking up people with have no cars entering into buses and military vehicles; in the interim, cars are following other military vehicles heading toward the hidden bases. It takes hours and hours until people worldwide reach the various army bases. Once they come to the military bases, people rush to the entrances of the military bases scattered as heads of the military personnel with bull horns exclaim loudly, "Please, we need everyone into four separate orderly lines! The doors to the military base will only open when we are in an orderly fashion, people!"

People are hysterical, loud, and confused as military people try to line up orderly. As the military bases' massive steel doors open slowly, many impatient people are trampling others. Therefore, there is an imperative need for the army personnel to step in quickly as people wait many hours to enter the four lines. Several military members with bullhorns shout, "Please follow the color corridor with the assigned color strips down the ramps. As soon as you arrive at that area, our leaders will brief you and show you holographic explanations of the reasons for the extraction of our race."

People talk among themselves with concern about what is going on. Others are scared. Still, others are confused, and some are a bit hysterical. "We're going where?" shouted a few people.

"Let us know! Please give us a heads-up now!" A few hours after the public arrives, single males and females, families with children, and geriatrics are crowded into small areas. Holographic brief communications appear out of thin air, controlled by airwaves in these small areas adjusted by these categories. While the public struggle with various disturbances and disruptions, talking loudly among themselves, without warning, tons of brief comms appear out of nowhere as the general public is startled a bit by this technology. Where some are amazed, others stare and gaze.

In contrast, others look upon it as striking or exciting. Suddenly, the president and other leaders appear to be discussing why they are there. The president relays the critical message to the public, while the other leaders portray the same note. "Do not be alarmed, people! We're going to get off of our planet Earth. Some civilians stayed behind because they believed the threat was no danger, but I must divulge the importance of why you are here. You are here because our race must be a race to preserve our future. There is an alien race that wants to wipe out the distant ancestry. But remarkably, we have been doing exotic projects that have given us your technologies of today's progress throughout the years.

"We are the ancestors of all these aliens. Since we were the first race created, there has been an alien race called the protectors who have been taking Earthlings to various universes for centuries and who live within these universes that have transformed through their terrains into foreign entities. We must flee to these universes to replenish them with alien life again. But this time, we have some protectors, and a race of beings called the Legendaries who will develop a new hybrids team to help fight this enemy off. Until then, we must flee as a human race through a portal called the G300 that will transport many of you to these universes. If you have a loved one you would like to take to a galaxy, please hold their hands or belongings. Otherwise, you will be separated from each other, landing on different universes on different planets lost forever, so I ask that you hang onto each other in this transition."

Yarmin and the president tell the importance of the enemy, "The enemy's goal is to eliminate us or take us hostage to worship their leader, who is more than a tyrant but an overlord who gets his kicks out of games of terror. So with no further words, please head down to the sliding doors that will bring you into a facility where you will meet these creatures. Besides the evil creatures mentioned, some Legendaries will lead your journey, which is a precious alien race. In addition, some protectors will go to these universes to help with the transitions and comfort of the terraforms and teach humans which nutrients are safe to consume."

A few Legendaires show up on the pop-up comms, "*As well as technology to transform the human race into various hybrids that will eventually fight against the menace of the universes. All of you will be a history remembered from this time forward to the future of your sacrifices for the sole survivorship of the human race.*"

Yufer and some Union People say through the pop-up comms, "And then the human race is met by scientists and doctors who take them through the portal's transition as families gather each other." Some families shout out for each other to get together to go through the G300; others let go of some to give them hope as they journey along the way, and some hold their young children. People are chatting, while people shout other comments.

"Over here! Hold on for me! Please wait for me! No, no, awe, they left without me! Help, I can't find my daughter or my son!"

And others are just happy they are going and starting a new life.

During this time in space, Faloosh studies humankind intensely by his appointed leaders. By relaying the message back to the main ship's computers, Faloosh and his family have been monitoring the planet's surface. One of the leaders speaks to the galley on board. "*We seem to have a settlement on the planet with different kinds of combat technology. We don't know if it's more superior or less superior than our technology. We need to look closely at the planet's surface.*"

Another leader, Stunner, suggests something that may make their surface task force more resourceful. "However, *we should scout the areas with the Madrones first to find any resources that may suit our species prolonging their existence. That is the first step we need to accomplish, Draker.*"

Draker punches in some calculations where their systems are beyond holographic simulations but with more advanced technology. You can feel the same environment on the ship, almost like a 3D world. You can walk around in it and taste the environment's surroundings. Draker, after he punches in the calculations, pulls up a terraform of greenery grass, along with a body of water, preferably a large lake, and adjusts in the order of sending not only the Madrones but the Spy ships.

Draker, in an alien language, says, "*Before you send the Madrones, we also need to send the Spy ships to comb the area for threats and other unique items that may be useful for the taking if possible.*"

Another terraform appears in the Middle East as the alien leaders walk around the holographic 3D terraform, smelling the atmosphere and walking through the desert. They see camels and giant camel spiders in the dunes. Draker punches other calculations into their computer system, indexing these creatures along the terraform.

They pull up deep ocean terraforms of giant creatures unknown to humanity and index them. They finally bring up several terraforms of mountains, skies, industrial areas, buildings, and farmlands and index them all. During those studies, they have come across humans and begin to study them through their computers. Decisively, Draker turns toward Stunner and a few other leaders and realizes something.

"These pink and dark-skinned creatures don't seem to be a threat. They fight among each other in wars, destroying and killing each other. They seem to have no regard for each other. On the other hand, we have no relations to other alien species but our own and those with our blood within them to destroy those who come against us. Unlike us, these beings seem to love each other. We have only hate for those who love. They have nothing to offer. Send out the scouts!"

Then, Stunner also notices the humans in another way. "*They seem to have pink skin and maybe a delicacy of some sort.*"

Draker appears to agree. "*They might be.*"

The Inquestorians have not realized yet that they are in the home world of their forefathers. But they have heard in their folklore that humans have something to do with their forefathers, so they are researching on them. Stunner feels deep inside about the humans. "*They seem to be no threat to us. We probably can easily overcome them.*"

Draker reports back to Faloosh as he heads to his leader's chambers. As the rooms open up, Faloosh enjoys entertainment from females on the ship. Draker interrupts him in his alien tone, "*Faloosh master, we come to find out that the pink and dark-skinned creatures below seem to be no threat.*"

Faloosh licks his tongue as he speaks. "*I want to know more about this race. They know of the ancient race.*"

Draker replies, "*From our study so far, Master, their surroundings are light and displacement within various terraforms. They seem to kill each other and love each other.*"

Faloosh lashes out, "*Love each other!*"

Draker kneels to the master. "*Yes, Master, love each other.*"

Faloosh shouts, "*Love! Love! No love will be left in this universe when I complete my task with this solar system. Send the scouts as soon as possible! I want to know more about their evil ways.*"

Draker also says, "*The waters are at least 90 percent of the planet, landmass 10 to 15 percent.*"

Faloosh, feeling disturbed too much, says, "*Get back to the research room and get me some information on minerals from the surface. Again, send out the ships already.*"

Draker quickly gets up from kneeling, and says, "*Yes, Master.*" Draker returns to the research room as he prepares for one of his scout leaders to head the scout team on the surface.

Draker and Stunner will have to discover about the humans as Thorgus, the scoutmaster, will tell them once on the planet's surface. "*I suggest we manipulate the pink and dark-skinned race to determine how they adhere or whether they become immune to the many chemical elements thrown at them through the 3D simulator, would be immune or turn them to become a threat to each other.*"

The doctor keeps her vials in a case in a dark area in the back of the simulation room. Thorgus approaches the spot. Pulling the door open with a push button, he grabs a vial that he isn't sure is correct. Through the 3D simulation, he assumes the vial in Draker's hand is the right one and entrusts him with performing a task on several humans. Draker blows the contents into a vial of human baits to see their effects on them. Stunner looks at Draker blowing the chemical on the subjects to see the results and notices an intelligent remark as he points to another human in the simulation running backward. He stares while talking to Draker. "*Hahaha! That's so funny. He is got his stomach upset!*"

However, Draker views it as only making human behavior a little unpredictable. Draker calls the doctor via a liprod, a tiny gadget attached to his clothing. Draker completes a miniature whistle. Draker's liprod slowly floats to his mouth. The liprod approaches Draker's mouth and turns to the side while Draker adjusts his lips to begin talking into the mouthpiece. Draker calls Munedane, as Munedane happens to be mixing a chemical with an associate of hers. She makes a final adjustment, telling the associate to grab an instrument.

"Can you, Petra, hold the performerine ring so I can put the final mixture of Horin together with the comperine compound? Will give this the standard adjustment we need for the Cameron chemical that requires the cure of the abnormal fetal fetish of the younglings."

Petra grabs their performerine ring and hands it over to Munedane.

Munedane, who has swirled the mixtures together, looks at the chemical with a bright indicator that turns the chemical into another color. Petra states a small comment, *"Looks like the chemical is taking part and performing well, Munedane."*

Munedane gets a call on her liprod as she says one more thing to Petra, *"Petra, we finally have it. We're off to a good start. All we need is a subject in which I have one in mind."* Munedane's liprod is receiving a call from Draker. As the liprod floats toward her mouth, Munedane begins to answer the call, *"Draker, what is the nature of this call? I know it has to be something serious. How can I help you?"*

Draker, on the other line, responds, *"Munedane, do you have that compound called Bustill, which is from the planet called Nubius from the eighteenth universe we had conquered? Do you presumably have that or not?"*

Murdune, thinking specifically about where this vial's location is in her office, pushes a button to open all the doors and stumbles upon it where there are several vials with the same name. She scans through her vials, grabs the one closest to what Draker wants, and tells Petra to keep on task., *"I'll be back. Keep working."* Petra nods her head in a yes motion, as Munedane leaves the room through a frosted door where she can see out, and no one can see through. Munedane travels along several corridors, passing several other species interacting with each other. Among them is a troop training facility where the military practices defensive moves. An area for childbirth is visible on our way. Walking past a classroom where the young are taught not to empathize with those around them, we come across a 3D simulation room. The younglings should have thick skin where nothing disturbs them, even a tiny cry; otherwise, they treat them with stern adult voices and whippings from the teacher behind closed doors. Assuredly, Munedane comes around to the 3D simulation room. As the door opens, Stunner makes an honest funny remark about another human victim of the previous compound used.

"This creature can't stop performing odd moves with something that sounds like weird beats."

One other leader chuckles a bit as well. Draker gets a bit frustrated from the outcome of the compound as he waits patiently for Munedane, who quickly enters the room. Draker talks to himself regarding the last vial as Mundane hands a new compound vial into Draker's left hand and Draker chuckles a bit. "*The species we have been studying ahould respond to this vial, Mundane, since I knew you would come through. This Bustill compound should do the trick!*" While he blows the mixture into some humans, Darker grins almost devilishly. "*Hahaha! Yes, yes! I think it is working!*"

Thorgus looks upon the different human hosts as they inhale the compound, noticing something is not quite happening yet. "*Don't see any coloration in their pink skin!*"

So Draker, who thought the combination would work, becomes a bit too discouraged and turns toward Stunner with a confused look. "*Why is this happening? Why can't we find a vial to make these pink and dark-skinned creatures lust for evil intentions? Why! Why! what is wrong with these beings!*"

Thorgus, also with a confused look on his face, also reminds Draker of the purpose of why they conquer universes. "*We are to beat this thing called love from all galaxies and planets.*"

Stunner interjects a bit, having an odd look, "*They are weird while their pink skin feels like some blockage to the chemical. It seems too bizarre and very complex in their texture.*" Stunner happens to feel the surface of the human skin and also acknowledges something strange to his touch. "*A strange feeling comes over me as I feel their arms having a cold sensation. They are clammy and almost feel reptilian to my touch.*"

Thorgus, hearing Stunner describe the human texture, comes up with a plan. "*Wait a minute! Let me call the scientist, Dunada.*" So Thorgus, on his liprod, makes a call to Dunada, who in return answers quickly on her liprod.

"*Yes, Mashee Thorgus, how may I help you?*"

Thorgus, feeling he can get his way with Dunada, suggests, "*Dunada, please bring me a compound called the stimmer. We must figure out a way to influence these creatures with evil intent.*"

Dunada returns with a hurtful comment, "*I've got a better suggestion for those creatures from the green planet. The chemical mixture is called minenum. Whether or not the minenum works on these creatures is undetermined, but it is stronger than the stimmer.*"

Dunada takes hours to reach the room where the 3D viewing location is. Draker runs after some human creatures in the road when she enters the room, grabbing one and holding him down. As Dunada stumbles over the cord, Thorgus grabs a large tube out of her hand and says, "*I'll take this!*" As Draker is holding a few humans down, Thorgus begins to blow the mixed chemical into the human's nostril, and the lungs fill up, and their chest expands. Munedane turns to Thorgus with an evil smirk.

"*The pink skins are turning reddish. It seems to be making them more aggressive with malicious intent is what we want.*"

One human begins to giggle a lot as his eyes turn bloodshot red with a tint of blue hue. One other human begins to smack the other in the back of the head, almost making the other human swallow his tongue, in which he begins to babble a bit and spit up chunks of a greenish spew out of his mouth. All at once, without warning, Draker, Stunner, Thorgus, and Munedane all say simultaneously, "*I think we got it!*" Meanwhile, Dunada sits back, enjoying watching the two humans battling it out, wrestling, hitting each other hard in a way that leaves bruises and cuts.

Thorgus has a spontaneous idea. "*We must develop a perimeter in that small town.*" The 3D simulator machine moves to a small rural area as the computer programs the data, automatically giving a small border of a city and scoping the zone. Draker realizes the chemical worked in the 3D simulator and could work on the actual human.

In a low tone alongside Thorgus, Draker suddenly remarks, "*But what if it didn't work on the virtual creatures who seem resistant to some of our compounds?*"

Thorgus remembers a war way back. "*Remember the battle of Tanion, where the talon-fighting creatures were immune to some of our compounds through the simulator? When we went to the planet's surface, they weren't resistant to them. Do you remember that war?*"

Draker, with an evil smile, says, "*Yes! Yes! I remember. Let us proceed further, Thorgus.*"

Thorgus grins back. "*Yes, let us move, Master Draker.*"

The perimeter surrounds a town in Texas called Seymour. Draker blows another vial consisting of another chemical into the 3D simulation atmosphere. Many humans are attracted to the initiative toward the new chemical, like bees to pollen, which affects them to the liking of the Inquestorians' evil ways.

The children, the tiny humans, are not affected in this case. Therefore, Thorgus and Draker discuss manipulating a chemical that may affect little humans. Stunner hops toward the vial dispenser cabinet and gracefully grabs one as he turns around quickly with a nasty look. His face is close to Munedane's face. His eyes are toward Draker and Thorgus, raising his hand in belief.

"What about this one? I believe this vial is a good fit for small tiny humans. Let's give it a spin. Why don't we."

Munedane grabs the vial out of Stunner's left hand with a surprised look as she glances at the compound's name on the vial. "*Wow, I don't believe this!*"

Draker, while talking to Thorgus, is interrupted by Munedane's thundering voice and is suddenly distracted. He turns around with a jolt toward Munedane's direction with an odd, weary look. "*What! What is it!*"

Munedane explains that Stunner has come across something that can help them with the puny humans. "*Stunner here has stumbled and picked up the correct vial for the tiny humans where we can experiment on them.*"

Draker wants to know exactly the name of the compound that Stunner came across 'cause it is unlikely Stunner gets anything right. "*What combination did so-call Stunner come across.*"

Munedane reassures and gives Draker the compound's name as she walks toward Draker. "*The name of this compound here is called clustic. This one may seem to work on small humans. Let's see what it does.*"

Meanwhile, as she hands Draker the vial, Thorgus grabs it from her. "*I'll take that.*" At that instant, although it was for Draker, Thorgus walks in front of Draker and begins to blow the vial compound onto the tiny humans within a 3D imaging simulation.

Dunada suddenly comments, "*We need that compound to work on the puny humans because if we were to conquer this planet, we want all the creatures big and small to worship the overload Faloosh.*"

In the interim, Thorgus blows more of the vial's compounds on the various tiny humans in the simulation. The small humans beget their evil intention on the small town by smashing toys, kicking cars, bashing in windows, and even playing sick games of jokes on each other. Thorgus and Draker, appointed by Faloosh to test theories on the planet, begin to address a different part of the planet, more toward the western parts of Africa. They notice that these humans have darker skin; some have tones of red hue and others of purple hues, and some dark skin have different-colored hairs and eyes compared to the lighter-skinned humans. They use other vials and notice that humans' dark skin seems immune to them. They have used identical vials on the dark-skinned humans that they had on the lighter-skinned people and noticed that they have difficulty finding the suitable compounds that affect the darker-skinned humans.

Thorgus, noticing a familiarity of the dark-skinned humans, reminding him of a species some millenniums ago, starts to talk as he gets the attention of the male counterparts within the 3D simulation room. "*Wait a minute! Why do these dark-skinned creatures look so familiar? Like we conquered these beings before.*"

Stunner, who has a different outlook on these dark humans, says, "*I don't know if we did.*"

Draker agrees with Thorgus about some familiarities to a race they once conquered before. "*They look so familiar to another universe of species many millenniums ago.*"

Thorgus, with deep thought, comes up where he had seen these dark humans before. "*They come from a universe called Siribius. They had the element of surprise when they almost defeated us in the war, which was very similar tp the battle of chelonians. What do we do with such beings? What vial do we use on them?*"

Draker frowns toward Munedane as though he doesn't want to battle these beings again. "*What do we do!*"

Thorgus looks at Stunner, then Draker. "*I don't know!*"

Munedane turns to one of her helpers and, without hesitation, has an idea of what vial might work on these dark humans. "*Go grab me the vial called the caffon, and hurry, please.*"

The helper, with no hesitation, runs to the science lab and looks around as her eyes move quickly among the moving cabinets. Seeing in alphabetically, she happens to grab two vials of similarity and heads back promptly to the 3D simulation lab. She hands both over to Mundane. Munedane looks at both vials, which say caffonA and caffonB.

She quickly hands over caffonB to Draker quickly. "*Let's try this one.*"

They smile at each other wickedly.

CHAPTER 27

STUDYING THEIR ADVERSARY

Draker remembers this compound had some effect on the dark creatures from their war a long time ago. "*I think the mixture you have given me, Munedane, the caffonB here will affect these dark humans. We recently defeated a parallel universe with a dark skin tone and a greenish hue.*"

Munedane, in response, also recalls similar battles with different creatures. "*Remember other creatures with a white hue and a pinkish-reddish glow around them?*"

Draker remembers. "*Yes, they were the ones we defeated after the dark creatures.*"

Mundane agrees with Draker. "*That's right, Draker.*"

Draker feels good about the compound Munedane has given him. "*We conquered them with both compounds combined. They slowly subdued to our commands.*"

Munedane agrees again with Draker. "*Yep, that is correct, Draker.*"

Draker proceeds with the vial as he slowly sprinkles it toward the dark humans. "*This compound here should get these dark humans to do our bidding. It turns their skin into a lighter hue we can control.*" Thorgus grabs the other vial from Munedane's hand, the caffonA. Another dark human gets on his knees and starts praying as Thorgus blows the sediments of the compound on him. As the dark human becomes a pale yellow to purple hue, the human suddenly becomes very evil and superhuman, tearing apart wild animals, robbing villages, hauling cars, and throwing them on other humans. Draker and the others smile evilly and are satisfied. Even though the Earth as a globe is moving peacefully; little does it know what level of destruction and disaster awaits it. It's just a matter of time.

Thorgus and Draker, with evil, look toward each other with a weird handshake, congratulating each other on their evil accomplishments as they exchange words on the evilest intents on humankind. Thorgus says to Draker as he gives a peculiar handshake, "*Now that is what you call progress, the most vicious of them all! Hahaha!*"

Draker responds, "*Yes, my evil brethren, I call it conquering of the colorless creatures to abide by our rules and serve our overlord. Ha, ha!*" As they continue with the compounds on other dark humans, some become drunk, stumbling over each other as their task becomes eviler and eviler between each other and things in their way.

Thorgus laughs a bit as he sees the humans stumble when he makes a cruel joke toward Stunner, "*They are such an inebriated look like they are stumbling over stairs you can't see in the dark.*"

Stunner laughs a bit and comes back with an odd comment, "*Yes, like charcoals that light up on a grill.*"

Draker looks at several dark humans, then turns toward Thorgus and Munedane. "*Those that are confused seem to be at times falling over. I don't think those types of creatures would be an asset to our army. It's like wasted material.*"

Dunada agrees with Draker. "I agree with you, the great one."

They turn the 3D simulator toward another planet area toward the United States forestry. They come across the red Indian tribes with unusual dressings on their heads, and Draker suddenly says, "*Catalog them.*" Draker takes his right hand and whizzes through the holographic catalog to find out what type of beings wearing these weird dressing on their head could be. He bumps into a portion of the record and comes up with the name of these odd beings. "*They're called American Red Indians.*"

Thorgus says, "*You mean engines.*"

Draker repeats, "*No, Indians.*"

Thorgus is a bit confused. "*Engines, machines.*"

Draker breaks it down to Thorgus. "*Okay, they are called In-di-ans.*"

Thorgus finally understands what they are and asks, "*Okay, since they are called In-di-ans, what do these have to do with the creatures on this planet?*"

Draker pushes some buttons on the computer and, with a confused look, says, "*They are similar to the pink- and dark-skinned creatures, except these seem to blend a hue of red as well! I am totally in awe here.*" Next, Draker asks for another vial that would confuse the Indians. "*Give me another vial!*" Munedane, who has have several vials around her belt, turns to a vial that would confuse the American Indians and hands it to Draker. Draker talks to Thorgus, Munedane, Stunner, and Dunada.

"We have to get them to loosen up by this vial because if we were to capture them, we must know if they would follow Faloosh and worship him."

Munedane walks over to the holographic storage room and examines various vials. *"If we still can't find what we need, we'll try again."*

She takes a vial out of the holographic storeroom, naming it checkief. She hands it to Thorgus, who blows it toward the Indians on the stage in 3D holography. Their size gradually shrinks as they start smashing things and getting into cars, like a bunch of little clowns just wrecking things. Thorgus, with an evil laugh, says, *"This is good. Faloosh would laugh at this. He would love these."*

Draker is rubbing his hands back and forth. *"Yes! Yes! He would!"*

The aliens discuss the tragedies of the human race with the different compounds of vials. Finally, Draker talks to Thorgus, when he says, *"Thorgus, we need to have some strategies to deal with these pink, black-skinned, and red hue creatures before we go onto the surface."*

Thorgus, in turn, remarks, *"These vials our Spy ships will take. If these pink, black-skinned, and red creatures were to attack us, these would come in handy. They would fight among each other then we could take the evil ones aboard that would worship Faloosh. What do you think about that?"*

Stunner begins to grin more and more. *"That is a good idea, Thorgus."*

Draker starts to think of another strategy. *"We can also use it on them in turn of not only a war that breaks out but a precaution as well."* Thorgus and Dunada nod their heads in agreement with Draker's strategy.

Thorgus says admiringly, *"However diabolic and clever, we must run more simulations before we run the stages of our plan, which is to find minerals, and if the pink, red, and dark-skinned creatures are more of a threat, we will be ready. However, our purpose is to make all universes worship Faloosh and his people."*

Draker further acknowledges, *"We shall embark within this unique program where the pink, red, and black-skinned race will become our minions that will do the bidding for Faloosh. If it comes down to that, Thorgus. Unfortuntely, it might take years to get these creatures under our control cause, according to the 3D simulation, just one creature takes hours for any compound to affect them."*

Stunner adjusts on the strategic planning computer while looking at a plot of the computer's strategic plans on the human race. *"From looking on the computer here. It seems it will take a shorter time than that, Thorgus. I believe it may take instead of years, maybe months."*

Thorgus, with more of an agenda for the human race, discusses the strategies of overcoming the human race. "*Since our genetic type is for us to rule, and whatever gets in our way will eventually do our bidding, they will abide with the law because we are the law. I must now make our way to this dangerous endeavor as soon as possible, Master Draker.*"

Stunner laughs evilly, almost like a Muppet but a bit more profound. "*Haha, ah huh, hahaha! Yes! Yes! These aliens will do our bidding, yes! Master Draker. Oh! I must ask Master Draker. I want one of these aliens in my chamber, eventually doing a little workout for my pets while entertaining myself.*"

Draker looks at Stunner and says, "*For real! What kind of entertainment would that be? You're usually dancing around the room doing acrobatic things or just being a momma for you! Hahaha!*"

Stunner laughs some more then explains the human use in his living quarters. "*Haha! Hum, ah, yes, Master Draker, the pink, red, black-skinned creatures are used for my amusement and entertainment by being my slave. If you and Faloosh give that wish to me, that would be the evil intent of all the armies of Faloosh. I think, why not!*"

Thorgus laughs at Stunner, amused at the possible human enslaved beings. "*Haha! Give me a break! Hahaha.*"

Thorgus continues with the ramification of the 3D simulation probability to stabilize the human race regarding their alien compounds. "*According to the 3D simulator, we are at 55 percent probability of conquering the pink, red, black-skinned creature race. But if we up that probability to 85 percent, we have a great possibility of destroying them with the compounds we had used in the simulator together if mixed correctly. Only one knows when the ships are out scouting the area and the effect on the pink, red, and black-skinned creatures.*"

Draker fills in with Thorgus about the conquering of the humans. "*We must have a way of disarming these pink, red, and black-skinned creatures on a massive global scale which is eminent to our success of taking them over if need be. Despite having superior weapons, we cannot underestimate these pink, red, and black-skinned creatures regardless of whether their skin is pink, thick, black, or yellow. We have to conclude that if they attack us, we would have to cloud the atmosphere with the compounds we have tried through the 3D simulator to find out if the compounds work on the anatomy of the pink, red, and black-skinned creatures.*"

Stunner, with an odd remark, has to get his two cents in on the conversation. "*These pink, red, and black-skinned creatures are like peeling the fruit off of a vine.*

They will be our minions to rule over. Hahaha! Ah, we will be the juggernauts of this world. We will rerun the simulation to finalize this tactic."

While Stunner is saying this, Munedane looks at Stunner, staring at him. Then turning her attention to Draker, she says, "*Draker, I think I got it. Why don't we push the limits of the 3D simulation to harness the full potential of the compounds on the pink, red, and black-skinned creatures? It will give us better judgment toward conquering them, even though we will eventually take over this world and subside it with Faloosh laws. But if they resist, we will kill them through our war games."*

Thorgus turns toward Draker to begin working again on the 3D simulation; getting the idea from Munedane recharging the simulation with a more considerable percentage of compounds over the human specimens. Draker starts to plot a more advanced task that will give them the power to overcome the human species. Draker is pouring the blends.

"*This should work, Munedane, and it will tell us a better probability toward the confirmation of actually conquering the pink, red, and black-skinned creatures for good."*

The computer starts saying. "Calculation of compound effect is 100 percent accurate." The 3D simulation calculates as the humans in the simulator take more drastic measures as the compounds work over time, affecting the humans in a more nonrational, violent way.

Munedane also comments on Thorgus, who seems to carry on with Stunner, "*Continue with the research and stop talking garble stuff.*" Munedane hits Thorgus and Stunner in the back of the head and says one last thing as an evil joke. "*You're not reigning supremacy. Yet you two, the only thing you both lead now is a snomoboors similar to white rats, except as you both know, the leader of the same fury fast snomoboors with saber tooth's gnawed on the leader would be the black snomoboor. Hence, the white ones take him over if he misleads them."*

Thorgus's eyebrows crisscross, as Stunner has a curious look as well. "*What is the reason for this lesson, Munedane? What do the snomoboors have to do with what Stunner and I were talking about or for that matter?"*

Munedane gives Thorgus the rundown of the scenario. "*Well, Thorgus, the snomoboor scheme is to get you two to know that no matter what you and Stunner are talking about, your troops always overrun you. Thorgus, they rarely adhere to your commands because you do remember a few battles back your men came up with a plan without listening to your orders at that time they won the war. You do remem-*

ber that, right? In other words, similar to the snomoboor leader, they took over that was eating you up inside for decades to come."

Thorgus laughs evilly and embarrassingly tells Munedane, "*I do remember that, except I called the final plan that gave the final blow to the enemy. After that, I initiated the rouge warriors before the giants that squashed the enemies."*

Munedane laughs and giggles as she says in a low tone, "*Yeah! Right!"*

Stunner gets Thorgus's attention regarding the Spy ships. "*Thorgus! We have to get the vessel out pretty soon."*

Entering the room is another alien. After a few minutes, Thorgus speaks to Stunner, "*Well! Right away, we need the Spy ships ready to launch."* Thorgus presses a button on a console as another alien enters immediately. Mapoh, the squad leader of Spy ships, is short in stature, and when he talks, he sounds like a small parrot. Mapoh, with attention, stands in front of Thorgus as he looks ahead toward the 3D simulation and begins to speak.

"*Yes, your eminence, what can I do for you?"*

Thorgus turns toward the front of Mapoh and salutes him with two hands across the chest in a crisscross position. "*Mapoh, I have a task for your fleet this week. I want you and your fleet to gain minerals that we use on the ship daily, and these compounds right here will be added to your ship's deposit dispensers so when your vessel is in trouble with the pink, red, and black-skinned aliens. It will cloud the area from above once projected into the sky over the zone. According to our calculations, in minutes, the pink, red, and black-skinned creatures will be in disarray and confused about what they are doing to the area and themselves. Got it, Mapoh?"*

Mapoh, with evil intent, shakes Thorgus's hand with one final request before he leaves his site to get his fleet ready to embark on Earth's surface. "*I have a request, Master Thorgus."*

Thorgus is trying to return to his duties. "What is it, Mapoh?"

Mapoh proceeds with the request. "*Well, I want to make sure if we find any odd minerals, can my team experiment with it, and if we find an unusual mean creature, can we have it as a mascot?"*

Thorgus smiles wickedly and says, "*Even make extraordinary pink, red, and black-skinned creatures your mascot."* And then he lets out a burst of chilling laughter.

Thorgus mumbles to himself as though they want a pet that Faloosh is against for any army personnel to have. Because it would defeat the purpose and make the military staff start to care about something instead of their ultimate evil intention to conquer all things. Thorgus gives the latter idea a no and the first idea a go. "*Hmm, well, Mapoh! If they find an odd mineral, your team can look at it. As for a mascot, Faloosh will not approve because we already have our mascot on board, and you know that already.*"

Mapoh asks differently why the mascot caters to his fleet only. "*We want the mascot only in regards to our fleet. We know we have our pet mascots Faloosh had appointed his family and all to worship him. We only want our own that looks out for our troops, Master.*"

Thorgus again reconfirms with a straight look, looking like a killer toward Mapoh as he gives his absolute disgust at what Mapoh wants for his fleet. "*No! Again it is a no! Captain Mapoh, that is all for now. We must get the fleet ready to dislodge onto the planet's surface immediately. Got it! Mapoh, now get ready!*" Mapoh pouts and then laughs as though he has an alternative motive that refutes Thorgus's decision. Mapoh leaves the 3D simulation room as a red and purple light starts whaling with a thunderous alarm, signaling the Spy fleet to board their ships.

Millions of little creatures start running toward the ship bays with no warning. The creatures are so crowded that they run as though they are stacked up, while some knock each other over as they swing toward their ship's entrance with its controls. The ships are shaped like pointy bows and arrows with a small haul for two aliens to move back and forth through. Tons of ships begin to rev up their engines as they descend from the main ship's haul. Tons and tons of Spy ships appear through the clouds of the Earth as they speed through the landmass as one of the foremost scouts scans the area. Then without warning, its computer picks up a few different minerals.

The scout reports to the main ship, "*We have found several minerals, one of them smithsonite. Also found plenty of zinc and calcium in the planet's crust.*"

On the main ship near the 3D simulation room in the scientist area, Munedane and Dunada are conversing as they get the results from the prominent scout leader on Munedane's liprod. Munedane tells Dunada about a particular chemical mixture. "*Take the minimal terk and mix it with the slime. You will get a torgu, which is helpful for the appetite of young teens. It should work.*"

Dunada is about to say something, but she is interrupted by Munedane's liprod. "*Well, I think, ah—*"

Munedane's liprod rings in as she answers it. "*Yes, Talon, what is it?*"

Talon, the lead scout, replies, "*We found smithsonite along with zinc and calcium within the planet's core.*"

Munedane feels like they have won the lottery, and runs to the 3D simulation room to tell all the leaders the excellent news. "*I have good news. We have struck into the planet's core and found smithsonite, zinc, and calcium.*"

Draker, who knows already, says, "*You're telling old news, Munedane. Someone gave me that news hours ago. And you're just getting it. Wow!*"

Munedane is confused about why she got the information later, which she usually gets before the leaders if they have to send a few ships out to manage the materials before the leaders get the word. However, since their computer upgraded centuries ago, the leaders now get word first before the scientists in case blockage prevents them from getting the materials. In this case, many Spy ships had flown through inactive volcanoes to get to the minerals.

In the short term, both Thorgus and Draker come across another type of human with slanted eyes in several regions of the Earth. Draker, who has no idea what they are, says, "*What strange and bizarre yellow-hue-skinned creatures seem like they have a hard time seeing with eyes almost shut.*"

Stunner says something ridiculous as he jumps up, shouting it out, changing his voice to fit a Chinese human with a slight alien accent, as Stunner's computer pronounces what they are in a machine language.

"They are Chinese."

Stunner says, "*The computer says they are Chinese. They seem to be on their knees. Extraordinary yellow-skinned creatures. On their knees, looking up at clouds, they must be waiting for something strange to hit them to move from their spots.*"

Thorgus looks at Stunner with a wild and peculiar look. "*Shut up, you stupid fool!*"

Stunner slams on the desk, and looks back at Thorgus with a mean look. "*That's what the computer calls them, and their pink skin looks a bit tighter than the other pink skins in the different regions of the world.*"

Thorgus makes a vile remark. "*I don't care what they call them. We must ensure we stay on top of our mission. The Spy ships comb all areas of the planet, and the compounds should be situated in case disruption occurs.*"

Munedane reaffirms Thorgus's plans for the Spy ships and keeps Stunner calm in his area on the computers. "*Stunner! Please make sure the ships are on schedule. Don't worry about these new pink skins. We have compounds that can affect them too. Also, some other weird brown skins near the south end of Africa are called Indians but seem to be a bunch of them that worship cows, which appears to be a delicacy to us. Only one would say in time! Get back to work, Stunner. Thorgus and I will see these various brown-skinned creatures and the compounds that will affect them. We need to make some more adjustments for future scouts to subdue these brown-skinned creatures, according to Faloosh and what he wants us to do at the time. Got it, Stunner!"*

Stunner looks down as though he got scolded, with eyes droopy. He begins to push buttons on the computer minding his own business as Munedane speaks to Draker about the minerals and lets Faloosh know more about it. "*Draker, since we got a word regarding to some minerals, shouldn't we let Faloosh know more about it and what action needs to take place?"*

Draker is studying the other types of humans as his attention is elsewhere asking Munedane to repeat her business. "*Please repeat what you just said, Munedane, because I am busy studying these other brown-skinned creatures with various compound usage needed to exploit their inner evils."*

Munedane, who hates to repeat herself, sighs and tells Draker again. "*Since we found minerals, shouldn't we let Faloosh know about it? Did you understand me this time, Draker!"*

Draker, who was handling some compounds in his hands, almost dropping them out of his hands, says frantically, "*Yes, got you now, Mundane. Master Chief Thorgus will let Faloosh know more about it on our next task."*

Thorgus receives a nudge from Draker as Thorgus turns toward Draker while inputting some numbers into the computer database. "*Yes, your leadership, what can I do for you?"*

Draker grabs Thorgus's shoulders and shouts, "*You know you need to let our warlord see the situation at hand and find out what to do next, Chief."*

Thorgus quickly turns toward the sliding doors and exits, and twenty minutes go by as Thorgus enters Faloosh's chambers. Faloosh has a few of his goons feeding his pets below his section. Faloosh is interrupted by Thorgus with the news that sparks an interest in Faloosh's monstrous ears.

"*Warlord! We have come to a planet with 90 percent of the minerals we need, like smithsonite, zinc, and calcium, which are huge layers that can last us millenniums! Unsuccessfully, we haven't found platinum yet. We're still looking diligently, Warlord. What should we do until then, Master?"*

Faloosh, in a slow-motion mechanical way, stands up slowly, thinks for a moment, and shouts with a burst of evil laughter behind it, "*Haha! Yes! Yes! Send out the Madrones right away! Now! Go, I want all of it! Go now!"*

Thorgus, religiously, backs away toward the exit, bows down toward Faloosh continuously. Once at the doorway, Thorgus turns around fast, runs down the hallways, enters the 3D simulation room where the leaders are, and starts discussing a strategy to get all minerals from the Earth's core. Meanwhile, Munedane explains to Draker, Stunner, Dunada, and the rest of the leaders what a volcano is.

"*Wait! Wait! You see right here.*" Munedane points her finger toward a mountainous area that seems to ooze some molten lava. "*On top of the mountain, pours out a hot liquid.*"

Glued to the area, Stunner and Draker focus theier attention, as Munedane explains Draker's left hand and reaches over the top, burning his fingertips. "*Ow! Ow! Now that hurts.*"

Stunner begins to laugh hysterically. "*Haha! Hehehe! Now that was a brilliant move! Haha!*"

Draker, not liking the jester joke Stunner just mentioned, as Munedane continues to explain what is spilling out of the mountaintop.

"*You see, this inward mountain that has this hot goo coming out of it is called a volcano.*"

Draker, very curious about this type of mountain, wants to know more about it. "*Exactly what does it do to the terrain here, Munedane?*"

Munedane explains why volcanoes exist to Draker, "*Well, Draker, first of all, volcanoes increase landmass by melting lava and expanding the planet.*"

Draker is again very intuitive with the scope of what a volcano does. "*Interesting, because most volcanoes on other worlds mainly eat up the terrain this one produces. That is a project I would like to intervene in one day.*"

Suddenly, Thorgus, without warning, enters speedily into the room. He seems out of breath as he tries to gasp for air. "*Huh, huh, hew, hew, whew, okay. Here we go!*"

Draker wants to hear what the overlord said. "*So what did he say! Tell us!*"

Thorgus gasps for air. "*Hey, Faloosh wants us to get all the minerals possible. He wants it all! He wants us to send out the Madrones right away. We must release the Madrones unto the surface right now!*"

Draker shows Thorgus an image on the screen from one of the Spy ships going down through volcano walls seeing smithsonite, zinc, and calcium walls.

Thorgus, satisfied and excited evilly, says so violently, "*Treasures and treasures! It's time to tear down those walls and get all the samples, so send out the*

Madrones immediately so they can start collecting them! Now! Draker, we have to proceed now!"

Draker, knowing Thorgus is in a time crunch, messes with him a little bit, as Stunner gets a kick out of the whole thing. "*Look, Thorgus on the screen, there seems to be a problem.*"

Thorgus wonders what the problem is on the screen where he doesn't appear to see a problem at all. "*I don't see a problem at all, Draker. Now let's proceed already.*"

Draker continues his farce a little bit longer. "*Looks like we can't get through all of the rock.*"

Thorgus, outraged, says, "*What! We don't want to disappoint Faloosh. Is there a way around it or not!"*

Draker looks into Thorgus's eyes and says, "*Yes. We are blasting the planet's entire surface with our highest technology weapons. But for this, we will need to talk to Faloosh and take his permission as we have with other worlds. This one has by far much more to offer inside its core.*"

Thorgus looks a bit scared now. "*I can't possibly go back to Faloosh with this piece of colorful rock. So you do it, Draker.*"

Darker is amused. In his words, "*Okay, on one condition I will.*"

"*Please, Darker, do this for me.*" Thorgus is furious but controls himself and says, "*Okay, please, Draker, do this for me.*"

Darker smiles wickedly as he confidently looks toward Faloosh's chambers, which is quite a distance to walk to, and after finishing the present task, he decides to do so.

Draker and Thorgus simultaneously input some numeric symbols into a holographic, syncing different computers and instructions for the Madrone ships. Decisively, they both input the final commands into the computers, as a gold and spiral shape color signal emerges throughout the spaceship to signal the pilots of these ships to board immediately.

The captain of the Madrones enters the 3D simulation room with a final saying as he enters.

"*Our mission from my wrist scanner says that generals and appointed leaders engulf all smithsonite, zinc, and calcium findings. If we bump into platinum, grab and deplete all substances, depleting this world's core.*"

CHAPTER 28

THE ANNIHILATION PLAN X

Thorgus, Draker, Stunner, Munedane, Dunada, and other leaders simultaneously speak aloud. "*That is right. Now get going and get the job done already!*" Draker, on the other hand, waits to see if his assumption of the Earth's intricate rock layers to core theory is right or wrong.

As the ships prepare to depart, all you can hear throughout the bay is "*Heard loud and clear, Captain!*" The captain leaves immediately out of the sliding doors to the ship bays as he directs his troops through a visual aid on their ships with the command at hand. "*Now, troops! As you read the holographic map, remember the order given to you to accomplish. Stay with that command until it's finished. Got it!*" The ships begin to depart from the ship's bay in the hundreds. They start to descend to Earth through the clouds and speedily through the terrains into the volcanoes as some vessels begin to open up a vacuum area of the spaceship that can pull hard metals off a mountain. Two ships enter the volcanoes at a time, pulling debris upon smithsonite, zinc, and calcium debris. All the minerals are uniformly distributed below the earth and toward the deep core. But it gets tricky as they try to go deeper for the more enormous and more valuable resources and their search for platinum.

In the meantime, the remaining humans hide behind massive objects and some underground facilities as they see these medium-size ships descending upon the planet. Mass hysteria begins, and humans try to hide from the invasion. One human looks up and says with fear in his eyes, "What the hell is that!"

Another human screams out loud, running in the opposite direction, "No! No! No! They are invading us!"

In amazement, another human freezes and stares in shock. "What in God's great Earth is that! We have to run! Run, people, run!"

Children are amazed and stunned, and some run toward the alien ships as the ships streak by fast. Some children are terrified, clinging desperately to their parents' hands. As well as military personnel who are ready to shoot them down if they pose a threat. An army soldier talks to his captain, who is by his side. The soldier looks to the sky to see if the ships are to shoot at the humans.

"Captain! They don't seem harmful. They might have come to learn about us."

The captain looks on suspiciously. "I don't know, Sergeant, but I...I don't think so."

Sergeant sees one of the ships scanning the area. "They must be observing us now to see if we're a threat, but they are definitely up to something."

Suddenly, the aliens who have been instructed to capture the remnant of humans left behind come and scoop up some of them as they drop them into huge nets on the ships below.

The humans' screams are heard in the distance, frantically, everywhere. Many human beings go into hiding, those who have been caught are questioned on the spacecraft's exterior, where they are questioned.

"*Faloosh is our leader. Are you ready to serve him and his siblings and children without questions or be left behind on this planet, which will soon decimate? We will cremate the surface of your planet by ripping it into shreds.*"

The majority of humans agree to board the spaceship. Additionally, those who disagree will get thrown into open volcanoes. Other people hiding and watching shuddered at sight of intergalactic communication. The original Legendary, a spy, reveals to the scientists about the various incidents and the threat of invasion of the Earth.

Meanwhile, Draker researches on their supercomputers that these humans throughout history loved to kill each other. Draker, with an evil laugh, says, "*So this is their weak point as it seems that the pink, yellow, red, and black-skinned creatures love to fight among each other, although they tried to fight our ships below. I love the part when these creatures fight with each other. It shows the girth of evil intentions. I love that part of these creatures, and they may make exceptional warriors among our armies when mixed with our blood.*" The other leaders in the room tend to agree with Draker.

Draker continues, "*We can mate those females with our warriors, making a species so violent in our army to do our bidding.*"

The other leaders chant, "*Evil rise, evil conquers, evil justified!*"

Thorgus inputs a bit, "*These pink and black skins can be helpful or even tactical in our army. Maybe take some of them to worship me.*"

Stunner intervenes with Thorgus. "*That might be a good idea.*"

Thorgus replies, "*I am intelligent, aren't I.*"

Stunner snickers a bit. Just then, Faloosh's server enters the room of the leaders. "*Faloosh has a message of concern. The news is, if this is the race of old, they must disintegrate. Make sure you all research that before as we take all their resources before conquering them.*"

Draker and Thorgus look at each other and communicate with the computer. The computer turns out with some odd news. "*Their technology is with a strange statement. Although ancient creatures may have been bold, their diabolic ways may have been cold. Make adjustments make surety. Trouble them, and they will fold.*" All the leaders look at each other oddly, thinking that the computer may need adjustment.

Thorgus says, "*We must recalculate before conquering these species.*"

Draker punches some numbers into the computer to get a recalculation of the humans for the mission of taking them over.

Some of the Madrone's ships go deep down through the pits of the volcanoes. Within that area, they get sediments of more calcium and zinc deposits off the walls and crevices of the walls and grounds. One of the head squadron leaders of the Madrone discovers a new and improved element on the inside of a narrow cave entrance of a volcano. That leader logs the information into their computer and then snaps it. The being heads fast out of the volcano to relay the message to the mother ship.

"*Leader Mapoh, we've found traces of a new element. Sending pictures of it now.*"

The computer transfers the picture to the mother ship. They get an image showing the image on their big screen once assigned.

In the interim, Munedane is chatting with an associate in the science room. "*Well, we would need to analyze the new material that we just received from the planet's core, to make sure it is a good fit for utilizing of our weapons and engines for travel and combat.*"

The associate puts her two cents into the discovery. "*Master Scientist Munedane, I've been looking through it. The related chemicals that are seen here that the compounds found on the planet seem to be a far superior compound that may supersede ours by one thousand to one hundred thousand, meaning it will last our people a lot longer than usual.*"

Munedane is surprised and beside herself, feeling very happy that her superiors, Faloosh's siblings, and Faloosh will be thrilled. Then, with shock on her face she says, "*Are you serious!*"

The associate reaffirms again, "*Yep, really, Master Scientist, ma'am.*"

Munedane smiles real big as she is interrupted by squadron leaders calling on her liprod hanging to the right side of her face, and a sharp beep hits her liprod as she tries to shake the sharpness within her ear. "*Yes! Yes! What is it, Squadron Leader Tirus?*"

Squad Leader Tirus's transmission comes through with a squealing sound, then slowly dissipates from Munedane's ears as he gradually relays his message to her. "*We have found a new element. It says here on my computer screen it is helpful for all technology. My computer also says it can enhance technology one thousand to one hundred thousand times its use.*"

Munedane, surprisingly happy with this outcome, has Tirus send her a sample through her holographic lab. "*Please send a fragment as quickly as possible so I can analyze it right away. Make sure it's a big enough piece too. Did you get that, Tirus!*"

Tirus responds, "*No problem, Master Scientist, it's on its way now.*"

Munedane disconnects from Tirus as she analyzes the glowing object. "*Let me see here. This mixture pulses in and out in a dark room.*" So she says to her assistant as her computer gives her the mix's name. "*When light hits it, it turns to almost a silverish color. Wow! Unique. It looks like we have something our people can work with.*"

The assistant tends to agree and further explores it, giving more reasons why they would need it. "*Look! It turns another two colors, green and orange. I can see why it is helpful because it probably can be helpful, like the squad leader said, for all technology through the versatility of the changing aura. I bet it will charge up our technology to be full strength with no problem for a very long period or maybe long enough for eons from now.*"

Munedane is amused at how her assistant analyzes the object, and the computer returns with the element's name. "*The name of the compound is larimar.*" Munedane speedily reports to Faloosh in regard to this new compound.

As that is going on, another squadron leader who had to relay a message to Mapoh found the same element in a different volcano. Mapoh, Draker, and the others all comment as they sigh in shock. "*What! That is exceptionally amazing! We must have it!*"

Mapoh steps too fast and says, "*Going to tell Faloosh about this. He may want insight into this compound.*" Mapoh leaves toward the doorway and, without warning, begins to race down the corridor toward Faloosh's quarters, bumping into Munedane, who seems to be going the same direction, almost knocking her onto the ship's floor. Mapoh continues toward the corridor as Munedane picks herself up from the floor and continues speeding toward the passage of Faloosh's quarters, as Mapoh enters. A few minutes later, Munedane enters Faloosh's quarters. They both are waiting as their nerves build up as Faloosh seems busy with other tasks. Faloosh is staring at some of the specimens he had collected from other worlds through his glass windows. Below the species seem to be attacking each other playfully.

Faloosh, with a calm voice gradually with no motion, turns around toward Munedane and Mapoh and yells frantically without warning, almost scaring his soldiers. All at once, the leaders in the room explode with an unremorseful voice, "*What! What! Is it?*" Faloosh reminds them of their duties. "*Haven't I told you what to do when you find the correct compounds!*"

Mapoh's throat slowly gulps a bit as he tells Faloosh what he saw. "*Master, we have discovered a new element that may be useful.*"

Faloosh looks down a bit, then up with curiosity. "*Well, what exactly is this new element? Tell me and its purpose!*"

Mapoh says with a frightful voice, "*Well, we haven't got to that point yet. Do you want us to analyze it?*"

Faloosh's eyebrows go down as though furious. "*Why would you come to my chambers without all that is needed? Why!*"

Munedane interrupts as she bows down to Faloosh. "*Master, Master, I have the analyses of this compound already.*"

Faloosh whips out a talon whip that flies by Munedane's head as it whips Mapoh's side of his face. "*You fool. You let our female scientists find out this information before our male counterparts. You are a disgrace to the male counterparts of our race.*"

Mapoh's head is down as though he is embarrassed by the female. He turns his head away from the sight of Faloosh's face as Faloosh tells Munedane to continue.

"*Please continue with the analysis you have discovered.*"

Munedane continues with viciousness in her voice. "*Master! What we have found is an element called larimar.*"

Faloosh frowns again and, with a weird and humorous look, blurts out, "*LARIMAR, LARIMAR! WHAT IS LARIMAR?*"

Munedane explains what it is and does. "*Well, Master! It glows and turns four different colors, two in dark light and two in bright sunlight.*"

Faloosh starts with a humorous statement, "*What are we having with this compound, a party or a parade? Sounds like nonsense to me.*"

Munedane approaches Faloosh slowly as she hands him a glance report on a holographic pallet. She further tells him the analysis of the compound element. "*Again! From just looking at it, it seems that it can enhance our technology from one thousand to one hundred thousand times efficiency, making all our technology last for eons from now. It may last us forever, from what my assistant and I concluded.*"

With his intuition, Faloosh happens to say after he looks at the holographic tablet and makes his conclusion from Munedane's reports, with a vengeful smile as greed hits him and his eyes turn a nasty dark blue with red and a tinge of green. "*I want it all now! Go and get it! Do my bidding, and my children do it now!*"

Munedane and Mapoh head back to their quarters to tell their squad leaders to get all the compounds as much as their ships can carry and bring them back to the main spaceships. Mapoh enters the 3D simulation room and quickly gets on his liprod at his station as he talks back to the squad leader.

"*Our master Faloosh wants all of the elements as much as you can find right away! Got it!*"

The squad leader's liprod lights up and slowly moves toward his mouth area as Mapoh gives him the information. "*Yes! Yes! I got it.*" The squad leader sends data to his team to retrieve as much of that element as possible and return it to the mother ship.

Meanwhile, Munedane calls Tirus on his liprod. "*Tirus, our warlord, Faloosh, made clear that he wants all of the elements as much as our spaceships can carry. He wants it all. Did you get that? I am sending schematics of possible locations to your computer now. Please advise your men to be careful with the element. We want them in their appropriate size and to never crush them. So we are sending transmission now.*"

Tirus gets the message as he says one other comment, "*Are we supposed to fill up the hauls with this compound than the others, Madam Scientist?*"

Munedane is about to hang up. "*Yes! Yes! Munedane is out.*"

Tirus relays the message to his squad, "*Okay, squad, new mission. We need the element that was last on our scanners to acquire. Carefully transmit them to your ship and return them to the mother ship. Unload cargo in the hauls as much as our spaceships can carry. Got it!*"

All squad gets transmission and command from Tirus as they start to carry out the mission; both Mapoh squad leaders and Munedane squad leaders gather as much of the larimar as they can carry, filling up the hauls much as they can. Other squadron leaders collect all specimens of smithsonite, zinc, calcium, and platinum. During the journey of one squad leader, he comes across assorted smithsonites that carry zinc and calcium in various colors from white, brown, gray, blue, yellows, greens, yellow-green, orange-green, pink, purple, and colorless crystals. This one squad leader reports to the headship the array of colors of the smithsonite that contains zinc and calcium. Squad leader with his liprod and video accessing the mother ship as he contacts General Draker.

"*General Draker, we seem to have a ton of smithsonite, sir.*"

Draker, not so amused, says, "*Okay, then collect all and bring and unload it in the assigned bays. What seems to be the issue otherwise?*"

Informed by the Squad leader, Draker sees report that the colors of smithsonite depend on how it crystallizes. "*The problem is that the compound smithsonite forms various crystals that produce a variety of colors. Among the colors available are green, orange, pink, purple, blue, yellow, and brown, we may see these of greater use for us, Master Draker. But how should I proceed with the type of information?*"

By using his liprod, Draker aims to collect the compounds and fill up the bays without telling Faloosh. "*You must assemble all the combinations, no matter what they might be, and fill up the bays. We'll adjust when all are collected. Did you get that report I just sent you, Master?*"

While flying, the squad leader adjusts the screen and his seat. "*I got that report, Master, and what commanded of us. Will do, General! Squad leader out.*"

Drabegers are the type of species flying the Madrones, so one squad leader says to the other squad leader, "*The planet is covered with so many calcium deposits that gathering them all would take at least fifty to hundred years. So, Squad Leader 2, what are your thoughts?*"

Squad leader 2 returns with an unusual outcome. "*Believe it or not, I believe it will take us roughly ten years to deplete most of it. After that, we would return to our home planet, disperse most of it through our teleportation machines, and eventually drain this planet's resources. Haha! Hehe!*"

Meanwhile, in Africa, two African people talking in their native tongue begin to worship the ships going back and forth through the clouds as though they are some gods. Without warning, one African chants a song in his native tongue as the other dances. An alien looks upon them inside the ship and raises his hands high as though intrigued by these people. On the other side of the spectrum in Russia are two Russian men dancing in the street as two of the ships hover above, communicating with each other about the weirdness of the dance.

One alien says to the other alien on the ship, "*Strange mating rituals. They seem to be doing the same thing.*"

With an evil laugh, the other alien says, "*Let's throw them a bone.*" The ship spits out a weird instrument at the two Russians, who begin to disperse as though it's a bomb, as military personnel begins to shoot at the aliens. The two alien ships see that they are hostile and report it to the mother ship. Alien writes to the mother ship through a holographic board, "*These creatures are as aggressive as we are! Look at the monitor. They are hitting us with projectiles repelling off our spaceships. What should we do?*"

Draker, on the other end, says, "*If they are attacking us first, we must send down our Mercy ships to combat the situation at hand.*"

Alien in the Madrone ship says, "*Should we engage or disengage?*"

Draker, who wants them to continue the mission, says, "*No, continue the task at hand. We will send out the Mercy ships if it continues. Draker out!*"

The two spaceships disengage with the humans and get back on track regarding the mission.

Munedane analyzes the various compounds from the Earth as the ships transport them to the different haul bays. Munedane, who has several fragments of the compounds, says to her associate, "Seems we are at 98.9 percent functionality with these compounds compared to the compounds from other universes throughout our transitions of elements found through the ages. What do you think, Diamor?"

Diamor, the associate, looks at the relativity of the compounds and, with a witting remark, says, "*When I input the mixture into this weapon, the aura these compounds have shown here tends to trigger a percentile so significant to a sextillion number. It quantizes our projection to be holding for eon years to come.*"

Munedane sends her reports to the leaders' computers with the outcome. The leader looks at this galaxy and wonders if this is an excellent galaxy to conquer. Thorgus talks to himself, "*Wonder if these beings are good enough to be defeated because what if we find other minerals of use that can last our species for eons and eons from now, or shall we enslave them?*"

Thorgus calls Munedane's liprod. "*Yes, Thorgus?*"

Thorgus, on the other line, says, "*Munedane, I wondered if these species have other minerals or compounds and if they are an excellent fit to conquer and mix them with our species. Those who don't comply will either die or realize through our dangerous games of worshipping and overlord Faloosh."*

Munedane, having her reports so far, tells Thorgus one final thing, "*I will let Faloosh know these species seem to be a species we should enslave to our liking, taking all their minerals as much as we can get, that is!*" Munedane goes into Faloosh's area to report the percentile.

"*Faloosh, sorry to disturb you, Master. I must relate the percentile to you.*"

Faloosh is impatient. "*What is it? Can it be 30 percent or 40 percent!*"

Munedane gives him the good news. "*Master, the percentile is 98.9 percent.*"

Faloosh jumps with an evil laugh. "*Wow! That's more than any other universe we have conquered, even my universe. That is unheard among our lifeline! But remarkably, it's time to conquer this universe. I want to beat these puny, tiny pink and dark-skinned creatures with ancient weapons. Also, I do not want to destroy this planet because it has plenty of resources for our guns and ships.*"

Munedane returns to her lab and sends the report to Thorgus and Draker. "*Faloosh wants to give these creatures a war that they can't handle. Faloosh wants us to conquer these little things and take their resources with many heaps loads we can carry on our ships.*"

Faloosh is talking among his beings on the ship. "*For all my children on the starship, worship me, Faloosh. I am conqueror of all universes and no one! No one! No one will ever come against me, for they will surely die if they do! Or creatures would have to play in my chaotic games of death! Hahahahaha!*"

CHAPTER 29

WARNING SIGNS

The Inquestorians are preparing for combat as Draker hits the machine. "*This dag gone machine will not work correctly. Nonsense is coming out of the computer with various gibberish garbage of mixed languages.*"

Faloosh looks down at Draker within his chambers and, with a strange and severe look on his face, gives Draker a pointing finger in the shape of a handgun and tells Draker with a loud, boisterous voice, "*We need to send out the ships as soon as possible to take over these planet creatures!*"

Stunner, in a very outspoken sort of comical way, gives a remark that makes Faloosh think he's pretty intelligent when Faloosh knows Stunner is a loose cannon when it comes to war tactics.

"*What if we swish them around like some cylindrical typhoon and guess where they land so we can hunt them down one by one, like their egg hunt during that particular point in their year? I think that would be a terrific idea, Warlord.*"

Faloosh again looks at Stunner as though he is a genius and stares at him for a moment, and, without warning, says, "*Ah no! I would need them where my men can capture them right away instead of seeking and hiding them in various places and trying to find them with our potent wind tunnel blasters. It will not work here. Now we set a plan to take over these creatures, and let's get that plan together, okay, my utmost fierce team leaders. Now we plan.*"

Draker, on the other hand, is trying to recalculate the machine, while Faloosh is chatting with the other leaders in the 3D chambers. Draker is calculating. "*Thorgus, I need your input to this machine to get the proper calculations regarding finding out with our warlords' instincts that these creatures may be the ones of old, so please, Thorgus, get over here and input your numbers already!*"

The grumbling voice of Draker interrupted the yelling of Thorgus while he was listening to his warlord Faloosh describing some wars he had fought and won eons ago. As Thorgus hears Draker calling him from an intermediate distance, his attention is interrupted. Suddenly, Thorgus turns around with an intense look as if he does not want to be disturbed, grins a bit, and shouts back, "*What is it, Draker?*"

Draker, trying to be patient, responds with a firm tone, "*I need you to input data, to put calculations into this stupid computer so we can find out if we are dealing with the creatures of old or not! Did you get that? So hurry up and get over here already!*"

Thorgus sighs a bit, and then walks in a rhythmic slick gangster walk and begins to walk over to the machine to punch in the numbers. Thorgus hits the numbers quickly along with Draker, and the holographic computer spits out an odd response.

"*Our calculations go round and round. Nobody knows, and we hit the floor as we go. These calculations aren't of the old. Nonetheless, you can conquer it with the old and the new, for it will exhibit a vibrant light hue. It will be a brilliant array of destructive light. Be mindful that the new will triumph without distress.*"

Draker is a bit pissed off. "*This darn computer.*" He kicks the side of the holographic computer box, losing his balance and barely tumbling down toward his left side. Draker looks at Thorgus, eyes wide open. "*Thorgus, what are we going to do!*"

Thorgus returns with a frown. "*Well, Draker—*"

Stunner is giggling. "*You guys, you should do what the master warlord says. Just send out the ships.*"

Thorgus continues, "*You know what! You're right, Stunner. Draker, let's send out the ships.*"

Draker quickly replies, "*I agree. Let's send out the ships, Mapoh! Send out the Mercy ships. Get Commander Rook up here.*"

Mapoh quickly acknowledges Draker's command. At that instant, Mapoh's liprod quickly calls, "*Commander Rook, please respond to the ready room at the 3D station.*"

Rook, on her liprod, quickly answers, "*Yes, Lord Draker, will be right there.*" Command Rook enters the ready room twenty minutes later, where all the overlords and warlord Faloosh make a minimal battle plan to take over the humans. Rook sees Draker at the far corner with Mapoh and asks Mapoh, "*Commander Mapoh, what seems to be the issue?*"

Mapoh looks at Rook as he approaches and responds diligently, "*Mrs. Commander Rook, we need the Mercy ships to infiltrate these creatures, gather them up like cattle, and prepare them to respond to our overlord Faloosh. If they do not respond or comprehend or commit to your subtle commands, then take all ships to the atmosphere and spray them with the chemical, and they should respond to our ways immediately. If you have rogue ones, either capture them or eradicate them instantly at your hands. Do what you must, isn't that right, Draker?"*

Draker and Faloosh say as though they were thinking the same thoughts, "*That is right. Do what I commanded of you, and you should have your way with these creatures as you like, Rook!*"

Rook, who has orders to know the likes and dislikes of these creatures, stares at Draker and Faloosh. Her job is to deal with beasts as she deals with critters who disobey Faloosh. Having decided to do what is essential to their species, Rook says one last thought to Thorgus, "*Okay, my role as a Mercy ship commander is to have my way with them if they don't respond, correct?*

Thorgus replies quickly, "*That is correct. Aren't you ready to leave already? Let's go already, Commander Rook. Get out of here and proceed with the mission.*"

With both hands on her chest, Rook salutes. "*Yes, Commanders and Warlord. I am on my way.*"

Faloosh says one final note before leaving the 3D simulation room, "*Okay, Overlords, release the Mercy ships from their locks.*"

With quickness, Thorgus, Mapoh, Stunner, and Draker simultaneously punch in some numbers to release the Mercy ships as Commander Rook leaves toward the bay areas of the spaceships. A vast silent whooshing sound goes through the corridors of the mother ship as the Mercy ships release themselves from the docking bays. Rook is in her spaceship, ten to fifteen minutes later, with an aerodynamic style and an unusual marking identifying her as the fleet commander. As she is the fleet commander, other commanders have similar markings but are slightly different. Because of this, if the Inquestorians ever came up against an enemy who beat them, the enemy could not figure out who was the supreme commander of the fleet. Continually, Rook gets to her spaceship as her men who drive the spaceship and gunners greet her when entering the spaceship ramp.

Rook, at the ramp, turns around at her beloved vicious male counterparts and says, "*Male warriors, we're to embark on this world and take it over, per overlords' and warlords' command. Are you all ready for this?*"

The men respond harshly, "*All hail Faloosh! We're ready to overthrow this planet and bring them to their knees, supreme leader.*"

Rook turns around and says, "*Fine, let's move on.*" Rook enters her command chair as many of her male variants enter the six-species craft where there are about five thousand spaceships in this bay area, and Faloosh has at least a thousand bay areas around both mother ships. Before embarking from the bay area, Rook gives the final command, "*Are you ready to embark, team!*" All ships' leaders respond by indicators on their spaceships from red to green. In addition, all ships get a message on board their 3D simulator.

"*We're ready!*"

Rook's ship embarks from the mother ship first before any other spaceship, and then the leaders of each squadron leave with the rest of the spaceships from the mother ship. Remarkably, all you see are squadrons and squadrons of spaceships leaving both mother ships and entering Earth's atmosphere. Spaceships are getting closer and closer to Earth by the minute. As they get about five thousand miles away from Earth, a newscaster comes on the television.

"I want to request your attention, ladies and gentlemen! Unfortunately, a severe emergency has arisen. We must all leave now! The final moment to go is now for those who wish to depart." The newscaster shows a picture of one or two spaceships coming through the atmosphere as people start to panic in their hearts.

One person says in her house, "Oh my god, look! He's not joking! These huge spaceships are coming through our atmosphere. I'm getting scared. Grab your things, Julio, and let's go. Grab the children. Hurry! Hurry! Hurry! Grab the children and grab the bags. Whew! Let's go, go already, come on down the stairs, get down, hurry up! Quick, quick, quick."

The female grabs the children and heads down the stairs, as the husband panics. Finally, Julio gets the soldier's attention. "Soldier, soldier, over here!"

The soldier sees the family panicking. Quickly, the soldier helps them up on the Humvee. "Okay, there you go, ma'am, and here are your children. Up you go!"

With the remaining humans left on planet Earth, about 95 percent start to leave and head toward the mountain. Another person who doesn't want to leave their pet behind asks a soldier, "Can I please bring my cat, Buckey? He is all I have."

One soldier says, "Leave it behind. I don't think these aliens will ever harm your pet."

A female soldier with a higher ranking interjects, "Go ahead and bring your cat. I'm sure it is your best friend. So go ahead and get him."

The man runs back inside his apartment and grabs his cat. The Humvee slowly gets crowded with some people going to the mountains, while there seems to be at least 5 percent of the humans left behind who are willing to stay to fight off these aliens. Five minutes later, the young man returns with his cat and puts it in a carrying case in the Humvee as some other people are taking their animals, like parrots, pigeons, and dogs that are dear to them. The military gets ready to go to the mountains, and the newscaster announces one more thing.

"Please, people, as you can see, more spaceships are coming through our Earth's atmosphere. I have no idea what their intentions are. They are bigger than the last spaceships, and when you see bigger spaceships according to movies, then we need to act fast right now. I will see you guys later." The newsman starts to run toward several Humvees that are leaving toward the mountains. The newscaster continues, "I'm out of here. There is no more news. The last piece of news in the history of our country will be this. If you get ledt behind, you will have to fend for yourselves. Good luck to you."

As a result, the continent of North America, South America, and the entire world are in a state of mass hysteria with a warning. There is screaming coming from everywhere. People start to say, "This way, this way!"

Other people saying, "No, not that way!"

Some people want to fend for themselves. "I want to stay as this is my house! I will not let any alien beings evict me from my house! It's not going to happen!"

Another human says, "They will not evict you, stupid. They might enslave us! They may eat us! Who knows? We need to get out of here now!"

Once again, the other human declares, "I won't leave my home! I worked all my life to have this house and this car. I'm staying behind. I'm an Earthling and an American. I'm staying behind, not letting no aliens evict me off of my planet. It's not happening! I have a ton of guns. I have ammo, and I have grenades. I was in the Vietnam War. I'm not letting these bastards take me out of here!"

In his final speech, the other human says, "Okay, you know what, have it your way! Due to the mountains, where we could hide, I'm not sure what to expect in the mountains or what the military has, but I'm getting out of here immediately! It's time for me to leave everything behind."

One last word from the Vietnam veteran, "Good for you. I'd like to wish you the best in your future endeavors."

The other human says his final goodbyes, "Love you! Take care, Dad! And good luck."

The father responds, "Good luck, and I hope you find destiny on the other side."

The son says his final goodbyes. "Love you too, Dad."

They both hug each other, and the son gets in a Humvee, while other people get into another Humvee, and all you can hear is more mass hysteria and people screaming. Other people don't want to leave precious, valuable things behind. Losing certain precious metals or cars can be painful for some people. Although many people are pulling out their materialistic stuff and carrying as much as they can carry in bags and sacks, other people are driving behind the Humvees. Many military people say, "No cars, please. Although vehicles are permitted to follow, they cannot enter the bunkers. There would be no other way in except to walk in. The cars cannot go through where you people are going."

People clamor among themselves, wondering what is through the mountains or what is expected of them as they are confused. One lady says with curiosity, "Why not!"

A female soldier gives her the reason. "Because, ma'am, where you're going, you wouldn't need a car."

Again the lady is a little confused. "Okay, where are we going then?"

Female soldier continues, "If you want to get out of here or stay here, it is your choice, okay! We're here to protect you until the very end."

Lady and a man seem more confused. "What do you mean until the very end? What are you not telling us?"

Male soldier says, "Whatever happens if there's a war and we were to succumb, or they were to scan us or get to know us or whatever! So we have to prepare ourselves."

Man on Humvee seems shallow when it comes to knowing the army is not too reassuring on the matter at hand. "This does not sound reassuring that we're safe. Vaguely, what are you not telling us, soldier?"

Soldier's trying to keep on beat with the plans. "If we need to go, we need to go now! So climb on board, and those curious, leave your curiosity to yourself. Thank you!"

A black lady calls out to her three daughters to come and get on the Humvee because the soldiers are about to depart. "Tanya, Jeannie, Sabrina, hurry up, we have to go!" She also calls out to two of her neighbors named Mike and Leroy to hurry up as well. "Leroy and Mike, hurry up! We have to go now! They are getting ready to leave already."

Leroy and the others run toward the vehicle; they all climb into the Humvee as one of the soldiers tells them where they are going. "Ladies and gentlemen, we're going to a hidden mountain base where they will explain further what is going on, okay." Finally, the soldier speaks and tells the driver to depart. "And please, ladies and gentlemen, we are in a rush. Driver, let's go!"

Several Humvees drive away as a small percentage of soldiers stay behind to ward off the enemy if they were to attack. Tons of people are getting into their cars, as other people hijack cars to follow the Humvees. The people following the Humvee take quite a few belongings with. There is more mass hysteria in China as you hear people screaming and scrambling to escape the imminent threat.

One Chinaman says in English to another Chinaman, "What's this! What...what is this? Please tell me it's not Godzilla, is it? What is going on here!"

Another Chinaman says, "I don't know. It seems like these aliens are trying to take over our planet."

The other Chinaman, Lero, says, "We need to go. There are a lot of military men out here. We need to go now."

The other Chinaman says, "I know, I know. Let me grab a few more things."

The other Chinaman, Lero, says, "No more grabbing. We need to leave now! We got enough. They said we don't need a lot of stuff where we're going. Where we're going, we are going to have plenty of things. Probably food, water, and many devices, so we must leave right now!"

The other Chinaman says, "Okay, we go! Oh well! I guess I will leave my stuff behind. It isn't vital. I didn't want to leave my apple iPhone 28. It has a big screen and a nice hard drive to download music and software from the cloud. Indeterminately, I wanted to take it."

The other Chinaman, Lero, says, "You probably are not going to need it."

The other Chinaman replies, "But I love that phone. It's the best iPhone Apple ever made."

The other Chinaman, Lero, lets him get his iPhone. "Hurry up and run up there. They're going to be leaving soon."

The other Chinaman sprints to his house, grabs his big iPhone 28 tablet, and rushes back toward the Humvees. Suddenly, as people scramble to get into their cars and Humvees to escape the swarm of spaceships coming through the atmosphere, you hear spacecraft screeching and flying across the skies, just landing in various zones of the planet.

Meanwhile, in Italy, two ladies in a department store are arguing over a designer jacket, and one lady says, "No, you cannot have this. I found it first."

The other Italian lady responds with a vengeance, "No, you cannot have this. It's my jacket. It may be the last one, but I found it first, and besides, I'm about to pay for it now!"

As the other calm lady says, both ladies tug at it for a while. "I took it off the rack while you snatched it from me when both my hands were on it, so basically, it belongs to me initially. Now hand it over like a lovely woman and politely put it in my hands!"

The other steamed woman says, "No, I will not let it go! Now give it!" Both ladies tug on it and rip the jacket in half.

Suddenly, an officer who has been watching them quarrel over the jacket steps toward them when they had pulled the jacket and, with a stern look on his face, makes a severe but comical statement, "Now, ladies, you see what you have done now. You destroyed a store item. Since you both destroyed a store item, you both have to pay for it. For instance, you ma'am have to pay the total price, and you ma'am have to pay full price too."

Both ladies look at each other as a ship flies by a window. Then, they both say simultaneously, "Ah, look outside. Let's leave! Hurry."

The male officer sees the ship landing nearby as he looks through the first floor store window. The ladies rush out of the store toward one of the military vehicles noticing an invasion; both hoop on an army vehicle. The military vehicle waits for a few more people to enter the Humvee's as it heads toward the mountain.

During this time, somewhere in Australia, an Australian man with his friends is supposed to go hunting today for some kangaroo, except the man notices the weather is rainy, as usual. Kangaroos hide during the rain; therefore, the man and his friends start to look up in the sky and notice spacecraft within the sky, as he continues to say, "I need to hunt, hunt, hunt. Where am I going to find kangaroo meat at this time?"

The man's other friend looks up at the clouds as it rains certain chemicals, where he begins to see ships cruising by within the skies. One of the ships lands nearby, as the man, with fright in his eyes takes a big gulp in his throat. "I think I know why the kangaroos aren't out. Look in the skies, guys. There seems to be an invasion. I believe those ships made the kangaroos disappear without a trace. I also have noticed military people in the area with tons of vans picking people up. We need to get out our gear and see what is happening. You do agree with that, right guys?"

Two of the three men start running toward the vehicles as the mountains begin to open up. They leave the first man talking to himself, a reaction from the alien chemical. The two men run home, gather stuff to take, and enter the vehicles. In contrast, the other man who was left talking to himself as he catches a drift of breeze whizzing by him, a small spacecraft lands near the enormous spacecraft, then he begins to run toward his home as though in a trance. He enters his house, grabs his wife and kids, and head toward the vehicles with their clothes on their back. With a step in a beat comes a zoologist with a bunch of animals in cages on a massive automobile that carries at least thirty-five animals, including elephants, giraffes, water dolphins, and various animals within six to seven huge vehicles that head toward the mountains. With those animals are the zoologist along with her helpers, military personnel, and what happens next is that massive caravan of animals enters the hidden military bases from all over the world, The transportation of all these assorted animals eventually goes through the G300 to various universes. Before that, the animals are cloned and sent to the different intergalactic dimensional universes and smaller animals, like dogs, hamsters, and various domestic animals, are also cloned and sent through the G300 to multiple universes.

Meanwhile, throughout the globe, among some of the remaining humans, mass hysteria is happening worldwide. Some military personnel have people jumping in vehicles like a clown car filled with clowns tightly fitting in the cars, and those with other motor vehicles people are trying to cram into them. As the people are getting out of their compressed cars and the military vehicles, a military personnel guides the people toward their respective lines and calls out to some of the people, "Wait, wait! Wait, we have to take time. Please wait! Don't pile up on each other, please! Move out of my way."

As the soldier moves toward the middle of the line where three people have decided to make their lines, the soldier screams at them right in their faces, like an army drill instructor, "Get in line! Do not make lines of your own. Either get in this line or the following, but we are not allowed to make our line, so get in a line!"

The two other people with eyes down slowly get back in the same line and their other friend. The soldier walks toward the front of the line as he mentions another thing, "This is not Christmas shopping. This is one by one. Please, people, obey our commands so we can get through this promptly. Please fall back, fall back. Ma'am, sir, fall back, please."

One gentleman says, "I need to go! Bad."

During that time, one alien says to the other on a spacecraft while the caravan of cars and military vehicles continues toward the hidden base mountain. "*I wonder where they are going?*"

The other alien says, "*Yeah, I don't know. They seem to be in a rush to go somewhere. Let's continue on our task, putting the ship down over here near these bushes and trees.*"

The alien on the trigger gun gets ready for combat as he states, "*Getting all firearms ready!*" He leaves his station and heads toward the small weapons room. As the ship lands, all eight aliens get out of the ship with weapons in hand. One of the aliens, who seems to be trigger happy, sees a human and suddenly, without warning, begins to shoot at the human with a fiery look on his face. The gun, with a swoosh sounding, annihilates the human, turning the human to dust. As the alien begins to laugh, the other alien hits him on his shoulder and tells him, "*We don't attack unless they attack first.*"

Over yonder, a soldier sees the alien attacking the human and the human turning to dust; he starts to report the situation to another soldier in ready stance for these aliens. That same soldier speaks to his commander as his scope records the attack. "Commander, an alien had started the bout already."

The commander looks within the range and sounds the alarm as other ships touch down around the globe while landing, spraying chemicals. The commander reports to the upper division within the mountains. "We're under attack, we're under attack! Some substances are dropping from the sky and making some people go crazy."

One frightened soldier says to his chief officer, "I don't know what superweapons these creatures have or what they are spraying, but I'm not standing around to find out, so I'm out of here."

His chief commander looks at him and says, "Get back here, soldier, or I will report you as being commissioned to do yard work in the wall from the unit, and you will be in a jail cell of another universe."

That soldier looks at his commanding officer, shrugs his shoulder, starts up the vehicle, and heads back to the mountain like a coward.

The soldier who leaves thinks to himself why he signed up to defend humanity when he needs to protect himself as he thinks of a plan to back up his squad for later battles. Several soldiers stare at a ship and notice this small muscular creature with a spiral head come walking out of the spacecraft. The being is talking to its officers. The beings begin to fan out the area to capture those humans around him that may comply with Faloosh laws. Mapoh, who is the creature with the spiral head, talks to his leading officers from his ship and through his liprod to all other Mercy ships, as his soldiers stand by, ready for any combat that may come their way. Mapoh speaks a bit in an alien language that interpreted says, "*The recording says that these puny creatures are no match for our weapons. Captain! Search all areas for all these pink and dark skins. Capture all and make sure none are in hiding. Surround the perimeter."*

The captain responds with a salute of two arms, hugging himself. "*Yes, your lordship.*" The creatures slowly engulf millions and millions of beings surrounding the streets and cities. Some humans try to hide in their closets, others hide in their basement, and still, others try to fend off the creatures. Others try to hide in cabinets, under sinks, and even in crevice areas of the cellars of their home. Some humans are intelligent and have underground compartments to hide from their enemies. The aliens go through houses and grab many humans, escorting them back to their ships. While this is going on, the remaining convoy transfers the humans through the G300 portal. Without warning, one of the creatures see the end of the convoy just disappear into the mountains.

"*Wow, are you for real did that happen that where the pink and dark-skinned creatures just vanished into the mountains?*"

The other alien responds, "*Yeah, they did.*"

The different alien looks at his partner and shakes his head as though jarring his thoughts together. "*I mean, we can get through certain things, but these creatures seem to disappear without warning, must relay a message to Mapoh and Rook.*" The being calls on his liprod to Mapoh and Rook to warn them of these creatures' ability. "*Mapoh, these pink and dark skin creatures just disappeared into a mountain site. What shall we do if they have those capabilities?*"

Mapoh responds on his liprod, "*What I want you to do is surround that perimeter as well, and if you see them come out, either capture them or destroy them if they fight back or don't comply. Got it!*"

The creature now knows what to do to complement the situation and hangs up his liprod with a final response, "*Got it, Mapoh!*"

Some of the smaller spacecrafts fly over the mountain and come down behind it even as many creatures close in on the perimeter of the mountains around the globe. A smaller convoy that sees many beings blocking the entrance has to go to another escape route. The escape route takes the rest of the convoy through some bushes and shrubs. As the shrubs move up, the convoy disappears into the patches to an underground facility. General Boulder, who had led the convoy away from the creatures to the hidden underground facility, furthermore, an alien sees way over and notices another set of human vehicles disappear into the shrubs.

While the human population is entering the hidden facility, General Boulder and Chief Peter are telling the people while escorting the people of the vehicles,

"People, please follow the lines where you were assigned while we were giving out the color pamphlets on the Humvees and while you all were waiting in lines, those pamphlets will take you to your destinations, where you will meet some scientists and doctors who will further explain what is happening."

General Boulder, Peter, and the rest of the people head to their destinations while meeting with scientists and doctors. Peter, along with Boulder, meets up with Lucas and Merna, who further explains what is happening to the people.

"This way, people, this way! People, you will be heading to another universe where the computer will justify the color codes on your cards and implement a status quo on that planet."

Some people are shocked that the government has been working on such a project, others are happy, yet others are sad that they have to leave the planet. Lucas interjects, "Please follow the lines, people. You, sir." Lucas points to an individual. "Please, sir, follow the yellow line. Take your family with you on this line. Thank you."

Merna continues, "No, no! Ma'am, you have to go on the pink line, yes! Please follow the instructions that we're giving you. People, follow the instructions. You will meet at the end of the corridor, where other types of creatures are allies to explain further what is going on."

The people follow the lines as soldiers guide them to different corridors. There are like fifteen to twenty corridors to go down. Just in this one facility, as the people enter the room at the end of the halls, they are met up with Legendary creatures who, to the humans' amazement, can speak the human language. One Legendary male speaks.

"Welcome, fellow humans. As you already know, you will be traveling through this G300 to different universes. Make sure you hold onto your loved ones and do not separate while traveling because, on the other side, you will be fulfilling the destiny of hybrids. These hybrids are generations from now that will confer with our species and one or two Praetorians, another specie that will guide these hybrids into a battle. Then they will be ready to take on the enemy Inquestorians that destroy universes through our knowledge and with the human instinct, and powers of the hybrids who will gain or confront the enemy within battle warfare. So in a nutshell, we need the human race to survive."

Then, like an earthquake, the enemy Inquestorians are knocking hard on the mountaintops, trying to find an entrance toward the compound sealed with top-grade alien technology beyond this world, which is unbreakable. Farther down the corridor, we see John and George, who are by the gates indicating if a person is coming to harm some humans, more like a metal detector, screening the people through the scanners. John turns around and says, "Wait a minute you, sir! Please empty your pockets."

The gentleman says politely, "I don't have anything in my pockets."

John then checks the man's coat. What comes out is a rifle. John exclaims, "Sir, you can't take this with you where you're going! I'm sorry, but we don't need violence where you're going, okay."

Knowing he is making a grave mistake, the gentleman tells John what to do with it. "Go ahead and leave it there with the guard. I didn't mean to alarm anyone."

George gently helps an old lady. "Please, ma'am, this way. Slowly, slowly step this way, okay, there you go." Unfortunately, the scanner doesn't pick up the old lady's switchblade, and she goes through the G300, not knowing what planet she will land on for safety.

CHAPTER 30

THE EXODUS

Millions of people are going through the scanners from corridors that seem to direct them way below the mountains. Along with many people are some soldiers who are not only going through the G300 but are highly classified clones of top soldiers. Finally, everyone is departing through the G300 to various planets in various universes. Some people come through this one section, where all meet up with Gale and Beth. Beth talks to the people on the left side, and Gale talks to the people on the right side. Beth says to the people on the left side, "What you're about to go through is a machine that will take you to another world and another universe altogether. Now, if you do not want separation from your family, I do advise you to hold hands and go through these gates. Now, if you happen to lose each other, you will be separated forever through different universes."

Some people are in amazement, and some people are shocked. People about to go through hold on to their loved ones and belongings tightly. It begins to fill with people as Beth turns up the power source. Beth again reiterates, "Please enter and remember to hold each other we're going to go to new worlds as this world is becoming an assaulted planet. There will be new life, new types of food, and new delicacies. So please proceed slowly."

In the G300, people enter. They start to disappear. All you hear is a whooshing of the tunnel within the room. Meanwhile, Gale, on the other end, is saying something of similarity: "Please take off your jackets. Some of these planets do not have cold weather. Still, some planets may have mediocre weather, others a bit hot, others a bit warm, and some a bit cold. Where you people are going to different universes on different planets, you're going to expect to live in a vegetarian and get used to the meats of those worlds. So, ma'am, you can take the chicken with you throughout centuries. As a result of mixing with the environment of that world, it may not be a chicken but a crossover. Hopefully, your pets will adapt to the new environment. A climate can either help them thrive or kill them. Do not let hands go if you're taking a loved one. If you let each other's hands go, you will separate from your loved ones, and they will land on various planets or universes, so please, I will not emphasize again, do not let your loved ones go! I will repeat, do not let your loved ones go! You got it, people!"

Many people are clamoring, and countless people say, "Yes, we got it."

Gale turns on her machine, and the apparatus starts making people disappear. The gadget makes a whooshing tunneling sound. In the interim, Master Chief Yufer, with a loud megaphone, is trying to get the initial 95 percent of the human race to come with them before it starts crawling with Inquestorians back to the mountains.

"People, people, I am begging you! You must leave now."

A crowd of people from their windows says, "We don't want to leave. My home is here! Why should we leave at all!"

Master Yufer says, "Sir, if you want to survive, you need to leave with us now! It will soon be crawling with an alien infestation, and there will be no place to hide. Sir, you may get strangled, eaten alive, or whatever their intentions are, you need to come with us."

The old man replies when he slowly gets out of bed, "I'm an old man. I am going to die anyway."

Master Yufer gently helps the old man out of bed. "Sir, you may live another twenty to fifty years. You have to see what is on the other side for you."

The old man jolts away from Yufer. He looks Yufer dead in the eyes. "Sonny, do you know how old I am? Huh."

Yufer, seeing the old man having some spike in him for such an old person, looks at the old man with caring eyes. "No, I have no idea how old you are."

The old man takes Yufer's left hand and rests his hand on his chest as the old man looks down and then looks up at him. "You see, sonny, I am almost ninety years old, and I am ready to go to my Lord and Savior in the clouds. What can be on the other side? Do I want to live another twenty to fifty years? I don't think so, sonny. I lived through World War VI and the Battle of Vengeance, about fifty years ago with Spain and Italy, what more can I possibly want in life, huh."

Yufer says with a stunning look on his face, "Well! What if the fountain of youth is on the other side, and you can reverse the aging process a little? You can live for hundreds of years, wouldn't you like to find out?"

The old man says, "Sonny, no one is taking me off the planet. I wasn't born to live on another planet that may or may not give me eternal life. Why would I do that when the Lord our God already gives us eternal life in Jesus, his Son who died for me. Nothing in any universe can give eternal life but Jesus Christ."

When Yufer realizes that the old man is stubborn he says, "If you change your mind, sir, just let us know, okay."

As much as the older adult is trying to rest in peace, he shuts the door behind Yufer as he leaves. Fear creeps into the old man's mind as he asks himself, "What if these aliens want to eat me alive? What kind of validation of letting myself be remembered like that when I can be young and productive somewhere else?" Finally, the old man looks at the picture of his wife on the wall and opens the door, smiling, calling out to Master Yufer. "Sir! Maybe this is God's way of showing me I can start over." The old man closes the door behind him and says, "I am only taking a picture of my dearly departed wife. Is that all right?"

Seconds later, Master Yufer sees the older man running toward him, almost like a young man, with complete shock and awe. Master Yufer hugs the older adult as if he were exhibiting the utmost respect. Yufer instructs his soldier on what to do next. "The ex-marine brings valuable cargo, so please take him to the mountains, Sergeant, and be careful with his cargo."

The soldier responds to Master Yufer, "Yes, sir! No problem!" Master Yufer convinces several other people to enter last minute onto the Humvee toward the mountains.

Almost 99 percent of the human race either left through the G300 or are traveling toward the mountains, where havoc happens to some of them while blocked off by the aliens, and still others are within the mountains getting ready to leave planet Earth. One percent of the human race that stayed behind are trying to fend for themselves against the treacherous aliens. Countless soldiers are left behind to fend off the enemy that may try to take the remaining humans with them. Master Yufer, at the underground passage to the mountains, gives a commanding soldier the responsibility for other commanding soldiers throughout the entire region.

"Soldier, I'm leaving you with the responsibility for the region of other commanding soldiers. If any fellow humans want to leave last minute, make sure you or another soldier take them to the mountains! Got that, soldier!"

A soldier salutes and says, in a yes motion, "Got it, sir! Yes, sir!"

As Master Yufer heads toward the mountains, there appears to be no threat of enemy attack. Then, suddenly, without warning, trees start to blow back and forth near the mountain's east side, causing an opening where a vehicle can enter through bushes without detection. General Boulder and Master Yufer meet. They saw the alien creatures by the mountains, General Boulder signals to Master Yufer that enemies are nearby. Master Yufer acknowledges the quadrupeds. Within the nick of time, the last vehicle enters the compound, and the enemies see something opening up, as they run toward that particular mountain area at full speed. In desperate attempt to subdue the compound entryway, the enemy continues banging and ramming the compound doors, which are now impenetrable.

During the interim inside the compound, mountain dignitary Yarmin says to Cokiko, "We need to prepare right now! The enemy is at our doorsteps."

Cokiko sounds the silent alarm throughout the compound to attract the attention of the Legendaries assigned for combat. As a result, a storm of Legendaries suddenly rises from every corner of the globe, marching toward the each compound's entranceways. In addition, the preparation of hybrids, in case of an intense war, are preparing their powerful ray lasers and cannons for military use. Currently, there are only the Legendaries with their massive ray-lasers. As a result, the Legendaries cn communicate wih each other in their native languages, giving them the upper hand over both humans and their opponents.

Furthermore, unless enemies shoot them, the Legendaries are protected by one Praetorian who can make them invisible. They had obtained the cloaking mechanism from the Praetorian species' injection of their blood into the Legendaries. The enemy would only discover the cloaking if the enemy continued to shoot within that particular perimeter until it had found the Legendary. Plus, if a bomb that uses napalm hits them, their outline will be noticeable. At each mountainous location, there are a few Praetorians who protect Legendaries and some soldiers who are preparing for battle worldwide. One Legendary says to his team of combatants, "*You ready!*"

Other Legendary says, "*Ready.*"

Then the team led by that certain Legendary says into one Legendary's ear sickle, "*Are you ready, all Legendaries?*"

As soon as the Legendary speaks into the other Legendary's ear sickle, it transfers into information, and all the Legendaries simulataneously say, "*We're ready!*"

Then the military head commander wants to make sure his team is in position and, through his helmet, can communicate with the rest of the military personnel. Commander getting his team to acknowledge his command. "Is everyone in place and ready for combat?"

The entire military personnel, through their head comm, responds quickly, "We're all in position and ready for combat!"

The commander calls his commanding officer, Snuff, who seems to be chatting with General Boulder; his transmission communicator responds to the incoming call. "Yes! Commander, are you in position and ready for battle strategies?"

The commander politely responds without any hesitation in his voice, "Ready to go? You can open the blast doors."

In the case of blast doors between the facility and the outside world, they open them, as the military and legendary personnel initiate their guns and bring their weapons up to ready status. Sergeant Bobo yells out loudly, similar to the adage of the British coming in a manner to start striking the enemy at the foothills of the mountain, "Okay, men, I'm going to be behind you, engaging the enemy as well. Onward, soldiers, prepare to engage the enemy. Ayah, move out!"

The blast door opens as a wind of a short gust starts to blow. The men stoop down. Sergeant Bobo makes a final statement before the attack happens. "Men, what we're about to encounter, we have no idea what to expect, be very careful because what is ahead of us is our lives, so protect one another. As our brethren engage the enemy, we must protect each other at all cost."

A commanding officer gets Bobo's attention as his guns point toward the outside of the door and tells his superior officer, "We must keep General Snuff informed through video. I'm sure he will see all the action that is taking place."

A few minutes later, Sergeant Bobo nods in agreement and continues to talk a little bit before they see action. "I've already understood that, Captain. Now proceed toward the enemy, Captain." Following his orders the captain steps out the door and begins attacking the enemies. Alternatively, Cokiko and the leading Praetorians will see how these enemies have updated their equipment, as well as whether these enemies are indestructible or not.

"When our Legendary friends and the army engage the enemy, we will see on the monitors if they are destructible." Cokiko says to General Boulder, "As time passes, the answer will emerge."

During that time, millions and billions of humans are going through the many G300 gates to get off planet Earth to a new home world, where they will have a destination toward a new life. In the command center, Boulder is speaking to the person who had opened the blast doors, which appeared to be thousands of feet away from the upper level of the original blast doors that led to the facility with bulletproof glass, two soldiers communicate with the outside world about the ongoing battle.

"Scout one, close the blast doors right away!"

The Legendaries, along with soldiers, feel a brush of wind gusting through their area, as scout number one presses three buttons, closing the glass doors slowly down. The blast doors are camouflaged and built with an indestructible alien shielding that would take billions of Inquestorians to pull down. That is how large and thick the blast doors are. A gust of wind hit the soldiers, as the blast doors close, and nothing moving except air, catching the enemy off guard. As the military and the Legendaries traverse the shrubs, it seems as though the enemy can't see them, almost as though they're invisible at this moment, but what happens is the Legendaries and soldiers slowly make their way toward the mountain, where the enemy lurks. On the ground, the military men crawl toward their opponents in formation. Since the military personnel within the bushes are like a chameleon through the grass and the dirt, the enemy cannot see them. Nevertheless, and the men have shrubs on them, so the enemy can only see shrubs and trees, making them invisible. Sergeant Bobo crawls behind his troops. After moving slowly toward and around the mountain area for some time, the men eventually arrive. At that time, the Inquestorians hear a sigh as they consider whether they saw anything move.

"Huh, hmm."

It appears that the grass does not move as the Inquestorians watch in the general vicinity, where the military men pause for a moment, then the Legendaries, invisible, move through the grass as it has never moved before. Crawling is not possible for Legendaries. Their only option is to stand up and go quietly toward the enemy as the military men slowly approach. Throughout the facility, General Boulder and General Snuff are communicating with the military, who are closing in on the enemy, and begin chatting among themselves.

A glance at the big screen prompted General Boulder to ask General Snuff, "What is going on? Is there any progress on these battle strategies?"

A message is being communicated between General Snuff and Sargent Bobo, "Sergeant, increase movement. A look elsewhere seems to be the enemy's focus."

On his headset, Sergeant Bobo says, "I agree. We need to move, soldiers. Get moving."

After that, General Snuff turns to General Boulder and says, "We have increased our movements."

That command tends to be accepted by General Boulder. The troops stand at the enemy's back door within an hour, waiting for instructions. In conversation with General Boulder, General Snuff, reveals the expectations for the battle strategies.

General Snuff, concentrating hard with thoughts floating in a cloud above his head, exclaims loudly, "The next step is to capture an enemy or bring them back and study them, or we can fight them. It all depends on our troops as to what can or cannot happen."

Therefore, General Boulder makes one brilliant statement concerning the hybrids that catches the attention of General Snuff. "Why don't we send out the hybrids capable of cloaking themselves and at least study one or more of the enemies into our facility?" he asked.

Amid General Boulder and General Snuff's lengthy conversation, General Snuff puts his right index finger on his cheek and thumb and thinks for a moment, before a member of Cokiko's comrades approaches him quietly to tell him something calmly that is urgent. Snuff stares for a moment as Cokiko's comrade is quietly telling him something, as General Snuff's mind finally captures what General Boulder is trying to say to him about the hybrids cloaking and catching one of the enemy soldiers.

"Oh, yeah, yeah, now that sounds like a plan, General Boulder. Let me pull back the forces before they engage the enemy and get the cloaking hybrids to take advantage of this situation."

Communicating on a specific frequency Sergeant Bobo's first and second commanders can pick it up. General Snuff calls into the speaker comm of Sergeant Bobo, while he is in the field, and explains the scenario to him, "Sergeant Bobo, do not engage the enemy at this time. I have an idea to implement. If possible, we plan is to capture one or two types of enemies to study them at the facility with the cloaking hybrids."

"Soldiers, stand down. In little while, we'll develop a plan of attack." Sergeant Bobo tells his team of soldiers.

As General Boulder speaks to Cokiko about the cloaking hybrids and how he and General discussed sending out amalgam to capture a few enemy units, he says, "Excuse me, Cokiko, but we have a plan regarding the hybrids. We were considering abducting one or two of the enemies to study them, and we wonder if we can get them on board."

Cokiko thinks to himself with regards to using the cloaking hybrids and puts his left hand on General Boulder's shoulder and looks him in the eye with a massive smile on his face and tells him with a benevolent look, "*Well, let's see here for a moment. Do we want the enemy to know we have this technology yet? If they were to unlock them, and if they find out, the enemy would be unstoppable and may find our universe and destroy us. I think it's best for them not to find out, my friend*

General Boulder, and to use them as a sneak attack. If a war were to brew that way, they would think you humans have some force on your planet that would push them back, so, my friend, the answer is no. For now, go ahead with your original plan and proceed from there, and if you're lucky to capture one in which my comrade already said one of our Legendary brothers has already been in one of their chambers, we are ahead of you. General Boulder, do not tell General Snuff. Tell him we said no and proceed with the original plan, okay."

General Boulder tends to agree with Cokiko, although not knowing that the Praetorians already have an enemy in custody; therefore, General Boulder walks back toward General Snuff regarding proceeding with the original plan. General Boulder walks toward General Snuff. As General Boulder gets about five feet away from General Snuff, General Snuff says with excitement, "Well, what did he say! Are you going forward with the plan? Because I think it is a lovely idea."

General Boulder smiles a bit, then, with a severe look on his face, exclaims with, "My comrade, unfortunately, Cokiko thinks it is not a good idea and would like your men to proceed with the original plan at hand."

General Snuff sighs and tries to reason with General Boulder instead of Cokiko. "Why! That is a good plan. We should use them. Why can't we use them? Is it because it is too early for them to be seen by the enemy if captured? Please tell me the reason, General Boulder."

Boulder seems to agree with what General Snuff would like to accomplish. But when it comes to reasoning with him, Boulder makes a consensus by telling stuff about the concerns of this technology getting into the enemy's hands. "Look, by releasing this technology, if the enemy were to capture one, all our goals would be forfeited by the enemy. Furthermore, since the enemy will know this advanced technology, they may eliminate every universe, including the universe of Cokiko, where all will be lost, and chaos will strive within all galaxies. They will take all their technology and use it for evil purposes. So we must proceed with the original plan at hand."

General Snuff is saddened but understands why Cokiko does not want to use the cloaking hybrids yet. In regards to the original plan, General Snuff calls Sergeant Bobo to let him know to continue with the original plan. "Sergeant Bobo?"

Sergeant Bobo answers quickly as his men are stationary. "Yes! General Snuff. What is the verdict, sir?"

General Snuff continues, "Proceed with the original plan. It is not a good idea to use hybrids yet. Just continue with the plans."

Sergeant Bobo understands General Snuff's command. "Okay, sir, will proceed with original plans. Sergeant Bobo out!"

Sergeant Bobo tells his first commander and Chief Peter to commence the previous command and continue forward. "Chief Peter, let us continue with the original plan and proceed with it."

Chief Peter responds to Sergeant Bobo and his men simultaneously, "Continue with starship destroyer sync as before, men. Let's do it!"

The entire military squadron proceeds slowly through the bushes toward the enemy, as the enemies are going back and forth in front of the mountains, waiting for the mountain to open up, the military come through an underground tunnel from the facility; without warning, one of the soldiers gets up like an idiot and starts to shoot at the creatures. In the meantime, a couple of the Legendaries are invisible. They also begin shooting behind him at the enemy. However, he is curious about the source of the other bullet. So while the enemy is shooting and hitting something, the Legendary, who seem to be a goofball, decides to stand in one spot instead of moving around, but has no idea what they are shooting aside from the crazy idiot military individual who went berzerk.

The Legendary will not move because he believes he can take on the enemy alone. In the interim, some of the other military men begin to shoot. Furthermore, as some of the military men get up and shoot at the enemy, the enemies start to think and have no idea what is shooting at them. A gasp of disappointment escapes Sergeant Bobo's lips. When General Snuff receives the order to shoot at the enemy, Bobo's team hears him sighs loudly.

"Sir, we have a moron that tipped off the enemy by commencing gunfire without permission, alerting the enemy to our location. Would you mind letting me know your position on this??"

General Snuff gives him the ultimate order. "If a soldier went out of your command, you must get cracking with the plan, Sergeant."

The strategy must be launched quickly by surrounding the enemy and implementing it.

"Men, we must promptly our troops around the enemy in advance with much caution and take them over as quickly as possible, men."

Forty-five minutes in, the entire infantry surrounds the enemy with caution as one soldier who seems to be not getting hit continues to shoot at the enemy and some Legendaries. Finally, the whole battalion moves into position, and Sergeant Bobo initiates the command for battle.

"Men, are we all in place?"

The entire squadron responds, "Yes, we are."

Bobo continues, "Okay, proceed with caution and go for it now! Start shooting, start shooting! Get them men!"

The entire squadron begins to shoot at the enemies immediately as more enemies of the Inquestorians move forward to that location to get involved in the battle right away. Enemy forces are shooting military units. A small cloud of smoke detects an outer shape that seems familiar to one or two enemies as the enemy fires napalm at some of the armies attacking the enemy, with the idiot and the Legendaries hitting their location.

There were many enemies, but only two reports the information to the mother ship regarding an outline that looked familiar to them: "*We have seen something extraordinary with the pink and dark-skinned creatures. We outline some unusual creatures that seem peculiar to something we encountered billions of years ago, Master Draker.*"

Master Draker speaking with Stunner, gets a notice on his liprod. "*Yes, Officer, you were saying.*"

The enemy officer repeats the same message to Draker again; this time, Draker responds quickly, "*Oh, okay, did you get a video on the information when you had to embark on the pink and dark-skinned creatures what this enemy may look like?*' Draker rages with fire in his eyes, as the officer on the planet sends him a picture of the napalm exploding within that vicinity, showing the creature's outline. But then, within the mother ship tower, Faloosh has no idea what is happening. On the surface of the planet except that his men are gathering the humans to worship his worthiness.

In the interim, Stunner also receives the message from the other officer on the planet, giving Stunner a more accurate picture of who these creatures are that could be shooting with the humans. Stunner interrupts his military officer and says, "*They have aliens among them, hmm! See if you can send another napalm in that area and look at what the outline might show. We need a clearer picture of those creatures fighting with the pink and black skins and find out what they are.*"

The Head officer that is talking with Stunner says, "*I will find out what they are, Master Stunner.*"

Stunner, who wants a closer look, gives an order to the commanding officer, "*Remember, get a closer look at these creatures, send me a 3D image immediately, and we will see what we can come up with.*"

The Head officer locates his 3D emulation video recorder within his helmet by voice recognition where he finally takes about ten seconds to identify and is ready to take a shot of those creatures that are fighting with the humans, "*I got the 3D emulator prepared to go.*" Master Stunner gives orders to officers to shoot the napalm within that area again. "*Please send napalms in the area again, and I want to ensure what is helping the pink and dark-skinned creatures." The Head officer says while looking for the footage. "I will record and upload it to you, Master Stunner.*"

Then Stunner, who does not know that Draker also received the message a bit earlier than he did, gives the Head officer a final command, "*Okay, remember I want that video as soon as possible. Master Stunner out.*"

The officer gets the last message and tells his soldiers to concentrate on the area where the invisible creatures location and shoot in that direction. "Okay, creatures, fire in the order the 3D pointer of my weapon shoots and keep firing the napalms in that area. Fire! Fire! Fire!"

The enemy saturates that area with weapon fire as the military tries to keep them off the target.

Stunner listening to what Faloosh and the others are saying, notices they aren't talking about what had occurred through his liprod with the leading officer of Rook, who is the leading officer to Rook. On the other hand, Rook has rounded up some of the humans and escorted them back to the mother ship to worship Faloosh; otherwise, if they don't worship Faloosh, they would have to perform life-or-death situations with Faloosh's insane death games.

The battle between the humans with the Legendaries fighting the Inquestorians continues as a human gets shot in his left shoulder, which is braised with blood seeping out quickly. The military soldier looks at it and asks another soldier, who grabs him up and starts to retreat to the facility with the wounded soldier, as the soldier turns his head to the left, "What is this? It is attached to my left shoulder and will not release itself. I am starting to feel faint. It is almost like a blood-sucker bleeding me out."

The soldier runs with the wounded soldier back to the entrance of the underground facility, where the enemy can't see him because the soldier seems to vanish within the bushes. One alien runs after them to see where he ends up. With the help of the Praetorians, the soldier with the wounded soldier turns invisible; all you can see is the bushes moving with windy air. A few seconds later, the underground blast doors open and quickly disappears, as the enemy looks around confused and sighs to himself as it continues to fight the humans. The wounded soldier is looked at by

Gale, who studies the instrument that lodges within the soldier's shoulder. As Gale touches it, the device seems to embed more and more within his shoulder, almost like severing his shoulder. Gale takes a sample of the instrument and puts it in a tube with some chemical liquid to see what the partial device does within the chemical. Without warning, the sample device seems to duplicate in an expounded measure increase. Gale gulps for a second and notices how fast it grows and how the chemical appears to feed it instead of destroying it.

"It looks like it grows and uses the chemical to feed on. Let's see what would happen to this device if we freeze it in sub below temperatures." Gale is talking to Penny and tells Penny to put the sample and the chemical inside the huge freezer doors. "Penny, please put this in the freezer. Hopefully, we can stop it from growing, and get this out of the soldier's shoulder."

Penny agrees with Gale, takes the sample, and puts it in a sub below a hundred degrees to see if the substance will stop growing. Within minutes, the soldier screams with agony and pain as his left arm detaches from his body, dropping to the floor as the soldier passes out unconscious. Penny and Gale wait approximately hours before returning to the freezer. The alien instrument expands and freezes at the final growth point as Gale opens the freezer. Gale looks with confusion on her face and tells Penny the outcome.

"Penny, it looks like the alien device has stopped growing, and it seems to be frozen, preventing the extra growth in its tracks. Can you see this, Penny?"

Penny, with eyes wide open, also looks at the device in disbelief as Penny hears the soldier in agony and pain. "Yes, it seems like we stopped it, all right. But, oh my, it seems the soldier is in pain. I have to get back to him. Let's go, Gale, leave the alien device in here. I don't think anyone or anything will be bothered by it as long as it is here. Don't forget to keep the door closed, Gale."

Gale rushes back with Penny to the wounded soldier. Gale grabs an alien device given to them by Cokiko's people. The device appears metal and a black cuff that looks like a giant coffee mug; it automatically fits or cuffs the soldier's severed shoulder as it heats up, clogging the blood, causing it to heal with the heat and cool it down instantly. The unconscious soldier regains consciousness as he catches his breath and sighs for a moment as he thinks to himself, *Was it a bad dream?* The soldier looks to his left arm. "Oh my god, it wasn't a bad dream. My arm is gone! Why, God, why!"

Using the golard requires placing the arm near the severed shoulder area. While attaching a severed arm, Praetorians used a golard, a technological glue-torch technique to help fix the severed shoulder area, where it hardens and clogs the site so that blood can flow again. Then using that same instrument as a medical device that sews it up with invisible casting that dissipates after a while. One Praetorian opens the freezer up, notices something familiar, and says to Cokiko, "The growing vector is back. It seems that the enemy improved on this technology."

As the Praetorian opens the door, Cokiko looks up and around the freezer. "*Yes, it seems that they did improve that instrument. Unfortunately, what else have they improved? It appears that we have our work cut out for us, Lieutenant.*"

Lieutenant Praetorian agrees as he also looks around the freezer. "*Yes, we do.*"

Gale, overhears them, asks, "How's that so?"

Cokiko tells Gale what the instrument looked like before. "*There was a noticeable difference in sharpness. In those days, it didn't embed itself. It just bled you out, and you couldn't get it out for any reason. So detachment of body parts occurred slowly.*"

Gale stares at it with awe and confusion. "Engaging. I suppose it is alive. A metal instrument with tissue. Strange indeed."

Cokiko tells Gale what it's called. "*It's a umagate.*"

Gale, with a confused look, asks, "A umagate!"

Cokiko, "Yes, a umagate like a fumigate, where it detaches the arm, and it probably sends a spray up through a hole in his torso toward his bloodstream. We would have to get this soldier to our scientist. They are Praetorian doctors."

The Praetorians come in with a miniature stretcher for the human soldier. They take the soldier back with his detachable arm and leave the room to a Praetorian mother ship to see what chemicals are in the soldier's bloodstream. They can probably combat that chemical during the interval on the outside. The military is in battle mode. The one Legendary keeps shooting and shooting at the enemy, not moving around but standing in that one spot, making him hard to kill; in turn, so are the Inquestorians.

One of the soldiers decided to throw a gyro geyser, a futuristic automatic heat sensor weapon that tracks the enemy's weakness, if there is any. A small miniature needle is sent after explosion of the gun that looks for a weakness in the enemy but doesn't seem to find one, and collapses when the enemy touches it. A military man that had sent that gyro gismo at the creature dies when the Inquestorians returns fire with one eye closed at him, aiming at the man that had fired it.

The war starts to get a little more intense as that one Inquestorian speaks to the other, "*Seems like they have superior weaponry because it made my body jump high. Must call command center regarding this.*"

The Inquestorian then calls the command center and speaks with Thorgus, who seems busy talking with Faloosh. Thorgus answers his liprod, "*Yes, Captain.*"

On his liprod, as he shoots and kills a military soldier, he says, "It seems that the pink and dark skins have a superior weapon for their archaic small-minded simple minds. What should we do about it. What if they have weapons that can destroy us?"

Thorgus, who doesn't want to be bothered, replies, "*Look into it further, Captain.*"

Captain replies, "*Yes, Master Thorgus.*"

Thorgus continues, "*Don't bother me unless the pink and dark-skinned creatures start to kill one of us, okay, eventually.*"

That captain is about to hang up the liprod. "*Got it, Master Thorgus. I will continue with the plan.*"

Before hanging up, Thorgus tells the captain to report to his superiors first. "*And, yes, Captain, make sure you write in your report to Rook right away.*" Thorgus hangs up. Captain respects the master and reports to Rook to let her know what is happening.

"*Commander Rook, the enemy has some seeking device that is looking for a weakness in us. They might have superior weapons.*"

Command Rook picks up her liprod, getting the message from the captain. "*I suggest you investigate further, and if possible, eliminate the pink and dark skins giving you trouble.*"

Suddenly, the trigger-happy captain panics, his men go crazy, and the battle goes on as many soldiers die. Then, after a shield blocks their barrier, the all-war continues with bullets, lasers, tanks, alien vessels, assorted alien weapons, and sophisticated exotic weapons on the human side.

Draker suddenly decides to look at the 3D imaging on Earth through one of the Inquestorians' image cameras. Draker thinks, *Why does that creature's outline look so familiar?* The remaining soldiers start shooting at the enemy after Draker sees a battle on the ground. Unfortunately, the invisible shield of a Praetorian does not protect these soldiers. In response, the enemies wonder whether the soldiers have superior weapons. So the soldiers begin running at the enemies. Some creatures begin to run toward their ships as the soldiers run toward them, about to engage and shoot them. The Inquestorians notice that they can see some of the pink and dark skins, and some can't see. So, the invisible soldiers take out their new weapons and start shooting at them as the Inquestorians try to dodge them, firing a soluble chemical that eats at anything. As the Inquestorians retreat to their ships, they regroup on how to defeat the humans.

As the battle progresses, more military vehicles appear, as well as extra large tanks and exotic foreign combat cars that the military has been researching for decades. Humans and minor legendaries ride alien motor tykes that can move sideways and hover over the enemy with an enclosed shielding. These tykes shoot clouded dust and spray the enemies with a cloud of chemicals, giving the enemy a hard time breathing, and making the enemy fall back into their ships. The humans seems to be winning the battle as you see streams of rays of light shooting across at the Inquestorians and the Inquestorians trying to keep their eyes on the prize of attempting to subdue the humans as best as they can. You hear weapons firing continuously among both parties throughout the planet. You see Russia, China, England, Scotland, Africa, Mexico, and all over the continents are battling the Inquestorians, and you can see one Praetorian throughout each continent embracing the humans with the invisibility of their synthetic blood within all the soldiers along with the Legendaries. The battles are vicious along the continents as our comrades move the aliens back to their ships.

While Commander Rook's spacecraft has maybe twenty to a hundred humans onboard, she starts to take off from Earth, and return to the mother ship after taking off from Earth. When Commander Rook signals her ship, two Humvees are firing at the spacecraft. As the ship'd weapons fire at the Humvees, the Humvee go up about a thousand feet in the air, exploding on the way down, killing the soldiers in a matter of seconds. Also, as the humans and Legendaries who are invisible close in on the enemy, the Inquestorians retract back to their ships. Draker's tone comes in quickly and loudly, announcing the attack.

Draker looks at Stunner with a confused epression as he says, "*Wait a minute! I know those creatures.*"

Stunner's eyebrows frown, "*I have no idea what are you talking about, Draker! How do you know what it is?*"

"*I know what those invisible creatures are!*" Draker says as he bangs his hand on the holographic table

In shock and stunned, Stunner asks, "*What are they?*"

"*They are legends!*" Draker announces with a more boisterous voice.

CHAPTER 31

LEGENDARIES RECOGNIZED BY ENEMY

Stunner repeats, "*Legendaries.*"

Draker looks in Faloosh's direction. "*Yes, Stunner, Legendaries.*"

Stunner looks upon the 3D image. "*Are you saying the ones we defeated on that inevitable planet billions of years ago?*"

Draker, concerned, replies, "*That is what I'm saying, exactly. So they are here on this planet, hmm.*"

As Draker discusses Legendaries with Stunner, Faloosh gets a bit of the conversation, where he quickly turns around with a booming voice, "*Who says Legendaries? We had killed them all!*"

Draker sighs a little and catches his breath. "*Master lord.*"

Faloosh answers quickly and with fire in his eyes, "*Yes, Draker.*"

Draker gives Faloosh the news about Legendaries on the planet's surface. Draker shows Faloosh the 3D image that outlines the Legendaries' skeletal structure. "*Look at the outline, Overlord.*"

Faloosh looks at the outline. At the moment, Faloosh's size is at regular height. He says in a low tone, with a look of bewilderment, "*Interesting. Legendaries on this planet. I wonder what they have to do with these pink and dark skin creatures. They wouldn't be here otherwise. Why would they be here unless they want the minerals too? I wonder if this is the planet, but I only see one or two Legendaries, so if that were the case, there would be many of them on this planet if it were to be the ancestors. Send out the spiral fighters immediately, Mapoh, but first, we must strategically make plans.*"

Mapoh responds in a salute manner to Faloosh. "*What are your goals, my overlord sire?*"

Faloosh sits with his shadow lords around a hovering table discussing their strategic plans for Earth. Draker sits down with a wise remark, "*Okay, Overlord, let's discuss the plans for this planet. What might that be, Overlord?*"

Faloosh begins talking about his strategic planning. "*Being that we have sought some Legendaries, we need Mapoh's spiral fighters to intercept any of these pink and dark skins, which are trying to attack back.*"

Draker, Thorgus, and the other overlords' eyes fixated on Faloosh. As with quickness, they say, "*Yes, your lordship.*"

Over the hovering circular, triangular shape table, a holographic representation of Earth's grounds displays pawns. The shadow lords, along with Faloosh, use the holographic pendulum suspended in thin air to fight the pink and dark-skinned creatures on the grounds strategically. While Rook's ships await orders from the shadow lords and Faloosh, Faloosh continues strategically positioning holographic pawns around Earth's forces to gain the upper hand.

"*The napalms must be sent down by Mapoh's fighters. I want to destroy them if they don't comply with your command. They made Rook turn around and go back and retreat. Rook is on her way back with some pink and dark skin creatures. Is that correct, Draker?*"

"*I believe that you are correct, my lordship.*" Draker replies with a shaky voice.

Faloosh proceeds as his face morns of defeat for now and says, "*Good. We will greet her spacecraft while the other ships hover over this planet, waiting for her commands when she returns. The pink and dark skin creatures I see now are celebrating as though they think they defeated us. We know they can't defeat us with those puny little archaic weapons. They have no idea what will rain down on their parade with our weapons. Lordships, we plan that the second and third waves will drench them down like a pile of rubble until they give up and worship me. You all got that so far, Mapoh, Thorgus, Draker, Stunner, Madane. You all have the idea, right?*"

Mapoh, Thorgus, Draker, Stunner, and Madane, almost like a singsong response, say, "*Right! We have the idea, Master Overlord.*"

Faloosh strategically plans the execution of Earthling forces that are trying to withstand them in chronological order on the invisible chess throne of eight layers. As Faloosh glides, his right hand appears from an invisible presence to an actual piece on the holographic board. As Faloosh continues, he tells Mapoh, "*I want you to cover the entire planet with strike forces. You'll initiate the napalms and corner their forces to central locations, around the planets, but we won't kill them unless they fight back hard. If they don't comply with your command, try to capture those for our games. With unmerciful weaponry, the Rook team is going to land. Again, oh, here comes Rook right now! We didn't have to meet her. She seems to have her eighth sense in line with what we're doing here. Welcome, Rook, we're trying to strategically take over these pink and dark skins in a way that doesn't slaughter them. Haha! What input can you put in for us, Rook, from what you had encountered on this planet's surface and the capturing of these pink and dark skin creatures?"*

Rook looks closely at the holographic board, taking notes and moving some of the pieces around to give Faloosh a great idea as Rook compliments the plan. "*Well, Master Overlord, from moving some parts here, I see that we can take them over by not harming them unless they wish to be destroyed from their existence or disintegrate within the planet. Having them worship you, my overlord, will significantly benefit our species."*

Faloosh picks up a great idea. "*I see here since you had put some guards around the captured creatures, it shows what our weapons can do. They must our laws, or else they will be destroyed. Very good, Rook, very good!"*

Another thing that Rook mentions is. "*So they have some potent weapons on this planet. I hope this works."*

Faloosh says with a demure tone, "*I see, saw it on the 3D screen, but your strike force team, We have some new weaponry we acquired using the minerals from this planet, so Mapoh, you should have your forces prepared. Then your team, Rook, will go down with those weapons. We will fight them to make sure they worship me. You all got it, right?"*

Rook quickly acknowledges, "*I got it, Overlord."* The others nod their heads in a yes motion.

Faloosh moves some more pawns on the holographic board and proceeds, "*After that, we initiate not only the strike force but catacomb the area for the destroyers. You got that, Thorgus?"*

Thorgus, eyes glued to the board, says, "*Yes, my Overlord, destroyers will defeat any weapons they might be using."*

Faloosh moves another pawn and says, "*We're going to take what we need to overrun this planet. We're not going to destroy this planet because it has way too many minerals, and the entire planet's surface and interior are full of these minerals. The whole world is a mineral treasure. The initial instructions you already had received. Now, you all must get ready."*

All warlords prepare for battle as Mapoh, Thorgus, and Rook all give separate gestures to Faloosh as a good sign response. "*Yes, Overlord Faloosh.*"

Draker makes a suggestion. "*On this pattern here.*"

Faloosh lets Draker change some things. "*Go ahead, Draker.*"

Draker proceeds with plans as the other overlords take charge within the bay area of the ship tactic plans provided by Faloosh as Faloosh gives the commands through their holographic hauls. Draker delivers the order through Mapoh's ship. Mapoh, with his strike force, goes down with the entire army but sends a few fleets to scan the areas to see what they are up against.

"*Do not bombard them with the napalms yet.*" Mapoh is looking at the task at hand, getting a call on his liprod. "*I got it, I got it. Not a problem, Draker, not a problem.*"

Draker tells Mapoh more about the plan. "*Then you're going to make a palm wave of fire across the entire planet, not hurting the pink and dark skin creatures but letting them know our power. Then, Rook?*"

Rook turns around toward Draker. "*Yes, warlord?*"

Draker explains to Mapoh about Rook's plan in a strategic battle way. "*Rook is going to come down behind the fire blazes. We're going to have the new weapons that can withstand any temperature that can burn, destroy, or disintegrate its enemies. We will take them over, okay.*"

In agreement with Draker, Rook nods her head yes. Mapoh also concurs with the plan as he screams toward one of his men, "*Not now, not now, General! Okay, Draker, I agree with the project.*"

Faloosh is busy making future moves regarding the Earthlings on the holographic chessboard, as Draker interprets the outcome from the board.

"*Stunner!*"

Stunner, making some computer adjustments to ship weapons, replies, "*Yes, Draker, how can I be of help?*"

Draker tells Stunner his position. "*Our teams—Mapoh, Rook, Thorgus and my team—go below onto the planet's surface while you, Stunner, will remain up here. Then, after Faloosh gives us the ultimate orders, I will take Thorgus and my team to touchdown our spacecraft at specific points on the planet. Then, finally, some men will take the weapons out of the ship to flood the globe with our species and take control of the creatures. Got it, Stunner! And others.*"

In between Draker's words, a strange sound accompanied him: "*We hear and respond, lordship, to the plan.*"

Draker turns to Faloosh with a smirk. "*Faloosh warlord, what will you like us to do with the Legendaries?*"

Faloosh, with an evil eye toward Draker and a burst of distinct laughter, says, "*Well! We wiped them out before. At least, I thought we did. But we'll have to wipe them out again, so if we find Legendaries anywhere on this planet, we will have to wipe them out one by one until we get rid of them all, which can mean one thing! Forfathers' planet. From what I remember, they no longer have a home world. At least, that's what I thought. We destroyed their entire species centuries ago. So there is no reason we can't explore this planet, unless more Legendaries show up. Madane, we'll find out their unique goal with this planet. What do you think?*"

Madane, with eyes confused, as Faloosh calls her attention. "*Yes, your lordship.*"

Faloosh looks to Madane for a particular chemical. "*Do you have that chemical called AIC Tarp? Let Draker get that for you, Madane.*"

Madane tries to tell Draker its location within the 3D facility near her bay area. "*It is the AID35, got it!*"

Draker looks repeatedly. "*All I see is the AIC TARP. I don't see anything else.*"

The location is shown to him by Madane. "*Here to the right of the AIC TARP, you have to go one up and two rows back toward the center!*"

As Madane hands the flask to Draker, Draker, on the other hand, hands it to Faloosh. Faloosh swishes and glides a live chemical that lives in the flask. He tells Madane and Draker what he intends to do with the chemical. "*Whatever Legendaries are on this planet, we're going to soak the air and snuff them out in the open area where we can capture them. Draker, as a last resort, will implement that task with the bombers' hyper-gliders. If the pink and dark skin creatures come full force against us, we may have to destroy some of them, but most of them, we want them to worship me.*"

Back at the facility on Earth, while Faloosh and his team are doing strategic planning, the Praetorians leak out a secret to the scientists of these enemies.

"*Yes, Gale, Penny, John, Lucas, Merna, let me tell you something about these Inquestorians.*"

All scientists nod their heads in a yes motion, with the quickness. "Go ahead."

The Praetorian continues, "*I want to tell you in that these creatures will not stop until they have entirely overthrown the planet. It appears that they have destroyed planets, based on our observation from our spy. As far as we understand, they have a colossal planetarian weapon, similar to a death star, attached to a vast mother ship that can implode planets up on contact. I don't believe they want to implode this planet because, as my colleagues told me, the whole planet has the minerals they want. The Inquestorians will not destroy it. They will maintain this planet and try to take control of the planet's resources, which is their goal."*

Merna says with a nervous voice, "Why are we leaving our planet if they want our resources?"

The Praetorian tells Merna why. "*By using up the Earth's resources, it will die due to depletion of mineral resources."*

Merna sees this playing out. "So you're saying once the planet depletes itself, they will implode the Earth."

The Praetorian is quick with a response. "*Exactly! We must leave and have a Legendary scout ship, a large one that the Inquestorians can see. When a wormhole opens up, the spacecraft will disappear into thin air, transforming the Inquestorians to hopefully follow away from planet Earth, leaving perhaps a few of their spacecraft behind. Hoping that the mother ship will follow us once we vanish into thin air when the wormhole opens up. In this plan, the Legendaries will be on Earth first, then the Cafalions can raom free on the Earth, with the remaining Inquestorians eventually defeating most of them. With regards to the hybrids taking on the colossal mothership vessels combating them from various planets to eventually the Milky Way galaxy in the future. Their neighboring planet was brutal for the Inquestorians to kill because they were ten times the skin strength of the Inquestorians, where they had at one point to fall back, but of course, they imploded that planet because of the threat that may overpower them one day."*

The Praetorian educates more about the Cafalions and says, "*The Cafalions are very hard to beat with their five-times-thick skin as the Inquestorians, where the Cafalions have leathery skin that is very impenetrable. You can send napalms and nuclear bombs, it will not hurt them, but there is some weakness we will not find out until centuries from now through the Cafalions, who may or may not conquer the Inquestorians alone. What those weaknesses are, we have no idea for right now!"*

Lucas gazes and stares at the Praetorians as he concentrates on what the Praetorian is saying. "So you are telling me that there is no way to defeat these guys. However, we're able to send them back to their ship."

Praetorian looks straight at Lucas. "*No! No! No! You didn't scare them away. You just made them much angrier. They are going to smother the Earth with their kind and take you by force as either enslaved people or destroy you if you are a threat, so you just encountered the first force wave. The second and third surge, and a possible fourth surge of stream of ships are still to come."*

John replies while he scratches his beard, "What do you mean a surge or stream of ships?"

Praetorian continues while swatting a bug nearby, "*I mean, surge streams of medium ships will cover the Earth's skies. Then, if that doesn't work, they will send out the fifth and sixth waves, the giants that will be the enforcers when they are in battle, and they can destroy everything on the planet. I mean everything, including underwater creatures and those of similarity. These giants are extremely hard to defeat. They are impenetrable, and they are monstrous. Trust me. You do not want to get to surge five or six. We must get off of this planet for now and revisit Earth in the future when the hybrids can defeat, alongside their allies, the Inquestorians in a raging battle to save alternate universes and the worlds that breathe life. Hopefully, throughout the centuries that there will also be giants on our side as well to take over these giants that are impenetrable as well. When you have two giants with the same width and problematic skin, it can be a battle that rages on for centuries to come, but we will find the weakness of the Inquestorians if it takes us decades and decades and centuries from now."*

Suddenly out of nowhere, comes Yarmin walking over toward the Praetorian with General Boulder and General Snuff as well as Cokiko, Wymoym, and without warning, Ballisto, the leader of the Legendaries. They all appear within the facility area of the doctors and scientists. Yarmin, without a fret says, "What is going on here!"

Cokiko fills in the military on what is going on. General Snuff, Boulder, and Yarmin are within the realm of Cokiko, who is telling the humans a secret about the enemy, the Inquestorians, whom the humans should already know something. "*So we're discussing with these doctors right here what these enemies are all about. Let me fill you in. These enemies are about their ultimate goal on this planet from my colleague, who will further educate you on their tactics."*

Ballisto interjects and interrupts Cokiko's speech. "*What I want to say, good doctors, scientists, and military personnel, is that we have found out through our Praetorian brothers the Inquestorians will not destroy this planet. They have a weapon to implode the core of a world, destroying it, leaving the world desolated and corrupted with the weapon that can eradicate any world."*

"I see," Yarmin says. "So what do we do about that?"

Ballisto proceeds further, "*They will not destroy your planet. The planet is full of minerals to hold them for decades and centuries to billions of years. For now, the only way to get them away from Earth is to send a Legendary ship through orbit through a wormhole. They would hopefully follow them when they see the Legendary ships leaving the planet. Their goal is to defeat the Legendaries.*"

The Praetorian intercedes hesitantly. "*As you can see, dear doctors and scientists, the Inquestorians will again not destroy this planet because it is full of minerals. Not only that, I will retell the situation to Yarmin, Snuff, Boulder, and the rest of the military personnel who are in this room right now. The Cafalions almost defeated the Inquestorians billions of years ago. Unfortunately, I will have to tell you a virtuos secret.*"

Overpowering his Praetorian brotherly comrade, Ballisto gives them the secret with his strong voice echoing throughout the room, "*That real secret is what the Legendaries have done with the Praetorian brothers. They were with the Cafalions, who got a warning sign from them that war was too immense on their planets. So the Praetorian brothers had gone with their extreme invisibility. At that time, through a wormhole came many other Inquestorians. Although they lost the battle, more Inquestorians came through wormholes that sought after the Cafalions to try to eliminate them. The Praetorian ships had landed on their worlds months before the war started, taking as many refugees as they could carry within their spaceships.*

"*They took among their ships younglings, primarily females, and some smaller males to rebirth their continued species.*

"*Therefore, the Cafalions are among the Praetorian home worlds getting ready and readying themselves for battle in the coming centuries when it will take place. It may take place during the time of the hybrids and how the amalgams challenges the Inquestorians will tell if the Cafalions are ready or not will be the final war for them. Since they are on the invisible planets of the Praetorian home worlds, you can see them only with Praetorian eyes. Otherwise, you can't see those planets. Once you land on the planets, you can see the skies, vegetation, mammals, and other assorted species. They have a total of twelve moons throughout their solar system. When you leave the planet, everything is invisible. It is almost like a two-way window where you can see out, but no one can see in.*"

"Hmm," says Lucas, Merna with enjoyment. "So you're telling me we can see from the planet's surface but can't see when we exit the planet's orbit."

Ballisto refreshes as he swallows some swine milk. "*That is correct.*"

"That is interesting. I would love to see something like that. It makes me wonder how the invisible spectrum works," stated Lucas.

Ballisto, with a slow smirk, replies, "*The invisible spectrum is unique. Our planets are magnificent. Our species are common ground and get along very well.*"

In his address, Ballisto shifts the spotlight to Professor Wymoym. "*Yarmin, ah, General Boulder, Sergeant Snuff, and all our military personnel, today is a day we can fight until our last man stands. If the enemy happens to surround us, then we must flee into the mountains and get off this planet as fast as we can. For those of you who would like to stay in the mountains, there will be plenty of nourishments to last several lifetimes, but if they happen to invade the mountains, you have nowhere else to go but to get off this planet before they burrow through the walls. We won't be able to escape the planet if we don't get them away as quickly as possible.*"

General Boulder and the military personnel within the facility and on the battlefield all acknowledge Ballisto's orders since they can hear what is going on through their helmets. Some of the military men are celebrating victory, and not paying attention to what Ballisto and the others are saying right now. One of the military men says to a Legendary, "We have our first victory!"

The Legendary looks at him and then slaps the military man in his rear without warning. One of the Legendaries says to Captain Bobo, "*According to what I know, they are currently putting together a strategic tactic plan. By now, if we had defeated them, the ships visible in the skies right now would have reached the mother ship. Instead, spacecraft like those are awaiting for commands to launch a devastating assault on us. The time may come when we will have to pull out some severe arsenal. It appears that the enemy is preparing a tactical strategy to overcome us.*"

"Are you serious?" Sergeant Bobo sighs a bit. "So we did not defeat them, right?"

Legendary tells more, "*No! They are brilliant. Once they have a tactical plan to take us over, they will ensure that you are slaves to them.*"

Sergeant Bobo is a bit frightened about that statement and stutters, "So we have to prepare ourselves for an extreme battle, correct?"

The Legendary nods his head in a yes motion as he agrees. "*That is correct! But luckily, our brothers, the Praetorians, are here to protect us from getting slaughtered. In other words, the first wave would have slaughtered you already, which means they would have killed off your species instead of us, the Legendaries, with our shields. So they had to regroup and make some tactical interventions to try to overcome us and your kind. Unfortunately, it took them to gain ground, not with waves three and four but waves five and six that defeated the Legendaries. Luckily, the Praetorians' brethren had lifted most of us out of the hellhole of a battle and saved most of our species. So the last two waves were the giants. So! Waves one and two were here already, gathering minerals and so forth. Wave three is above the skies right now, and we are waiting for waves four and five, in which we will be in a war for our lives."*

As the rest of the military from within the bunkers come out with more potent weaponry to bring the fight against the enemies, the Inquestorians, Sergeant Bobo, with eyes staring down at the ground in front of the Legendary, responds with concern in his voice, "I see, we will not be afraid of them. We don't want our planet destroyed, and we will do whatever we need to protect our world."

The Legendary says with a special concern, "*We did the same thing too. Our planet didn't get imploded because they found minerals vital, although they took ninety-eight percent of our resources, knowing that it can replenish itself. So, therefore they may be back later sometime in the future. We are so humbled that our brothers, the Praetorians, were able to help a lot of us escape off our planet right away. They are doing the same thing with this planet. Once they have depleted all minerals, they will most likely not destroy this beautiful globe."*

Bobo says again with concern, "Okay, I think I understand now. We will bleed them as best we can. Rah-rah! Men, are you ready?"

The men in ready stance are ready for battle with the newly charged intergalactic weaponry, prepared for the war that is yet to come after the small initial fight that happened already on the ground as the men face forward toward the blast doors. At the same time, back on the Inquestorians' ship, they continue their tactical scheme of things to come. Faloosh tells his overlords, "*Okay, everyone, did you all get your plans in sync. Mapoh initiated plan B."*

Mapoh gets his ships ready for battle as he receives plan B from Faloosh. "*Yes, Master Overlord, I am on my way! Rook, plan A belongs to you. Get the job done. Plan C is Thorgus."*

Not capturing what plan A is, Stunner asks Faloosh a silly question, "*Is plan A where the female Rook bows down and lets them capture her right, Overlord Faloosh?"*

Faloosh looks at Stunner, eyes wide open. "*Capture! Hahaha! Never will one of us ever be captured in any plan of mine. You idiot!"*

Stunner gulps a bit as Faloosh looks at Stunner with crazy eyes. Faloosh is belittling Stunner since he is so stupid.

"Plan A, dummy, is where Mapoh sends out a strike force first, using that strike force to strike at the enemy to see what kind of weaponry the enemy has to fight back while they try to knock us out. Then the battle will begin with the rest of the strike force. Then Thorgus's team, the raiders, will be part of plan D. If they are fighting back too hard, we would have to bring out the giants with Draker. Are you ready for that, Draker?"

Draker, without hesitancy and with quickness, responds, *"I'm prepared for anything, Master Overlord."* Draker punches his left hand into his right fist with an echoing sound.

Faloosh continues with the plans. *"First we must explode some napalms with the strikers protecting their surroundings as they land along with Rook's forces, blinding the Legendaries with the smoke so we can come in from behind and defeat them if possible this time."* Faloosh has no idea how the Legendaries became invisible to his detections. *"I have no idea how they became invisible to our scanners, but I will soon realize. I promise you that, so go, take the initiative."*

Stunner finally gets the scope of things. *"I get it now! I understand the plans now!"*

Faloosh tries to chase away Mapoh and Rook. *"Be gone, Mapoh and Rook. Go do my bidding."*

Thorgus says, *"Master Overlord, isn't Rook with my team instead of Mapoh's team?"*

Faloosh corrects himself, *"Yes, that is correct, Thorgus, that is right!"*

Mapoh is at the loading bay with his strike team getting ready for combat. Mapoh readies his team to disembark from the bay area of the mother ship and the adjoining second mother ship. Some of the striker ships enter Earth's orbit, and they initiate the strike force, but before he gives orders across the globe to ready the napalms, Mapoh says in an alien language, *"Drop the napalms in a circular motion, preventing the enemy from escaping."*

The military around the globe all say simultaneously, "Get ready for a battle. We think they will eventually strike first. Okay, people, get ready."

This time, several Praetorians are shielding around the globe, with invisible protection for many military personnel and Legendaries. The napalms start to hit the grounds of various military forces as the military troops scramble to get cover and aim at the enemies' flight engines, as some of the military men say, "Jam the signal, incoming! Run! Incoming! Run!"

During the napalm attacks, the Praetorian shields military personnel from injury. As Mapoh watches the napalms blow up in the air, his eyebrows curl in amazement. According to one of the military men, "Target in sight! Fire! Fire!"

All you see are midair explosions as the military men are trying to celebrate. Hitting some of the ships has no impact on the spacecraft. Then one of the military men looks up with amusement and surprise. "Look! Look! We didn't get them at all, people. Keep firing, keep firing!"

In this scenario, one of the military men fires an alien grenade gun at one of the ships, which strikes the ship and rocks it back and forth, but only leaves a small dent. Next, on the side of the Legendaries, many military men arrive with an alien triple-headed tank. With these tanks combined into one giant concrete muscle tank with exotic weapons on board and various types of lasers shooting at the strike force, a ship slowly drops with a trembling gait. An alien emerges from the ship and starts shooting at the military personnel. A fleet of Mapoh's strike force appears in the skies and starts shooting at both military personnel and Legendaries. Mapoh reports to the mother ship, telling Faloosh that reports have been coming in that more Legendaries are appearing around the globe.

Mapoh notes on a holographic tablet, "*Overlord Faloosh, my creatures have said that there are more Legendaries throughout the world.*"

Faloosh, with a mean look, replies, "*More Legendaries, impossible! How can that be? Maybe they are after the minerals too. Destroy them, Mapoh. I will be sending Rook to accommodate you in the battle!*"

Mapoh gets the command to destroy them. "*Okay, my team will focus not so much on the pink and dark skins, but on the Legendaries. So acquire and shoot them down through your target scopes! Ready, aim, fire!*"

The Legendaries noticed the enemy is firing on them only instead of military humans. With a forceful strike, the human armies cloud the enemy with ton of firepower so that the Legendaries can escape. Eventually allowing the Legendaries to fall back into the facility tunnels. The Praetorians at that very moment, camouflaged the Legendaries within the fields. Then the enemy starts to focus all their firepower onto the human military, thinking to themselves that the Legendaries again are eradicated while Mapoh's team celebrate.

"*Yeah! Yeah! We got them, Master Overlord.*"

Faloosh again with an evil eye. "*That seems too easy. They must be somewhere. Keep checking the area and scan it!*"

Rook's team comes to intervene in the battle. With her squad, Rook starts to shoot lasers and land on the planet where her team disembarks from the ships. Rook's men begin to shoot toward the military men with their lasers and different weapons, hitting a few men by luck through the force field; some men fall out as though unaware that the enemy has some weapons that can exceed and go right through a force field. Some military personnel engage with the enemy, shooting and firing back at the enemy with alien technology.

One military man says to Sergeant Bobo, "Sir, the men will engage the enemy. We're taking on fire, and we're jamming them with firepower. It doesn't seem to be doing anything but push them back. What can we do?"

Sergeant Bobo gets General Snuff on the helmet comm. "General, we're taking heavy firepower, although our weapons are just pushing them back. What can we do, sir? Heavy artillery vehicles are coming out of some of the other ships."

During the interim, Mapoh pulls out some heavy military vehicles that engage the humans' military vehicles. The triple tanks take heavy fire from huge vehicles, whipping firepower with speeds beyond light-years ahead of time. Some military vehicles catch on fire, while military men escape their military vehicles with their weapons taken on the ground forces.

Furthermore, Rook's men try to surround an area slowly as one of the military men seems to figure out that the enemy is attempting to edge them over. "Sergeant Bobo, I believe the enemy is trying to surround us. Can we come up with a plan to prevent this?"

Sergeant Bobo calls for reinforcement from one or two hybrids. "General Boulder, the enemy is trying to surround us. Therefore, we urgently need support with the directive as soon as possible."

General Boulder speaks to Yarmin with permission to get one or two hybrids around the globe, helping each sector of the world forces to debunk their plan of surrounding the earthlings. As Rook's men seem to get closer and closer, just when they are about to close in, surrounding them, without warning, the natural fast hybrid, with all his might, speeds around the enemy as fast as he can, drawing them back farther away from the military men.

Captain Rook says to Mapoh and the overlords on the mother ship, "*The pink and dark-skinned creatures have some weapon that keeps pushing us back and back further from them. We seem not to get an inch on them, but my creatures and Mapoh's team are trying to keep them at bay. So what do you want us to do? Because it seems we can't get ahead of the plan here, Overlord Faloosh.*"

Faloosh pounds his hands in anger on the table and calls for Thorgus to stand ready with his team, the raiders. Responding to Mapoh and Rook, Faloosh's face turns different colors as a base tone echos throughout his spacecraft with eyebrows furrow, *"Okay! Keep them at bay. Please do not lose sight of them. We must trample these puny pink and dark-skinned creatures and take hold of them right now. I am sending Thorgus and his team to intersect with plan C. It seems like we need more substantial firepower to overcome these creatures. On that note, Rook and Mapoh, keep the war brewing because reinforcement will soon help you two, and we will take them over one way or another. Got it!"*

Rook receives the intermessage from Faloosh, and so does Mapoh, who gives the order to keep the Earthlings at bay until reinforcements get there. Mapoh tells his strike force what to do. *"Creatures, keep the pink and dark-skinned creatures at bay. Do not let them escape or out of your sight! Does everyone understand!"*

Some of Mapoh's men get the hint by trying to push that invisible force forward, as the other hybrid throws giant boulders that he consumes within his stream of breath. The hybrid forms huge boulders as he moves roughly through the sea of military men. He then throws the boulders, helping to protect and surround the military men creating some blockade from the enemy. In the facility, Ballisto, Wymoym, and dignitary Yarmin plan to escape with the doctors and scientists once the war brews over or gets too intense. Ballisto is talking with the scientists and doctors.

"Okay, people, as you can hear and see from the soldiers' comms the war is brewing and getting more intense. We must start planning on our escape route to get off this planet as soon as possible. Everyone understands the emergency of the matter, right!"

Lucas and Gale simultaneously think the same thing, saying, "We know, except as we leave our home world, will we ever come back in the future?"

Ballisto explains what task they have for the good doctors and scientists. *"Where you will be going, you may age one year on planet Earth to ten thousand years. The Praetorians, our brethren, have lived for eons and our Legendaries have lived for billions of years. We don't know how you humans will yet accommodate or acclimate on the invisible planets. By not knowing how your anatomy will adjust, we have no idea if the human structure will last ten years to thousands. We have no idea yet."*

One of the doctors named Penny had a joyful excitement in her voice. "I don't care if I live to ten thousand years. It is more than what the Earth can offer us. When do we leave? I am excited to see something new. I have been traveling worldwide, even sea diving, and rented a submarine to see many parts of the ocean. However, I would like something fresh with a new vision to see."

Ballisto continues, "*Their planets are ten times the size of Earth. So it probably would take you eons to go through all parts of the planet. In contrast, it takes the Praetorians several thousands of years to see their entire planet because of their way of living. Their creations form from the core of their planets, similar to how volcanoes create new land masses. As soon as they are born, their essence leaves the old bodies and enters these new bodies where the old, as you call spirits, merge into a newly formed creature. The living planet somehow and someway gave us birth from forming with our ancestors. You see, if humans were to be on their planet, you might come across giant humans in the future. You never know, especially with their foods, which might activate something special in the human species. By mating, you can have either giants or dwarfs with a great deal of intelligence.*"

Lucas looks toward Penny with eyes of love. "I guess I can see the future toward a lovely lady. I don't know how it will pan out, but hopefully, she can see the end with me if it comes down to that."

Penny looks back and gives Lucas a bit of a smirk. "Yeah! But we must first focus on victory against the enemy and the scientific knowledge that we can provide our clones through telekinesis. Then, with our intelligence, the Praetorians, and the Cafalions and Legendaries, we can devise a plan to take out the enemies, eventually destroying them once and for all."

The Praetorians disagree with that quote. "*We don't want to kill them all. On the contrary, we want to preserve some of them for the good of their species because if we destroy all of them, we will be no better than they are.*"

Lucas tends to disagree with Ballisto and thinks they should wipe them out for good. "I think we should wipe them out entirely because they would be a threat to us all whether we save them!"

One of the Praetorian brothers tends to speak up to Lucas about preserving the life of another species. "*Well, we would like to keep this species and study them eventually. Then, hopefully, they will not retaliate and conquer our worlds.*"

John thinks it is a bad idea. "I think it is a bad idea. To begin with, they are evil and will remain corrupt. There is no way you can teach them goodness. Just like a pit bull, you can train it all you want, but it tends always to attack you, eventually destroying you or something you love."

The Praetorian says more, "*If that were the case, then we would finish them off in a way, as you would say, humanly as possible.*"

Ballisto tells more about the enemy to Yarmin, the doctors, scientists, and other military personnel. "*Now! This enemy will stop at nothing to get their point across, and if we don't comply right away, they will tend to wipe out the existing creatures on that planet. Let me tell you the particular secret that these Inquestorians have, which you should honestly know the extent of it all. At that moment, with research from the Legendary who died getting conclusive information, we discovered that the enemy has a miniature hole. We determined it to be near the back of its head. With such knowledge, when accessing this hole, we found out it can drive them crazy to the point of fighting among themselves and eventually driving them into confusion. With this pertinent information, it can conclude their downfall.*"

Yarmin wants to explain how it works "So, Ballisto, how do we get to that point of how to conquer them, or has it ever been done before?"

Ballisto scratches his ear, telling more of the story. "*According to the Cafalions, their strong claws almost got them right where they wanted them by their tiny fingernails, nearly piercing the enemy within those areas. They got conquered because the female giants, who rarely show themselves, hardly had any weaknesses that overthrew the Cafalions, taking them out many at a time. Until then, we must find a fault for the giant female Inquestorians. We can't win the war, but we can always slow it down. Other than that, we must try to get our hybrids up to par throughout the other galaxies and realms with potent battling weaponry and various skill sets to take the enemies over.*"

Gale and Lucas tend to agree with Ballisto. "We both agree that we probably need more time to draw out the females and see how well we can take them over in the long run, right?"

Ballisto scratches the top of his head as he sneezes. "*It will take many battles among battles to draw them out and test the waters to see if the female giants have any weaknesses. The worst of them all is Faloosh. He is cunning. The design of Faloosh's prime anatmoy is to the point of being invisible sometimes when he shrinks to a mere ant. In other words, he can shrink and grow to any size, which makes him incredibly hard to defeat. First, we would have to destroy his minions somehow, then his warriors, then the females leaving only him to conquer which can take millions of species to fight him off.*"

Lucas, Jewel, Merna, John, Penny, and other scientists and doctors who have stayed behind so far are in awe. In contrast, Lucas states with curiosity at Faloosh's powers, "Since he can get in our heads and grow to planet size, is there a way we can get into his head and defeat him from within, destroying him from inside instead of battling him face-to-face?"

Ballisto, with butterflies in his stomach, says, "*Wow! That is something to think about because going within would be harsh and rash, but I love you humans because you are innovative and come up with solutions that might work.*" Ballisto continues to tell more to all in the facility. "*On that note, back on the mother ship, Faloosh is preparing his task force to cripple the military humans surrounded by boulders that are barricading them.*"

Faloosh prepares a raider strike force. "*Okay, my trusty overlords, are you ready!*"

Then, all the overlords initiate and comprehend what Faloosh wants them to accomplish and acknowledge with a yes. Faloosh tells Thorgus with wide open eyes as though he just smoked some serious alien herb.

"*Please, Thorgus, you know the plan. Be done with these pesty pink and dark-skinned creatures already. They are starting to get to me now! We must trample them and take them over, although these types would make an excellent addition to my army because they are resilient and persistent, unlike the alien creatures I have now! So go, Thorgus, make me proud and bring back a host of them to worship and do my biddings. Now go!*"

Thorgus gathers his team of raiders and several captains in his troop as he appoints his captains in the ship bay area for a quick meeting of the minds and what they are supposed to accomplish throughout each region of the Earth. Thorgus orders, "*Okay, captains, we need to ensure you are all on the plan. We have sent the strategies to your ship monitors, where you will follow them to the tee. Just make sure we all stay on course and let's get this done and make our master overlord proud that we have conquered the enemy. Now let's move out!*"

The captains take heed of the plans and go aboard their huge raider ships as they start to rev up their engines. They take a look through their monitors, acknowledging the leader's strategy. Meanwhile, all you hear is roaring spacecraft throughout the bay area as Thorgus's ship leads the way out of the bay. The rest follows him as raiders' engines roar throughout space toward the Earth's atmosphere. Finally, Thorgus sends the command to drop a more vital chemical similar to napalm but with a more decisive blow onto the surface of the Earth as military people and other humans race to take cover from the bombardment of the huge drops. The huge raider ships are high-speed as they whiz through the skies, just dropping doses and doses of a weird chemical that makes the humans take cover and hide as military people hide in bunkers and other surrounding areas.

After dropping the chemicals, they land on the surface with more potent weapons as they exit the spacecraft's doorways. Next, Thorgus's creatures start shooting with a burst of lasers that, when your trigger pulls back, tend to last for at least thirty minutes, cutting through an enemy's torso. Then, back-to-back, Thorgus orders his creatures men to get closer to the enemy and break down the boulders.

"*Creatures! Destroy those boulders that are in the way of getting to the pink and dark-skinned creatures, and make sure they surrender before eliminating them.*"

Thorgus's creatures, Mapoh, and Rook's creatures are firing on the boulders. At the same time, the hybrid keeps replenishing the boulders around the military men, as the military, through holes within the boulders, are protected. They are firing at the enemy with full force as military vehicles, or as one would say, the triple tanks, are firing within the air over to the enemy with a bent laser beam that rebounds off the force field. Determinately, the force of the enemy's firepower starts to get intense, to the point that the enemy focuses fire on one spot and gets a bit through the boulders, hitting a few military men outside the force field, slicing them in half as they yell in agony.

During that time, a few military men leave the force field as the laser is still shooting in the general area. These certain military men bend down to drag their comrades from under the fire of the lasers to safety. In the general vicinity, one of the Praetorians, whom the enemy cannot see, grabs the two military men that are severed in half as they again cry out in agony, returning to the base of the facility to begin operations. The Praetorian holds several unique tools that would to put these soldiers back together, which only takes seconds in surgery.

Like chameleons, some Legendaries are intertwined with the same color of the boulder due to a Praetorian shielding them. The battle stew on as invisible Legendaries fire weapons of intense equality compared to the enemies' weapons, firing back at the enemy, eventually making some enemies push back a second time. With conviction, one Legendary yells in his native tongue, "*Get back and focus on the leaders. Focus all power on their leaders.*"

Thorgus, Mapoh, and Rook notice some invisible weapons shooting right toward them, so they try to hide from the lasers within their creatures. The Legendaries start to shoot within the vicinity of the leaders as some of the enemies scramble around their leaders and focus their shooting toward the invisible area, almost cutting one of the invisible Legendaries. Unaware of the truth; if the enemy were to find more or even a ton of Legendaries on Earth. By noticing they would indeed be at the beginning of creation, the mother of all life, Earth. Then the Enemy would overtake it, for sure. But keeping themselves hidden within the realm of invisibility, they only shoot again when a stream of military men are firing in a particular direction.

Without warning, the boulders seem to push closer to the enemy inch by inch as the speedster hybrid runs as fast as the speed of light while moving all boulders closer and closer to the enemy. The enemy forces' firing power on several more immense boulders as the boulders inch by inch get smaller and smaller, eventually penetrating the strong military hold as a sudden ray hits the hybrid a bit in its neck region. The amalgam then escapes into the facility as the enemy sees the boulders stop getting closer and closer. As the Inquestorians tend to think they have them trapped out of nowhere, from behind enemy lines is a solid line of hybrids that surround the enemy. They are invisible and start to shoot weapons of mass destruction at the enemies as the human amalgams make their tactical moves. As one runs fast, the other throws various boulders, and the third kind sneaks up on the enemy in a stealth motion toward them while being invisible.

Thorgus, Mapoh, and Rook get the intense feeling of almost defeat from behind their back that the human enemy has more technology than expected, so Rook, along with the others, speaks out in disbelief, "*What the heck! What is going on! I don't fathom this sensation. It seems that the pink and dark-skinned creatures seem to have more than we can encounter!*"

Thorgus calls for reinforcement, similar to Rook's call for support, but the Earthlings are giving them the run for their money as the battle rages. Seeing lasers going back and forth and some military men getting hit with them, just severing them in half as several Praetorians worldwide grab the painful army men who are just not paying attention to the enemy's powers. Thorgus calls for backup.

"*We can't seem to get through the enemy although we seem to be weakening their defenses. The more destructive power we push on them, the more they seem to fire on us! Draker! Draker! Are you getting my message?*"

Draker, on the mother ship, says, "*Yes, Thorgus, loud and clear! I am looking on the monitors at the battle of these puny pink and dark-skinned creatures who are starting to drive me crazy. I'm getting my team together right now! We will be there sooner than you think, Thorgus. Also, tell Mapoh and Rook to draw back a bit, and remember I will spray these pink and dark-skinned creatures with a toxic chemical that hopefully will make them act rash or confused. According to the computer out-*

put, if possible, it should make them respond erratically!" Draker hangs up his liprod as Faloosh gives Draker a hard-core sentimental look, almost like a look similar to kicking the human's butt.

Faloosh warns Draker, "*Draker, make sure whatever is helping the pink and dark-skinned creatures that we destroy them. I want whatever is helping them to go down in our history as a lesser threat to us. Now go! And make sure you get them to kneel before me, Draker. Please go!"*

Draker gets his team ready to board their spacecraft. Draker sounds his thundering alarm for his creatures as he forms his alliance with his beasts. He meets them at the bay doors on their liprods and announces the task at hand, "*Team, our goal is to exterminate the pink and dark-skinned creatures. If they do not comply with our rules, we will feed them to the deadly games if captured. Are you ready to descend onto the surface creatures?"* All of Draker's men acknowledge in a yes nod. Draker is aboard an even bigger spacecraft that houses at least a thousand aliens telling those aliens to drop bombs, initiate drives and descend onto the Earth's surface. With a powerful, monstrous sound, the thousands of bigger ships leave the mother ship bay, exit the bay areas, and descend upon the Earth's atmosphere. Without warning, Draker commands, "*Bombard all pink and dark-skinned creatures around the globe with the giant chemical weapons. Initiate plan D."*

All you hear from the air are bombs exploding within the atmosphere, releasing chemicals affecting the hybrids, where the crossbreeds had to fall back immediately. Thorgus, Mapoh, and Rook continue on the path of either capturing the various pink-skinned and dark-skinned creatures or destroying them, which they do not wish to do. But as the war continues, the humans seem to fall back a bit as the enemy gets closer and closer with their weapons of mass destruction.

Some of those chemicals the enmies were testing in the 3D labs have finally hit the planet's soiled grounds. The humans not within the force field feel the chemical's effects to the point that hysteria hits them so hard that their actions show prolonged response to the enemy's compounds from the substances that they had to fall back slowly into the base facility. Some humans are fighting hard, and some are being killed and destroyed with weapons that disintegrate them. Other humans without military left on Earth have been trying to fight back these heinous Inquestorians.

Out of Draker's teams that land on the surface comes one giant out of each ship that begins to overpower the humans with their gigantic weapons and spray the laser hitting many human soldiers, where the humans had to fall back within the facility base. As a result, countless military men are fleeing through the portals to other universes. Some military men are trying to fight the good fight to defeat this enemy but are having a hard time doing so.

CHAPTER 32

ENEMY ATTACKS ARE STRONG

Draker tells his men to cut off their enemy as they draw closer and closer to his comrades. "*Surround them, creatures! All of them! Do not let them escape.*" The Inquestorians almost have them covered with only one way out. Many humans, along with Legendaries, head back to the tunnels. They eventually have a few humans, surrounding them in a particular area. The Inquestorians first capture some military men and some average human beings who are still targeting the enemies on an all-wage-out war. Draker says to his captains, "*Initiate spider bombs.*"

The captain, who focuses on aiming at the enemy with his splice-cutting weaponry, acknowledges Draker's command. "*Yes, my overlord Draker.*"

Without warning, the intensity of firepower between the Inquestorians and the humans is very violent. Then you hear from the Inquestorian side spider bombs, where the humans, the Legendaries, and the Praetorians scramble within the foothills as they gently grow invisible toward the foothills of the mountains cloaked by the Praetorians. A few Inquestorians keep shooting along the general area where several different lasers permanently maim some humans. The lasers injure one or two Legendaries, although they are cloaked. Draker, the other overlords, and Rook are laughing while the Earthlings are losing to a slaughtering war one by one.

Back at the facility, dignitary Yarmin noticed the coming victory for the enemy, and without prolonging, he exclaims loudly, "It is time for us to leave this planet Earth! Now!"

Meanwhile, war is imminent outside the facility for the Inquestorians as they proceed with might and power, closing in on all corners of the human military. Some are within the three-tower tanks that pull to the front of the ongoing battle as the tanks keep shooting out its warring ray guns at the Inquestorians, causing the hybrids to back down and escape into the facility's mountainous areas toward the underground spacecraft of the Praetorians. Side by side, the Legendaries are also fighting against the Inquestorians while the military men back them up with lasers. The lasers are just whooshing by on either side. Draker calls for some of his forces to move forward as his troop goes deeper and deeper toward the humans, inch by inch, closer and closer, as though they are trying to get them surrounded to take them out.

"Okay, all creatures, troops, and gangers, pull in closer to the enemy's lines and destroy their machinery first."

The blaring tanks spray out lasers among the Inquestorians as it hits a small Inquestorians that, for the first time, seems to get a scratch from the tank's weapon. Draker and Thorgus, with almost fearful eyes, look at each other, as Mapoh and Rook start to intensify their shooting toward the tankers.

Thorgus mentions something to Draker as they are looking to pick off some of the military men in the distance. *"Look, Draker, why don't we pull out the giants now and get these tankers out of our battle with these various pink-skinned and dark-skinned creatures."*

Draker tends to agree with Thorgus but mentions something first. *"Why don't we wait until we can get our creatures to the point of destroying one of these tankers by exploding them with a shock wave heater canon."*

Thorgus looks at Draker, who pulls one of his creatures back while the battle continues. *"That sounds nice. We definitely should give that a shot."*

Draker tells his creature to pull out the canon. *"Hey, Lieutenant, get the heater canon and try to destroy one of those tankers."*

The lieutenant looks down and then up at his superior, Draker, and with a minimal sentence, he states, *"What about the razor canons? They can cut through that tank like a sheet of wet noodles."*

Draker looks deep into his creature's eyes and tells it with a harsh command, *"No! I want the heater canon, and that should do. Now get me the heater canon so that I can melt these tankers and get them out of our way of the war. You got it, Lieutenant!"*

The lieutenant slowly backs down as though he got scolded by a parent and quickly runs into the starship's bay door. The creatures searches different compartments within the ship to find the heat canon. During that time, the tankers are trying to draw back the Inquestorians bit by bit.

Then the Inquestorians' lieutenant looks at the bottom of the ship, finds several heater canons, and brings out about three for several of his creatures. The lieutenant runs back toward Draker as he hands the three units to his sharpshooters.

As the sharpshooters aim, Draker commands to fire, "*Sharpshooters ready! Fire at those tankers!*"

The sharpshooters start to fire at the tankers. Eventually, the tankers get so hot that some of the men in the tankers try to escape. The Inquestorians shoot their lasers at the men controlling the tankers and taking them out one by one. Some of the military men in the tankers rig the tanker to keep shooting without anyone driving them. Therefore, similar to autopilot on the tankers, the heater canons continuously fire at the tankers. In conclusion, with the intense heat, one of the tankers explodes and flames disperse everywhere, with embers of ashes sprinkling down slowly hitting the ground.

More military men start to retreat to the mountainous base just as one military man says, "Revert to headquarters! Again, retreat!"

Sergeant Bobo orders some men to leave and others to stay and keep firing. "The rest of you follow the others that are retreating. I am hoping not to repeat it. Again revert to the facility base quickly. These enemies are far too strong for our weapons."

Several more tankers take fire and release fire upon the Inquestorians as more and more Inquestorians become injured. The men who retreat have new technology from the Praetorians, who keep them cloaked from the enemy's fire as the enemy thinks they have killed and disintegrated them for good, not wondering if they are alive.

Since the tankers are firing back with intensity, Draker calls out the big guns of bodyguards. "Release the bodyguards." Some men on the ships move out of the way as giant beings come off the spacecraft, bending down out of the bay doors of the spaceship with their knees bent. They stand about fifty to hundred feet tall when they are entirely out of the ship. Draker gives the giants commands with several hand signals. "*Attack the pink and dark-skinned creatures!*"

As the military is fighting, they notice the ground shaking as one of the military men sees a giant being in the distance. "Retreat! Retreat! There is no winning this battle! Retreat, I say retreat!"

Other military men are standing up, and the Inquestorians think they are picking each military person one by one when indeed, the Praetorians are cloaking them as they escape into the facility. When one of the Inquestorians notices the mountain moving back and forth, he wonders whether the Inquestorians see a ghost. By continously looking back and forth, the Inquestorians wonders whether they are winning or losing the war by killing the humans. Finally, the Inquestorian thinks to himself, *Huh, what! Wait! I don't understand. Is it possible that the pink-skinned and dark-skinned creatures are turning into a ghost and living in the mountains? I don't comprehend. Oh no, my mind is playing tricks with me.*

Overpowering attacks from the Inquestorians are extreme for the humans. Swinging their colossal gantlet size weapons back and forth, wiping out the tanks one by one on the ground as the Inquestorians' troops surround a few of the military men and women, capturing them all of a sudden in the area near the mountains. In other parts of various continents, there are giants, just sweeping military personnel like batting flies with a fly swat. A massive giant creature shoots its laser in one shot and explodes an entire area of humans and military vehicles with explosions so intense that it looks like an atom bomb shaped like a mushroom cloud. The military men are shooting at these giants, and it doesn't seem to affect them in any way.

Several Legendaries flee the scene as one Legendary says to some military men, "*Time to leave! The giants are on their way. We must abandon now! We can't combat them now. We don't have enough hybrids to take them over.*"

The other Legendary says, "*I agree. We don't have the right hybrids to take on the giants yet. I get it!*"

A military man tells his comrades, "Move faster, move faster, get out of here!"

As military men and women scream with fear, they all start running for the mountains toward the underground facilities.

Mapoh, Draker, Thorgus, and Rook laugh once again. By taking over the Earthlings. On the other hand, the giants wipe away the vast tankers, other vehicles, and jets in the air, crashing down the planes as they slam them down to the ground. During that time, other humans within their homes fight off the aliens with some military personnel to keep the remaining humans safe.

With his 9mm-gauge shotgun, a declining older man shoots at the aliens with no effect on the alien. The alien laughs and comes forward a bit, grabbing the older man as tenants in the apartments try to beat the alien off him. Likewise, the alien gets bombarded by the other humans, and at that very second, the alien drags the older man down the stairs and to his spacecraft. He then puts the human into one of many chambers for the captured inferior beings who will face Faloosh. A squad of military humans tries to surround one of the Inquestorians, whereas other Inquestorians are almost at the sight of capturing some of the humans. Some humans lurking in their homes are trying to keep the enemies at bay with their ancient weapons of guns and arrows and trying to beat the enemies of the captured humans.

Trying to ward off the enemy, a military man tells his soldiers, with some of the remaining humans on board their vehicle, "Let's get out of here! We will not win this battle with our weapons, people! Move! Hurry! Move!"

The few captured women and men are struggling and screaming to escape from the clutches of the enemy's hands as the enemy drags them along the ground as though they are either captured meat or carried like some cavewoman on the Earth. A man hauled by an Inquestorian starts to pray.

"Dear God, forgive me of all my sins. Take me yonder and in your presence as these dark creatures consume my body. Oh Lord, I pray that you forgive them and take my soul!"

On the other hand, the woman screams and tells the old man to be quiet. "Shut up, old man! We don't know whether they will eat us alive. We don't know what they have in store! So be quiet while my days are closing in because of my age, old man!"

When the alien drags the woman and the man into the spacecraft, some previously captured humans are frightened by the alien's presence. The woman screams as the alien pulls her into the holographic chamber with the man. Another old man is being dragged by Rook's men in a frightening voice.

"No! It's not a good idea to take me! I don't want to leave Mother Earth! Nooo!"

There are no children on the Earth anywhere. Remarkably, the Inquestorians are trying to figure out where all the puny humans went. One of Rook's men says to a commanding officer, "*Where did all the tiny pink and dark-skinned creatures go?*"

The commanding officer responds, "*I have no idea. Maybe the napalms killed them probably! Huh!*"

The other Inquestorian officer replies, "*Hmm! I don't understand, or could they be invisible, just roaming around us, laughing? Do you think that can be a possibility?*"

The commander again states, "*If that's the case, then they have supremacy better than us.*"

Commander Thorgus, on the other hand, has his creatures round up any females they can find on the Earth, which they do. One of Thorgus's creatures about to capture a woman tells the other one of Thorgus's creatures about the female struggling, "*Hmm, it looks like this female is giving us the run for our glolumbs.*"

The other creature states, "*Seem to be wiggling and wobbling back and forth.*"

During this time, the female is screaming for her mother, who has no idea that she's left back with some of Thorgus's creatures, who, without warning, turns her to dust, as the woman yells, "Nooo! No! Ma! Mama!" The woman tries to fight the aliens off her while they are dragging her by her feet. Inescapably, the aliens take her feet, hold her up against another alien's back, and tie the woman down.

Meanwhile, whatever military is left behind, the rest of the military personnel take heed to escape the onward slaughter of the humans losing against this powerful enemy. Convincingly, one of the military people gives an idea to their superior.

"Well! I have an idea, Sergeant. There is a place where we can hide since they have surrounded all the bases, and there is no way to get in or get back without them recognizing us."

The sergeant asks his military woman and sighs, "What place is that, Private?"

The private tells the sergeant, "There are tunnels all around the world that leads to the waterways where we should find a few submarines waiting for us and can house the remaining population until the aliens are done with our planet or flee from our world."

The sergeant looks at the private with eyes of surprise and relief in a condescending manner and tells the commanding officer, "Okay, Private, let's see how far or how close is it since we are miles and miles away from the ocean. So you tell me, Private! How are we supposed to transfer all these people on Earth who are left to fight? On a fast route? Tell me, Private, how do we start, or do you even have a starting point?"

The private gives the sergeant a clue. "Sergeant! The way to go is right here!" The officer points to a building that seems to drive downward into a parking lot. The sergeant is very concerned that the officer might lead them into a trap.

"I don't know about that, Private. I think there is no way out of our situation by going under a private building. We could get trapped there where the enemy will annihilate us one by one or even capture us and probably use probing devices on us."

Private, not concerned about being trapped, tells the sergeant to drive toward it. "Sergeant, trust me! Drive toward it quickly, and there is a surprise to get us to a tunnel. It will prevent us and everyone else from being captured. But, nevertheless, it will lead us right to the submarines."

The sergeant looks at the private with his left eyebrow up as to how this officer is so optimistic that he really can't trust her. He is concerned that she might be a traitor. "I'm concerned, Private, are you sure there is a tunnel? Are you pretty confident? Because if not, I would think you're working for the enemy and letting them capture us."

Private, shaking her head in a no direction, tells the sergeant sternly, "Look, Sergeant! Please trust me! There is a tunnel! You will have to see and believe me.

Other than that, if I am wrong, you can shoot me and head back to the mountains, okay."

The sergeant notices that the private is sincere and begins to drive the entire bunch of vehicles toward the building down the ramp into a private garage. Then suddenly, the sergeant meets up with Sergeant Bobo and his men. The sergeant is surprised at the outcome of people and military there. He pats the private on the back as they open a door that travels down a tunnel. Sergeant Bobo then commands all people, "Let's go! People, hurry up before the enemy finds this location."

The people start to pile into the tunnels as fast as they can as they follow the military men who had entered first, going down the corridors. The last military man closes the giant maintenance hole to the tunnels as one of the Praetorians covers it up with an invisible shield. Seconds later, the sealing of the last quarter portion of the top of the utility hole become invisible when the enemy gets there a bit too late and notices that those people seem to disappear, as well as the small humans.

An Inquestorian male says to Rook, who was the one that led them there, "*No way! How is that possible? Gone, vanish in thin air!*"

Rook reports to Draker, "*Draker, the rest of the pink and dark-skinned creatures seem to have disappeared into thin air. What should we do?*"

Draker, pissed and teed off, gives the order to his creatures, "*Search all areas, tunnels, doorways, stairs, galleys, mountains, and airways! Find them! And bring them to me.*"

Draker's top creatures are almost like sniffing dogs. One of the creatures looks at Draker and, with a deep tone, says, "*Yes, Master Overlord Draker, we will find them and bring them to you.*"

Draker acknowledges, "*Good!*"

There are tanks left with men who want to fight the good fight until the end that remains in the tanks and fight on and on; they are considered worthy adversaries. But Draker sends out his giants again and sweeps the tanks to the side like toys. Ninety percent of the Legendaries head back to the mountains, where the enemies have a foothold. Many Legendaries run around with tremendous speed and agility along with invisibility due to their counterpart, the Praetorians, helping them. The doors open quickly and close quickly as some of the Inquestorians notice the doors to the mountains have sealed shut. A lot of the Legendaries go through the portals with some Praetorians. Numerous Legendaries head to the Praetorian's spacecraft, and Ballisto heads to his ship, modified by the Praetorians to go into hyperdrive and disappear into midair quickly. With invisibility, the Praetorians have disappeared and seem to be heading toward the mother ship within the mountains; the Legendaries only have 2 percent still fighting with some of the military men within the tanks.

Draker tells the rest of his creatures, "*Either kill them or capture them!*" Draker's creatures get close to the remaining military personnel and bombard them with weapons. Many of the creatures surrender, while others keep fighting around the globe to see if they can get these aliens off planet Earth. A lot of the military are either captured or killed on the spot. Draker tells the giants and his creatures to grab the Legendaries.

"*Capture the Legendaries and bring them to me!*"

The Legendaries are very quick and hard to capture. With every turn, the Legendaries run like a lion on their tail, crisscrossing the enemy left and right, where the giants almost get them and escape numerous times. The Legendaries are very good at hiding. Some Legendaries try to sneak behind the enemy when the enemy goes by them, having little effect on them. Some Legendaries almost get captured but get away and slip away from the enemy's hands. At times a Legendary may try to sneak behind. Still, the enemy is so keen that if they try to sneak up on one Inquestorian, the other is waiting for the Legendary attack. This enemy is pretty intelligent and cunning.

The Legendaries are smarter than the Inquestorians, although the Inquestorians have a way of baiting the enemy. For example, one Legendary says to the other, "We must get out of here!"

The different Legendary responds, "I agree!"

The last Legendaries escape through the tunnels where one Praetorian keeps them and the humans invisible for the last of humanity to go through it. Within the tunnels, Sergeant Bobo exclaims loudly, "Move, people! Move fast! Let's get to the submarines as quickly as possible, move!"

Yarmin and the others, along with the scientist and doctors, are all aboard the spacecraft, ready to ascend to space. Sergeant Peters and his team of tanks, along with others around the globe, are the only combats remaining to fight the enemy. The battle is intense, with the giants slamming tanks and the human military with their battle-axe guns while shooting at various enormous tanks, taking them down one by one.

Back at the facility on a ship, Yarmin questions one of the Praetorians, "Are we leaving yet?"

The Praetorian quickly responds, "*I want to ensure all Praetorians are within the facility.*"

As the enemy captures some of the military personnel and some of the military women personnel, the war comes to a close as the enemy takes down the last tank. The enemy wave their guns and shake it like they don't care. Within that time, the people in the tunnels finally reach the submarines, where other military navy personnel waiting for them to get on board. As they come running down the hallways of the tunnel, people climb onto the submarines' ladders and gently go down the opened submarine ladder on top into the submarines' hulls.

Draker states a real quick comment, "*We won! We won! We beat this enemy!*"

Thorgus tells Draker something, "*I don't know where all the pink-skinned and dark-skinned creatures have gone too, but search everywhere, creatures, and find them!*"

Thorgus and Draker's creatures are looking for the remaining humans throughout every inch and cranny of the Earth. Lastly, Mapoh tells Draker where the humans might have fled. "*It seems like the pink and dark-skinned creatures fled into the mountains, Draker!*"

Draker, a bit angry, says, "*Tear the mountains down and find these pink and dark-skinned creatures!*"

The giants walk toward the hills and start pounding them to try to open the barricaded doors. The doors are so complex that it is hard for the giants to get through because of their alien development; Praetorians have developed an exotic alloy that seems more potent than steel or titanium. These robust doors are impenetrable. Even the mighty Inquestorians would have problems opening them, especially the giants since the doors are ten layers thick. It would take at least months to break through them as long as they keep banging on those doors.

Days go by. The giants pound the mountains for months and finally get through one of the barricaded doors by denting it and tossing it to the side as Draker, Mapoh, and Thorgus discuss how the giants are having issues getting through those giant steel doors.

Mapoh tells his creatures, "*All military go and help the giants and bring those doors down, please.*" Mapoh's creatures start to shoot at the blast doors with their ammunition. Thorgus, knowing that Mapoh and the giants are having issues bringing down the doors, begins to gather his creatures with stronger weapons to help bring down those stronghold doors.

"*Creatures, take your guns and get that door down right now!*"

Thorgus's creatures, with all their firepower, are also having issues bringing down the doors for a certain amount of time; therefore, Draker also sends in his creatures along with Rook's creatures. *"Okay, Rook's and my creatures will go ahead and help the giants and bring me those pink and dark-skinned creatures!"* Both Rook's creatures and Draker's creatures, with all their firepower, try to get a second door down, which they finally do after hours and hours, almost two days of shooting and pounding. The double door cracks open as they continue to get through the third and fourth. It takes the Inquestorians days and weeks to get through the titanium steel doors. Suddenly, the mountain caves in and gives way for the enemy to invade. The giants move all the dirt and debris out of the way so that the Inquestorians can invade the facility. They get to an open corridor.

Yarmin and the others who hear a crash from the facility say, "Everyone through the portal quickly! There is no one left!"

The final Praetorian sneaks right by the enemy since he is invisible. He gets to his mother ship to fly out as soon as possible with the scientist and doctors along with 99 percent of the Legendaries, where 1 percent is left behind on the submarines. A vast number of escorted human prisoners are taken to a spacecraft flown to the mother ship. Aboard the mother ship, the caught humans are in single file, getting off the spaceship with the Inquestorians in lines as the humans march down between them toward the overlord Faloosh, who seems to be an average size at this time.

Within the scope of things, Sergeant Bobo, along with his men, is traveling throughout the deeps of the waters to a hidden base that is far below the depths of the deepest part of the seas. While traveling within the deeps of the blue sea, Sergeant Bobo talks to the citizens along with several Legendaries and Praetorians about the secret base. Sergeant Bobo tells all on the ship, in the ship quarters' hallways, "Ladies and gentlemen and beings, we are going to be approaching a secret underwater base where there is a celestial of water creatures in our headquarters that are from the underwater world that we communicate with. For example, we speak with mermen and mermaids along with octomen and octowomen. These creatures are a breed of humans that were created within our facilities and roamed around our facilities on the outside protecting the realms of the underwater base. We're about a hundred miles from headquarters at this moment. Does anyone have any concerns or words?"

One human young lady has a sort of twisted tone to her voice that she stutters every other word that comes out of her mouth. "Well, I-I would like to, ah...ah, know about how they came to form, begin with. How is that...that possible?"

Sergeant Bobo gives the young lady a lesson as the other humans are in a trance with unbelief. "Well, now, young lady, when we arrive at the facility, I will show you around personally and give you some type of insight to the surroundings, okay."

The young lady nods her head with a big smile.

Hours later, the giant sub with huge windows starts to reach its destination. The humans on board see mermen and mermaids and other creatures protecting the outside perimeters of the facility. As the facility's giant glass doors with a dark mirrored dome open the blast doors, the enormous titanic half sub, half thick glass submarine enters, slowly draining the water levels down as another blast door opens, entering with giant robotic grippers gently grabbing the submarine as it slowly pulls it in as close to a gangway that attaches the sub's hallways to that device as people slowly get out with their few belongings.

As each person exits the gangway of the submarine, there happens to be someone or something that greets them as an unknown presence. Now, this strange presence is nothing more than a humanoid creature that looks half man and half fish, more like a whale. The man stands ten feet tall and with a prominent lurch voice says, "Right this way, all! I will get you to your quarters."

Now walking along with this creature are a few other sea creatures and some humans taking each visitor to their quarters and showing them what their quarters look like. For instance, one quarter is as huge as five thousand square feet of living space. Now within that living space are holographic symbols that generate food, drinks, clothing, and even shopping apparels. In view are a few robotic entities where the robotic characters are used to implement the choices from the holographic machines where these choices have to be chosen by the guest when shopping or dining that a person or creature may want. If you can think it, you can get it. Just imagine the amount of stuff one can get from the imaginary to the known stuff. Sergeant Bobo, at this time, calls the holographic intercom to reach all the visitors in their chambers to discuss several strategies regarding if the hidden base ever gets attacked. Sergeant Bobo is appointed commander in charge. Since his commanding officers are leaving the planet and heading to distant worlds, he discusses his plans with the elders of the underwater base.

"Greetings, all people new to the facility and creatures of all! Today I want to discuss our strategies for protecting this planet."

Sergeant Bobo, along with a Praetorian, discuss the emphasis of the creatures that invaded Mother Earth and have infiltrated Earth, making Earth's people disappear off the planet's surface.

Sergeant Bobo begins with what these creatures are and what they look like if they expect to come against the water creatures and the facility. "Well, let's see here. This is a holographic image of what these creatures that invaded the Earth look like. On the upper-left-hand corner is one called Faloosh, who can strangely shift shapes and can imitate anyone of us. From what I know he can grow huge and shrink small, also can shape-shift. This creature is tough to beat. That is why I am going to let our Praetorian brothers tell you more about these creatures."

Praetorian looks for a minute at another creature from the sea takes off its divers mask and says, "These creatures are deadly and unbeatable. Their skin is a thick armor that is impenetrable. If you look at the back of these creatures, there seems to be no type of weakness regarding the rear portion of these creatures. These assorted creatures are from various worlds that have been conquered by these evil beings where ones are transformed to are called Inquestorians."

"You see, people, these beings dominate many universes, and they mate with the females of those universes where the offspring either worship Faloosh, or they are killed or transferred to another universe if they make it out of these games you see on the holographic screens here."

As the Praetorian shows the horrific killing of a creature from a distant universe from many eons ago being killed and eaten by some beings, during that time on the surface while the Praetorian is telling the story about these Inquestorians and their wicked ways, gathering enslaved creatures to do Faloosh's bidding, more of Draker's creatures are saying to themselves, *"Why these pink and dark-skinned creatures who are puny and not strong enough to be in our great army of destruction, their frail little bodies couldn't deal with our vital blood. I feel like annihilating them already! Why would our master want anything to do with these pink and dark-skinned creatures? If it were up to me, I would deplete this planet of all its minerals and then kill them all because they would be useless to our army. What would you do?"*

The other Draker soldier tends to somewhat agree with his superior in the matter of should the humans survive or the planet dies. *"Well! I think that the pink and dark-skinned creatures should be amusement in all the games except the gala spirit games. If they survive, they could end up being some type of threat in the future. I think with the glass container game, we can move our pieces to certain spots and watch the great menace of a creature devour them slowly, what do you think of that?"*

The soldier looks at his superior at the moment and nods his head in a yes motion, with almost a disagreeable face upon him as he pulls his weapon upon his shoulder more and points it in the direction of the human enslaved people, making believe that he is killing them off one by one. As the human males are startled, they put themselves in front of the female humans as though taking a bullet for them. The Inquestorian soldier begins to fret about how the male humans are protecting their females.

"Move, you male pink skins, move! Let me blast those females after I mate with them! Hahaha!"

One male human screams out with a burst of hatred at one of the Inquestorians who seem to be pushing at him with his weapon. "*Move along, pink skin, move along, now!*" That same male human tries to combat the creature as the human waits until the living being goes by him and, without warning, jumps with a front flip toward the being as the creature's back turns away from the human. The human male flips right unto the creature's back. The Inquestorian begins to jerk and turn faster and faster as though the human is riding a bull but ten times faster. The human clasps his legs around the creature's neck. As the human is swinging back and forth, another Inquestorian comes running by and, with a quick flick of his wrist, sends the male human flying across the grassy area.

Back at the underwater facility, the Praetorian is discussing more plans to deal with the Inquestorians if the facility happens to get hit. "*As I was stating, the fact is these creatures have no mercy whatsoever. To deal with them underwater would slow them down unless they have a creature that can swim and defeat our mermen and octomen and others. We're generally safe within these depths.*"

One lady asks a rhetorical question, "Why can't we drown them in the waters and see if they can swim?" The entire audience begins to clap with excitement.

A man jumps up with excitement. "Why not! I think that's a great idea, drown them all and have the war come to the ocean, where the giant beings can swallow them up."

The Praetorian begins to swallow a bit and slightly gulps. "*You're forgetting Faloosh can grow into a monstrous giant and tiny as an ant. With his help, the Inquestorians can defeat us. I think we should remain here throughout generations and hope that the hybrids will find their way back home to us, killing off these evil intent creatures for good.*"

The people in the audience agree with the woman, but they totally forget about the one colossal problem: Faloosh himself alone with his giant females of destruction. A Legendary speaks up about a tactic that can revolutionize the situation with the help of the hybrids in the distant future. The Legendary master that stayed behind takes over the awareness of the plans of these creatures.

"*Furthermore, these creatures, through a specific game, can track other beings by a victorious victor getting through a particular game and then disappearing into thin air. Where they use that victor as a tracking device to seek other universes.*"

A merman questions the integrity of the hybrids being discoverable throughout generations. "What if the Inquestorians capture these hybrids and tries to kill them off one by one defeating the purpose of conquering these beings? The future, I guess, will be upheld and foretold."

The Legendary master proceeds as he stares into the audience at the possibility of the hybrids being undiscoverable. "*On that note! The amalgams are not like that dangerous game because, unlike the victor, that victor is transported to new worlds, whereas the hybrids are on the old worlds. According to our calculations, the Inquestorians do not have reverse technology to go back to those universes and reconquer them because the enemy believes all the lives that were already conquered and left behind, which of course, are eradicated back in time from these vile, evil creatures except for us Legendaries, where I am sure Faloosh thought we were defeated with no trace of our species until he came to planet Earth. From what I know, I don't think he knows that this is the great ancestors. Otherwise, Faloosh would destroy it provided he gets enough of the Earth's core minerals.*"

An assorted being from the ocean floor in the room with an interpreter device around its neck wants to know more about why the Inquestorians are here and what purpose would they want with the minerals. This odd creature that's in the room with a cone-like enclosure that embeds the floor of the deck of the underwater see-through facility has the beast in it looking only toward the pulpit area.

"What do these Inquestorians want with our minerals in the first place?"

The Legendary master clears it up for the odd creature. "*You see, their technology works on minerals from other planets since their planet depletion of minerals is gone within their first eon of life in the first place.*"

A human man asks a trivial question, "Why did their planet get depleted in the first place?"

Legendary clears his throat and takes a big gulp of air. "*First of all, the reason from our old tales is that there were divisions among them that they were greedy, and with greed came conquering the weak where the strong took over the weak and either killed them off or the strong raised pets to destroy them through heinous games of what they call entertainment in their world of excitement."*

The human man sighs a bit then recovers with a yes-motion nod as he slowly wipes his face off with a white napkin. A merman in the bubble divider wonders and thinks to himself, floating with a fish coming out of his mouth, *What are those bloody games about anyway?* The Legendary explicitly clears his voice again and shows on the holographic image coming from a device around his left hand, showing what the games are all about, showing a clip of the outline of the game with holographic pieces. Of the hideous game called the lottery. The Legendary tells all who are in the audience, including Sergeant Bobo, the name of the game, and what it consists of.

"Humans and species the object of this game which is called lottery consist of the Inquestorians betting on one species surviving that game and moving onto the other game or executed within that game. Of course, they gamble with their currency and with the outcome they at times get one hundred to one and so forth."

Sergeant Bobo responds with a defensive way about himself, "If they were to put me in one of their games, I would survive them because I love punishment, and my body can withstand anything, except being eaten of course."

Legendary begins to laugh, and the entire crowd laughs as well. Sergeant Bobo's head bows down, and his chin almost hits his chest as he walks out with shame on his face.

On the surface, the Inquestorians, especially Rook, the female Inquestorian leader, walks upright and with authority, shoulders forward, as she walks toward a male hostage, looking deep within the human's gray eyes. She puts her index finger onto his chest, belches out loudly with a roaring type of voice, *"You male pink-skin, stop whining unless you want something from this whip that I have in my right hand. With this whip I can slice you in half, so stop screaming and carrying on about missing home. The family, we're your family now. You either listen to us or suffer the consequences."*

With fear in his eyes wide open, the human male moves his eyes to the left and down with his chin as though he got scolded like a child. "Okay, okay, I won't talk and cry about it."

Rook, with eyes squinted and fearsome face, says, *"Good! Now carry on and move within the line."* Rook then walks down the line of the many humans boarding the ship, as her commander is getting a fight from one of the humans who doesn't want to cooperate within the line.

"Move, move, now! I said move."

The human man and woman attack the commanding Inquestorians captain as Rook approaches in time. "*What seems to be the trouble here, Captain!*"

The captain tells Rook as he points to the two suspects, "*These two will not cooperate with our commands.*"

Rook looks at them with one foot in front of her and the other foot behind a bit as she tries to scold the two humans, "*Look, you two, you either come to your senses and listen or deal with the consequences of my whiplash. Let me prove something to you.*" Rook takes an elder human, which means nothing to the Inquestorians, and with a violent stroke of her wrist, she lashes the whip around herself and hits the ground. They hear a lightning roar from the whip, like the whip whizzes through the air just barely touching the neck of the old man, as it slices his neck in half, making the man's head to slowly fall off his body. As it lands on the ground behind his body with eyes wide open, the body voluntarily moves in various directions with minutes before it finally falls to the ground. Both the humans, in shock, turn around and, without resistance, start to face the line and begin to listen to the commanding officer.

Rook keeps walking down the line of the prisoners and comes across a commanding officer with a high-pitched tone, noticing that she wonders to herself if it is a female or a male with a high pitch. The officer struggles with moving the humans who are laughing at the soldier's high-pitched voice, whereas the humans are not taking the soldier seriously at all. Rook, again wonders to herself, can this be a jarguardian? To an Inquestorian, a jarguardian is what humans call a transvestite creature that has not been developed fully into a male Inquestorian, or it can be one of the queen's children that they hide as a soldier, preferably a female war queen. Rook tells the solider to remove a garment of clothing.

"*Soldier, can you please remove your helmet and your top garment now!*" The jarguardian removes slowly by gently pulling the helmet and shoulder garment off its body. "*Soldier, do it now!*" The soldier fringed a bit and took off their garments as carefully as she took off the helmet and gently put it on the ground. At the same time, bent over, it takes the shoal off its shoulder and gracefully raises its head forward as Rook jumps back and kneels to worship the creature; Rook suddenly praises it. "*Almighty Fuwishna, what can I do for you, Your Highness!*"

Fuwishna, with a tiny tone of voice, says, "*Get up, Rook, you are doing a fine job out here. I want you to build a dome out here because, like my dad, Faloosh, I want to have or create a game out here! You got that, Rook!*"

Rook responds with the objective, "*Got it. We will build a game for you, Your Highness!*"

Fuwishna is tapping Rook lightly. "*Good girl! I trust you will get a game that I like and love with the horror between.*"

Rook and Fuwishna both laugh with evil intent. Both speak about a game plan for a warrior game that she would like with one or two monsters in them, which would be her pets. Rook making plans with Fuwishna and talking about a game centuries ago that she had loved as a baby that her dad used to have her watch. Fuwishna tells of the game and organizes it with Rook.

"*Now! The game consists of logical squares where each square moves. One square may have safety to a maze to escape, but both the upper squares and bottom squares have creatures that devour them. These pets of mine love warm scared blood and can sniff them out. The upper part also has a creature on top as well, with these pink and dark-skinned creatures who aren't worshipping me can be a part of my game. Okay, have the rest of them stay back and see who worships me and who are in my game.*"

Rook agrees with Fuwishna's plans and starts gathering her creatures to build the grounds from the ship's supplies. The creatures whip out some awesome technology that automatically builds the site's construction without using any workforce from any Inquestorians or humans. Rook then guides the remaining humans toward Fuwishna to see who worships her and who goes into the game of death.

Rook tells one human, "*Do you worship our princess or not?*"

The female human is scared and has no idea what to do with trembling hands. "*Yes, I will worship you, my princess.*" And more and more humans want to worship the princess. Now knowing that these humans would definitely worship Faloosh. The ones that didn't worship the princess like this gentleman who swears up and down that he only worships the one true God and refuses to worship an alien goddess will not kneel to her.

"I will not worship any image greater than my God!"

Rook pushes on the back of his knees with her leg to make him kneel toward Fuwishna, and the human man's head knocks into her frontal toes. The man exclaims loudly, "My God, my God, please help me! I didn't ask for this! Help me, my Lord!"

Fuwishna throws her feet toward the human and grabs him lightly. "*This one is special. I will keep him for my corridors.*"

The man looks into the creature's face and says right to the Inquestorians' princess, "Evil bestows you, and with envy comes your sudden destruction. It may not be anytime soon, but it will be sooner than you think in eons from now!"

Fuwishna chuckles a bit and chains the man to her side as she discusses the game of lottery with Rook. Rook commands her officers to get the gremgin machines to create the game for the princess and how she wants it constructed. "*How about building it over here near the lake and form a circular elevation from top to bottom, with an exit at the sand dome area. If they make it out that is.*" Rook and Fuwishna laugh and slap each other in amusement. Several of Rook's creatures bring out the equipment called gremgins, which are substantial holographic equipment that, when aimed, actually creates the holographic inputs out of whatever terrain or metals around the surface area forming that actual creation out of that substance from the the planet surface. So it is a holographic input that is similar to a 3D printer. Rook's creatures slowly take the colossal device equipment out of the ship as it glides through the grass and dirt at a fast pace upon the grassy terrain. Rook tells her creatures exactly what Fuwishna wants. The creatures input it into the machines, taking roughly hours and days to build the authentic replica of Fuwishna's dome of doom.

At the other outpost where Draker and Thorgus are, they are also gathering prisoners for their ships, where some of Draker's creatures and Thorgus's creatures have already left to the mother ship with other prisoners. Draker, on the other hand, is mainly gathering male humans so that the Inquestorians can extradite to holographic electrical cages, where you can put five people at a time in. If a human is to put their hand's through the holographic cell, it would cut their hands off. Since Rook is way on the other side of Draker and Thorgus, about fifty miles apart, Draker throws back his red cape and walks along the line of the captured humans that are boarding the ships and grabs a male stature human and tells the human in a soft tone with eyes on the human's chest, "*The next time you do that, I will turn you into dust, you hear me, dark-skinned creature!*"

The tiny human man cinches down a bit with fright in his eyes. "No, no problem here."

Draker moves down the line to see who is weak and who is strong. Although the skinny stature man is carrying a lot on his back in accordance to Draker, he is strong. But the weak ones is dealt with another lash of Draker's dust transcender gun. Quite a few of the humans catch the case of the trial and jury from Draker. Draker would ask each weak human a question, and that question would be, "*Do you worship Faloosh or not?*" If a weak human says no, Draker would use his dust gun and turn them into dust; otherwise, he notices that the weak ones wouldn't make it through the games of destruction.

Thorgus, who is not too far from Draker, has his men semicircling the humans and have the humans strip down their clothes to make sure they don't have any alien technology that can hamper the mother ship or their ship. Thorgus's creatures bring out a holographic scanner that, when scanning the various human bodies, would make a whistle tone if that human had any weapons embedded into them. Thorgus's creatures bring the holographic scanner to scan the humans, as Thorgus makes several statements in regards to holographic scanner and the humans.

"*Today you pink and dark-skinned creatures must undress to your nakedness and walk through this scanner to make sure you have no metals that can harm our ships or our people. Furthermore, I need you pink and dark-skinned creatures to only carry your bodies and leave the rest of your belongings here. What we have in store for you is far beyond what you need for clothing.*"

A female human talks, "What about my pregnant child here? she has two broken bones and a metal splint in her ankles. What about that?"

Thorgus coughs a bit and points at the pregnant child. "*We will firmly and sparingly let your child have the baby and, if it is a boy, train it in our army from birth or, if it is a girl, birth her with our male babies when she gets older.*"

The female lady looks at the creature with a disgusting shock. "Are you kidding me, mate with one of you instead of our own? That is disgusting!"

Thorgus again replies to the lady, "*The only way we will prolong your race on our ships is if you worship our overlord, Faloosh. Otherwise feel the wrath of our most evil war games of destruction that, with detail, has the devouring creatures we own as pets on our ships.*"

The human lady cringes at the thought of being consumed by alien creatures. Rook, Draker, and Thorgus round up the humans to board the ships, except Rook keeps her humans on Earth for the games regarding Fuwishna.

Moreover, Draker and Thorgus are formable friends who agree that the Inquestorians' cooks should take these pink and dark-skinned creatures for food. Since their overlord, Faloosh, would like them to serve him, they have to deal with their superior, who has reigned over the Inquestorians. Therefore, all humans enter the enemy's spacecraft. In contrast, all spacecraft tend to take off into the atmosphere, except Rook's ships. Furthermore, the enemies from around the globe gather some of the remaining 1 percent of humans left on Earth to face Fuwishna's game of death.

CHAPTER 33

THE FINAL FATE FOR MANKIND

As soon as all ships enter the atmosphere, Fuwishna takes the people who do not worship her into the game of death, which has several levels in which the human has to trick the beast into letting them escape. Most humans are food, and the weak ones will worship Fuwishna. Meanwhile, Draker is getting all his creatures together onto the ships, setting up the holographic cages, one by one. As they enter the spacecraft, the human people enter the cells, while other humans try to fight some of the Inquestorians as the Inquestorians' hard armor stuns their hands. Most of the humans are chained together like enslaved creatures. As the enslaved people enter the spacecraft, the chains are detached. They have put the humans into a holographic cage, where the captains of the ships at this point communicate with Stunner, who is aboard the mother ship.

One of the captains tells Stunner while talking through his liprod, shares his visual holographic screen, "Stunner! Calling Stunner!"

A bleep comes in with a holographic image of Stunner, as Stunner responds on his liprod, "*What is it, captain!*"

The captain begins to tell Stunner, "*Stunner, we'll be leaving shortly fromthe planet's surface. We're just gathering up the rest of them, sire!*"

Stunner regroups with a heavy tone and a serious look. "*When you get to the mother ship, then, I will send out my squadron toward the mother ship bay to assist you in relieving the prisoners off of your spacecraft.*"

The captain at this time from the ship says, "*Will do! I will have the dark and pink-skinned creatures situated for the entrance of your squadron once we land on the docking bays of the mother ship.*"

With a twist in his mouth area, Stunner replies, "*Okay, thank you, Captain!*"

Draker, on the other hand, exits his ship again, whereas his other ships seem to withdraw from Earth's atmosphere through the clouds and then hit space as the various vessels enter the mother ship, landing on the docking bays. While that is going on, Fuwishna's games around the globe are proceeding with humans that aren't worshipping her entering the game of doom. So Thorgus halts his humans as he stares over with a small eye scope. The view of the scope goes for millions of miles; Thorgus then sees Fuwishna in the distance. Thorgus talks to one of his captains, telling them to abandon two ships from the exiting orbit and to stay behind.

"You two captains stay behind with your prisoners. I may have a plan!"

The rest of Thorgus's ships exit Earth's atmosphere, while Draker's ships exit as well. The two captains salute Thorgus and agree to stay behind. Thorgus notices Fuwishna is on Earth, whereas she isn't supposed to be on Earth. Thorgus, on his liprod with a visual holographic image in front of him, reports back to the hall of the mother ship as he communicates with Faloosh.

"Overlord, your daughter Fuwishna is on Earth, and she has a game of death going on. What would you like me to do, Overlord?"

Faloosh on the mother ship with a strange and obscene look on his face. *"my daughter has a game upon this planet? What kind of game? Find out what game she is running, Thorgus, and get back to me as soon as possible!"*

Faloosh laughs a bit as he returns to what he is doing. *"First, prepare the pink and dark-skinned creatures to battle our creatures within the games of death."*

Thorgus responds with hesitation, *"Okay, Overlord, I will find out and get back to you!"*

Faloosh is a little wary of the situation with his daughter and a bit concerned for the humans because although his daughter might get those to worship her, she may see a few weak ones and put them in the game anyway. Thorgus rides on the outside hinge of one of his ships as they fly low and toward the ground. The ships get a bit closer to one of Rook's ships just hovering above the ground, Thorgus jumps off and walks toward Fuwishna and, with a big smile on his face, asks Fuwishna some questions.

"Hello, Fuwishna, I see you have a game. What kind of game are you performing for these pink and dark-skinned creatures that do not want to worship you? The council does not recognize this game. What is it called?"

As Fuwishna, who doesn't see Thorgus, slowly turns around and looks right in Thorgus eyes, she says, *"What are you doing here, Thorgus! Aren't you supposed to head back to the mother ship already! Aren't you supposed to care for the enslaved creatures?"*

Thorgus bows down a bit. "*Your Highness, I have some more slaves for you in these two ships.*" Thorgus points to the two ships as Fuwishna smiles a bit. Then, Thorgus walks away for a minute to call Faloosh back. "*Faloosh, your Overlord, I see that Fuwishna is performing some old game, I guess!*"

Faloosh bangs his hands on the table. "*Find out what game it is and get back to me, or do I have to do it myself, Thorgus. Now get it done!*"

Thorgus, a bit scared, responds, "*Yes, my Overlord. I will get it done.*" Thorgus walks back over to Fuwishna and asks a subtle question, "*What exactly is this game, Fuwishna? What exactly are you doing?*"

Fuwishna smiles a bit. "*I'm having fun!*"

Thorgus looks around at the game from a distance with his scope. "*Awe, I see that. Would this be a game of the old?*"

Fuwishna points at a ninety-degree angle while the game proceeds with two humans almost getting away from a creature as another human gets swallowed up. "*Did you see that, the human got swallowed within one chunk. Now that was funny!*"

The other human fights his way through the second layer of the game as the human falls through a barrier. Thorgus questions Fuwishna's ways of the games. "*Why the old games instead of the new ones? This is an old game, right?*"

Fuwishna, with a giant devious smile, replies, "*Yes! It is the game of old, Thorgus. Why?*"

Thorgus has a suggestion. "*Why the old games instead of the new ones? The new games are exciting. So why not use them instead?*"

Fuwishna, who seems a little far from daddy's rules, is a bit more deviant. "*The reason I don't want to be like my daddy is that my grandparents believed in the old ways. So I want to bring them back. It is all I am doing, and the ancient traditions are better than the new traditions. The old games started the new ones. Remember, back on our planet, we had games similar, and we had a lot of warriors that survived these games, but these are very interesting to me because the pink and dark-skinned creatures got devoured and smashed up. You see where I am coming from, right, Thorgus?*"

Thorgus, with a smirk on his face, says, "*Oh, you like the terrible games.*"

Fuwishna says, "*Yes, I do!*"

Thorgus, however, calls back Faloosh. "*Faloosh overlord, we have an issue. It seems that princess Fuwishna is using a game of old called the horizon zeta game.*"

Faloosh is stunned. "*Hmm, we haven't seen that game since I was baby eons ago. Proceed, Thorgus, how is it coming with her.*"

Thorgus is surprised. "*Looks like Fuwishna is doing an excellent job with it, except she is taking the weak ones that already worship her to the games.*"

Faloosh is a bit pissed off. "*What! Shall I come down there, or will you take care of it, Thorgus!*"

Thorgus, a bit frightened by Faloosh's voice, replies, "*I will take care of the situation, my Overlord!*" Thorgus hangs up from his liprod and proceeds back to Fuwishna and explains to her the reason the weak need to worship Faloosh.

"*Fuwishna, I understand you are terrified of the weak, but the weak can worship your father, and he will make them strong again with a meaning to live and worship Faloosh. With this much, it will show honor and dignity and regain his trust in you if you let the weak worhsip him, okay.*"

Fuwishna is a little confused with a backlash. "*Why should I! I enjoy these terrifying games of death. Let's explore whether they survive or become snacks quickly using the weak. Let's assumke a theory here, shall we? I have never seen one weak one survive the games yet. So why should I give them over to my father, Thorgus?*"

Thorgus agrees to disagree. "*Okay, I understand your way of bringing the old games, but why not see if they can handle the new games as well! Give it a chance, and if they get eaten, you can laugh. Otherwise, allow them to worship your father, the overlord, and since you are the princess, wouldn't you be looking for a prince that can soothe your ways. and probably these creatures can alleviate that way from an Inquestorians and creature hybrids that can accommodate your ways of life. You two can do evil things together, okay!*"

The eyes of Fuwishna look up to the sky as she examines the situation and realizes that Thorgus may be right when she crouches down to fix her shoes, "*I think you are right, Thorgus,*" she says to him. "*Okay, I will go with your plan, Thorgus, and take some of the pink and dark-skinned creatures up with me toward my father's ship and see how they would play out in the games of now.*"

Thorgus and Draker's men arrive on the mother ship halls as they all land simultaneously throughout the bay areas of the spaceships. Suddenly, Draker and Thorgus's creatures walked out of each spacecraft as the doors opened slowly. Draker's and Thorgus's creatures grab each human from the holographic cages one by one and line them up in a line as they form a line with Stunner's squadron who are all lined up on the left and right side of each spacecraft. The humans exit the ship entrance forming a straight line, as Stunner's creatures are on the left and right sides of the humans. The humans walk up the middle to make sure that none of them try to run or escape.

The captains from Thorgus's and Draker's ship tell Stunner's creatures what to do with the humans. "*We need to take the pink-skinned to the holding blocks or the hidden barracks.*"

Some of Stunner's creatures tend to agree. "*I agree, Captain.*"

Various Stunner's men take the prisoners toward a holding area or some barracks that holds a hundred human prisoners at a time. Two guards for every human are carried through a corridor down a pathway throughout the spacecraft, where the spaceship has dim to not-so-dim blue lights throughout the ceiling portion of the ship. Then, they take the human prisoners to a dark area where air opens like a compressed door lock. In this dark blue-lit area, the humans with a bit of oxygen have to wait out to see what happens in the cold, gloomy region of the ship. A sergeant from the military who can withstand the chill looks at several of the females shivering. Concerned for the women, he hands over two jackets that he has on.

"Ladies, please take my coat. It will warm you up."

The two ladies gracefully accept both jackets as each lady puts each arm through the sleeves and, with a smile and warmth, pays the man with a reverent smile. "Thank you, sir! We greatly appreciate it."

The rest of the humans take heed to warm each other up by snuggling with each other, although each person is a stranger. Some humans rub their hands together to get friction, and others blow on their hands to get warm heat from their breath. Some of the women get close with their legs crossed over each other. A few of the Inquestorian guards from Stunner's group guarding the doors watch through a thick piece of glass on the door outside of the locked-down doors. There are 1.2 million humans that the Inquestorians from around the globe captured. Those same Inquestorian soldiers and others, begin to open the trap doors. As the doors open, some humans rush toward the front of the door to get warm air to come through as the humans bombard the Inquestorian soldiers to get warmth. The soldiers start to push the humans back with their tough armored skin as the humans bounce off them. The soldiers grab as many of the female species as they can grab with their hands as the women start to scream and kick as though someone is raping them. Each Inquestorian male that is in Faloosh's army holds a female human and takes that human back to his housing station, where the door automatically senses its dweller and opens the door for that soldier. At that present moment, the Inquestorian soldiers begin to mate with the human females. Terror of cries come from the women as some of the men and women that are locked away are hearing agony and pain so horrific that the rest of the human's stomach starts to hurt them as though falling over in pain.

The cracking of vertebrae at the housing of the male soldiers who took the human women has drained them to the point of feeling like they are dead, with a limp of a major cramp; it takes the women over again, who begins to cry in agony once more. The Inquestorian's helpmates gather up the limp female humans and take them to an incubator room so that the human women can give birth to the Inquestorian's babies in a matter of several months compared to human's nine-month gestation. But right away, after the Inquestorian male rapes the women, they are already hauled back to the birthing room as their stomachs are within the six-month gestation period. The nannies then put the human women in an incubator cycle until the women give birth.

Months have gone by, and the women are ready to give birth. One of the women screams like her body is on fire when the babies are born. The women cry a bit, and suddenly one of the women starts to giggle and laugh. One of the nannies slaps the woman as the woman laughs some more. The nanny starts to discard the woman like she is a bad seed from a factory plant, shooting the woman down to a lower level of the ship with giant bugs that devour her flesh as the woman is still laughing while getting eaten alive. The babies are born and then carried to quadrants called training bays, where the female babies are grown up with other females and nannies. In contrast, the male babies are put in an area for training and battling with each other so that the strong can survive, becoming soldiers later on within the army of Faloosh.

In the interim, the men either worship Faloosh or enter the games of death. Each male is bought forward toward Faloosh as one of the male humans tells Faloosh, "Why should I worship an ungodly being that wants to destroy our world! Why should I?"

Faloosh looks at the puny human with a deep look in the human eyes. "*Because I am your God, and you will either worship me or die worshiping me. Either way, you will worship me or die!*"

The human man stands up to Faloosh with a grin of meanness in his eyes. "I'd rather die than worship an ugly being like you!"

Faloosh grins, jaws wide open, and slams on the holographic chair within his chambers. "*By the gods, you will worship me in death then! Guards, take him immediately to the games of death. I would love to see this one get swallowed up by my pets of destruction.*"

The guards take the human man toward an open corridor that slides the human down a chamber to a locked door area; as the door drags the mortal man toward the floor of the available space, where two creatures await the human man. The human man must try to escape as Faloosh looks through the side of his chambers down through a big glass as the guards and Faloosh's people cheer on the creatures to devour the human. It takes approximately several hours within the game as the human ducks and dodges the beast, hiding within the small cubby holes. The creatures wait patiently as the human makes one mistake by putting his left foot out within the area to see if there is anything in front of him. The human tries to dodge, but at rest, one of the creatures grabs the human man's foot and, without warning, devours him whole as the man jerks and screams as though in severe pain. The men who refuse to worship Faloosh put them in an area or arena postdated for games, and when the games start, they tag them with specific dates for the games throughout Faloosh's journeys.

One of the guards calls out two men within these arena areas. "*You! And you! Follow me or be shot! Now follow me!*"

The Inquestorian soldiers are walking with the two humans down a corridor, going down some dark steps. Once they reach the bottom of the steps that curved around, they come to a path area that seems to have a drop millions of miles down. The two human men follow the two guards; one of the humans is a lieutenant from the military forces, the same gentleman who gave the women their jackets. The one guard walks across a holographic bridge as though he is walking in thin air. The weaker human tells the lieutenant about the drop.

"I am not going across that. I may fall! There is no way I am crossing that. I will die."

The Inquestorian creature tugs the man toward the invisible plank area as the Inquestorian tells the human male, "*Walk across it. You will be all right! Now move, you little dark-skinned creature, move it!*"

The mortal man, feeling the pressure, begins to move toward it. "All right! All right! I'm going. Don't kill me right now, please! I'm going."

The lieutenant tries to halt back. "I'm not stupid. I'm not crossing it. There is no way I am. Maybe you creatures have ways of floating within your feet, but we mortals will die! I'm not going across. I tell you I'm not!"

The guard nudges both humans toward the invisible bridge's plank area as both humans realize that they are floating in thin air. The weaker human shouts out,

"Holy crap, are you kidding me! Look at this, I am walking in thin air! All right, I think I am balancing this platform. How wide is this?"

The Inquestorian soldier does not worry if the humans fall. "*Don't worry about how wide it is. You will not fall off unless we program it for you to fall off, and besides, it has protective fences.*"

The lieutenant tries to inch his way across to the sides of the holographic bridge to find out that it is pretty big, and the handrails are ridiculously far apart. "This is ridiculous that these railings are far apart. Wow, this technology is far beyond us."

One guard sees that the lieutenant is holding up progress, and the guard catches what he said. "*Yes, it is! Far beyond your comprehension indeed!*"

The other human runs across the bridge as though he is scared he might fall off it. The other Inquestorian guard walks across the bridge like nothing. Both guards take the human prisoners down some escalator elevator device that leads them to an open ground floor of a game arena. These two humans do not want to worship. They'd rather die than worship a tyrant of a creature. The guards let the humans down the escalator device as they hit another ground floor area. Once on the ground floor, in a dark room with a mere light of purple gaze, a dark object that feels like a cold steel door starts to push both humans as though they are about to be crushed. They are met face-to-face with another door just slightly about to be destroyed. The doors facing them starts to open slowly, relieving them from being crushed to an open playing field, where the humans are met with creatures in the audience cheering on the beast within the game. One of the humans wants back in and is in tears, as one of the soldiers speaks out loudly, "*Get in there! I said get in there!*"

The Inquestorian soldier points the man toward the upward balcony with shielded windows of thick glass. The crowd screams and laughs as the game of death begins for the two humans. The human that isn't the lieutenant gets a bit scared of asking the other human a question. "What is that screaming and laughing all about? It seems to ring my eardrums. It is so loud."

The lieutenant thinks to himself and tells the other human that seems to be very scared at all the excitement around the enclosed glass areas, "Look! I have no idea what is happening, but we better prepare ourselves for what's coming." In a soldier-ready stance, the lieutenant prepares himself for hand-to-hand combat if it is one of the Inquestorians, but what comes next frightens the two humans. These giant white storm doors open up slowly on the other side of the game of death arena as light shines in with a glow so bright that it barely blinds a person. Out of the light comes from the rear of the dark corner of the doors, where something is pushing the doors open slowly, and slowly.

The human man asks the lieutenant, "What are they doing? Are we going to see what comes out of those doors, or what! My nerves are killing me!"

The lieutenant is trying to calm the man down. "Please stick with me, and you'll be fine, my friend!"

Feeling relief, the other human begins to calm down as the lieutenant sticks by his side to see what big thing is coming out of those doors across the hallway with several obstacles. The scared human, trying to get out of the arena, somehow tells the lieutenant, "A man like me if very frightened by what's to come. I want to worship the almighty Faloosh. I want to get out! Can I get out, please? I will worship Faloosh!"

The great white doors push wide open as the crowd cheers some more as the lieutenant grabs the man by his shirt. "Come on, man! Fight through it, man!" The weak human begins to find the courage and stand in his ready stance as though prepared to fight what comes out on the other side. This game is called the glass container, where the humans have not noticed how clear the floors become once a particular chemical smoke transpire throughout the arena along with a smog that grazes the floor.

The weaker human sees something huge with a bunch of teeth. "What the hell is that!" He looks down between the floors at the beginning area of the deck before he steps on it. Lieutenant jumps back a bit onto the hard flooring that can barely hold two feet on it as the doors slide them onto the glass floor that seems to be moving back and forth, not knowing there is a considerate drop.

The lieutenant tells the frightened man to follow him. "Follow my steps as I step through since my eyesight seems stronger than yours, okay!"

The other human agrees with him in a yes motion. Both men step carefully one by one as they move step by step through the maze, stepping on the clear glass that seems to close in from bottom to top glass. It can be tricky because one false move, although the glass may look like it is overlapping, can screw with a human's mind. As both humans reach the middle of the platform, both glasses move faster and faster as they get closer and closer to completing the task. The lieutenant almost feels like he is running through a maze, as the other human tries to follow him as fast as possible, trying to keep up with him as he begins to get dizzy and dazed as he tries to keep up with the lieutenant.

About a half hour later, through the transparent maze, the lieutenant makes it through to the other side, as the other human, who is very nervous, starts to make mistakes, almost trapping his feet as he fights his way out of it. Then suddenly, without notice, he springs from one trap goes right into another trap, making that vital step while falling into the murky alien waters as the creature swallows him whole. He screams for dear mercy as the strange creature chews and chews the man, spitting bones onto the playing platform. The lieutenant looks with eyes wide open and with disgust, almost throwing up as though he ate something raw.

"The poor innocent man was so scared of death that this became his final way out, being devoured by an illicit strange, and disgusting creature instead of going out in our human way by at least a whale that swallowed Jonah. That would have been dignity and honor within our human race. The best way for me would be a whale instead of going through these horrifying creatures' teeth."

The lieutenant makes it out alive as the floor moves the lieutenant back toward the doors, hoists up from the game floor to a see-through balcony, and one of Faloosh's creatures greets him. The creatures detain the human lieutenant and take him to face Faloosh, whom he hasn't met yet. The two guards walk with the lieutenant down some corridors of the spacecraft, where he is grabbed quickly by Faloosh's creatures toward some automatic sliding doors. Faloosh is talking to another beast, and the guards try to get his attention.

"Faloosh our overlord, we have the prisoner detained and probably ready to worship you, my Overlord."

When Faloosh begins to turn around, the lieutenant's eyes widen as though chills of fright come over him with a dizzy feeling as though Faloosh is going to eat him. The lieutenant becomes numb as Faloosh speaks; the human hears a deep, powerful ear-aching sound come out of Faloosh that scares the lieutenant badly.

"Do you worship me, pink-skin!"

The lieutenant, with blurred vision, tries to focus as he looks at Faloosh with a glare. "I will not worship such an ugly creature as yourself! I will never worship such a thing as you. There is no way I will ever worship you on God's green Earth!"

Faloosh says with a resounding voice, "*You will worship me as your* God."

The lieutenant takes a deep breath and holds his ground. "I worship only one God, the almighty God ancestors worship, and you would be considered a demigod or false god. There will be no image to be honored because our God of the Bible is jealous."

Faloosh states the same statement again as Faloosh gets in the face of the human. "*You will worship me and bow down to me. If not, then you will die in one of our most exciting survival games of all time.*"

The lieutenant pushes out his chest with hands behind his back, and eyes trying to be focused and open. "Why should I worship you? There is no way I would honor you! I will not bow down to you no matter what!"

Faloosh sees that the human has a stubborn heart, and Faloosh deals with this in another direction. *"Okay! Since you will not worship me, you will be our entertainment throughout the death games and amuse my people and family. Have it your way! Guards, take him!"*

The two guards take the lieutenant to a holding area, where he is kept away from the other humans in a dark place on the ship with doors closed behind him. Faloosh also lets one of his other guards in the room. *"Guard! Prepare that pink skin for the next upcoming game!"* The guard, who seems to be sleeping on the job against the ship's wall, gets wind of Faloosh's right hand slamming into his chest. *"Guard, prepare that pink skin for the next game!"*

The guard opens his eyes with shock as sweat rolls down his arms and face. "Yes, Faloosh, right away, my Overlord!"

Several other humans are taken from the holding block in a different area of the ship by a leading Inquestorian captain who leads some of the humans to another game called water Neptune. A few Inquestorian soldiers take several humans that will not worship Faloosh or his team to a steel room area of the ship. Next, the creatures take the humans down a circular staircase where three Inquestorians are in front of them and three behind them. Then, walking in a line formation, they all head toward a maintenance hole area of the ship with another set of circular staircases leading down to another hall area of the spacecraft. The humans enter this utility hole and exit into a bright-green room that seems like green goo. From within the green goo are slithering creatures that look like giant electrical eels. Its mouth is like piranhas and the soft snake skin that sheds within and out of the green goo. Except they do not give out electricity but a smoky mist of green cloud covering either the top of the green goo, blinding its prey.

The Inquestorian soldiers guide the humans, showing them a specific direction as they follow some guards to a gallery with pictures of some writings made by the Inquestorians throughout their history. Finally, one of the soldiers stops as a rising door with giant nails opens up. The soldier points toward the door, telling the humans to enter that area. *"Now! Pink skins follow that black line, and it will take you to your freedom unless you will now worship Faloosh. If not, enter, for this is your last warning."*

All six of the humans enter the arena area because they, at this time, chose not worshipping an ugly creature. The humans enter the arena in a circular motion to protect each other from the dangers that come their way. As the door closes behind the humans, they feel a firm, strong breeze, almost like a miniature hurricane blowing the women's and some men's long hair back and forth, almost making them stand unbalanced. The humans inside the arena are captivated by the enormous holographic maze, where they have to cross the green goo fast. Otherwise, they get eaten by the creatures underneath. One of the humans tells the other humans how to manage this maze to the best of his knowledge.

"Okay, people, we must go through this maze in teams of two people to get out, and be careful of any traps. Okay!"

The other humans acknowledge this human and head through the maze in two teams. The first two humans lead through the holographic maze, being careful of any traps, as they slowly enter the holographic maze with the green goo as they are all wearing boots up to their knees. Then, carefully, the following two teams enter the labyrinth, tiptoeing throughout it without making a sound as they see something moving below them in a giant form.

The middle two are getting through the maze inch by inch. One of the humans from the third team makes a vital step and falls into the slimy green goo as one of the creature's gills opens up, clouding the human from seeing the holographic maze to try to get back into the labyrinth and swallows the human whole. As the human screams with severe pain and suffering, the creature starts to chew on the regurgitated bones for some time as several humans escape through some small puddles of green goo, where both beasts can get them, just missing the point. One of the creatures has noticed the last human passing through that part of the maze, and the creature grabs for the human's left ankle, just missing him by inches. So far, there are five humans left, with one defending himself throughout the maze, except he makes one mistake. That mistake is when he makes a right turn in the maze instead of a left turn, trapping him in an area where the goo climbs to his waist as it eats at his flesh underneath his clothing. The man yells for help.

"Help! Help! Someone get me out of here!"

During that time, one of the other humans tries to save him, and both are trapped. The creatures go back and forth real fast as though about to jump through a Hula-Hoop. But instead, the two enormous beasts attack the humans. At that very second, the holographic wall blinks in and out as though there is a glitch in the system; both beasts quickly devour humans as they chump slowly on their bones.

The leading human and one other human meet on a path. One path leads to freedom, and the other leads to death. The one human goes down the path of death to find out it leads to a dead-end with the green goo that would go up to his neck. This human takes a chance to try to swim through the green goo as the green goo slowly eats at his skin, while he's screaming and paddling, trying to get to freedom as one of his legs just come off. One creature grabs the leg. As the human reaches for safety, the other creature slowly drags him back into the green goo as that creature swallows him whole. The last remaining human makes it out alive, captured by Faloosh's creatures and escorted by the two to the upper surface to meet Faloosh. When he meets Faloosh, his stomach begins to hurt him as though hard-core butterflies are fluttering quickly. His stomach churns with nerves, seeing Faloosh's face for the first time. The human's eyes begin to widen with fear. Faloosh looks at the human and, with a deep, roaring voice, says, "*Puny pink skin, do you worship me? I'm your master and owner!*"

The human stares with disbelief and stutters, "Na! No! No!"

Faloosh turns around and flicks his hands at his guards, telling them to leave his sight.

The guards take the human to a holding block, where the lieutenant is in a holding cell until the next game of death. The next game the Inquestorians have fun with is the game of Chaplin, or in other words, the game pretty close to the game of the glass container, where four Inquestorians play a sort of chess game with a person dressed in gold, another in silver, one in red, and the last in blue. This game has a bunch of creatures that the Inquestorians strategically put in specific locations of the game. The game design has a four-stage holographic quadruple tower played similarly to chess but backward. The humans are pawns and can move in different directions without being captured by the creatures. The four soldiers perform this game. First, they must enclose a human, forcing the beast sideways, vertically, and horizontally. If that creature sees the human on any platform or the human's shadows, that holographic window opens up. The human is trapped, causing the beast to kill that particular human. So the Chaplin game is similar to the glass container with many routes and escapes if the humans can get to them fast. Some obstacles are either traps or traps triggered by an object. Some blocks are above, and when they drop, you can be trapped between the different holographic floors if you don't move fast. If the humans make it through this game, they will meet their final destination in the game, ogala spirit, where they may have a chance to survive and be accessible to the freedom at the moment or meet their maker by dying at the hands of Faloosh.

Either way, they will expire immediately or when they find them at the new galaxy in Chaplin's game. There is a sergeant, a lieutenant, and several other humans in the game. As the Inquestorians put their creatures at certain spots of the game, those same Inquestorians control the holographic settings for the beast to win, of course, and the humans to die in the game.

One Inquestorian soldier pushes at their prisoners to enter the holographic arena. *"Move! Move! Move! Get in there, get in the passageway, puny pink and dark skins!"*

The sergeant and lieutenant are not sweating as much as other male humans, a female trapped in a corner has no way out within the arena. As the blast doors close on them, escaping the impossibiliy is within four tiny corners of the stadium. Loud, obnoxious noises begin to bring ear-piercing rackets from within the arena. When very evil creatures come out, humans can't see the beast.

The Inquestorian soldiers go to their control panels above the arena as they control the holographic floor booby traps. At the entrance comes a booby trap about to slam on them as the humans scatter on the floor, waiting for the next surprise, moving one space in each direction, about a block across a vast arena. Within the hall, there are nine humans, and three of them shield each other; the sergeant, lieutenant, and women all seem to give each other a chance for survival. Here comes another booby trap. This time the sergeant, who appears to hear something from a distance, comes swirling in like a diving plane.

"Duck! Duck! Quickly!"

Some of the humans with a second to spare, duck, and two seem to get their heads chopped off as a creature from below jumps up and grabs the two humans; this creature has eight arms or legs and is gross looking, almost like some alien gargoyle.

With seven humans left, the sergeant is in black since he is the leader, while the lieutenant is in gold, and the girl in a red uniform that is made entirely out of a material that appears to be bulletproof and shiny. So humans argue to go in a specific direction. Finally, one human says, "We should go east. That's the exit."

Another human on another platform says, "We go south."

Unfortunately, the sergeant, lieutenant, and the girl are on different platforms and communicate by sign language because they can't shout. However, they got lucky earlier since the creatures were making wailing noises to throw them off their game. The beasts have different color traits on their stomachs, almost like various colors lizards' underbellies have. Their faces similar to gargoyles with eight arms or legs and wings that allow them to move above the floors, except they are trained not to move in the way of obstacles. Another part of the game is a holographic floor that seems to sputter signals to the beast to capture its prey, tearing them apart. The rest of the obstacles are rigid and more powerful as the humans gear toward the middle of the playing field. Again we see two more humans trapped, and the holographic stage begins to flicker, signaling to the creatures to swoop down and catch and destroy their prey in which they do, as the two humans scream for a second in agony and pain. Now we've lost one human from each color, leaving the Inquestorians trapped on what next color to take out, giving the confident Inquestorians leadership for the next battle.

We now have left the sergeant, lieutenant, and the girl, with one blue and one red. The girl almost gets trapped by the next booby trap, spike balls rolling in their direction, as the sergeant yells to the lieutenant, "Get down there and help her before that traps her on that level!"

The lieutenant runs fast as one of the creatures comes swooping down toward him. As the lieutenant slides on the holographic floor as if stealing third base, the creature misses the grab and turns back toward the human. This time, the lieutenant jumps really high and then slams his body down, causing the holographic floor to flutter as he crosses onto the woman's area. He grabs her quickly by her arm, and both run toward a faraway entrance where the creatures came out of since an Inquestorian guard mistakenly left that door open. The sergeant sees it and runs toward it as the other two humans run after it too. On two holographic panels, the sergeant, lieutenant, and the girl are in frony. They both make it through except the other humans that couldn't keep up got annihilated by the creatures, ripped apart and devoured by all four beasts. The three make it alive from the game. Three Inquestorian guards meet them, but not the original ones; there has to be a challenge by the gold and red Inquestorians on the ogala spirit conquest to see which one will prevail in a quick war to see where the lieutenant and the woman will be going. In other words, they will go to separate galaxies to sacrifice as pawns to locate Faloosh's targeted new worlds or universes. Faloosh thinks humans are equal to ancestors and wonders if he's in the right galaxy.

Fuwishna and Rook are playing a deadly game on Earth with old mixed with new throughout the dome structure. Draker, whom Faloosh demands to find the hidden bases they did find earlier but could not penetrate with the giants. Draker gets a beep from Faloosh on his liprod.

"Scout the area for any other hidden bases. You had pounded initially on one of them! I want to know where the Legendaries have gone. Find out now!"

Draker immediately answers, "*Yes, my Overlord! I will proceed in that vicinity and get the giants to proceed with caution!*"

Faloosh garbles a bit. "*And make sure you get any intel right away!*"

Draker strategically plans with the giants how they will rip those doors open. "Yes, your Overlord!"

Draker plans with the giants. "*Okay, you big thugs, time to use you guys to keep pounding that entrance we have found earlier throughout the months.*"

With a roaring, one of the giants says, "*Yes! We will pound it out, Draker!*"

Draker flies his ships to the Earth's surface again and calls one of his lead captains. "*Captain Lopar, report to the main hall, pronto, and make it fast!*"

Captain Lopar hurries to the hauling area of the ships and faces Draker. "*Yes, Draker!*"

Draker, with a deep thought of concentration, says, "*Captain Lopar, I need you to do something. We were hoping you could go back to the base before, where the giants were pounding in earlier. Unfortunatelyy, we had to leave and take the pink and dark skins to our mother ship. I need you to do is return to the planet and keep pounding that area until you get through it with the giants, okay.*"

Lopar responds with subjectively, "*We will do our best to get through that base area, sire!*"

Draker further instructs, "*Make sure the giants get through and get again any intel that you can dig up on where the Legendaries' new home world location is. You got that, Lopar?*"

With a concerned look on his face as though feeling a bit sorry for the Legendaries that the Inquestorians will once again destroy, Lopar takes his troops as he leaves Draker's side. "*Yes, my lordship, will take that with precaution.*"

Draker says one final word, "*And, Captain, don't forget any of the giants this time.*"

Lopar replies, "*Yes, your lordship.*" Lopar and his scout ships rev up their engines and fly out of the hull of the warship and mother ship. Then flying down to the Earth's surface in alignment, all spacecraft around the globe get to the areas of those hidden bases. Once landed, the giant doors to the back of the ships open up. The small front doors open up, letting the brigade and the giants come out of the spacecraft toward the hidden bases. As the giants get closer and closer to the remote command center, the men chant, "*Go be on it, giants, and pound out those doors.*" The giants go to the area of the hidden base and start to pound out some more doors. With extreme pounding, the giants hit another type of thickness that weighs about ten million tons of heavy steel doors. These door designs have different kinds of anthurium metal between them, forcing the two giants to pound them out worldwide for at least weeks. It involves just one door being dented and thrown to the side by both giants.

One of the scout troop's temperament throws his voice as a commandment to the giants who feel the harsh commands, saying, "*You lousy giants, get in there and pound those doors. Get in there!*"

One of the giants looks at the soldier and kicks him to the side as the giant has to move to get the right angle to pound the door on that side. While in the facility, Wymoym and Cokiko both say to each other simultaneously, "*It seems like they are getting into the doors slowly but surely.*"

Wymoym tells Cokiko and his comrades to set some traps. "*Set the traps. Set the traps right away. We don't want them to get any information on the computers. Wipe everything out. Go! Hurry, we have weeks to get it done. It will take them weeks before they penetrate through. Now hurry! Hurry all!*"

Ballisto gathers his people and makes sure all material transfers to the mother ship. His people heed to give fake material in place of the original material that is transferrable by hitting several buttons on their holographic computer instance, on their arms and hands. Cokiko and his team set traps by the doors and the rest of the facility that will trap them in the mountains, and it will take a miracle for them to get out of the traps or maybe eons before they can get out, with automatic explosives that can read movement once set.

It has been several weeks from the ten steel doors, and they get through two steel doors with eight remaining. It takes them months and months to finally get through to the last steel door. Lastly, the final steel door is blasted open. Suddenly, nothing but roars and whooshing signals fill the air. In some portals, aliens leave with Legendaries and never-before-seen creatures. One of the Inquestorian troops tries to run after the last of the Legendaries, while other troops try to gather data as quickly as possible to report back to Draker as soon as possible. A final group of Praetorians leave through some portal as one of the Inquestorian troops tries to run after the last of the Legendaries. The giants, especially Faloosh's other giant daughter, Diamond, hit a booby trap. All you can see is dust and bombs going off as the cave of the facility caves in, leaving the giants trapped and some of the troop creatures in shambles, caught between rocks, and buried alive. The spaceship and the final ones in the facility get out in time as the spacecraft reeved out of the top of the mountains with the original scientists buckled up in the Praetorian mother ship.

All other Praetorian mother ships enter into space, whizzing by the Inquestorians' ships with a streak of light as the ships are invisible.

During that time, Inquestorians notice some bright lights leaving Earth's atmosphere. Faloosh notices it when he sees the final two leaving Earth. Draker tries to contact his creatures on Earth, where there is no transmission, and Draker says a final goodbye to his troop.

"Goodbye, troop. I hope all is done well, for we got some information and not all downloaded but will go off that material and eventually come back for you all in the future."

Stunner sees the last two spaceships appearing to take off with some other vessels and tells Faloosh, *"Overlord, there are two types of spaceships leaving the planet. Do you want us to follow it?"*

Faloosh pounds his fist on the holographic table and angrily grunts, *"Follow them! If we can see the blue streak, follow them."* Faloosh has left a few creatures back on Earth, along with Draker's troops, trapped in the mountains. As Faloosh and his spaceships prepare to follow the unknown vessels, as they start to follow, both the unidentified vessels, they go into hyperdrive and disappear. Faloosh's spaceships do the same thing, except this time, they can't see the strange spaceships because they are invisible. Faloosh doesn't have that technology, and Faloosh again slams his hands down.

"Darn it, I lost the possibility of finding these last Legendaries. Send the pink, red, yellow, and dark-skinned creatures to the ogala games. We must see them through that way."

Faloosh's ships slow down from hyperdrive and are ready to set the pink, red, yellow, and dark-skinned creatures up for the ogala games to locate the final Legendaries. Faloosh roars like a lion spitting his final statement out, *"I will, by the gods, find these pesky Legendaries and their newfound friends if it's the last thing that I do!"*

Will Faloosh locate the pink skin and dark-skinned friends until the next book, or will he forever fall victim to the hybrids? The series is just beginning, and a lot must occur before the final conflict. Either Earth falls victim to Faloosh or Faloosh falls victim to the amalgams. We won't know until the next set of books, so keep reading and discover what happens. The turn of victory can be a bleak site for the Milky Way galaxy or a fascinating light for humanity.

End of Story

ABOUT THE AUTHOR

Shaun R. Desouza is from a small town in New York City, where he went to Harry S. Truman High School and graduated in 1986. Throughout high school, his GPA suffered, but in English is where his love for writing flourished. Creating several writing genres in school made him a person who loves fantasy and science fiction. He has loved science fiction and fantasy since the days of *Star Wars*. In addition, he loved shows such as *Battlestar Galactica* and *War of the Worlds*.

He moved from New York and ended up living in Florida in Fort Lauderdale, where he went to college at Broward College. At that college, he accomplished his two-year degree in computer science. He learned from one of his English teachers at the north campus that he had a skill in fantasy writing, and the professor told him that he should write for a living.

Shaun R. Desouza's two famous fantasy and science fiction idols are George Lucas and James Cameron. Their work alone has molded Shaun R. Desouza into an exciting writer with turns and twists within his fantasy-and-science-fiction writing style. Furthermore, Shaun R. Desouza moved to Arizona in 2004 and is residing in Arizona today. He finished his schooling at Northern Arizona University with a BA in technology management and an MA in leadership.

Printed in the USA
CPSIA information can be obtained
at www.ICGtesting.com
LVHW090321010624
781673LV00001B/89

9 798885 057097